Stone
Feather
Fang

A.G. Rodriguez

Winnipeg, Canada

Editor: Christina Bagni
Proofreader: Francisco Feliciano

Published June 2024 by Deep Hearts YA, home of diverse young adult fiction and an imprint of Story Perfect Inc.

Deep Hearts YA
PO Box 51053 Tyndall Park
Winnipeg, Manitoba R2X 3B0
Canada

Visit deepheartsya.com for more great reads.

Publisher's Note:
Stone Feather Fang contains scenes of violence and death.

Stone
Feather
Fang

The World of Ke'
Ultan-Mere
Tir-Ulen
Itibanen
Bi' Chone'o
Cike'o
Stone Point
Cike'o
The Andolins
Vento Zaeri
The Summer Sea
Hal'e Archipelago
Sandria
Sandria

HILDY

The Dream

"Now, who can tell me the name of the cemi of death?" I asked the small group of six-year-olds sitting before me, each one forced to have a religious education thanks to their devout parents. They mused silently until a little girl named Gia raised her hand.

"Hildy," she started then shook her head.

"It's Behique Hildy," her friend Flor scolded from her side.

"Behique Hildy, is it Guayaba?" Gia asked.

I smiled widely at her, "You are so close! Guayaba is the cemi of Coabey, or the land of the dead. That's a good guess, Gia. Remember, there is a different cemi for death and for the underworld. They are two separate cemi." I looked over all the curious little faces, scrunched up in thought, furiously trying to remember the name. It made my heart happy.

Isadore was present also. My best friend and carib sat at the back of the room, cross-legged, raising her hand on her tattooed arm emphatically. Her dark, braided hair fell to one side of her head and the beads and stones adorning the braids jingled as she shook trying to get my attention. She shaved the other half of her head as close to the scalp as she could. Her cutlass at her waist clinked against her dagger and the stone floor of my room. Her boots tapped like woodpecker on a ceiba tree. She made more noise than any of the students.

"Izzy, you're not a p–part of this class," I stuttered with a shake of my head. The children turned to look at her and all giggled. "And I'd be shocked and frankly ashamed If you didn't know the answer. You're here just as much as they are."

Isadore grinned and leaned to close to the nearest student, a boy named Hermilo. "I can give you a hint if you need it." This prompted more giggles.

"Anybody care to b–be as b–brave as Gia here and take a guess?" I asked. Santo, a chubby little Borinken raised his hand cautiously and with more than a little reluctance. "Yes, Santo?"

Santo cleared his throat and said, "Is it Maboya, Behique Hildy?"

I gave the boy a wide smile and a short round of applause. "That's right, Santo! Maboya is the cemi of death."

"That's what I was going to say," Isadore chimed in. The class of six-year-olds giggled.

"Do not listen to the Anacaona at the back. We all know they care not for the cemi, except for you Memo, you are b–brave to do so." I smiled at Isadore's cousin. He smiled back and blushed. There was no denying their heritage. Both had smooth, dark skin like onyx and beautifully shiny, tightly curled hair, or at least Isadore would have had she not braided and shaved hers.

"Now, b–before I let you go for the day, I want you to remember, we Andoli, whether B–borinken or Nitaino, Jibaro or Kiskeyan, do not fear death. Death is a gift from the almighty Yaya. It is out ticket to the third cave. And who remembers what awaits us in the third cave?"

"Feasting!" Isadore shouted. The children jumped at her outburst then laughed hysterically, repeating her call.

"Okay, okay, now off with you all. Your p–parents are all waiting!"

Isadore and I walked the group of students from our little study nook in the temple to the arboretum where the fifteen of them ran to greet their smiling parents still feeling the effects of the cassava pipe. The sun shone brightly onto the flamboyán and ceiba trees that grew there. Small stone likeness of the cemi stood in their respective alcoves, complete with stone or copper bowls for offerings. Candles surrounded some, silver and copper Andoli marks littered the feet of others. Andoli of every walk of life knelt at their respective family cemi, praying for whatever blessing their cemi imparted.

"I used to wonder why my bibi and baba hated coming to the temple," Isadore said quietly, leaning closer to me. "I mean, they loved to smoke cassava as much as the Suma Behique. And since its part of the rituals, you'd think that would have been right up their alley."

I shrugged. "B–but had they attended the temple rituals, what would have happened to the famous Anacaona impiety? I don't think anybody judges you or your clan for not b–believing in the cemi."

"I'd hope not!" Isadore said. "So, is this all you had to do today, teach these runts about scary Maboya?" She emphasized the name with her deepest, most haunting voice.

"Yes, it was, and I'd ask that you stop interrupting my lessons with your antics, Isadore Anacaona."

"Yes, Behique Hildy Campos," she said tongue in cheek. "Where to now? Should we hit the city and ogle at all the tourists arriving and wandering the streets? I heard the dance troupe from Fajardo has arrived! Do you remember them from the last festival of Areíto?"

"Were they the ones that danced in nothing but p–paint smeared over their b–bodies?"

"Of course, you remember. Who could forget that?" Isadore said pulling me close.

"We can do that, b–but..." I trailed off.

"But?"

"I need to speak with the Suma B–behique first," I said. "I had that dream again."

Isadore grimaced. "The one about you, Jenaro, and Maboya?"

I nodded. "It was the same, but also different, strange. I can't make out the meaning and I want her opinion."

"Then after that, we go watch the dance practices?"

"Yes. I'm surprised you didn't recommend lunch."

"Oh, that's on the itinerary."

Eighth-day afternoons, or Atabey as we called it in honor of the mother goddess of our people, the Suma Behique, head priestess of my order and administrator of the Temple, spent in quiet solitude. Her week, filled with study and service, speaking at the Temple of the Cemi, and pressing flesh with the few faithful still in attendance, drew most of her time. But for as long as the Temple of the Cemi existed, even as far back as when behique more closely resembled shaman than priests, Atabey existed as their day to rest. The current Suma Behique, who sacrificed her own name to better serve the cemi, was no different from her predecessors. Her place of rest and relaxation was known only to a select few. Luckily, being the daughter of the previous cacique and sister of the current leader of the Andolins, provided me with access to useful tidbits of information not available to others. When I first told Isadore the Suma preferred to garden on her eighth day, she didn't believe me, until we snuck in and witnessed it with our own eyes. The punishment that followed left me with dish-pan hands I thought would never return to normal.

"Are you sure she's going to be okay with us interrupting her day of rest?" Isadore asked. "Last time you had to wash the Temple pots and pans every meal for an entire week."

I nodded. "I know. B–but if I know anything about the Suma B–behique it's that she will be expecting our arrival."

Pedestrians and carts packed the seastone streets of Puerto Zafiro. The city bustled on a normal day, but now, so close to the Festival of Areíto, you could not move without brushing arms with a tourist or bumping into a member of the city guard. Yet, despite the ballooning population of the city, and the raising of countless, colorful banners and decorations, things seemed normal to my eyes. Friends and families greeted each other on the doorsteps of their seastone bohios exchanging warm embraces and planting heartfelt kisses on every cheek and forehead. Farther down mountainside, merchants and traders filled the market square and engaged in shouting matches, attempting to outbid one another for prized goods. At the docks, merchant marines unloaded their vessels from lands beyond the horizon, casks of wine and barrels of ale rumbled down gangplanks. Cranes affixed with nets emptied ship holds brimming with freshly caught fish and shrimp. Jibaros guided their mule-driven carts laden with slop and refuse from every home and business in the city toward their farms and ranches outside of the city proper. The smell of their passing wrinkled my nose as it mingled with the briny sea air that cooly breezed up the streets and alleys and around the buildings.

Izzy and I took the long way from the temple to the cape where the Suma's garden grew, circling through the city and past the Batey del Albizu, the largest park in the Andolins, where a multitude of work crews assembled tents and stages throughout the grounds. "You would think the next three days were just a normal eighth day weekend if not for the view of the b–batey," I said as we walked past the wrought iron fence that enclosed the grounds. "Nobody seems to even notice what's going on in there, or the b–banners and streamers decorating every lamp p–post and street crossing, or the vendors cramming their way through the city gates, or the inns nearly b–bursting at the seams with dance troupes and b–batu p–players and tourists. It's like a normal eighth day."

"For the most part it is," Isadore replied. "The carnecerías and panaderías still have to butcher meat and bake bread. Those children who were fortunate like us will be in lectures at the temple, the others will be helping their parents with the looms or the plows. I even heard that the caciques menores were commanded to meet with your sister today and tomorrow. Tomorrow! On the first day of Areíto! She can't even let them have the day off for the holiday."

"I'm sure they're all thrilled about that," I said with a grimace.

"Just adds more fire to their already raging hatred for her."

"Do you think we could not talk about Luisa today?"

"Of course," Isadore said with a smile.

The cape on the western side of the city, once the site of a glorious and stately lighthouse and military lookout, had long since transitioned into a botanical garden home to the flora from every realm in Ke'. Maple and live oak from Ultan Mere, cactus and enormous flowering succulents from the arid wastes of Itibanen, palms and blooming shrubs from the isles of Hal'e and the continent of Sandria, even the slowly burgeoning stately ironwoods from the tundra of northern Cike'o. I never understood how plants from every imaginable biome in Ke' could live and thrive in the tropical sauna of the Andolins but thrive they did.

The garden itself was kept by the behique, more specifically under the watchful and careful eye of the Suma. She would spend all eighth day afternoon among the flowers and ferns, tending the plants and pruning the bushes. It was her secret joy and one that connected her back to the cemi. "All the cemi can be seen in nature," she once told me, "Yaya, in the creation of life, Atabey, in the nurturing and growth of each plant, fed by the waters of Boinayel, germinated by Yucahu's winds. Even Maboya visits every plant in their due time." Isadore and I stopped at the gates, scanning the paths that curved around planters and through the twisted roots of a towering ceiba.

"I...I don't know if I'm comfortable doing this," Isadore said. "I know you're close to the Suma, but she gives me the jibblies."

"Don't be silly," I said. "I told you; we're expected. And anyway, the worst that can happen is we're sent away."

"I hope you're right," Izzy said with a shudder.

We didn't even make it to the first guidepost before a pair of my brethren, the behique Tonio and María, appeared from farther down the path. They hurried toward us struggling to appear calm and simultaneously move with a sense of urgency. They both huffed and puffed as they came to a halt in front of us.

"Tonio, María," I said, giving them the palm of peace. Isadore did as well but positioned herself slightly behind me. I know she hoped I wouldn't notice but when I turned my head to look at her, she smiled sheepishly at me and took a step forward to be next to me.

"Hildy, I hope there is a good reason for this intrusion. It is the Suma's day of rest," María said, exasperated.

I looked at Izzy who said, "You did say she was expecting us."

"Not us, just you, behique," Tonio said. "She would like for me to escort you to her. Your carib can wait here."

"Now, hold on," Isadore started but hesitated when I grabbed her shoulders and turned her toward me. "It'll be okay. I won't be long."

Isadore folded her arms across her chest. "I know you'll be okay; I just think it's rude that she knew you were coming but didn't see me with you."

I tried to hide my amusement but failed. "Izzy, I love you. You're my best friend and you are so sweet. I guess I'll have to do this alone."

Isadore breathed a sigh of relief and mimed wiping sweat from her brow. "Thank the cemi. Be safe." She threw me a smile then turned to María. "So, what'll it be, behique? Should we play daggers, or would you rather show me which of these plants produce useful toxins?"

"I beg your pardon?" María gasped.

"We gotta pass the time somehow?" I heard Izzy say as she and María disappeared around the corner.

I turned to Tonio, bowed my head, and said, "Lead on, behique."

We walked through the garden, following the twisting dirt paths around a veritable orchard of fruit trees, growing high and shading our way with their foliage. The shade smelled sweet with ripening mango and papaya. The flamboyán trees bloomed brightly, crimson petals decorating the path like a red carpet. When the shade parted, Tonio had led us to the last tree on the cape, hanging precariously onto the final chunks of soil before the edge of the cliff. The ancient ceiba clung to life, roots cascading down the cliff face toward the waters of the bay. Fingers in the earth, sun visor on her head, dagger slicing small roots from around the tree's base, knelt the Suma Behique. She didn't turn around to see who approached nor did she stop what she was doing to greet her guests.

"Thank you, Tonio, you may leave us now," the Suma said, wiping her blade on the sleeve of her shift.

"As you will it, Suma Behique," Tonio said with a bow then scurried away, leaving me alone with the head of our order.

A terrible fear suddenly washed over me. What if Isadore was right? I shouldn't be here interrupting her only day of rest. Areíto started tomorrow, the three-day festival only celebrated every three years would monopolize her time for the rest of the week. How selfish of me to think she would gladly see me, a novice behique whose only duties were study and teaching the youngest students what I learned…and occasionally cleaning the temple. I may have been the daughter of a cacique, but in the temple that meant nothing. I wasn't any different from the other novices. In hindsight, I knew I had made a terrible mistake.

"Come here, behique, and sit with me," the Suma said, moving from her knees to sit cross-legged against the roots of the ceiba, shading herself from the harsh midday afternoon sun. Her copper skin glistened with sweat. Stray strands of white hair parted from her waist-length braid and stuck to the slick skin on her face and neck. I hurried over to her. "The cemi told me I would see you today. I thought to myself, surely not Hildy. She would not interrupt my day of rest."

I inhaled sharply before noticing the sly smile curling the edges of the Suma's mouth. I tried to smile back at the tease but felt the weight of my decision. "I'm so sorry, Suma Behique."

The Suma waved away my words. "There is nothing to apologize for, child. If I am not available to my own behique, than what use am I? Now put aside the shame you feel and speak. Whatever weights on your heart must be an incredible burden."

I finally took a seat across from her, swallowing hard before I spoke. "I had a dream. I mean I've dreamt before but this dream, it isn't the first time it has come to me. Every time it happens, I wake up in a cold sweat, only this time, well it was different."

"Tell me this dream," the Suma said. She reached over and

took my hands in hers. Her skin was soft and warm, not like a gardener's hands, and the way she held mine to hers sent signals of love and comfort to my brain. I looked into her dark eyes and felt a sense of calm. Taking a deep breath, I recalled my dream.

"In the dream, I see a boy, young, no older than eight or ten years. He's a stranger to me, yet I feel connected to him, as if I know him, as if I've met him before. His face is stained with tears. Someone close to him has died. He's in the manse, or what used to the be the manse, the gallery and museum now, and climbs the tree in the Cacique's garden. I'm standing at the base of the tree, watching the boy climb, scared that he's going to fall and hurt himself. Thankfully, he doesn't. He reaches his favorite branch and perches there, back against the trunk of the tree and cries. Yet he is not alone. Sitting in the tree with him is a giant maja, body coiled and twisted up within the branches. I watch the snake slither its way to the boy's tree limb. I'm scared, I yell out, but the boy doesn't hear me. The maja moves in close and begins to whisper into the boy's ear. It's forked tongue flicking with each syllable. I can't hear what its saying, just the hiss of the boy's name, Jenaro, but I know the rest of the maja's words can't be good. So, I begin to climb. Higher and higher I go, until I'm in the clouds, watching birds screech as they fly by. I manage to climb to the branch just below Jenaro. He's arguing with the maja. I yell out again, trying to get their attention. Jenaro still can't hear me, but the maja turns it head. I can see its eyes, hypnotic, cycling from gold to green to silver and back again. It speaks to me, but I can't make out what its saying. Whatever it says startles me and I lose my grip. It ends the same way every time, with me falling out of the tree.

"Last night's dream started much in the same way, the young Jenaro, the manse, the ceiba, and the maja. When the snake turned its head to me and hissed, I could finally make out its words. You've

awakened. The time has come, daughter of dust. I need your help.' The words hit me like a gust of wind and sent me flailing from the tree."

After I finished the retelling, we sat in silence. I thought for a moment that the Suma had fallen asleep. She sat so calmly, barely moving, barely breathing. I opened my mouth to speak but she spoke first.

"It seems to me the cemi are sending you a message," she said.

"What message?" I asked. "And what cemi? The maja would be Maboya. Oh, Yaya be good, Maboya is the last cemi I want speaking with me. And if that's the case, why is he so cryptic? Why does he come to me in a memory that is not my own? It doesn't make any sense."

"Many times, the word of the cemi fails to make any sense to us. You and I are simply borekua to them, their mortal creations, beings to worship and entertain and fulfill their deepest desires. Yet, to be visited by a cemi in a dream is not for the outsider to understand. Those dreams are for the dreamers."

"So, it has to do with me. B–but, why dream of Jenaro? It felt so real, as if I was transported b–back in time to witness a moment in his life, one of p–profound sorrow."

"The cemi will not often use languages we understand. It is up to us to interpret their messages."

"B–but how, Suma?"

"Think of everything I've taught you. The cemi no longer communicate openly with us and when they do speak, it is through visions or flashes of insight."

"Maboya is trying to get my attention b–by showing me my distant ancestor, b–by giving me a look at the traumatic loss of his mother." I paused for a second. "Is he trying to tell me I, too, will experience the loss of my mother?"

"I do not think Maboya taunts you with what will eventually come to pass regardless of his involvement or not. Perhaps it has to do with Jenaro. Perhaps your distant ancestor's life will bring about change in your own life. For that, fundamentally, is all death is, transformation, change."

I hmphed and mused over her words.

"Do not dwell on it for too long, my child. Sometimes the answers come to us when we least expect it. Maybe Maboya will speak to you again. And maybe he will not. Maybe he brings about great change and maybe not."

"Yes, Suma B–behique," I said with a heavy exhale.

The Suma smiled widely. "Now the cemi's message to me has been made clear. You will perform the Telling at this year's festival of Areíto."

"What?" I shouted, pulling my hands from the Suma's grasp. "The Telling? No, I can't do that. That honor is reserved for senior members, b–behique who have trained for years, not a novice. And I stutter! I can't speak in front of a crowd of Andoli stuttering over my words."

"The last time I checked, it was I who claimed the title of Suma Behique not Hildy Campos," the Suma replied softly. She smiled widely once more. "I, too, had a dream, or rather have had a dream for many nights, recurring just as yours. Weeks it has tormented me. It has been the only thing I've seen in my sleep. I will not bother you with the details, yet only last night did I realize the face I saw in my dream belonged to you, Hildy.

"The telling is your own. I've heard you teach to the children about cemi and the old majicks. I've seen their faces, how you engage them. I know you will do well. I have no doubt, child."

I sighed, slumping my shoulders. "There's no getting out of this, is there?"

"I will send word back with Tonio to have your duties for

the next three days assigned to one of your peers. Fear not, child. All is well. I have the utmost faith in you. Now, do me a favor and help and old woman to her feet. I need to check the roots of the other ceiba for wild cassava."

Books and Breakfast

When I returned to the entrance of the botanical gardens, I found Isadore chatting with a duo of city watchmen. She saw me from a distance, saluted both, and jogged to meet me.

"So, how'd it go?" she asked.

I shook my head. "I…I don't know what happened. One minute I'm discussing this dream and the next minute the Suma B–behique is telling me I will be p–performing the telling at this year's Areíto."

"What?!" Isadore screamed. "Hildy that's incredible! You'd have to be the youngest behique ever!"

"I am," I said.

"To give you such an honor, the Suma must be so confident in you!"

"She is."

"Hildy! This is incredible! Exciting! You know how many Tellings have been given by crusty old behique that don't even know what batu is?"

"All of them?"

"All of them!" Izzy shouted. "But not this year. Wow. Fifteen years old and giving the telling." Isaodore gasped. "Your bibi is going to lose her mind."

I felt my heart drop to my stomach. "My b–bibi…do…do I absolutely have to tell her?"

"No, but I'm sure she'll be incredibly proud. You are her eldest daughter."

"B–by a year."

"And I'm sure she'll be ecstatic."

"It's just that if I tell my b–bibi she's going to tell Luisa and I really don't want to tell Luisa. The last thing I need is for her to show up and critique me."

Isadore groaned. "Ugh, Luisa. How you two are related is beyond me. Your natiao, Arecibo, and you are the same, kind, caring, loveable. But her?" Isadore clenched and bared her teeth then mimed choking herself. "She's making the caciques menores miss the first day of the festival for some ridiculous meeting."

"I know. She continues to not do herself any favors."

"The people talk about her as if she is an Ultan spy, planning to have our islands invaded after they were kicked out centuries ago. You and Aré on the other hand, the people love you two."

"Let's not talk about Luisa. I need to head b–back to the temple and get to the archives. If I'm going to give the Telling, I at least need to p–prepare something…anything. Can't stand b–before the p–people and talk about majick like I do to the children every week."

"Why not?" Isadore asked.

I gave Izzy stare that made her laugh and hold her hands up in defense. "So, no dancers today?"

"I'm sorry, Izzy. I'm sure we'll have time tomorrow."

"It's okay, Hildy. But we still need to eat. I'll accompany you to the temple then run over to the batey to see if any of the vendors have started selling yet. I know it's a day too soon, but sometimes they cook for the set-up crews."

Behique Inez placed the last of the eight books I requested on the table. The enormous, weighty tome made the aging wood creak and groan. Even a cloud of dust rushed away as she dropped the book to the surface. We both held our breath and waved away the cloud.

"Here's the last one," Inez said. A short, mousy Borinken with crude glasses dangling on the tip of her nose, Inez started at the temple two years before me and already achieved the rank of apprentice. Seeing her work the archives meant she aspired to replace the current archivist one day.

"Thank you, Inez," I said with a nod. "Yaya be merciful, how heavy is that b–book?"

Inez wiped the sweat from her brow, nearly knocking the glasses from their perch. "You wouldn't believe it. I'd wait until your carib returned to move it. It may take both of you to lug it open."

I wanted to laugh but knew the tiny Inez would think it was at her expense. Instead, I agreed with her and waved as she headed back to the circulation desk two floors above me. A mighty sigh left my lips as I examined the eight books and one scroll resting on the archive table. My hand instinctively went to my braid as I leaned back in the chair, reluctant to start the research process.

The weight of my task didn't immediately overwhelm me. Yet, after only a few short minutes, I found myself staring at the same page, reading the same paragraph over and over again. Every word made sense on its own but none of them made any sense together. I considered giving up and dropped my head to the table with a groan of discomfort. I could have stayed in that position if not for the faint argument I heard in the distance and the sweet aroma of freshly baked bread and sliced ham. Isadore had arrived and no doubt started an argument with Inez over food in the archives. A few minutes later, Izzy placed two wrapped sandwiches on the table next to me.

"That bad?" she asked.

I turned my head to her and groaned.

"Would a sandwich help?" Izzy asked. "Sandwiches always

help me. If I'm hungry, sandwich. If I'm tired, sandwich. If I need the energy to train, sandwich."

"Yes. No. Maybe." I sat up and grabbed the sandwich, quickly unwrapping it to take a bite. The salty goodness of the ham made me moan in delight. "Ugh, that is good."

"Right?" Izzy, mouth full, agreed. "So, what's the hang-up?" she continued after taking another bite.

"I just don't know what to say. What do I even write about? What am I supposed to tell these p–people that they haven't already heard twice?"

"Did the Suma have any advice?"

"I didn't ask. I was too shocked to even think about asking. Do you think she would write it for me if I asked?"

Izzy scooted her chair close and grabbed one of the books from my stack. "Well, let's think about the last Areíto. What did the behique who performed the Telling speak about? How was it received?"

I pushed the book in front of me out of the way and grabbed my notes with my free hand. "B–behique Osvaldo, seventy-four years old, related the story of creation to the life cycle of the caguama."

"Cemi be damned, that sounds miserable," Izzy cursed, a little too loudly which drew a hush for silence from a passing behique. We exchanged a grimace of embarrassment.

"B–before that, there was B–behique Sarai who spoke about the way corn fields grow. She was eighty-two years old." Izzy groaned in pain. "I even found my great aunt in here. She had a telling years b–before we were b–born. Her Telling likened the creation story to the war with the Ultans five centuries ago."

"Oof, a history lesson? I thought your clan was more creative than that."

"Yeah, so did I," I said after swallowing another bite. I shook my head in frustration. "It's hard enough getting fifteen six-year-olds to listen to a lesson on the majicks. How can I get a group of adults to p–pay attention to three nights of instruction?"

"Do you have to talk about the creation?" Izzy asked. "I mean, is there any rule that says it must be about the creation? What if you talk about batu, or dancing, or pernil? That would be a delicious Telling."

"Too b–bad you're not the one giving the Telling."

"I mean, I could, but only if you want."

I took the last bite of my sandwich, let out a whine, and dropped my head to the table again. "I don't know what I want," I moaned.

Isadore chuckled and said, "You're so cute when you're pouting." I shook my head then balled up and threw my empty sandwich paper at her. She only smiled and hurried away to find a waste basket.

The rest of the day passed with my nose buried in various dusty tomes and my hand attached to my pen, desperately trying to find some inspiration for my telling. Traditionally, the Telling taught people of our history and our culture by relating it to something the people would understand. Heavy theology too often meant a crowd of sleeping speech-goers. It was the Teller's discretion as to what they wanted to speak on. Thus, each telling became an extension of that person. Dreams, desires, beliefs, hopes, and fears all presented themselves in the Telling, all meant to teach a valuable lesson about the cemi. I wracked my brain trying to think on one thing, one simple story of my life that could bring the people closer to the cemi, but not a single idea was born. I was only the daughter of a cacique. I lived my fifteen years in relative comfort and ease. What would I know of the toils of the Jibaros, planting their fields, or the daily struggles of average

Borinkens, who lived on the east island, in Puerto Zafiro, raising families in a city that suffered from its own growing pangs?

I looked up from my book, across the table at Isadore. My best friend and carib sat there, face scrunched up in that cute way it did when she read something she didn't understand. She didn't have to be here. She could have left me in the relative safety of the archives, deep under the Temple, and ran to the batey to watch the dancers arrive, drooling over the men and women with their honey skin and dark hair, glistening in the setting sun as they practiced their routines one more time, but she sacrificed her evening to be with me. I didn't deserve her. I looked back at my notes. My scratchy handwriting said, "flute?" Izzy mentioned music during another one of my meltdowns. My flute playing brought me comfort and joy. Surely, I could make that an interesting talk for three nights. I took a deep breath and began to scribble down notes until the sun disappeared beneath the horizon, until the city lamps were lit, until the archives shone ocher in the artificial, mirrored light. Before long, I felt my eyes grown heavy and my head begin to drop.

"Maybe a little nap," I murmured to no one. Isadore already sat with her arms folded on the table and her head nestled softly atop. She snored lightly and muttered an unintelligible conversation to herself. I smiled and soon faded into sleep.

Dreaming. I stood in front of the ceiba once more. After taking a moment to examine my surrounds, the grass, the garden, the walls that surrounded it, I looked up and high up in the branches and saw Jenaro. The boy sat with his back against the trunk of the tree. His tears rained down on me like a passing storm. I started toward the trunk, intent on once again climb the great sentinel, when I spotted the maja. It slithered down to Jenaro from a limb just above the boy.

"You've been here before, Hildy," I said to myself. "You've done this before. Just walk away. Walk away or wake up. Wake up!" I put my feet back on the earth. "Well, that's new. I can move. And my stutter is gone."

The hiss of the maja grew louder. I looked back up to where Jenaro sat, only the boy faded away on the breeze like a wisp of smoke. The maja descended the great ceiba, wrapping its enormous body around the trunk. I shook my head and turned to walk away. That was when I heard the maja speak.

"You've awakened. The time has come, daughter of dust. I need your help."

I continued to walk until the garden faded to nothing. Yet the words continued to follow me. "You've awakened. The time has come, daughter of dust. I need your help."

I woke the next morning with a start. Inez stood next to me, shaking me by my shoulders. "Hildy, did you spend all night here?" she asked in a whisper.

I rubbed the sleep from my eyes and noticed Isadore had pulled her chair up next to mine. She slept, leaning against my side. "Yes, Inez, I guess I did," I said with a yawn.

Inez looked troubled. "Oh, I hope Behique Marta doesn't hear of this. She'll think I failed to do a final check of the stacks!"

I smiled gently and took her arm. "It's okay, Inez. I won't tell a soul."

Inez nodded uncomfortably. "Okay. Well, it is dawn. I only wanted to make sure you two were okay."

"Thank you, Inez. I think we'll take a b–break from studying and go get some b–breakfast." I said quietly so as not to wake

Isadore. "Should I b–bring the b–books up to circulation?" Inez nodded then hurried off. I turned my face and gently rocked Izzy until she groaned with reluctant wakefulness.

"Is it breakfast?" she asked.

I giggled. "Well, it is morning, and it is time for b–breakfast, so I guess you can say it is b–breakfast."

"I could eat an entire pig," Izzy said, rising from her chair.

"I think I'd like to go to the manse this morning if you don't mind. I thought about what you said, and I think you're right. I should tell my b–bibi about the Telling."

"Of course, I'm right. Aren't I always?" Izzy asked, tongue in cheek. I pushed her and she rolled herself from the chair and crashed to the floor. A cry for silence immediately followed.

I shook my head. "I need to get you out of here before they ban me for life. Can you imagine a behique denied entrance to the archives?"

"You'd be a laughingstock, Hildy," Isadore said with a wink.

"And it'd be your fault."

The excitement of Areíto was everywhere the moment we stepped out of the Temple. Streamers flew from every lamp post. Confetti and flower petals floated on the briny morning sea breeze that rushed over the island. Everyone on the street of Puerto Zafiro, dressed in vibrant colors and patterns, moved to the Batéy del Albizu for the opening festivities. We heard the music clearly from the temple steps, even over the roar of the crowds. The smell of festival food filled the air and made our mouths water.

Despite the pedestrian traffic that choked the streets as well as the innumerable amount of tourists, rickshaws, and carts, Isadore managed to find us a ride to the manse. The boy pulling an elaborately decorated carriage for two, complete with flags, streamers, and noise makers on the wheels, gave us a brilliant smile and excited nod of his head when we told him our destination.

"Yes, behique, I know the quickest route," the boy said, bursting with pride. "I'll get you there before long." The feathered hat on his head resembled the mulit-colored inriri of Yucahu and bobbed, flapped, and shook as he spoke. On any other day, I would have giggled at the show, but the dread of returning to the manse struck me hard. Isadore answered for me and helped me to my seat.

It wasn't that I disliked home. I loved the manse and the people who worked within. I loved my family, even though our dynamic shifted drastically when my baba died, and Luisa ascended to sit on the dujo of the Cacique. Too often I felt alienated in my own home. I knew I shouldn't let my youngest sibling bother me so much, but Luisa had a power over me and without Arecibo to defend me, often I simple shut my mouth, nodded, and went along with everything she said.

The cart darted through the crowded streets, narrowly missing other carts and pedestrians. The kid was talented I couldn't deny him that.

"Would you mind playing a song, behique?" he shouted as he ran.

"I'm sorry?" I asked, both embarrassed to be put on the spot and shocked that I would be embarrassed.

"A song! To celebrate Areíto and put a pep in my step!" the boy shouted.

"I don't think you need any more p–pep, but okay. Since its Areíto. You'll to keep the cart steady, okay?"

"Of course, behique. Steady as she goes!"

"What should I p–play" I asked, turning to Isadore.

"El Tiburón," Isadore said with a grin.

I started the up-tempo tune, and the driver indeed gained a pep in his step. I couldn't help but think how ridiculous and incredible our bird-like cart looked and sounded as it coursed through the city, with nothing but a melody left in its wake.

The boy did not lie. It was the quickest trip to the manse I ever made. I handed the boy a silver Andoli mark, but he refused saying, "It was an honor to serve you, behique."

"P–please, I insist," I said, but the boy shook his head and held up his hands. "Then can I at least have your name so I can offer a b–blessing to Yaya in your name?"

The boy's face lit up. "Lalo, behique. Lalo Lopez."

"Well, Lalo Lopez, I will offer this silver mark to Yaya and p–pray he showers you with b–blessings."

Lalo bowed repeatedly and seemed on the verge of tears. "Thank you behique, thank you!"

"Funny boy," Izzy said as the cart sped away down the hill, back toward the city proper. "You probably made his week, no month."

"I couldn't let him leave without something," I replied.

"See? This is why the people love you. Luisa would never do something like that."

I frowned. "Yeah, you're p–probably right."

"Are you good to see your bibi alone?" Izzy asked. "I think I'm in time for the security briefing. The city watch always loves when the carib are present. We kind of act as a buffer between the watch and the Guazabara."

"Go ahead," I said and tried to smile. "And good luck!"

"Oh no, you take all the luck. I'll be fine. You though?"

I froze. "Do you really think I need all that luck?"

Isadore smiled and hurried back to my side. She put her hands on my shoulders, smiled widely, and said, "It'll be fine. It'll be easy. It's just talking to your bibi. You do that all the time. You got this. And your bibi is great. You don't need luck. So, I take it all back. Give me all the luck."

I tried to smile. "Thanks, Izzy."

"Now go! I'll meet you out here after."

It was business as usual inside the manse. Guazabara, the elite royal guard who answered only to the Cacique, stood watch at the door. Gardeners carried urns full of water to each planter and hanging pot. The housekeepers marched in a single file line from the dining hall to their next destination. I frowned knowing I missed breakfast but knew I could head to the kitchen and grab some leftovers from the chefs, Feliz and Marcos. The air in the halls smelled floral. The walls, floor, and ceiling shone glossy and clean as if a thin layer of water sparkled on every surface. I kept my head down and walked as quickly and quietly to my bibi's chambers. She liked to have a bath after breakfast saying it helped with her indigestion. When I made it to her quarters, the guazabara stood guard while Celia, Isadore's aunt and my bibi's sworn carib, stood outside.

"Hola, Hildy," Celia said as she embraced me and kissed both my cheeks.

"Hola, Celia," I replied. "Is my b–bibi free to talk?"

Celia frowned uncomfortably. She put a hand on my shoulder and guided me out of the earshot of the enormous double doors to my bibi's chambers and the heavily armed guaza that stood guard. "She is in one of her tempers, mija. Is it urgent?"

I shook my head. "No, I just have some news and I wanted to share with her."

Celia nodded. "I can pass on a message if you like. Or I can deliver a note."

"You really don't think she'd accept me right now?"

Celia shook her head. "She had a rather vocal argument with

Luisa this morning and ordered the Cacique out of her chambers."

I cringed. "If we're b–being honest though, Luisa and b–bibi are always at each other's throats."

Celia rolled her eyes. "Who doesn't that girl argue with? A cacique should have more even a temper," she said then immediately bit her tongue.

"It's okay, Celia. I'll write her a quick note." I reached into my pouch for a blank note card and my pen, then scribbled a little message:

Bibi,

I know how important it is to you having a daughter in the Temple. I wanted to tell you that the Suma chose me to perform the Telling at this year's festival. I'd hope it makes you proud and I hope you feel well enough to make it out one night."

You are the moon of my life and the stars of my forever.

Hildy.

I folded the message and pressed it into Celia's palm. "P–please tell her I would still love to see her tomorrow for our second day b–breakfast, if she's feeling well enough."

"I will, Hildy," Celia said then kissed my cheeks once more.

With my plans thwarted, I walked back to the main hall and made my way to the kitchens. I heard Marcos and Feliz arguing before I even made it to the door.

"I said two tablespoons per cup of rice, not four!" Marcos shouted, fighting Feliz for a spoon and jar. "You'll over season it!"

"I put three per cup last time and nobody complained. I even heard the Cacique say it was better than usual," Feliz said coolly, with a grin plastered on his face. Feliz was the younger of the two chefs and had only worked in the manse for three years. He hid his luxurious auburn locks underneath a handkerchief that matched the wild colored, geometric print of his pants. He was thin but had an angelic face and always wore a smile no matter the situation. I believed it was that smile that most often drew the ire of Marcos.

"I don't care if it tasted better to one person. I've measured the ingredients out perfectly. That jar is supposed to make ten pots of rice. The way you're going through it it'll only make six!" Although old and heavy, with short, cropped hair and a nose that looked broken in three different places, Marcos was surprisingly light on his feet.

"Which is it, chef, over seasoned or I'm using too much? You worry too much, my friend. I'll make more if it runs out."

"I am your chef, not your friend," Marcos said, jabbing a stubby finger at the taller man's chest. "Two tablespoons from now on, understand?"

Feliz snapped to attention and saluted Marcos.

"I don't know why I put up with you," Marcos said then noticed me standing in the doorway with slight amusement on my face. "Hildy! Come in, come in! What can I get for you?"

"Hola, Marcos. Hola, Feliz. I missed breakfast and wondered if you had any leftovers?"

Marcos directed me to the island in the middle of the kitchen where a small pile of breakfast pastries was stacked. "A few sweet breads are all. Take your fill. What we don't eat will go to the poor."

"I also have some tocino," Feliz added and slid a plate piled with bacon to me. "Take whatever you want Hildy. It's all yours."

"Thank you so much. I'm so hungry," I said then stuffed a sweet roll into my mouth.

"So, what brings you to the Manse this morning?" Marcos asked. "Did the Suma Behique finally give you a day off?"

I shook my head. "No, I mean yes, b–but that's not why I came. I just wanted to see b–bibi."

"Ah. Poor timing then," Marcos tsked.

"You heard about it too?" I asked. "It must have b–been an epic shouting match."

"Lots of yelling, from what I heard."

"Did either of you hear what it was about?" I asked.

Marcos shook his head, but Feliz shrugged and bobbed his head side to side.

"Mas o menos," Feliz said.

"Well?" I asked for more.

"I think Luisa is considering disbanding the Temple, outlawing religion. I don't know how or why. I didn't even realize the cacique could do something like that, disband an entire religion."

I couldn't believe what I was hearing. Disband the Temple? That surely would have caused an argument. Bibi is still devout, but Luisa has always had an issue with people not giving her the respect she feels she deserves. And I know from experience that she and the Suma Behique had not seen eye to eye. But to disband the Temple? Would she really consider doing something so stupid?"

"Cállate, Feliz. Nobody would do something that stupid," Marcos said, taking the words out of my mouth. "The Temple gives people hope, provides for the poor, teaches the children, and let's not forget her own sister is a behique. Why would she even consider that?"

Feliz held up his hands. "I only repeat what I heard. Don't stone the messenger."

The two chefs grew quiet and turned their attention to me. Marcos's eyes went wide. "Hildy are you okay? You've gone white as a sheet!"

I swallowed hard and looked at the chef. I wanted to speak

but I had no words. Feliz walked to where I sat and put a hand on my shoulder. "Let me get you some water, Hildy."

I shook my head, grabbed two pieces of sweet bread, a handful of tocino, then stood up. "I'm sorry. I have to go. Thanks for the food." I shot from the kitchen as fast as my feet would carry me.

The Festival of Areíto

My heart pounded, threatening to burst from my chest. My stomach churned itself into knots. Suddenly I felt like I needed to vomit or use the toilet, or both simultaneously. Disband the Temple. Why would she even consider that? The nerve! The insanity! It's no wonder bibi was not feeling well. I had to go confront Luisa. Maybe I could talk some sense into her.

I hurried to the main hall and saw the clock above the chamber doors. Nine a.m. She would have started their council meeting by now. All the caciques menores would be in there. I felt sick again. "You can't just barge in there," I thought to myself. I looked again and saw the doors still open. She hadn't started yet. "Go, Hildy!" I commanded myself. "Go now!"

Gritting my teeth, I hurried up the steps. I knew not what I would say to her or even if I would have the self-control to keep my cool, but I had to say something, anything. I reached the landing and the two guaza holding the doors open for the caciques menores quickly began to close them shut.

"No, wait!" I said through ragged breaths.

The two guaza stopped and the man on the right approached me. "I'm sorry, behique. Today's meeting is a closed session, by order of the Cacique."

"Okay, I just need to speak with my sister. It won't take b– but a minute."

"I'm sorry behique, I cannot let you through," the guaza said, arms crossed on his chest.

I looked around the beefy guaza and pointed at Luisa. "She's right there. It'll be quick, I p–promise," I said, trying to pivot around him, but he stuck out his massive tree limb of an arm and barred my way.

"Really?" I said in disbelief.

"Really, behique. I can send word to you as soon as they have ended the session but until then I cannot grant you access."

I clenched my jaw and took a step back. I watched as the guaza closed the doors, watched as Luisa welcomed the twelve caciques menores, watched as her eyes caught my red and sweaty face full of anger. Her face lit up with a smile and a nod as if to say, "Too slow, sister. I win again."

I stood in front of the closed doors, staring at the guaza with righteous indignation. After a brief moment of scowls I had hoped translated my anger and frustration at them, I turned around, stuffed another sweet roll into my mouth, then slowly made my way down the steps and out the front doors of the manse.

Izzy had yet to leave her security brief, so I plopped myself down on the steps, angrily eating some slices of bacon. I'm sure I looked like a pitiful sight, especially to the first groups of tourists arriving for the tour of the old manse building, the traditional caney of the caciques of the Andolins. But I didn't care. My anger and disbelief at Luisa burned hot. I knew one thing, I wanted to be as far away from the manse as possible. Luckily, Isadore came skipping up.

"Greetings, Behique Hildy," she said formally, with a stiff bow.

I exhaled sharply. "Please don't do that. Not now. You know I hate it."

"I'm sorry," Izzy apologized. "Did something happen with your bibi?"

I shook my head. "I didn't even get to see her. Apparently, she and Luisa had it out at b–breakfast."

"Speaking of breakfast, is that for me?" Izzy asked, pointing at the sweet bread and bacon.

I nodded and handed the food over to her. "Feliz told me something disturbing, but I don't know if I believe it. I don't want to believe it. I won't."

"Oooookay, care to share?" Izzy asked.

I shook my head. "Not now. Maybe later. Can we just get out of here?"

"Sure. Where do you want to go?"

I shrugged. "Nowhere. I mean somewhere. I know I need to go over my notes one more time. And I feel like I need to b– bathe. Maybe a soak will do me good."

"A soak and a quiet room to go over your notes. Bath house? Or we can hop right next door to the compound. I'm sure my bibi wouldn't mind drawing some hot water for us."

"I know she wouldn't, b–but I'd rather not give her any more work."

"Bath house it is then!"

The attendants of the fancy bath house that Isadore brought me to were surprised to see a behique at their establishment and even more so to see the sister of the cacique there. Business was slow now as almost everyone in Puerto Zafiro was either at the batéy or on their way there. This meant we were able to bathe in the most luxurious private room they had. I offered to pay, as did Isadore, but the hostess flatly refused to accept my marks. Izzy and I vowed to leave our coin in the room for whoever cleaned it after us.

The herbal and mineral soak felt amazing on my stressed body. I could feel it all fading away, even though the words "Disband the Temple" still crashed around my head. Izzy told me about her briefing as we bathed, glossing over the juicier bits she couldn't tell me without "having to kill me after," she joked.

After my fingertips turned to prunes, I stepped out of the bath, threw on a robe, and sat with my notes, scanning over everything I had written the previous night. Isadore remained in the bath, sprinkling handfuls of water on her arms which rested on the stone floor before me.

"What did you end up on for your Telling?" she asked. "Majick? How dogs naturally obey the members of your clan because your people worshiped Opieyelguabiran a thousand years ago?"

I grinned and nodded in agreement. "That would have b–been a good idea, b–but no. I used your idea about music. B–but it isn't any good. It's terrible. Are the people even going to know what I mean when I start discussing musical theory? I barely understand it and I've p–played the flute for ten years now."

"Remember what I told you a couple of years ago when you said you were a terrible liar?"

"No, but I don't know if I like where this is going."

Izzy grinned. "I said if you can say it with confidence, you can literally say anything and have anybody believe you."

"Hmm," I muttered.

"Did you know the first dance troupe to perform at Areíto were actually accompanied by flautists?"

"No, I didn't know that. Really? How did you know? Wait."

Izzy smiled. "See, it's that easy."

"It's that easy for you. You're naturally charismatic."

"You are too, Hildy," Izzy said, gently splashing water at me. "You just don't have the confidence. But it's okay. I'll believe in you even when you can't believe in yourself. That way, if you can't believe in yourself, you can believe in the me that believes in you."

I chuckled and shook my head. "Thanks Izzy. I don't know if I tell you enough, but I love you."

"I know."

The rest of the afternoon went by in a blur. We moved from the bath house to the gardens of the Temple where I practiced my first night's speech over and over again, stumbling over words, stuttering, and simply hating everything I wrote. Each mistake increased my fear and anxiety completely erasing all the good the bath house had accomplished.

Isadore sweetly listened to each trial run, never judging, or giving me pointers unless I asked. I changed words here and there on her suggestion and tore up whole cards after I stuttered over every word I had written. As the sun began its descend toward the horizon, I could feel the panic setting in. The cheerful shouts from the batéy could be heard all over the city. The people began to file that way to watch that evening's fireworks display. Yet the only thing I wanted to do was crawl under my covers and sleep for three days. And no sooner did I confess that to Isadore did the bells around the city begin to chime. The first hour of night and the official beginning of Areíto was announced and with it my dread peaked.

We had already begun our walk to the batéy when I looked at Isadore and said, "I change my mind. I don't want to be a b– behique. I don't want to do this anymore." Isadore stopped in the middle of the street and stared at me. The crowd of people moved around us, only slightly perturbed by the blockade. Then, with an evil grin, Isadore circled around me and put her hand on my back. "P–please don't p–push me. I don't think I can't do this," I croaked, fear dripping from every stuttered word. My heart pounded clear out of my chest. My palms quickly grew slick with sweat. To top it all off, my knees locked as if my body, in a sudden show of solidarity, agreed with my panicked sentiment.

"Hildy, don't be ridiculous," Isadore said as she stepped ahead of me and turned to face me. "Yes, giving the Telling is the biggest opportunity you've ever had in your fifteen years, and yes, you may have trouble speaking in front of crowds…"

"Is this your definition of a p–pep talk?" I interrupted.

Isadore grinned wickedly and continued. "But I've seen and heard you practice this speech all day today. You are more than capable and definitely prepared for this."

I shook my head. She was right, of course. I kept telling myself that being chosen for the Telling was an honor, to be sure, and doubly so to be the youngest behique the Temple had ever chosen. But I didn't feel prepared and as I stood before the gates to the Batéy del Albizu, watching all the people with enormous smiles plastered on their faces, walking, skipping, and some even running into the biggest and most beautiful park in Puerto Zafiro, I couldn't help but feel the opposite. The gates, iron behemoths with "Batéy del Albizu" displayed proudly at the top, were not the entrance to the best holiday celebration on the islands. They felt more like cage doors, threatening to slam shut and trap me as soon as I stepped foot inside.

"I want to agree with you, b–but look at me," I held out my shaking hand. "My hands are shaking and this…damned stutter."

Isadore grabbed my hand. "You want to agree with me, so quit arguing and agree with me." She smiled the genuine sly smile only she could give. "Plus, it is my solemn duty as your best friend and carib to make sure you make it there safe and on time, so let's go!"

She pulled with all her might, but my feet were planted firmly to the stone street. Isadore tugged, but I shook my head and pulled back. She let go of my hand and I began to turn around, only she quickly ran behind me, placed her hands on my back, and turned me back toward the gate. My feet were no longer stuck to the stones like glue. Thanks to Isadore's pushing, I slid almost effortlessly through looming black gates. I am positive we looked absurd.

Suddenly, an explosion of fireworks, in breathtaking and spectacular hues of turquoise and gold, lit up the night sky over the batéy. The people around me cheered, yet their shouts sounded like a miserable cacophony. It made me jump in fright. Isadore pulled me out of the way of a crowd of festivalgoers just before they ran into me.

"What's gotten into you?" Isadore asked. "You're skittish like a stray cat."

I shook my head. "It's not nothing. No, I lied. It's what Feliz told me, what he overheard at the manse."

Isadore frowned. "What now? Is Luisa trying to flex her muscles as Cacique, even over her own kin?"

I shook my head.

"Do you not want to talk about it?"

I shook my head again. "I'm sorry," I whispered, lowering my head.

"Don't be," Isadore said, placing fingers under my chin and lifting my head. "Just forget about it for now. Let's try and have a little fun on the way, okay?"

I nodded. "Yeah, okay."

We walked the cobblestone paths, along with most of the city's population, through the Batéy del Albizu. Children ran several paces ahead of their parents, squealing in delight as they weaved through the crowd. Jibaros from the countryside, with their wide straw hats and dark chestnut skin, sauntered in packs, each man chewing a piece of sugar cane and laughing. The city watch mingled with the guazabara, both sets of soldiers clad in their most colorful ceremonial garb. There were other behique, too. The brothers and sisters of my order scurried about in their usual plain grey robes, carrying flags, transporting barrels of water, or giving aid to the elderly who braved the crowds for the festival.

Seeing other behique made my breath catch in my throat. I pulled my hood over my braided, brunette locks and immediately patted my own robes, hoping I had not forgotten anything at the Temple. I slid my fingers into the pouch attached to my belt and felt my folded-up notes along with a few Andoli marks, in case I wanted to buy anything. I touched my prized flute, reddish orange in color like the flower of the flamboyán from which it was carved, tucked safely between my belt and my robe. I thought I heard Isadore speak, so I impulsively said, "What?"

"I said, you know what my favorite part of Areíto is, Hildy?" Isadore asked with an enormous grin as she pulled me close and bit her lip in glee.

"I b–believe the entire city knows of your ravenous appetite for p–pernil," I replied, trying my best to smile.

Isadore giggled and clutched at her chest as if holding something dear close to her heart. "There is no part of that glorious twisty-tailed, snout-faced animal that I don't enjoy."

"I am well aware of that," I responded with an amused shake of my head. "Remember the festival three years ago? The fiasco with the merchant?"

"It was not a fiasco," Isadore argued through her laughter. "I paid for the meat. The old man thought he could cheat me out of two whole ounces."

Another round of fireworks detonated overhead and a roar of applause washed over the Batéy. Once again, the noise made me jump. "The fact that you can feel the difference of a few ounces can make is the most fascinating p–part of that story."

"Carib are trained to be precise in everything," Isadore said, licking her lips.

I tried to smile, but the old memory only reminded me of a time when I didn't have such responsibility weighing on me. "That year was the last Areíto I could celebrate without any cares or worries. I miss running the streets of the b–batey with you before these obligations to the Temple."

Isadore squeezed me tight as we walked. "You know, we can still run the streets of the batey without any obligations. We're only fifteen! Let's celebrate like we did when we were twelve."

"You mean argue over pernil? Or do you mean steal feathered b–bracelets from troupe tents and sneak into the b–batu championship?"

"I mean have fun!" Isadore cried. She grabbed my hand and pulled me to the nearest vendor. "Come on, Hildy. The meat is on me."

I sighed. "Eating doesn't sound like fun to my stomach."

Isadore insisted though and bought us both small plates piled with salty pernil. I ate one piece and immediately regretted it as nausea swept over me. There was no calming my stomach. Izzy graciously ate my portion which I think was her plan all along.

"I don't know where you fit all of that," I said as she stuffed the last piece into her already full mouth.

She shrugged. "Dah mea heps buil ma mushuls," she mumbled through stuffed cheeks.

We walked slowly through the Batéy del Albizu, the largest park in Puerto Zafiro. Puerto Zafiro was the capital of the Free Islands of the Andoli Empire, or the Andolins as we Andoli referred to it. The batéy, an enormous rectangle spanning nearly five and a half kilometers, from the borders of the manse district, down the mountainside was its crown jewel. The batéy was as close to a paradise as you could find, which is impressive for a park in the middle of a tropical utopia. Acres of trees, ponds stocked with fish, ball courts where the batu tournaments were held, and several amphitheaters could be found within the grounds. During Areíto the batéy became a haven for tents and flagpoles in every color of the spectrum, thrusting above the treetops. Each big top housed traveling companies of dancers or that year's cook off participants, or cots for visiting ball clubs. Every manner of performer danced, pranced, and sang their way down the cobblestone paths. Candy-makers spun sugar or stretched taffy for adults and children alike, filling the air with sweet, decadent delight.

We happened upon a small crowd just off the path we followed. The twenty or so people surrounded three dancers and clapped a beat as they moved. The troupe was clearly Nitano by their elaborate and obviously expensive dress, while the crowd gathered was mostly average, working-class Borinkens. Isadore smiled widely as she grabbed my hand and pulled me toward the group. She joined in, clapping and shouting when a rather jolly, rotund man, with no shirt, pointed at the flute tucked snuggly into my belt.

"Behique!" He called to me then bowed. "Can you play us a tune; perhaps 'Baile de la Grulla?'"

The woman to his right added her voice to the cause. "Yes, behique! Play us a tune!"

Several others joined their voices, and it soon became a chant. I flushed in embarrassment at the attention and shook my head, raising my hands and backing away, but Isadore, ever the reveler, cried, "Yes, she can!" and pulled me into the center next to the dancers. I tried to walk back into the crowd, telling them I only really play for my bibi and at the Temple, but Isadore grabbed me by the shoulders and planted me front and center.

My jaw shuddered as I reluctantly released my flute and started to play.

I hit the first notes and a cheer ran through the small crowd. The dancers threw their arms up and began to gyrate their hips. Isadore leapt in excitement, twirling, and kicking along with the troupe. The jolly man sang at the top of his lungs and nearly all joined in on the chorus. *You can do this, Hildy. It's just like playing in the Temple. You've done that loads of times.* That was when I missed a series of notes. I cringed and pulled my flute away from my mouth, staring at the delicately carved wood with disgust. It was as if the instrument inherited my stutter just to mock me. I tried to pick up the song and join in at the end of the second verse, only my fingers trembled with fear causing me to play out of tune. The crowd continued regardless and when the singing finished everybody clapped ecstatically. The dancing troupe bowed with a flourish. Even I received a few grateful bows and palms of peace as Isadore and I left the group, although I could tell they were given out of pity. My confidence shattered to pieces.

"Don't you just love Areíto?" Isadore asked, slightly winded, her beautiful, burnished bronze skin slick with sweat from her spontaneous performance. Her eyes, which nearly matched her skin tone, beamed with joy. "Andoli from every walk of life, together in harmony!"

"Yeah…" I mumbled. I slid my flute back into my belt and kept my eyes glued to the path.

Our conversation slowed the closer we got to the plaza at the center of the batey. The buzz of revelry also faded the farther from the crowds we got, yet it still sounded harsh and shrill in my ears. I could feel a headache forming. My stomach clenched and tied itself into tighter and tighter knots. I hated the feeling. This was Areíto, after all. I should be filled with joy and happiness like the countless citizens that surrounded me. My mouth should be watering just thinking about the pork, or the fried mango and banana, or the skewers of camarones and bacalao. I should be eager in anticipation to watch the batu tournament, or dance with the troupes, or just lay back and watch the fireworks that illuminated the night sky. Yet all that, when combined with my fight with Luisa and the possibility of ending the Telling, filled me with uncontrollable dread. I felt completely inept for the task ahead.

"Isadore," I called.

Isadore stopped and turned to face me. "Uh-oh," she replied.

"What do you mean 'uh-oh'?"

"You only call me Isadore when you're in need of sage advice."

I frowned and motioned to a bench just off the trail, avoiding her gaze. We sat and she bent forward to rest her arms on her legs, clasping her hands together. It took me a moment to gather my thoughts. My mind raced back and forth bouncing from worry to worry so fiercely I could scarcely form coherent sentences, let alone have them pass my lips. Finally, I took a deep breath and said, "I know I should not always burden you with my anxiety."

Isadore *tsked*. "Hildy, I am not simply your carib, your protector, I am your friend, your BEST friend. You *never* have to apologize for wanting to talk."

I forced a smile and nudged her with my shoulder. "I am going to stutter. I know it. My tongue trips over itself when I speak in p–public."

Isadore placed her hand on my knee. "You're doing just fine right now. It's barely noticeable."

I wanted to believe her but found it impossibly hard to.

Instead, I buried my face in my hands. I could feel the tears welling up. "Oh Yaya, give me strength."

Isadore scooted closer and wrapped her arm around me. "It's just the nerves, Hildy. You'll do fine. And I'll be right there with you."

I lifted my head, wiped my eyes and my nose on my sleeve, and looked at her for what seemed like a quiet eternity. "Thank you, Izzy," I finally said. "B–but that's not the only thing. Luisa is considering altogether eliminating the Telling from the festival."

Isadore's face contorted with confusion. "Why would she do that?"

"I don't know. Maybe because nobody attends the Telling any more. People come from all over the islands for the food and the tournament, but most have forgotten the reason why we celebrate Areíto in the first place. Not just that, but you know my sister. She has never been the biggest supporter of the temple. It's a major point of contention b–between her and the people she governs. The caciques menor have already voiced their displeasure with this idea. I've heard the rumors but, she is adamant that as the Cacique of the islands, she can do as she wishes; she only needs to consult the menores, not heed their advice. I'm afraid things will get muddled if she goes through with it. And I don't want my Telling to be the last Telling in history. What if I mess up? What if I'm the reason the Tellings end?"

Isadore nodded. "I can see why you're nervous. But if you look around at all the people in the batéy, it looks like none of them are even worried that any of that will happen."

"I know it is tradition, b–but something b–buried deep inside me is screaming. I want *my* Telling to be different. I want p–people to see that it's not just some myth from our p–past b–

but a living narrative; one that shaped our past and continues to shape our future." I paused and shook my head. "Maboya take this damned stutter," I mumbled as a few stray tears rolled down my cheeks.

Isadore stood from the bench and lifted my head in her hands, tenderly wiping away the tears. "If that's what you want to do, then I say do it. Yaya speaks to you in ways I never would have imagined. If you feel so strongly about this thing buried deep inside of you, then it must be a message from Yaya."

I shook my head, "I don't know, Izzy."

Isadore lifted me from the bench and embraced me. "Don't worry about Luisa. Just focus on the Telling." After our hug, she kissed me on both cheeks and gave me that same sly smile from earlier. "You'll be great, and if anyone says otherwise," she punched the palm of her hand. It made me genuinely smile for the first time that day.

The flags and tent tops that surrounded the batey shrank away with each step. The circle plaza of the batéy was once the centerpiece of the entire celebration of Areíto, but now was largely ignored in favor of the excitement in the rest of the park. I was painfully aware of this as we neared. The paths that, farther from the center, teemed with Andoli of every color, shape, and size, were now virtually abandoned. The few people Isadore and I did encounter were heading away from the center plaza in an inebriated stupor, the latest victims of too much snuff and cassava juice.

The path widened and came to a halt at the plaza, a perfect circle with stone walkways and gardens surrounding an ancient batu court. The tents of the Temple of Behique sat on the grounds of what was largely accepted as the foundation of the caney of the caciques of old; before Marohu's war with the Ultan-Meres. The behique transported countless cemi representing tribes and clans old and new and placed them in the tents. They said it was so our people could perform the worship rituals to their respective god, yet I never saw evidence of this.

The ball court was a different story. The center plaza ball court was the largest in the entire Batéy del Albizu and until relatively recently, within the last fifty years, hosted ball tournaments every day of the year. The surface was polished seastone that glistened pearlescent in the sun and glowed with the moonlight. It was enclosed with similar seastone walls about shoulder high. Each panel bore the likeness of a cemi carved directly into the stone so the gods could weigh the outcome of each match. The court lost popularity in favor of the open grass courts that dotted the Batéy. It was transformed into a statuary well before the birth of me and my siblings. Several giant cemi stood watch in the courtyard; Yaya as revealed to our ancestors, a loro alighting on a tri-faceted stone with a strange face carved on each facet. The voluptuous form of Atabey, mother of nations, astride her mighty caguama stood to Yaya's right. To the left, and completing the triangle, was Maboya, dark and shadowy cemi of death coiled within an equally dreadful looking maja. The cemi stood watch like armed sentries, their gazes fixed on the black marble memorial stone in the center.

"Let's stop by the statuary b–before we go in," I said to Isadore. It was meant to be a statement but came out as a plea.

"Of course, Hildy," Isadore said, grabbing my hand and leading me in.

We bowed and paid our respects to Yaya, Atabey, and Yúcahu. I made sure I touched Opiyelguabiran, who was the dog cemi responsible for seeing souls to the afterlife, and strangely enough, the patron cemi of my clan, the Albizu–Rios clan. We stopped at a black marble memorial stone, and I quietly read the inscription aloud.

"The Stone of Jenaro Albizu del Rios, son to the great Marohu Josue Albizu del Rios first Cacique of the Free Andoli Kingdom; a gift from the Mason's Guild, Scholia Regium in remembrance of Jenaro's deeds to all nations of Ke'."

"I always wondered what it must have been like to serve him," Isadore said. Her voice seemed far away as if she spoke in a dream. "Agostin Anacaona was a fortunate man."

"Agostin was just as prominent a figure in the legends as Jenaro was," I replied, squeezing Isadore's hand.

"That he was. Their fabled friendship was bigger than either man."

"Do you think there was ever an Albizu–Rios and Anacaona that didn't b–become b–best friends?"

Isadore chuckled at my inquiry. "Impossible. Since the Oath, families are bound. Our family lines have quite literally grown up together, just like you and I."

She loved the old stories of our clans. The tales of danger and adventure never failed to make her smile. "It's almost time," I said quietly.

"We go in together, side-by-side," Isadore said with a nod.

I nodded back and took her hand.

The Telling

Banners waved proudly atop the monstrous, weather-worn canvas tent where I would spend the next three evenings. There were more lamps surrounding the tent than traditionally called for. I also noticed a detachment of guazabara guards standing watch by each entrance. I shuddered. The presence of guazabara could only mean one thing: my sister had come to the Telling.

Why is she here? Coming to tell me she decided to disband the Temple—or simply to gloat about how she's bibi's favorite? I cringed and pulled my hood lower, hiding my face as we quickly brushed past the guaza. I made a beeline to the rear of the tent hoping I could make it to the anteroom where I would make my preparations before Luisa spotted me. I reached the room, burst through the tent flaps, and quickly tied them shut. I made it without running into her.

"Hildy!" Luisa shouted as she embraced me.

I nearly leapt out of my skin at the sound of her voice and shrieked at the surprise hug. *So much for avoiding her.*

"Luisa!" I cried with a mixture of surprise and horror. "What are you doing here?"

Luisa laughed as she released me from her embrace, yet still clung to my shoulders.

"Oh Hildy, my favorite sister," she said, her voice needlessly high pitched. She hugged me even tighter.

"Your only sister," I grumbled, to which she quite ominously didn't respond.

"I just couldn't let you perform the Telling tonight until you heard just how proud I am to be your younger sister. A del Rios woman has performed the Telling at least once every generation. You bring honor to our family." She placed a gentle kiss on my cheek. "It is only fitting that one of our clan would make the *final* telling." The way she emphasized the word "final" made me gulp.

Luisa wore a smile that thinly veiled her foul mood and only barely caged her viper's tongue. Her eyes twinkled with false pride. The game she played may work wonders on the caciques menores, but I knew the truth behind her saccharine façade. She still bristled with anger. Her showing up to the Telling was not out of family pride but a threat.

My wanted to poke the coals and stoke the fires of the smoldering fight, but my brain declined the invitation. *You have given me enough to deal with already*, it told me. *Don't pile it on.* So instead, I smiled back, hugged her once more and said, "Thank you," then slowly moved toward the table at the far end of the room. I emptied my pack onto the table, placing my notes and my flute next to my ceremonial vestments that one of my fellow behique had laid out for me.

"Are these your notes for the Telling?" Luisa asked as she approached my side and reached for them. I hastily gathered each leaf and tried to stuff them into my robe pockets but only succeeded in dropping them all over the ground.

"No, no they're not," I said as I dropped to my knees to gather them up. "I mean, yes, they are…I don't know why I lied. Aren't you late for the crowning of the dancers?" I asked in a futile attempt to free myself from Luisa's meddling. "It is customary for the Cacique…"

"Since when does a behique lecture the Cacique on what is customary?" she fired back. I looked at her face just in time to see her clenched jaw and blaze of anger quickly subside. "Why sister!" Luisa cawed, her high-pitched, honey coated tone resurfacing with a vengeance. She even placed her right hand on her chest feigning offense. "Are you trying to be rid of me?"

I sighed. "Of course not, Luisa, It's just…I have to get ready and changed into these vestments–"

"This terrible thing?" Luisa asked, reaching and grabbing the sleeve off the table. "You don't have the body for this. Your hips are too big and your boobs too small. Had I known the behique got to wear this, I might have joined the temple as well."

There are only two people in my life who find a need to comment on my body and unfortunately both are my kin. My bibi's comments are subtle and passive-aggressive while Luisa always preferred a more direct approach. I inherited the shape of all the women from my baba's side, thicker through the hips and thighs with not much on top, and, if I'm honest, outlandishly large ears. Meanwhile, Luisa was "blessed" with my bibi's figure. She was a statuesque goddess; tall, buxom, and shapely with high cheekbones, dainty ears with a multitude of small ringlet piercings, big hazel eyes, and a sharp, avian nose adorned with tastefully placed stud piercings. She braided her raven hair and bunched it together on the back of her head, adorned with wild, elaborate shells, colorful beads, and stones. Her skin was perfectly sun-kissed. Even her opulently tailored dress seemed paltry in comparison to her natural beauty.

"Yes, Luisa," I said through clenched teeth. "It is revealing and calling attention to it doesn't help my nerves. I need to go over the p–preamble once more and my stutter is uncontrollable today."

Luisa placed her hand on mine. "Oh, Hildy." Her lips pouted ever so slightly in a way I'm sure the boys found irresistible. She didn't have to say it, but I could feel the pity seething from her flesh.

Despite all this, it is true: I love my sister. She has always been like a second mother, but when added to our already overbearing mother, this meant I had always been given little room to breathe. To make matters worse, she was a full year and one month younger than me, which made her mothering all the more difficult to bear.

"Thank you for coming, Luisa. I mean it. I only wish you could stay," I found myself saying, hoping she would not and praying she took the hint.

Luisa rose from her seat and gave me another hug. "You'll do fine, sister. When you finish tonight, will you come straight home to the manse? Our bibi has been asking about you."

I rolled my eyes. "I am having b–breakfast with her in the morning, dear sister."

She held me at arms-length once more then kissed my forehead. "You are the moon of my life," she said.

The words my baba once said to us every night before bed felt cheap and tawdry coming from her loathsome lips. My already nauseated stomach churned a bit more as I responded in turn, more out of necessity than anything. "And the stars of my forever." *If he was still here, he would be sitting at the front, by the stage, with the biggest smile on his face.* I thought as I watched Luisa strut from the room. The curtain opened. That's when I spotted Isadore speaking to her own sister, Luisa's carib, Liliana. They shared a quick hug, much to Luisa's chagrin, then Isadore hurried into my chamber.

"The Suma Behique is getting anxious," Isadore said. "I think she's feeding off of your energy."

I groaned. "P–please don't tell me that Izzy."

Isadore grimaced, grabbed my hand, and gave it a squeeze. "I'm sorry. I didn't mean to." She glanced over to the table at my ceremonial vestments. "Did you need help with those?"

I shook my head. "Not unless you can convince hundreds of

years of cultural history and the countless religious legalists that it is unnecessary to dress in such ways."

Isadore eyed me and smiled. "I actually like the vestments."

I squinted and pursed my lips. "Get out."

She laughed. "I'll be right outside," she said and left me alone.

I removed my robe then my silken breeches, camisole and my undergarments. Then I lifted the skirt from the table and scowled as I slipped into it. It covered a shockingly small amount of skin, shielding my most intimate areas from prying eyes, but leaving the entirety of my legs bare. The rough fabric could have at one time been considered white. The top resembled the skirt in make and color, rough leather, short, and faded white, almost gray. Feathers hung from beaded strands of hide that attempted to conceal my torso. When I reached up and undid my hair, I noticed the vest lifted a little too high. *Great. I'll have to try and keep my arms as low as possible.* The crown was simple; sea stone with tri-faceted beads representing Yaya. The Suma Behique left me a small jar of ermine colored paste. I smeared it on my arms and my cheeks, my torso and legs. It's not perfect, but it isn't supposed to be. We are imperfect before Yaya, she taught us. The final pieces were the ceremonial pipe and retch rod, which were not used much if at all these days, especially during Areíto, but were still considered necessary. I opened my pouch and grabbed one in each hand then finally turned to the door. Isadore stood there with a big smile on her face.

"How long have you been spying on me?" I asked, arms akimbo, face askew.

"Well, that is simply insulting," Isadore responded, mimicking my pose. "I am your carib. What I do is not called spying. It's called guarding."

I shook my head and forced a smile. "How b–bad is it? B–be honest?"

Isadore averted her eyes and rubbed the back of her neck. "Not great."

My shoulders slumped.

"But," Isadore continued, "I don't believe that's going to matter much. There's exactly five Andoli waiting for you."

My eyes went wide.

"Only five?" I asked in exasperation.

We both rushed out of the room and around the corner to the main area of the tent. I peeked through the flaps and was greeted by a nearly abandoned tent. Isadore was correct. There were exactly five people seated cross-legged on the stone floor of the plaza, two of whom looked drunk off mango rum and cassava juice.

"No, there needs to b–be more than five!" I cried. "This will just b–be another confirmation that Luisa's decision is the right one. Gah, can you imagine the gloating she will do?"

"I can try and rustle up some more people," Isadore said with a shrug. "There's bound to be a few exhausted elders or curious tourists nearby."

I shook my head. "No, there isn't enough time for that. It's already time to b–begin."

Isadore placed her arm over my shoulders. "If you insist. But change your mind and I'm gone in a flash. Just remember, you're amazing and talented and whether there are five people or five hundred people, you will give a Telling for the ages."

"Thank you, Izzy," I said.

"I'll be at the back. And hey, you should have no problem seeing me!"

I pushed her through the curtain into the main room. I stood for a moment surveying all the empty space. *Baba would have been here. He wouldn't have cared if I gave the Telling to such a small crowd. It's like my own private Telling, he would've said.* I was so wrapped up in my own thoughts, I didn't hear the Suma Behique approach.

"Are you ready, my dear?" she asked while gently touching my shoulder.

I tried to smile but could not find the strength. Fear gripped my entire person. My reluctance to speak ballooned to bursting. Yet, to only have five souls present was worse than having a full room. There were a million reasons for the low turnout bouncing around in my head. Maybe it was me. Who would want to hear such a young behique give the Telling? If the Suma Behique was slated to speak, would it be a packed house? Or maybe the citizens of the kingdom have just given up on the Telling. There was no need for oral tradition when we had such a beautiful written word. It hurt to admit, but maybe Luisa is right in wanting to completely cancel the Telling...

The Suma Behique's voice broke through my thoughts. "Hildy?"

"I can't do it, Suma B–behique," I admitted to the head of my order. I never shied away from candid conversation with her, but it felt wrong so close to the Telling. "I am not as strong as you. The spirits don't speak to me or through me like they do to you."

The Suma Behique smiled. "I communed with the cemi this morning. They showed me a vision. In it, I saw you, standing before a great multitude. A strange, metamorphic wind began to blow. It swept around you and tossed all else aside." She smiled. It was a genuine smile, full of the kind of love and hope and a caring I had only ever experienced from baba, my father.

I shook my head. "B–but Suma B–behique, there is not a great multitude out there. There are five p–people, six counting

Isadore. And what if I mess up? This could b–be the last Telling and…and…"

The Suma Behique reached for my hands and held them, pressed together, in her own. "I have never once doubted what the cemi show me. I refuse to do so this evening."

She pulled me into an embrace. I felt a strange warmth pass from her to me. Even after she released me, the warmth surrounded me and held me tight, the same feeling I used to get from my baba. It was the same feeling I get when I'm alone with Isadore or when Arecibo returns home. I took a deep yet shaky breath and nodded. *I can do this.*

I marched through the tent flaps and into the main assembly. The five Andoli present all turned their eyes to me. I nodded solemnly as I stepped into the speaker's circle, then took a deep breath and raised my arms, remembering not to raise them too high.

I clapped the pipe and the rod together.

The three sober Andoli responded by drunkenly clapping their hands.

I cried out to Yaya in the ancient tongue.

"Yaya send your b–blessings down upon your p–people!"

"May we live in your favor," Isadore responded from the rear. She was the only one.

I brought the rod to my mouth and mimed swallowing it, then lowered it to my side.

I brought the pipe to my nostrils and inhaled, only it was not lit and there was no snuff inside.

I turned slowly and placed both pipe and rod on the table of relics behind me. I reached for my notes but noticed they weren't there. I had left them in the room. My heart skipped. I could feel my cheeks turning red. My breathing began to quicken. My teeth chattered. I trembled from head to toe. I took several deep breaths. *Don't panic*, I told myself. *You know this story. Everyone knows this story.* I slowly turned back to the congregation.

"I b–b–begin with the first cave," I began. I snapped my trembling jaw shut before my voice once more betrayed me. My heart jumped. I glanced over the congregation. I couldn't tell if they noticed or not, but I felt their eyes glaring at me. They were silently judging me, embarrassed by my impediment, rolling their eyes that they had to hear the Telling from me. I began to feel nauseated. I looked again and saw Isadore standing at the entrance to the tent, leaning on the pole. She smiled wide and waved.

I closed my eyes and tried to picture the words to the Telling. When I opened my eyes, I could see through the entrance of the tent to the memorial of Jenaro Albizu del Rios resting in the center of the plaza. At that moment it seemed odd that a memorial to a man considered to be the heroic symbol of my people would have such a minimalistic shrine. Batu stadiums have grander statues to past players than Jenaro's cube of black marble. I imagined his likeness, standing tall and confident, mid-stride. I could see his roguish smile flashing to onlookers. In one hand he would have his lute, the other would be reaching down, reaching out to whomever stood in its presence, beckoning them to take his hand and join him on the adventure.

Without warning an idea formed. I could feel it taking shape in my mind, weaving through the memories of my baba and the tales he would tell. I could see the Telling, the narrative of our people, reflected in Jenaro's life. I turned once more to Isadore and raised my hand to her to signal I was okay. I was going to perform this Telling MY way. I took a deep breath. *Yaya, give me strength*, I prayed silently.

"The first cave," I repeated. "The first cave is creation."

THE FIRST CAVE: CREATION

In the Time Before

Marohu Josué Albizu del Rios sat cross-legged on the ground of his caney and smiled from ear to ear. It was an infectious smile. Anyone who looked upon it found themselves smiling back for no reason at all. In fact, the kindness and generosity represented in Marohu's smile was known throughout the Andolin Islands. It was one of many reasons the people trusted him. It was one of many reasons the people followed him. On this day, though, Marohu's smile was not for the people he ruled. It was for the child he held in his arms; a newborn, the first child of a union that brought peace and prosperity to his people.

Marohu's dark brown hair was pulled back tight and knotted near the top of his head. His skin was a deep olive and his eyes a polished mahogany. He was above average height for an Andoli, and lither than was normal. He was a strong and powerful man yet cradled his newborn son with all the grace and gentleness of a mother.

"He is more beautiful than I possibly could have imagined, sweet sun of my life." Marohu whispered to his wife.

Helena smiled weakly from her labor bed as the behique performed her cleansing rituals. She was from Hal'e, the island nation across the Summer Sea from the Andolins, and was representative of its half-Itiban population. Helena stood tall, a statuesque woman with soft features. Her skin shone like fresh honey and her dark hair rivaled the blackness of tourmaline. Her eyes resembled the sky after a storm, cool and gray. Her ears tapered to a gentle point. Helena reached out touched Marohu's face. Marohu turned his eyes to his wife and smiled. He was crying.

"If I am the sun of your life, he will be your moon," Helena said sweetly.

"My moon," Marohu whispered through silent tears, "and the stars of my forever."

The behique finished her tasks and bowed to the new parents. Marohu nodded in thanks and moved from the ground to the bed. He and Helena lay together in silence; Marohu with his head resting on Helena's shoulder and their son nestled tightly between them. They remained that way until the shadows grew long and the lamps were lit.

Helena was fast asleep when Marohu emerged from his caney with his son cradled safely in his arms. It was a clear night and despite the lamplight outside his abode Marohu could count the stars. He walked slowly down the steps outside his home, crossed the batéy, and reached the plateau that overlooked the city below. His men were working overtime assisting in the recovery effort. Their torches lit the city like a thousand garnets strewn across a navy sheet.

"My son," Marohu whispered, "my moon and stars forever. I have created the foundation for a great empire. I united the clans under one flag. I brokered a treaty with the Hal'e restoring our once powerful alliance. I led our people to victory over the Ultan-Meres, expelling them from our islands." He paused for a moment and turned his attention to the baby in his arms. "Yet, all my accomplishments pale in comparison to you."

Marohu's son nestled himself deeper into his arms. Marohu kissed him gently on his forehead.

On the third day following his birth, Marohu and Helena

brought their son before the local behique. In the sight of the cemi and those citizens of a now free Andoli nation, the child was named Jenaro Marohu Albizu del Rios. His life was dedicated to Yaya, greatest of all cemi and creator of all that surrounded them. He was then blessed by Opiyelguabiran, cemi of the del Rios clan. Murmurs of approval swept over all who were present.

Less than a week passed before Octavio, Marohu's best friend and sworn carib, and his wife, Ines relocated to the batéy. They had a newborn son, named Agostin, and promised that he would serve and protect Jenaro as Octavio had Marohu. It was repayment for a life debt. Marohu once saved Octavio from the brink of death. A caney was built alongside that of Marohu and Helena. It was a temporary shelter, for construction of a manse fit for the new Cacique had already begun.

Andoli masons and carpenters completed the new manse of the Cacique and much of the reconstruction of Puerto Zafiro on Jenaro's sixth name day, erasing the last vestiges of the filthy, pale faced Ultans who once ruled their islands. There was an enormous celebration. Andoli from throughout the two islands gathered in Puerto Zafiro. It was as lively as an Areíto, complete with a batu tournament and a Telling. The people danced and sang in the streets. It was well accepted that all this was possible thanks to Marohu's stewardship. The people anxiously looked ahead to a new era of prosperity in the Andolins.

At the end of the day, Marohu stood from his new balcony and surveyed the city which he liberated, the city he helped rebuild. It was once again the beautiful jewel of the Andolins. Yet, he could not shake the feeling that something was missing. He swore to voice his concerns to Octavio the next day.

Octavio joined Marohu on his balcony the following afternoon. Marohu was lounging in a cushioned chair. Octavio reclined in a similar seat opposite of him.

"The business of running a nation is more talk than I imagined," Octavio said with a sigh.

Marohu chuckled lightly. "Politics is not for the weak of spirit that is for sure. I imagined our time at war would have prepared me. I thought wrong."

Octavio smiled. "You mentioned you had a private matter you wished to discuss?"

"I do," Marohu answered with a nod. "It has only been six years and I fear we have already experienced our first failure as leaders of the Andoli."

Octavio was shocked. "I cannot say I agree, Marohu," he replied. "The city is rebuilt, better than before. The shops have reopened. The harbor is bustling. People are returning to their lives and thriving. Andoli are even enjoying diversion once more. Have you seen the number of batu tournaments being played and bards plying their trade?"

Marohu nodded but remained preoccupied. "It is true, Octavio. Peace and prosperity have taken hold of the people, yet I cannot help but think they are missing something important, something vital."

Marohu stood from his seat and walked to the balustrade. Puerto Zafiro bustled below. A distinct chatter resounded from the city. "What are the people of Puerto Zafiro missing that you and I both were fortunate enough to have in our small mountain village?"

Octavio joined Marohu by the balustrade. "Crisp mountain air," he said.

Marohu chuckled. "Do you remember the behique, To'guey?" Marohu asked.

"How could I forget her," Octavio replied. "The woman never could get me to pay attention to her lessons."

Marohu laughed. "I was thinking about her yesterday as I

walked past the Telling. It was a strange Telling, not anyway resembling the Tellings we grew up with. It was full of references to the god of the Ultans and stories passed on to us by our oppressors." Marohu thought for a moment. "Our people need a return to what was once ours, to live by the gods of our ancestors."

"You desire a return to tradition?" Octavio asked. "It seems counterintuitive to our ideas of progress."

"I desire to see our people proud of our history and heritage once more. If To'guey taught us anything, it was that the Andoli are just as strong and just as important as the Ultans. We are not lesser beings."

Octavio nodded. "To'guey would want us to lead our people back to our heritage."

Marohu clapped his hands together. "It is settled then. Tomorrow, we make our way back home to Cidra. We will meet with To'guey, offer her the title of Suma Behique, and charge her with restoring our people's faith in our culture and heritage."

Octavio nodded. "I will begin making the preparations."

Later that evening, during his private lessons, Marohu broke the news of their trip to Jenaro. The boy was excited to travel and more than eager to learn about his family history.

"Baba," Jenaro said, "Agostin says his family doesn't believe in the cemi, that he thinks it is silly of our family to pay tribute to a hound and a bird and a turtle and a snake. Is this true?"

Marohu laughed heartily. "Only an Anacaona man could be so bold and brash with his impiety." Marohu smiled at Jenaro. "Yes, my son, the patron cemi of our family is indeed a hound, or rather takes the shape of a hound. But it is not just any old dog. Opiyelguabiran is more of a spectral hound. He guides the souls of the departed to Maboya's wharf where they begin the final journey to the third cave. Have you not learned this from the behique?"

Jenaro's face twisted in thought. "We learned about a few cemi and the thirteen gods of the Itiba, but none as powerful as the one true god of the Ultans."

Marohu felt his stomach turn and his face twist up in a scowl. "Well, my boy, it is a terrible oversight that your education of the cemi should be neglected. That is one reason we are traveling to Cidra, to meet with my old behique To'guey."

"Ha ha!" Jenaro shouted. "My first adventure! I'm going to be a real adventurer!"

Marohu smiled. "That you are, my son."

"Wait until Ago hears this!" Jenaro smiled. "Who is To'guey, baba? Is he my new teacher?"

Marohu nodded, "She," he corrected, "will be your teacher and, if the cemi will it, the new Suma Behique. Do you know the significance of that title?"

Jenaro shook his head.

"It means To'guey will lead the behique and oversee all their training and teachings. It is to be a very important position."

"Where is Cidra, baba?" Jenaro asked.

"Cidra is in the mountains to the south and east of Puerto Zafiro. It will take several days to reach it, so I want you to take some time to pack up tonight, before bed. I will check on you to make sure all is ready."

"Yes, baba," Jenaro said with a smile. "Can I bring my books and my lute?"

Marohu nodded as he rose from his seat. "Of course, my son, of course you can. Now, finish your lesson then start packing." He leaned over and kissed Jenaro on the head. "You are the moon of my life."

"And the stars of my forever," Jenaro replied.

That night, before heading to bed, Jenaro met with Agostin in his mother Helena's private garden. It had several manicured lawns, flower bushes, and a fountain placed at the base of a young and spry ceiba tree. There were several lampposts scattered throughout the garden, lighting the path with a soft, flickering glow. The boys lay side-by-side in the grass next to the fountain, staring up at the night sky and listening to the gentle rippling of the water. The coqui were out *en* masse serenading the rising moon.

As for the boys, the six years they had spent together meant they were as close as a behique is to their cassava. They spent nearly every waking moment together and even some sleeping moments as well. Agostin developed into a clown, always entertaining Jenaro, even at Jenaro's own expense. Jenaro, though, took it in stride. He smiled and laughed at each joke.

The boys were each fast becoming spitting images of their fathers as well. Jenaro had Marohu's dark, wavy hair that curled when it grew long. His eyes were the deepest brown and his skin a dark olive. Agostin, it seemed, inherited his mother's height. He was taller than most boys his age. Everything else about the boy harkened back to Octavio.

"Do you think the moon enjoys the song of the coqui?" Jenaro asked as he tossed blades of grass skyward. The ripped pieces spun and floated down over him and Agostin like verdant feathers.

Agostin giggled. "No, dummy, the moon doesn't have ears. And it's just hundreds of high-pitched croaks, not music."

"Well, I think she loves it. Why else would she shine so bright when their song fills the air?"

Agostin had no response, so instead he segued to a new topic. "My baba told me that the air in the mountains near Cidra is so clean and crisp it can heal those with lung sickness."

"My baba told me there is a spring near the peak of the mountain that bubbles out steaming hot water," Jenaro said.

"Like bath water?" Agostin asked.

"I guess."

"Are you excited to go on this trip?" Agostin asked.

Jenaro nodded. "Oh yes, Ago! It will be our first in a long line of adventures!"

Agostin smiled and laughed. "I've never been on an adventure before. Will I have to protect you from danger? Because I think I could. Look how big my muscles are getting!" He sat up and flexed modestly. Jenaro oohed and the boys laughed. "I should probably get home though. Baba said I need to get plenty of sleep because sleeping on the road is hard."

Jenaro brushed the grass from his chest, sat up, and gave Agostin a hug. "See you in the morning, Ago."

"Bye!" Agostin yelled as he ran from the garden.

Jenaro lay back down in the grass and continued to stare at the moon while the songs of the coqui rose to the heavens. Jenaro let his mind wander and his eyes close and soon, he was fast asleep.

Helena found her son not long after and carried him to his room. She placed him gently in his bed and kissed him on the forehead which stirred him from his slumber.

"Bibi?" Jenaro murmured softly. "Can you sing me a song?"

Helena sat on the edge of Jenaro's bed and leaned close. "Of course, my little sun."

Jenaro smiled as Helena's delicate soprano filled his ears. She sang in Olelo, her native tongue, a lullaby she learned from her mother.

"Sleep little child of angels above
For rest is what your heart needs.
Without it your body will not grow strong;
It will not sprout both its wings

The moon moved across the night sky
Dropping tears on the earth below.
We took to our wings to fly,
Just as they did long ago.

A child needs their wings to visit the sky.
Without them a child may cry.
The moon weeps for children who have not their wings
For she cannot meet them in the sky.

The moon moved across the night sky
Dropping tears on the earth below.
We took to our wings to fly
Just as they did long ago."

Helena knew Jenaro had fallen asleep before the end of the first verse but couldn't resist singing the entire tune. She loved it as much as he did. "My sweet little moon," Helena whispered, gently sweeping Jenaro's hair from his face and placing a kiss on his forehead. Carefully and quietly, Helena extinguished the lamps and tiptoed from his room. Waiting just outside stood Marohu with a sweet smile on his face and the twinkle of love in his eyes.

"Sun of my life," he said as he embraced Helena, kissing her on her forehead, both cheeks, and her lips. "How is our moon?"

"Exhausted," Helena said. Her smile quickly faded though. "Tell me honestly, Marohu. Is it truly necessary he travel with you? Cidra is a long way, through jungles and up mountains."

Marohu nodded. "To'guey will insist on meeting the boy, of that I have no doubt."

Helena tsked and turned her head away. Marohu placed a finger under her chin and sweetly lifted her face to his. "You have no need to worry, sun of my life. He will not go alone. Ocatavio and Agostin are joining us, as well as a couple of Guazabara."

"I have no need to worry because I am going too," Helena said. "Our boy will accomplish great things in his life. I don't need him falling off a mountain beforehand."

Marohu knew better than to argue with his wife. With an enormous smile, he answered, "I would not have it any other way."

Blessings

The caravan to Cidra left shortly after breakfast the next morning. There were three horse-drawn, covered wagons carrying everything from tents and travel supplies to food and water for the thirty travelers. Helena, Ines, and the boys rode up front while the cooks and two attendants rode behind. Marohu and Octavio walked ahead of the wagons. Andoli were not fond of horses and preferred to travel on the strength of their own legs. Surrounding the caravan were Ana, a former comrade-in-arms turned guard captain, and nineteen of her best soldiers. The Guazabara, as they had taken to calling themselves, always traveled light and required only the permission to hunt and forage for themselves as they had taken to doing during the war and to save the weight of additional food and supplies.

"How long will it take us to get to Cidra?" Jenaro asked over the rumble of the carts and the clopping of the horses. The caravan had just exited the city gates.

"It is a five day walk if you were to head there by yourself," Marohu answered his son. "I imagine it will take us a bit longer with carts and wagons and so many people."

"What will we see along the way?" Agostin asked from beside Jenaro.

Marohu smiled wide. "Lots of things, Ago; jungles, mountains, rivers and waterfalls, plains and pastures. We'll pass through the towns of Caguas and Bayamon. We may even see some wildlife on the way."

"Wild animals?" Agostin excitedly asked.

"Possibly," Marohu said with a shrug. "Although I doubt any will show their faces with all the noise we're making."

"I want to see a yamuy!" Jenaro shouted.

"Oh, me too!" Agostin cried out.

Octavio chuckled from Marohu's side. "You do not want to come across a yamuy. Those cats would tear us to shreds. Why do you think the guazabara wear their skins? It's not because of their spots."

"Because they're ferocious?" Jenaro asked.

"Because they're ferocious," Octavio agreed with a nod, "and only the guaza dare hunt them."

The boys entertained themselves for most of the day. Jenaro played his lute and sang songs with Helena and Ines. He and Agostin ran alongside the wagons until they tired. They ate lunch on the move and didn't eat again until the caravan stopped for the evening. Tents were set up by the guaza and fires started. The cooks prepared the evening meal and the guaza spread out creating a perimeter.

Before turning in for the evening, Jenaro sat with Marohu and admired the stars. The night skies over Puerto Zafiro were always teeming with constellations, but on the road, in the mountains away from the city, Jenaro was flabbergasted by the number of new stars he saw.

"Is the sky like this in Cidra?" Jenaro asked from his place in the grass.

"The sky lights up even more brilliantly in Cidra, if you can believe it my son," Marohu replied.

Before he finished his sentence, they heard the screech of a bird.

"What is that?" Jenaro asked, quickly sitting up.

"It sounds like a mucaro," Marohu answered. "I wondered if we'd hear one."

"A mucaro? The behique said they are called night eagles since they hunt when all other things sleep. Is it true they are good luck?"

Marohu sat up and shook his head. "No, Jenaro, not good luck–great luck."

Jenaro smiled.

The days on the road continued in much the same fashion. Jenaro and Agostin talked and asked questions. Marohu and Octavio would do their best to answer. Jenaro and Helena would sing and even dance in the wagon. Octavio taught the boys how to play daggers, despite the disapproval from their mothers.

"They're too young to be tossing knives in the air," Ines moaned. "What happens when one of the knives bounces off the target and back toward Ago? Hmm? Or Jenaro?"

"They have adult supervision," Octavio replied with a sly smile.

On the sixth day, the trail to Cidra ascended at an even steeper incline. The dense jungles gave way to sparser copses amid high plains. After a day of travel, the wagons were circled and Marohu declared that because the air was growing thin and the horses we're struggling mightily with the wagons, only a small group would continue on. Ines volunteered to stay behind as did the cooks and servants, and most of the guazabara.

"I am coming with you," Helena demanded.

"Stay with Ines, my sun," Marohu pleaded. "It is only a short hike from here to the summit. No harm will come to him, of that I promise."

"Swear to me, on your life," Helena replied.

Marohu placed a hand on his heart. "May Yaya condemn me to a life outside the third cave should any harm come to Jenaro."

Jenaro, for his part, was grateful for the break, but as the guazabara took their time preparing camp, he grew restless. His heart longed for excitement on his first adventure, more than simply riding in wagons or walking up mountains. He grabbed Agostin and pulled him aside.

"You want to go exploring?" Jenaro asked his friend. "I can't stand one more minute of sitting, or talking, or walking. This was supposed to be an adventure!"

"Then let's go exploring!" Agostin said eagerly.

Filled with anticipation, the two boys snuck away from camp and bolted into the nearest stand of trees. Jenaro ran ahead of Agostin. Despite Ago's pleas for him not to, he darted through the sparse, patchy jungle and lost Agostin in the process. Thrice he had to double back to find his friend. Each time Agostin angrily chided him to remain by his side. Together, they soon reached a clearing with a panoramic view of the valley.

"I think I can see Caguas from here!" Jenaro exclaimed.

"Your eyes aren't that good," Agostin ragged.

"Says you," Jenaro shot back. "I bet I can run to the end of this field and still see how many fingers you're holding up." Jenaro began to jog away, but Agostin groaned.

"Stop running away, Jenaro! Next time you bolt, I may lose you and never find you!" Agostin called.

"Come on, Ago, just head to the opposite end and hold up some fingers, any amount!" Jenaro took off before hearing Agostin's response. He reached the other side and turned to see Agostin begrudgingly trudging back the way they came. He smiled, tongue in cheek, and hopped around waiting for Agostin to stop and face him.

That was when he heard a spine-tingling hiss. Immediately after came searing pain and a shock that ran through his heel and up his leg, straight to his chest. He had been bitten.

Jenaro gasped and slowly turned around. He saw a giant

maja slithering its way back to the jungle. The maja was enormous; at least as thick around as Jenaro's neck and as long as a horse and wagon combined. Its scales were deep, dark, grayish brown with accents of slate and black lines running along the entirety of its body–except for near the tail where its scales turned to chestnut. Its eyes were silver and shone in the sunlight and its forked tongue was as dark as night.

The maja eyed Jenaro with interest and seemed to beckon him into the jungle. It turned and slithered back under the shade of the trees before turning its head and eyeing Jenaro once more. It then did the same head-shake beckon and slithered away. Jenaro found the maja's movement quite odd and decided to follow. The first few steps came easy, but each step that followed shot excruciating, burning pain up his leg, through his knee and into his hip. Regardless of the pain, and driven on by his curiosity, Jenaro gritted his teeth and soldiered on.

Even in the semi-darkness of the jungle canopy, it was easy to spot the trail of the maja. It left wide rivulets in its wake. Curiously enough, it also seemed to char and kill the grass and underbrush that touched its scales. After a while, a rare and peculiar mist set upon the jungle. Jenaro began to second guess his excursion alone, especially with the continually degrading state of his leg, but continued. He desired to know where the maja headed, no matter how purple and swollen his ankle grew.

Jenaro limped until the mist cleared, slowly revealing a small glade. The air smelled pleasant, a scent Jenaro could only describe as incense. The long grass felt soft to the touch. It tickled Jenaro's good leg and foot as he walked. The sounds of the jungle dwindled, except for a babbling from a murky and aromatic pond near the opposite end of the glade. Jenaro slowly approached the edge. The dark, muddy waters popped and burbled. A layer of steam rose off its surface and made Jenaro sweat. All manner of insects flitted and floated above the water, dragonflies and darners, gnats, and flies.

Jenaro took a seat next to the waterline and noticed a decent size stone off to his left. It was pyramidal in shape and appeared as granite. Resting peacefully, curled atop its pinnacle, was the maja. Its body was coiled tightly, except for its tail that dangled down the stone and rested in the grass. It had a smile on its serpentine jaws.

There was a pang on Jenaro's heel from where the maja bit him. He looked back at the snake, its heavy eyes teasing sleep. Yet, before he could move, an aguila pescadora swooped down, talons gleaming, and landed with one claw on the maja. The snake hissed as the bird's talons sank into its flesh and attempted to strike the aguila, but the bird brought down its other foot on the snake's head, preventing it from striking. Jenaro suddenly felt a wave of pity for his adversary. The maja only bit him because Jenaro frightened it. It was simply defending itself. It didn't deserve such a death.

He got to his feet and shouted at the aguila, waving his hands and yelling for it to leave. The bird was startled by the noise—it shrieked at Jenaro then lifted off. The maja was left bleeding on the stone, using its forked tongue to lick its wounds. It stopped for a moment and analyzed Jenaro with curiosity. Its eyes studied him, its tongue flicking energetically, trying to decipher his scent. Then with a nod of its serpentine head, it uncoiled off the stone and slithered away into the tall grass of the glade.

The contentment lasted only a moment. Jenaro glanced down at his heel. The wound had turned purple and black. The colors webbed out from the fang punctures and wound their way up his leg, past his knee. He began to feel light-headed. The smells of the pond made him nauseated. He tried to take a step, but his knees buckled wildly, and he collapsed to the ground. A violent cough shook his body. He convulsed and vomited just before the world went black.

When he awoke, he noticed the glade appeared different from how he last remembered it. The glorious white light from the sun disappeared, replaced by a dark, night sky complete with innumerable stars beaming in colors Jenaro had never before experienced. Translucent strokes of turquoise and tangerine shot across the heavens like sheer veils over an open window. The insects around the pond continued to fly; only now their bodies glowed like lanterns. The waters of the pond were calm; a shimmering gold light emanated from within. Jenaro sat upright and took a deep breath. The air was fragrant, like flowers and fruit. A blinking, golden dragonfly zipped around his head and toward the pond. He noticed that the entirety of his leg below his knee was purple and swollen, save for two dark circles where the maja's fangs had so surgically injected its venom–but the pain was gone. He tried carefully to stand and found he could do so easily.

Jenaro slowly walked around the glade, investigating the strange new realm he awoke in. His first instinct was to find the maja. Surely it had not slunk too far away. He walked in concentric circles, his hands floating just above the grass. Each blade tickled his palms. The ground was soft and warm under his feet; he dug his toes in and smiled as the warmth grew in intensity. The trees that surround the glade glowed green as if each was majickally lit from the inside, and countless birds sat perched in the trees, inriri, mucaro, toucan, and aguila pescadora. A cool breeze swept through their branches causing their limbs to dance about.

Finding no trace of the maja, Jenaro returned to the pond and noticed the large triangular stone was gone. He turned his eyes to the treetops and spotted a curiously colored aguila, feathers of emerald, ruby, and sapphire, perched high above the glade. Its head twisted and bent as it studied Jenaro with great golden eyes. As he watched the bird, a shape just beyond its feathers began to grow and change until a luminous pillar of cloud formed. The cloud descended past the aguila and wafted just above the surface of the water, stars twinkling within its veil.

"Who are you?" Jenaro felt compelled to ask. "Where am I?"

To his surprise, the cloud responded. "I have many names, but I believe your people call me Yaya."

"Yaya!" Jenaro exclaimed. "You are the creator god, father of all that is and ever will be!"

The light in the cloud wavered and pulsed quickly as the voice chuckled. "Yes, child of dust, that I am. As for where you are, you stand in my garden amid the third cave."

"How come I can't see you?" Jenaro dared to ask.

The cloud migrated toward Jenaro, floating gently to his side. "My true form is too great and terrible for one such as you to even conceive. To gaze upon it would send you spiraling into violent madness. You would be stricken incurable and pass from my realm into nothingness."

Jenaro frowned. "But can't you change? All the cemi in the stories can change. Yúcahu can turn into all sorts of birds but favors the aguila and the inriri. Atabey can swim the waters of the world as a caguama. Maboya can be a maja or a shifty skeleton…" Jenaro's speech faded, realizing what he was saying. "The maja…"

The voice in the cloud laughed. "The simple mind of a child is a delight! If it is what you desire, I will take a form more suited to your mind."

The lights in the cloud blinked and flashed brightly. He turned his head away and shielded his eyes with the palms of his hands. There was a noise like rushing water followed by a roaring wind that knocked him to his backside. When the calamity ceased, Jenaro opened his eyes and beheld Yaya.

Its body had a head above its shoulders, arms that ran parallel to its trunk, and legs that jutted from its pelvis to ground, but that was where the similarities to humankind ended. Yaya's head was a tri-faceted stone, like the one the maja had rested upon. It was wider at the neck and rose to a sharp point nearly a foot above the chin. Each facet bore a fearsome face with three eyes that saw in every direction. There were three arms protruding from the body and three legs. The skin looked as if it were made of granite; gray and black and gold and orange pressed together. The multitude of birds in the trees surrounding the garden began to sing and squawk at the stone-man. The strangely colored aguila drifted down and rested on its right shoulder, while an inriri alighted on his left. They stared at Jenaro with amusement. Similarly, an inriri alighted on his left shoulder.

Jenaro looked upon Yaya with curiosity. "You don't look so terrible, Yaya," he said with conviction.

"I am glad you think so," Yaya responded. His voice had changed. It was many voices in one, atonal and ethereal. Each word resounded in Jenaro's ears. He took a step forward then sat crossed legged on the ground across from Jenaro. He landed with a muffled rumble like a stone hitting the ground. "What brings you to my garden, young one?"

Jenaro was bewildered. "I–I don't know," he muttered. "I was playing with Agostin. I ran. I saw the maja. It bit me and I chased it to the glade. I passed out and woke up here." Jenaro paused and looked at his ankle and ran his fingers over the bite marks. They were raised and sore to the touch.

"It was a grievous wound, young one," Yaya said.

Jenaro said nothing. He looked to the stone-faced god and allowed a single tear to fall from his eyes before whispering, "The bite…the glade…you said we are in the third cave…I understand now."

"Do not weep, child of dust," Yaya consoled Jenaro. "Death is but a small part of your journey. Soon you will be greeted by Atabey and properly welcomed to the third and final cave where there is feasting and dancing."

Jenaro shook his head and wiped the tears from his eyes. "I am not afraid, Yaya…" he trailed off.

"What is it?"

Jenaro shook his head harder. "I don't want Agostin to be scared or sad. He is my best friend and I left him alone in the jungle. It was a terrible thing to do and only now do I see. I don't want him to cry for me. I don't want him to get in trouble for what happened to me. It was my fault, after all."

A smile grew on each of Yaya's stone faces. It started slowly, a barely noticeable twist of the lips at each corner, but soon his lips parted and his teeth began to separate. Then he broke into a loud and boisterous chuckle. Jenaro jumped and gasped. He held his breath as the cemi's laughter roared throughout the glade. The multitude of birds flew off in a flock of shrieks; all except the aguila and inriri on Yaya's shoulders. Jenaro's fear was soon overcome with pure joy. Yaya's laugh was infectious and soon Jenaro was laughing along with him.

Yaya rose from his seat. "You are an inspiration, young one. Truly, no greater sentiment can be had, for when faced with death, your thoughts are not on your own mortality but on the well-being of those you love and left behind."

Yaya reached down and lifted Jenaro to his feet. Jenaro felt a strange tingling on his ankle. When he looked down, his normal coloring had returned. His leg was no longer purple nor was it swollen. The two fang punctures remained, only they were scars of what once was. He turned to face Yaya and smiled.

"You are Jenaro Marohu Albizu del Rios, are you not? First-born son of Marohu Josué Albizu del Rios and Helena Meleloa?"

"I am," Jenaro answered with a nod.

Yaya raised his hands to the sky. The starlit canopy parted at his command and the warm, white light of the sun once more beamed on Jenaro's skin. The jungle trees swayed gently in the breeze, the pond burbled and babbled once more, and the air smelled again of moist earth and incense. Jenaro was back in the glade.

"Jenaro, son of Marohu, you have the blessing of Yaya, greatest of all the cemi, creator of all things. Carry my light with you, always."

Jenaro was unsure what to do or say, so he simply bowed. "Thank you, Yaya but…" he paused and looked down, ashamed he did not know the significance of what the Yaya had done. "What does it mean to have your blessing?"

Yaya smiled. "You are the symbol of my power and mercy in this world, the world you call Ke'. Part of you will be always with me as part of me will be with you. You will be tested in many things. Many trials and tribulations will you face, yet it is my blessing that will protect you. You will draw the light to you and all my creation will be attracted to your light until your appointed time."

Jenaro's mouth curled, and his brow furrowed. "I am not sure I understand…" he mumbled, yet there came no reply. The stone-man that was Yaya crumbled and collapsed to the earth sending a loud crash through the glade. The only evidence of his brief existence was the maja's sun stone by the shore of the pond and the aguila taking flight and soaring above the treetops. Jenaro knelt next to the stone and saw three miniature charms floating above its pinnacle: a pyramidal stone, a feather, and a fang. Jenaro gathered up all three charms and inspected each one. The stone was tri-faceted, with an elaborate face etched on each side. The feather was a metal alien to him. It had a shimmering color that shifted from the cold blue of steel to a strange blackness that seemed to consume the light around it, and the weight and feel of an actual feather. The fang was the least unusual. It felt like bone and looked like it once belonged to the maja. Jenaro placed each charm in his pocket then turned and left the glade.

He followed the jungle back to the field where he bolted from Agostin. When he stepped out of the tree line, he noticed Agostin in the distance, pacing frantically.

"Jenaro!" Agostin's voice echoed, carried to his ears on the breeze.

Jenaro smiled and ran to his friend. "Here, Ago, I am here!"

"Jenaro?" Agostin cried again, only this time the panic was replaced with confused delight. "Jenaro!"

Agostin sprinted toward Jenaro. The two slid to a stop, inches from each other. Agostin's face was tear streaked and smothered in sweat.

"Why did you run off, you bobo?" Agostin scolded with a punch.

Jenaro winced and rubbed his arm. "I'm sorry, Ago. It was a dumb thing for me to do."

"So dumb," Agostin agreed. He leaned in and embraced Jenaro tightly then recoiled with he saw the scars of the snakebite on his ankle. "You were bitten!" Agostin yelled. "Oh no, you were bitten! I failed to protect you!"

Jenaro chuckled and placed his hand on Agostin's shoulder. "Ago, it's okay. Everything is fine. Yaya healed me."

Agostin's face immediately morphed to skepticism. "Yaya," he stated in disbelief. "I think the venom is affecting your brain."

Jenaro shook his head. "Yes, Yaya. He came to me. Not in a

vision, Ago, like the behique, but really came to me. Come on! Let me show you!"

Jenaro led Agostin into the jungle back to the glade, only to find it empty. The bubbling pond was no longer there. The stone was gone. There was no maja nor were there inriri or aguila in the trees. It was no more than a simple clearing.

Agostin snickered. "You sure it's not the venom?"

Jenaro punched him. "It was here, I swear it. Look," he said, pulling the charms from his pocket. "Yaya left these for me."

Agostin looked at the charm, but was unimpressed. "Yaya, creator god, left you trinkets? Why wouldn't he leave you something better like a knife, or an unquenchable fire, like in the stories?"

"I don't know, I didn't have time to ask. He just–*poof!*– disappeared and here they were."

Agostin laughed.

"I'm serious, Ago!" Jenaro shouted.

"Okay, okay, you saw Yaya and he left you little trinkets. I believe you. Can we go back to the caravan now?"

Despite this, Agostin continued to pester Jenaro the entire walk back to the caravan. Jenaro desperately tried to convince him, telling him intimate details of his encounter, but Agostin would only poke and chide his belief in fairy tales. He laughed at the idea of beings that could transform into birds and maja, at stone-men with three faces and arms and legs. Jenaro shook his head. Agostin was just like his father in that respect.

The two boys returned safely to the caravan and were immediately met by Octavio. His face was turned up in a scowl and his fists were gripped tightly around his cutlass.

"We have been waiting for three hours for you boys to return," Octavio rebuked as he sheathed his blade. "I even sent scouts looking for you."

Agostin moved in front of Jenaro, head bowed, ready to play the martyr for Jenaro's mistake. Jenaro knew it was wrong and grabbed Agostin's hand, pulling him back.

"It was my fault, Octavio," Jenaro said, dropping to his knees. "I was foolish and ran off without Ago. He spent his entire afternoon looking for me because he is a great friend, something I am not. He is innocent of any wrongdoing."

Octavio's face quickly turned to shock and just as quickly returned to his ever-present stoicism. "That is a very adult thing you have done, my young lord." He turned to Agostin and nodded at his son. "By the tears on his cheeks, I'm sure his panic was punishment enough."

"They're not tears!" Agostin shouted in embarrassment.

Octavio and Jenaro exchanged glances then broke into laughter.

"Run along, you two. I'm sure the cacique is ready to leave and will want you both with him at the head of the column."

Introductions

The column of six arrived in Cidra at sundown. The village was small. A mere five caney surrounded a dirt batéy that showed obvious signs of disuse. The uneven ground humped and divoted between the walls. Grass and weeds grew unchecked. Mud mounds surrounded the village, each brimming with sprouts; of what, Jenaro could not tell. The cacique, called Abey, greeted them immediately outside of his caney. He was young, a teenager, and had the look of a del Rios about him.

"Abey is your cousin, Jenaro," Marohu said. "He is my nephew by my sister, may her soul rejoice in the third cave."

Jenaro smiled and raised the palm of peace to Abey, only Abey pulled him into an embrace instead.

"I had no idea I had a cousin in the mountains," Jenaro said after Abey released him.

"And I had no idea I had a cousin in the city," Abey responded with a smile.

Abey led Marohu, Jenaro, Octavio, and Agostin into his caney. The guaza stood guard outside the entrance. It was a modest, round building constructed of ceiba planks with a multitude of palm fronds as a thatched roof. Jenaro saw little in the way of comfort. A simple mat of straw served as his bed. A short, knee-high table held a lamp, plate, and pipe. A small fire crackled and burned opposite the entrance. Abey motioned for everyone to sit. He grabbed his pipe from the table then took his seat next to the fire.

"It is good to see you, Octavio," Abey said, nodding toward the carib.

"Last I saw you, Abey, you still wore diapers," Octavio said with a chuckle.

"And your hair had less gray than it does now," Abey smiled, laughed then puffed on his pipe. "What brings you back home, tío?" Abey asked of Marohu.

"I have come to call on To'guey," Marohu said. "I assume she still resides near the mountain peak?"

Abey's cheeriness faded and he nodded. "Yes, she is still up there. She rarely leaves her hut, preferring to spend all her time smoking cassava and talking to the cemi. I don't know how much use she'll be to you, tio. She's been nothing but a burden since I became cacique." Abey passed Marohu his pipe. Marohu accepted it and inhaled deeply.

"Do you suppose she will still see guests?" Marohu asked.

Abey shrugged. "Possibly. Knowing the guest is a del Rios may act in your favor." He paused until the pipe passed from Marohu to Octavio and then back to his hand. "I wouldn't expect much, though."

Abey offered the use of his caney, but Marohu declined, deciding to sleep under the stars. They camped in the batéy and woke with the cock's crow. Abey had a meager breakfast prepared for the four travelers and their two guazabara consisting of eggs, beans, and sweet potato all fried in the same skillet. Marohu thanked him profusely for his hospitality and led the way out of the village of Cidra and up the mountain slope.

During their hike, Jenaro shared with his baba his meeting with the cemi. He wondered if his baba could tell him more about what Yaya meant. "Ago didn't believe me," Jenaro said.

"I wouldn't hold that against him," Marohu replied.

"But you believe me, right baba?"

"It is an incredible tale, and you have no reason to lie, least of all to me. I'm sorry I cannot give you more insight as to its meaning, but perhaps To'guey can." Marohu nodded at Jenaro then leaned in close. "Also, do me a favor, don't tell your bibi about the whole snake bite thing," he said softly. "That's a detail we can keep between us."

Jenaro noticed the air was cooler and the jungle smelled differently as they climbed. The moist and acrid smell gave way to cleaner, briny air, like that near the coast, as if the altitude summoned the ocean breezes that swept over the island. As the sun rose, he could see nothing but mountain tops in every direction. Rain clouds crept their way over distant peaks and dropped their contents on the slopes below, slowly disappearing in the process.

They reached the peak just after midday. The path they followed circled around the pinnacle and ended in front of a small hut next to a pristine pond. Although, calling it a pond was generous. It was more of a large puddle. The entire place looked abandoned, or at least its owner was absent.

Marohu announced their presence. There was no response. He looked back at Octavio and the guazabara then stepped inside the hut. After a half a minute, he exited and shrugged.

"Have you taken to petty thievery, Marohu?" a voice asked from the pond.

Standing by the water's edge, just beyond the tree line, appeared the grizzled figure of an old woman with a jagged dagger in one hand, a fistful of cassava root in the other. Marohu thought her shorter and stouter than he remembered, with graying hair that fell in wild tangles from her head. Her dark and leathery skin served as evidence of a life outdoors, and she wore a plain canvas skirt and a hooded tunic showing much of her rotund mid-drift.

The woman took a step forward, bare feet entering the pond,

and pointed her dagger at Marohu. "I asked you a question, del Rios. Why are you sneaking around my abode?"

Jenaro watched as his baba circled the pond and knelt before the old lady. He spoke to her, head bowed, in hushed tones. She remained still and silent, gripping her dagger in an aggressive stance. After Marohu's whispered speech, the behique concealed her blade.

"Up, up, you fool. There's no need to prostrate before me," the behique said as she walked around the pond to where Jenaro stood. Marohu was several steps behind her. "Your baba tells me you are Jenaro."

Jenaro nodded slowly. "I am, behique."

She shook her head, "I am no behique. Call me To'guey."

Jenaro looked confused. "Baba said you were a behique?"

"I was, once; now, just an old hag, living in isolation on the mountain whence she was born," To'guey replied. "Come; let me have a look at you."

Jenaro stepped forward. To'guey reached out and placed her hands on his face. She moved his head up and down, left, and right. She dropped her hands to his shoulders and squeezed them, then gathered his hands in her own. She brought both hands to her face, one at a time, and studied them for an unusual amount of time. After letting his hands fall to his side, To'guey grunted and turned back to Marohu.

"He is indeed your son, del Rios. I must speak with him alone. Only then will I give my answer." To'guey did not wait for Marohu to respond, but ambled off to where she appeared only moments before.

Marohu chewed his cheek and looked at Jenaro. Jenaro stared back, the very picture of serenity. Marohu smiled at the boy then turned to To'guey and called after her. "Take as long as you need, behique, provided I have your decision before sundown."

Jenaro looked up in the sky and spotted the sun. It was still several hours before nightfall. He frowned at the prospect of keeping the old lady's company for such a long time. Regardless, he waved goodbye to Agostin, smiled at his baba, and followed To'guey into the trees.

To'guey was old, but ambled faster than Jenaro was used to walking. She had a strange air about her, almost as if she could read Jenaro's mind.

"Keep up, Jenaro," she said the moment the thought popped into Jenaro's head.

They walked for several minutes away from the prying ears of Marohu, following the tiny stream that fed To'guey's pond. The trees swayed in time with To'guey's pace. The birds sang along to Jenaro's breathing. A sweet aroma wafted in the air. He could hear the gentle rushing of a nearby waterfall.

Soon the jungle parted ways. The trees revealed another pond, this one larger and much deeper than a puddle and fed by a bubbling spring near the rock face of the mountain. Surrounding it were flowering mango and papaya trees. In the middle of the pool were three standing stones. Each stone bore the faded likeness of a cemi, though because of their weathering, Jenaro could not make out which three.

On the near end of the pool was a small, handmade bench carved from ceiba wood. To'guey took a seat on the bench and motioned for Jenaro to join her. She inhaled slowly, and then spoke in almost a whisper, words meant solely for Jenaro's ears.

"You have seen him, haven't you?" To'guey asked. She outstretched her arm and pointed to the center stone. "You have met Yaya."

Jenaro nodded. "How did you know?"

To'guey's somber expression grew in intensity. She exhaled violently through her nose. "I am sorry, young one. It is not fair for a mere child to be saddled with such a terrible burden."

"Why do you say it's a burden?" Jenaro asked, puzzled. "Yaya told me I am one of his blessed."

"My child, what do you know of the cemi?" To'guey removed her pipe and packed it with snuff.

"Only what I've been taught by the behique in Puerto Zafiro, and briefly by my baba. My bibi is not from our islands. She doesn't worship any gods."

"Most likely sunshine and rainbows," Toguey shook her head, lighting the pipe with a flint lighter. "The behique have been poisoned by the religion of the Ultans. It twists the true nature of the cemi into something unnatural." She exhaled a thick cloud of cassava smoke. "Not all cemi are benevolent beings, Jenaro. Some cause harm while others simply look the other way. The Yaya is indeed our benevolent creator, but he is also cruel. It is true, he created the reality in which we live, but he also created evil. He pitted his sons against one another which resulted in the sealing of the first cave. He created death and evil and allowed it to flourish. He ignored the suffering of his people for generations. Did your teachers ever discuss the symbol of the coqui?"

Jenaro shook his head.

"Of course, they would remove that from the teachings. There were once two schools of thought on why Yaya and Atabey created the peoples of Ke'. All sentient life on Ke' is represented in the ancient drawings as the coqui, our beloved tree frog. The first school of belief felt that as small and weak creatures, the coqui needed guidance. The cemi, thus, loved and protected the coqui, allowing them to multiply and cover all of Ke'. The coqui, of course, represents all people of Ke'. There are Itiba Ara', the great ones, those closest in likeness to the cemi, who once ruled all of Ke' with their mastery of the majicks. Next came the Cibao Ara', the people of the mountains, those who never knew the cemi. Finally, the Borekua, mankind, encompassing all other races of Ke', from the Ultans and Meres to the north to the Sandrians to the south. And of course, the Andoli."

"What did the second school believe?" Jenaro asked. He was now at the edge of his seat, eyeing To'guey with curious exuberance.

"That our lives being mere coqui to the cemi is a slight against all peoples. The cemi see us as lowly, frail, easily manipulated beings. As nothing more than frogs. They delight in keeping us under their heels."

"Why would a blessing be so wrong then?" Jenaro questioned To'guey. "Would it not mean a reprieve from such an existence?"

To'guey exhaled another thick cloud of pipe smoke. "Yaya has deemed your life of special interest. He will watch you and thus you will forever be scrutinized by the cemi. Your soul will never fully belong to you, Jenaro. Half of who you are was left behind with Yaya. He did mention this, did he not?"

Jenaro shrugged.

"Do you know what happens to someone with only part of a soul? They are doomed to witness the workings of the cemi in our second cave. You will be privy to exactly how they operate in our world. As a result, your life is only half of what it should have been. You will leave the second cave before any of us, Jenaro. Only, you will never enter the third."

Jenaro turned his face from To'guey and looked to the pool. A dragonfly skipped over its surface, creating ever expanding ripples in the crystal clear, shallow water. There was a turtle at the edge, testing the warmth of the pool. Several coqui leapt from the water's edge to the trunk of the mango tree. He heard the tap-tap-tap of an inriri and spotted the bird pecking away at the trunk of an aged ceiba.

It was silent for some time before To'guey spoke once more. "Do you know why your family worships Opiyelguabiran as their patron cemi?"

Jenaro shook his head weakly.

"Opiyel is a spirit guide. Of all the cemi, its loyalty lies with the lives and souls of people of the second cave. It is concerned for us. That is why it guides our departed souls to the third cave. Your bisabuelo realized that of all the cemi, Opiyel's character most closely matched his own. Everything he did was to serve the people of the coqui, to serve the Andoli and all other races of Ke'."

Jenaro turned and faced To'guey, his face full of confusion and fear, anger and sadness. To'guey raised her hand and tapped Jenaro's forehead with her thumb. "Yaya made a mistake when he chose you. He will expect you live a life of servitude to him, wasting away like some hopeless, hapless hermit, spouting the good word of the creator. You will not succumb to the curse of the cemi. You will be a guide, like Opiyel; one to lift our people just like your patron cemi.

"Your baba requested I join you in Puerto Zafiro, take on the title of Suma Behique, and lead the people back to our rich heritage, forsaking all that was forced upon us by the Ultans. I will accept his offer. In the time I have left, I wish to help you, to guide you to a newfound knowledge of the cemi. I will teach you how to live for the good of your people, not only for the delight of the cemi."

Jenaro rubbed his eyes and forced a smile. "Did you also guide my baba?"

To'guey nodded solemnly. "I taught your baba, and his baba before him. They also sought my guidance, especially in the most desperate of situations. But those are tales for another time." She rose from her bench with an exceptionally loud groan and reached her hand out to Jenaro. Jenaro took her hand and the two walked back to her hut.

When they returned, Marohu was pacing around the pond. Octavio was sparring with Agostin while the two guazabara sat sharpening their blades. Jenaro did not realize they were absent for such a long time. To'guey announced their arrival with a cough. All eyes turned to her.

"This new temple you plan to build must be built like the old ways, ceiba and stone, none of this fancy quarried seastone and gold. I will have the specifications drawn out for you."

Marohu nodded. "Consider it done. Do you have any other requests?"

"Only one," To'guey said quickly. "I need a litter or a carriage of some sort. I hope you don't think I'll be walking the entire way back to Puerto Zafiro."

Marohu chuckled. "We have wagons just outside of the village."

"Good," To'guey said. "Then what are we waiting for? Stand up you two," she pointed to the guazabara, "you'll have time enough to sharpen your swords once we are on the road. And you, Anacaona," she nodded at Octavio. "I expect to see your young son in my classes as well. I don't care how much you hate the cemi; the boy needs an education."

Octavio's face lit up with delight. "It is good to have you in our lives again, To'guey."

To'guey scoffed. "Save your falsehoods for someone else, Octavio. I haven't forgotten about you and Marohu's atrocious behavior growing up."

Jenaro looked at Agostin and the two boys burst into laughter.

Another full day of hiking and Jenaro was reunited with

Helena back at the caravan. After To'guey was introduced and given a spot in the wagon, Jenaro spent hours in whispered conversation with his bibi. He told her everything he experienced, including his visions of the cemi. Helena gasped in horror and shot Marohu and angry glare at knowledge of the snake bite. Marohu could only smile sheepishly as she motioned toward the puncture wounds on the boy's ankle. After he finished, Jenaro remembered the three charms in his pocket.

"Here, bibi, I want you to have these," Jenaro said proudly as he produced the charms.

"Oh, my son they are beautiful!" Helena exclaimed. "This stone looks expertly carved, and I doubt I have ever seen a feather this magnificent."

"Don't forget the fang. I think it belonged to the maja," Jenaro said with a smile.

Helena held them close to her chest and kissed Jenaro on the forehead. "As soon as we return home, I will have them put on a gold rope and wear them forever."

Jenaro smiled and gave Helena the biggest hug he could muster.

New Beginnings

Once To'guey moved to Puerto Zafiro, Jenaro spent four hours a day with her in personal instruction outside of the general teaching she gave him and Agostin. To'guey became his mentor, instructing him in more than just the nature of his curse. Jenaro learned to read, write, and speak Itiban as well as Cibaonan. To'guey even polished up his Olelo, much to the joy of his bibi.

Within her lessons on language, To'guey loved to pepper Jenaro with the history and politics of Ke'. He learned of the War of the Gods which led to the downfall of the Itiba Ara' and the disappearance of the majicks from Ke'. He discovered fascinating facts on the Cibao, especially the Scholia Regium where all the most talented artisans in the world studied. Jenaro found it notable that even after the majick essences waned, the Cibao continued to train majick users. To'guey claimed that because of their refusal to participate in the War of the Gods, the cemi turned a blind eye to their continual, albeit meager, use of it.

"But To'guey, the Andoli did not fight the cemi. Why can we not use majick?" Jenaro asked.

To'guey chuckled. "Our people did not need the essences to experience the cemi. We communed directly with them."

Jenaro thought about that for a moment. His face scrunched in painful concentration.

"You have more to ask?" To'guey inquired.

Jenaro shook his head.

"Come now, child. The only questions not worth asking are those to which you already know the answer."

Jenaro frowned. "How did they commune with the cemi? Was it like my experience?"

To'guey scratched her chin. "Not much is known about that. We assume it was similar to what you experienced. Some put importance on the cassava snuff, but no one knows for sure."

"Okay," Jenaro replied in a mutter. Disappointment painted his face and his shoulders drooped.

To'guey grimaced. "Manipulating the essences was dangerous. Those skilled in the majickal arts were often consumed by them. You see, to use the essences, something of equivalent value must be given, the stronger the offering, the more powerful control over the essences. Men lost their souls, and their lives, for such power."

To'guey instructed Jenaro in math and the science of healing as well. Each school day ended with assignments, which were often extensive readings of dusty, ancient tomes. These lectures were on top of Jenaro's religious education. To'guey ensured that Jenaro understood everything about the blessing he received.

Six days a week, Jenaro met To'guey in the temple just outside the gates of the manse. It was built to her exact specification: a single story, ceiba and granite building. What it lacked in height, it made up for in expansive square footage. The largest area was, of course, the worship hall, built to accommodate close to five hundred Andoli at a time. Likenesses of the cemi lined the walls under windows that allowed the sun to shine down on each statue. There was a cloister separating the worship hall with the rectory where most of the behique lived, ate, and slept. On the opposite side of the worship hall were the archives. The archives were the only part of the temple to have basement levels deep in the earth housing the accumulated knowledge of the Andoli.

From within the walls of the archives, To'guey taught the

boy the history of the cemi, their character traits and the different ways the Andoli worshipped their gods. Jenaro read from the scriptures, not to gain favor or to increase in piety, but to glean an understanding beyond that which the common Andoli knew.

He listened intently as To'guey told of men and women throughout the history of the Andolins who were previously blessed of Yaya. They became great behique or spiritual leaders and lived pious lives full of worship, cassava smoke, and retching rods. Always, they died young.

"They were all fools," To'guey told Jenaro. "And why?"

"Because the blessing of Yaya is a curse," Jenaro repeated, "because the cemi do not care for our people."

To'guey nodded. "You will break this cycle, young prince. You will not be another victim of their deception. Your life will not be cut short to satisfy their egos."

Jenaro's childhood was not without misery. During his ninth year, his mother Helena died giving birth to a daughter, named Helena in her honor. Jenaro mourned the loss of his mother and hated his new itu d'itu, preferring to call her anki, or demon, out of spite. During this period of mourning, the boy was once again visited by the maja.

It was the first Karaya, or seventh day, after the death of Helena. Jenaro had spent the week since her death hiding from his baba and his carib. Alone, in darkened corners of the manse, he sobbed. His cries intermingled with moans of torment, like the howls of an animal mourning alerted all to his position. Soon, he was back in his mother's garden, climbing their favorite tree.

He clutched his knees to his chest and buried his face between his legs. Jenaro continued to cry, only now, silently. His tears rolled down his face and fell to the earth below. Slowly, his heaving gasps returned to their normal rhythm. His head began to pound and his eyes to burn. When he finally lifted his head, he noticed the maja was now sitting on the branch with him.

"Go away," Jenaro hissed and kicked.

The maja recoiled, dodging Jenaro's strikes. It backed up, giving itself room, then gathered itself up in a tight coil, head resting on its body, eyes gazing at the boy.

"To'guey told me my blessing would allow me commune with the cemi, whether I wanted to or not. So, I guess you're just here to torment me?"

The maja blinked its large, hypnotic eyes. Its sinister tongue flicked.

"Why did you have to take her away from me, Maboya?" Jenaro asked the maja in between sobs. "Why?"

The maja's head lifted from its body. "I did not take her life from her, child of dust," it spoke. Each word was long and drawn out. Each syllable was emphasized with a flick of its forked tongue.

"You are the cemi of death," Jenaro replied.

"Yet it is Yaya who numbers your days," the maja hissed. "I merely retricve departed souls."

Jenaro's brow furrowed. His eyes narrowed. "You tried to kill me! That's not merely retrieving departed souls."

"I did," the maja hissed with a nod of its head. "Only to keep you from going any further. But foolish boy, you followed me anyway. It would have been a swift death from my venom and would have ensured your place in the third cave. It is unfortunate that your soul will never find rest. Half of you exists with Yaya now. Half of you will forever exist with him."

Jenaro's skepticism began to fade. The maja spoke the same words that To'guey had told him. It was just as his teacher had said.

"What do you want, Maboya," Jenaro finally asked.

The maja hissed again. "You and I…we are bound by the same twisted fate, dustling; a fate neither of us chose or desired. A fate only Yaya could devise."

Jenaro's face tightened. He moved to a cross-legged position. "I don't believe you."

"Believe it or not, it is the truth. Help me and maybe together we can fight against fate."

Jenaro stared at the maja, then with an outburst of anger kicked the snaked off the limb, screaming, "I said leave me alone!" He watched as the snake tumbled from the tree, only it never hit the ground. The maja vanished into thin air. Satisfied, Jenaro remained silent for a time, until Agostin called out from below the tree. Jenaro looked down at his carib.

"Can I come up, Jenaro?" Agostin asked.

Jenaro took a deep breath and said, "No, Ago, I'm coming down."

Young Love

As Jenaro grew, his hatred for his sister waned. Other matters began to take precedence in his young mind over his grudge. He spent more and more time away from the manse, always with Agostin, at the temple of the behique, or watching batu matches together. To'guey also made sure she occupied Jenaro with plenty of hours of study. Not a week went by in which the behique did not assign translations of long dead languages from ancient tomes or written reviews of economic treatises written by Itiban and Cibaoan scholars. Yet, chief among these new interests was the allure of the opposite sex.

It started with Sharae. It was not an immediate realization. He did not feel struck by lightning, nor did he fall in love at first sight. In fact, Jenaro despised Sharae for the better part of a year. Sharae Campos was the daughter of Alonso and Yahima. When Jenaro first met Sharae, she was a tall and swarthy youth, with curly black hair she kept braided in front and flowing at the back. Her eyes were warm brown, almost cocoa colored. She was sharp and agile of both mind and body. Jenaro could not help but be drawn to her.

Her father, Alonso, played batu professionally for the city club. He was an all-pro and captained the team representing Puerto Zafiro in the last five Areito Festival tournaments. Yahima, her mother, was a seamstress and proprietor of fine silks and linens. Even Jenaro owned tunics and jackets made by her hand. Sharae accompanied Alonso to all of his batu matches. She stood courtside, handed out towels, and served water to the team. Sometimes, if another player's son or daughter wished to take on these duties, she would step aside and sit in the stands, cheering loudly for her father. It was during one such occasion that Jenaro and Agostin first met Sharae.

At first, Jenaro was impressed with her knowledge of the sport. She knew players by name and could rattle off statistics better than he or Agostin. She knew strategy and would sometimes even call formations before the coach. Yet this devotion to the sport simultaneously irked and rubbed at Jenaro. He never understood how or why she could be so involved in the game.

"There's no way you know so much about batu," Jenaro derided her after a match. "You're a girl. Shouldn't you be more interested in girly things?"

"Girly things?" Sharae asked, offended. "I think you're just jealous because I know more about batu than you could ever dream of knowing! And don't think that just because you're some soft, royal brat that I won't talk back to you!"

"I'm not a soft, royal brat!" Jenaro shot back.

"Oh yeah? The fact that you have a carib following you around everywhere says otherwise." Sharae responded, sticking her tongue out and walking away.

"Well, he's also my friend…so you're wrong!"

Agostin chuckled. "That was a weak response, Jenaro."

Jenaro punched Agostin in the arm and glared at Sharae as she skipped to her father. "Shut up, Ago. You're supposed to be on my side."

Yet her derision didn't stop Jenaro from showing up to every game the city club played. If she sat courtside, he would simply enjoy the match, keeping watch on her movement from the corner of his eye. If she sat in the stands, he would find some excuse to sit near her and start fights.

After the batu club of Puerto Zafiro won the championship,

Marohu invited the entire team and their families to the manse for a celebratory feast. It was a casual event held on the ground of the ancient batéy, site of the original settlement of Puerto Zafiro. The party felt more like a giant family reunion than anything. Each of the fifteen team members, the three coaches, and the club president were present. There was plenty of laughing and carrying-on. Children ran and played. Teenagers practiced their best batu moves on the old court of the batéy, imitating their fathers or mothers.

The chef and his crew had their work cut out for them. Yet, they proved more than up to the task. The sweetest and most savory aromas descended upon the batéy in mouthwatering clouds. Three of the fattest, healthiest pigs were covered in mango and peppers and roasted, along with fifteen chickens, and a fifty-pound sack of shrimp. The tables were piled high with grilled peppers and onions. Enormous iron pots with seasoned rice and beans were set about the feast tables. Pastries and candied fruit rested on their own separate table and were eyed by all in attendance. Marohu even tapped several casks of Andoli dry, rum, and the last of the Meren mead left by their former oppressors.

Jenaro, who normally never missed his opportunity to gorge himself on sweets, spent most of his time eying Sharae from across the batéy. When she decided to peruse the selection of desserts, Jenaro pointed out his favorite, the candied mangos. Sharae ignored his recommendation, grabbing a jelly stuffed roll, and left without saying a word. When she was with the other boys and girls playing batu and reliving the highlights of the championship, Jenaro approached to join in the conversation. She suddenly decided to find another form of diversion without even introducing him. Jenaro even joined her on a tour of the manse. When he offered to show her the private gardens, Sharae ended her part in the tour and returned to the feast. All his failed attempts left Jenaro discouraged. He decided to sit alone to sulk and brood.

Agostin noticed Jenaro's displeasure. "Are you upset because she seems to be ignoring you?"

Jenaro gasped, offended. "I don't care what she does or who she speaks with, Ago."

"Don't worry, Jenaro," Agostin offered, "girls like it when you show interest in them, even if they refuse to show it."

"I am NOT interested in her, Ago," Jenaro blurted out. "She is arrogant, over presumptuous, outspoken for no reason, and rude. I don't like the way she walks or talks or pretends to know it all."

Agostin smiled. "Would you like me to fetch her, my lord?" he asked with a ridiculous bow.

Jenaro glared then punched Agostin in the arm. Agostin laughed, punched back, and ran away.

Later that evening, after all the food was consumed and the barrels of alcohol emptied, the team each took their turns thanking Marohu for his hospitality before stumbling home. Jenaro sat off to the side of his baba as he accepted palms of peace and grateful chatter of all fifteen players and their families. He watched with interest as Alonso and Yahima Campos reached the front, Sharae standing dutifully between them. Jenaro craned his neck, attempting to inconspicuously hear their words when Marohu called his name and beckoned him to his side. Jenaro sighed and dragged his feet.

"Jenaro, have you met the captain and star of the city batu team, Alonso Campos?" Marohu asked. "This is his wife Yahima and their daughter Sharae."

Jenaro bowed his head to each and showed the palm of peace. "I have watched many of your matches, captain Campos.

You are the greatest batu player I have ever seen," Jenaro gushed. His eyes briefly met Sharae's before averting.

"I am honored by your words," Alonso replied with a bow. "I hear you have already met my daughter. She claims you have interesting insights into the game."

Jenaro jumped, startled by his words. His eyes shot to Sharae. Her cheeks were flushed, and her eyes glued to her sandals. Jenaro remembered Agostin's words. Maybe she did enjoy his company. What's more, he started to believe he might actually be interested in her. She was pretty, after all, and he did feel compelled to spend time with her.

Jenaro swallowed, "Oh no, Señor Campos. It is your daughter who has all the great insight. I only agree with her."

The adults all chuckled at his response.

"Alonso, why don't you join me in the morning for breakfast?" Marohu said. "Bring Sharae. I'm sure Jenaro here would enjoy discussing batu."

Alonso bowed low. "I would be honored, cacique."

The next couple of years were spent in constant contact with each other. She would spend Karaya at the manse, talking to Jenaro about the recent batu match, playing the game of daggers, or listening to him sing and play his lute. When Jenaro would bring other girls to the manse, Sharae never got upset or angry. She encouraged him to love as fervently as possible. Jenaro returned that sentiment, sometimes even joining Sharae and her new love interests on outings or for meals. Their relationship worked. That is, until the arrival of a delegation from Hal'e.

A Dragon on the Horizon

Jenaro celebrated his sixteenth name day when the delegates from Hal'e sailed into Puerto Zafiro. He, Agostin, and Sharae sat atop one of the lower walls of the manse, sipping on mango wine, enjoying the warm, early autumn breeze, and admiring the billowy white sails of each and every ship in the bay. Jenaro liked to play a game, guessing at the cargo and port-of-call of each ship, weaving elaborate stories of Itiban khufus ferrying majickal items like eternal fire and seeker stones. Sometimes he imagined Ultan frigates flying the red and white hound of the Andolins and captained by brave Andoli privateers, returning from their long stretch as sea, laden with spoils of war. He even got Agostin and Sharae in on it. Agostin often guessed correctly.

"What about that one," Agostin pointed with a bottle in hand. "I've never seen a ship like that one before."

"Go ahead my friend," Jenaro patted him on the shoulder. "It's your turn anyway."

"I thought it was my turn," Sharae said from behind Jenaro. Her arms were wrapped around his waist, legs dangling from the edge, and her head resting on his back.

"I had the last one and you the one before that," Jenaro answered sweetly.

Sharae kissed the back of his neck.

Agostin thought for a moment. "It is a diplomatic ship from Hal'e, ferrying some beautiful princess longing to be wed to you."

Jenaro laughed, but remembering Agostin's curious power with the game, decided to investigate. Initially, Jenaro could not place the vessel. He gazed at the slim and majestic long ship with wonder, commending its sleek appearance and oddly shaped sails. The hull was a color he was not familiar with, possibly the wood of a tree from another land. He squinted and noticed the pale blue standard with a white dragon flying from the mainmast.

"Do you tease me on purpose, Ago, or are you truly clairvoyant?" Jenaro asked glumly.

Agostin turned his head to Jenaro. Sharae lifted her head from Jenaro's back and placed it on his shoulder.

"It's a long ship from Hal'e."

Agostin barked with laughter. "Maybe I am clairvoyant!"

Jenaro cursed. "I swear to all the cemi, if that ship has a princess of Hal'e aboard, I may ask To'guey to bind you and sacrifice you to save us all."

"Should I be worried?" Sharae expressed mildly, with a tiny smirk curling the edge of her lips. "It's not like I'd marry you anyway. I don't believe in it."

Jenaro shook his head, twisted around, and kissed Sharae on the forehead then stood from his perch. "I'm sure we all have nothing to worry, you least of all. Let's head back, Ago. We may have to change into some more presentable attire if we are to receive foreign dignitaries."

Agostin finished the last drop of wine and smiled.

"Are you planning on joining us?" Jenaro asked Sharae.

Sharae yawned and shook her head. "I actually have plans for this evening with a young gentleman from West Andolin."

"A westerlie?" Jenaro played impressed. "Do be sure to show him how us city-folk enjoy our time."

Sharae giggled and jumped off the wall. "I'll be sure to tell you all about it over lunch tomorrow."

Jenaro waved goodbye to Sharae and lowered himself down the opposite side of the wall. He and Agostin hurried back to the manse. Jenaro was still amazed and appalled by Ago's gift of ship-guessing and his decidedly overconfident in his power of perception. But the fact of the matter was that a ship from Hal'e had indeed arrived. Jenaro's stomach churned and his heart raced at what that could mean.

The manse was practically abuzz with life when they entered. Servants ran back and forth down the halls. Octavio directed a group of guaza carrying a solid oak table into the Great Hall. When he saw Jenaro, he called him over.

Jenaro bowed his head, as did Agostin.

"The cacique is looking for you, Jenaro. He's at his table in the Great Hall. Agostin, will you assist me?"

"Of course, baba. See you soon," Agostin called to Jenaro.

Jenaro nodded and rushed away to the Great Hall.

"Oh, and Jenaro," Octavio called out.

Jenaro turned back to the carib.

"Be gentle with your baba. He is in a mood."

The doors to the hall opened smoothly to a bustling hive of activity. Tables and chairs were being placed. Incense was added to the censers. A gardener placed a fresh array of flowers in every wall mounted vase. Jenaro kept to the wall, trying his best to avoid the onslaught of dutifully panicked servants. He ducked around a couple mopping the glistening granite and danced his way to his baba's table.

Marohu sat amidst a tower of parchment, shaking his head, and cursing. His hands shuffled between two pieces of correspondence, both with the pale blue seal of the Hal'e royalty. His jaw was set tight, and his brow furrowed. His eyes darted nervously across line after line of Oleloan script. His eyes looked up from the writing for just a moment and briefly acknowledged Jenaro's presence before returning to their place on the page.

Marohu grumbled, just above the chaos of cleaning. "Helena, your bibi, attempted to teach me how to read her native tongue. I never could grasp it. I mean, an entire language with so few letters and I'm to be able to decipher inflection and tone which can change the meaning of one word into any number of other definitions…"

Jenaro sat down next to Marohu. "Here, allow me, baba."

Marohu shook his head. "I cannot figure out if this phrase means 'should be' as in a request or 'will be' as a demand."

"Often times, you have to read it in context of the complete document." Jenaro eyed the parchment. He skimmed from top to bottom, mumbling a word here and a phrase there. He reached the line Marohu was stumbling over and gasped. "Why does this correspondence from the Queen of Hal'e say she is sending her daughter, my *betrothed*, to Puerto Zafiro *for the ceremony?*"

Marohu cursed under his breath. "I was afraid of this. Queen Hannah is impetuous and begrudges my marriage to your bibi."

Jenaro rose quickly from the table. "Baba, that does not answer my question. Why is a princess of Hal'e arriving in Puerto Zafiro and why does this parchment say she 'will be' announced as my betrothed?"

"My son, this has been a long time in the making, I just," Marohu bowed his head, "I just could not find the strength to tell you after Helena passed on to the third cave."

"So, your defense is that you are a coward?" Jenaro asked in anger.

Marohu inhaled sharply. "Watch your tone, Jenaro," he warned. "I am not only your baba but your Cacique. You will show respect."

"How can I respect a man making decisions about my life without even involving me?!"

Marohu slammed his hands on the table with such force that every single piece of parchment was thrown from its surface. The noise sent such a shockwave through the room that each servant froze in place. It caused Jenaro to jump and hold his breath. His body tensed up. Marohu stood still, his face turned to stone, his palms flat against the table. He slowly, deliberately turned his head to his son and spoke with calm intensity. "A Cacique does not owe an explanation to his son concerning the reasoning of his will. If he wills it, then his son will comply. Is that understood?"

The flash of resolve and righteous indignation Jenaro felt melted away in the incinerating glare of Marohu's eyes. Jenaro felt every ounce of defiance wither and die. He tried to open his mouth, to form words and answer his father, but his lips refused to part. Instead, he nodded and bowed low, prostrating himself before his baba, the Cacique.

"Now, if you will, please inform your itu d'itu that we are to have guests this evening and her presence is required in the Great Hall." Marohu stood up straight and adjusted his tunic. He ran his right hand through his thick, dark hair, fixing the stray strands that fell free from his outburst. "It is a formal gathering. I trust you will come prepared."

Another quick nod was given then Jenaro marched himself out of the Great Hall. The walk to his room was swift and only upon reaching it did his voice return. He slammed the door and cursed wildly. In a flash of rage, he threw everything from his table, pounding his fists against the now bare wood. The crashing and yelling reverberated off the seastone walls as Agostin ran in.

"Peace, Jenaro! Peace!" Agostin cried as he bear hugged him, pinning his arms to his side.

"Unhand me, Ago," Jenaro grunted.

"No, my friend, you must calm yourself first."

Jenaro struggled in vain to free himself from Agostin's grasp. His carib was simply too strong for him. After a couple long minutes of struggling and crashing around the room, Jenaro went limp and Agostin released his hold. The two immediately moved to Jenaro's bench.

"I need to go see Anki, let her know of the state dinner this evening," Jenaro said through ragged breaths.

"I can do that for you," Ago said as he rose and started for the door. "Anything else you wish of me?"

Jenaro nodded. "You can make your way to To'guey and have her perform an exorcism on you, you witch."

Agostin grinned. "The ship was ferrying a foreign princess? Truly?"

Jenaro nodded once more, entirely unable to match his gleeful expression. His heart pounded with fear. His lips trembled with rage. "Truly. As it happens, I am betrothed to this princess."

Smile fading, Agostin took a deep breath and bowed. "You can tell me more when I return."

Jenaro sat and stared at the mess he created and was immediately overcome with shame. Such outbursts were unbecoming. He let out a loud sigh and dropped to his hands and knees, cleaning up the shards of his now broken vase, shattered wine bottle, spilled flowers, journal, dagger, and myriad of other trinkets and gadgets that dotted the surface of his solid ceiba wood table. His journal with original songs was leaking old stale wine now. He moved his table back to its original position, scooted his chair to its place, and gently nudged the planter back to its spot.

Once everything was gathered up into his wastebasket, Jenaro sulked his way to his bathroom and drew water for a bath. He bathed quickly and then hurried to his wardrobe, choosing his fanciest Andoli ceremonial dress. He oiled and slicked back his hair, tying it tightly with an elegant wrap adorned with mucaro feathers, and wore his mother's three charm necklace around his neck. An ornate cream sash with gold trimming running from his shoulder to his waist covered his otherwise bare chest. A medium length skirt woven by premier Andoli weavers and fastened with an oiled black, full-grain leather belt wrapped around his waist. The skirt fell to just above his knees and was crimson and ermine brocade with a likeness of a hound's head stitched in gold on the front. He shod his feet with strapped and laced sandals that rose to his knees. Feathery musaraña fur fringed the top of each sandal.

It was well past their normal dinner time when Agostin entered Jenaro's room. Jenaro had just finished dressing and slouched uncomfortably in his armchair. Agostin was also dressed in traditional Andoli garb, but of more reserved fabrics and colors. His blades hung at his waist. He coughed and waved his hands in the air as he walked through a thick cloud of sandalwood and cloves.

"You think I should strap a dagger to my belt?" Jenaro asked with a grimace, thinking of the oleloan blade given to him by his bibi that rested in a trunk in his closet.

Agostin shrugged. "It wouldn't hurt. It may let your betrothed know you are handy with a blade and can protect her if need be."

Jenaro shook his head and flashed a dirty gesture at Agostin. Agostin chuckled.

"How does it look out there?" Jenaro asked.

"Like Areíto came a year too soon," Agostin answered. "The Hal'e have been preparing for the feast in your bibi's old quarters." Jenaro cringed at the news. "What are you going to do?"

"What can I do? Betrothed to a princess of Hal'e. And without even a care for how I feel about it. I don't want to get married, be the Cacique, take the throne from my father. It's as if all my hopes and dreams of a life of adventure are vanishing before my eyes."

Agostin approached Jenaro, pulling him to his feet. "You don't know that."

"I do. And the Hal'e are stuffy, prudish, moralists. I highly doubt my new wife will look kindly upon my desire to travel the world much less my love for Sharae."

"It's doubtful that she'll be interested in being a paramour either," Agostin added. Jenaro let out an exasperated breath which prompted another slap on the shoulders from Agostin. "One thing at a time. Let's tackle this feast. Then we'll worry about your new bride and Sharae."

The guazabara lined the walls of the Great Hall like sparkling toy soldiers. Banners from each of the islands' caciques menores hung on the walls. Hanging proudly over the dujo was the Andoli standard and del Rios family banner. The polished and stained ceiba wood tables gleamed in the light of the braziers that hung from the vaulted ceilings. The aroma of flowers, perfume, grilled meat, and peppers punctuated the air. Jenaro's old lute instructor was present, performing up-tempo Andoli numbers with his small quartet. A small crowd of partygoers were dancing to the tune and made Jenaro wonder how such a lively guest list was thrown together so quickly.

Jenaro spotted Marohu, standing on the dais and talking to Octavio. On the opposite side of Marohu was To'guey. The behique appeared to be the only Andoli dressed in plain, unflattering robes despite the pomp surrounding the event. Anki and her carib, Agostin's itu d'itu Marisol, were chasing each other around the dinner tables, screaming and giggling as eight-year-olds did. Jenaro noticed another girl accompanying them, an Oleloan about the same age. Her long black hair trailed behind her as she ran. When Marohu noticed his son, he raised his hand

and drew him to his side. Jenaro nodded and pulled at Agostin's arm.

"What is it?" Ago asked.

"My baba calls," Jenaro said. "Where will you be?"

"I'll stay close by; in case you need me." Agostin bowed.

"Why don't you go get us some wine. I think I might need some here shortly."

Agostin waved his hand in a flourish, signaling his approval.

Jenaro took a deep breath, adjusted his sash, and started for the dais. Octavio bowed and backed away once Jenaro arrived next to Marohu. He bowed his head to both Marohu and To'guey.

To'guey inclined her head. "It is truly a blessing to be in your presence, Jenaro."

For a moment, Jenaro thought he heard sarcasm in her voice, but when their eyes met, he could see the severity of her words. He smiled. "It has been too long, To'guey. You should stop by and visit when you aren't with Helena."

To'guey nodded.

"I'm glad to see you taking this seriously, my son," Marohu said without looking at Jenaro.

"I didn't have much of a choice," Jenaro replied, smiling at a passing servant carrying a platter of empty wine glasses.

Marohu leaned in close. "Petulance is unbecoming. You always have a choice. The truth of the matter is whether you are man enough to live with the consequences of those choices."

Jenaro rolled his eyes.

"Did I ever tell you how your mother and I met?" Marohu asked.

Jenaro shook his head. "I figured you went to Hal'e to enlist their help in the war and came back with a treaty and a wife."

"That's only partly true. I did sail to Hal'e to breathe new life into our alliance, but I never intended on returning with a wife. I met your mother and knew she would forever be the sun in my skies. My decision to leave Hal'e with Helena nearly ruined our chances of Hal'e support in our war. But that is a story for another time."

Jenaro turned to his father, confusion painting his face. Marohu smiled somberly.

"And what of the woman you were meant to marry?" Jenaro asked.

"She is now the queen of Hal'e."

"And is this the first time you'll see her since?"

Marohu shook his head and hmphed. "She didn't deem it important enough to travel with her two daughters."

"Two?" Jenaro asked.

"The girl playing with your Anki," Marohu nodded at the trio still weaving in and out of the crowd.

Jenaro took a breath and hazarded a question. "So, you also shirked off your royal duties?"

Marohu's face said Jenaro had stepped over the line. The fury faded quickly though, and he said, "You are the moon of my life, my son, truly."

Jenaro inhaled and responded, "And the stars of my forever."

Marohu opened his mouth to speak again just as the delegation from Hal'e was announced. The throngs of guests in the Great Hall separated, creating a pathway to the dais. Leading the procession were two women dressed in shimmering white fabric decorated with pink and pale blue hibiscus blossoms. They wore crowns of yellow and white flowers and carryied the pale blue standard of Hal'e.

Following the standard bearers were four soldiers carrying spears twice their height and white kite shields painted with pale blue dragons. They each wore strange spherical helmets with strips of dyed cloth and strange feathers. Jenaro could not see their faces.

Immediately behind the soldiers came two women. The first was a stately matron about the age of Marohu. She wore no crown of flowers atop her jet-black hair, which was styled high with thick strands falling on either side of her lovely face, but instead had a single pink hibiscus resting behind her ear. The other was young a girl with a chubby face and a body still clinging to her baby weight. Her lengthy black hair was curled and draped in tiny white flowers and prismatic feathers. Her cream-colored dress complemented her deep caramel skin and on her breast perched a shimmering blue dragon brooch with eyes made of pearl.

"She looks young," Jenaro voiced his concern. Marohu only glanced at his son.

The procession reached the dais and split to the left and right continuing until the matron and the girl were standing before Marohu and Jenaro.

The matron inclined her head ever so slightly before addressing them. "Marohu Josue Albizu del Rios, Cacique of the Free Andolin Islands, I am honored to present to you, Hildy, daughter of Hannah and Lunalilo Hal'e, firstborn daughter of the Queen and King of the Hal'e empire; promised to your firstborn son per the alliance of nations made by you and her grandfather, King Hilohilo the second of Hal'e."

Marohu bowed in a strange manner, one Jenaro could only assume was the preferred greeting of the Hal'e. He then stood and presented the palm of peace to Hildy and the matron. "May the blessings of the cemi pour down this day. May your days among the Andolins be brimming with peace and prosperity."

With that, Marohu extended his hand to Hildy. There was a moment of hesitation before the girl reluctantly took it and stepped onto the dais. Marohu took a step back, guiding Hildy to his spot between To'guey and Jenaro. Her face was pale and grim, her eyes glossy with a well of tears. She smelled of coconut and jasmine. Jenaro tasted bile.

"May this union bring continued peace and cooperation between our two great nations!" Marohu declared.

A cheer erupted from the Great Hall. The applause echoed off the granite and seastone. Almost immediately, the doors were opened, and the feast was brought forth. Jenaro and Hildy were escorted to their seats at the head of the main table. Marohu sat next to the matron. To'guey had slipped away and was speaking to Octavio.

Conversation between Jenaro and his new betrothed was slim. He learned she was merely thirteen, a full three years younger than him. She liked to paint, enjoyed the taste of fish, and before arriving in Puerto Zafiro, had never been away from the Hal'e archipelago. Their wedding was to be in two days. For the third time in his life, Jenaro felt helpless.

"So, um, how's Kauhal'e this time of year?" Jenaro awkwardly asked in between bites of food.

"Nice," Hildy stated. She pushed her food around her plate with her fork, barely touching anything she had been served.

"My bibi was from there, the capital. But she never spoke much about it."

Hildy forced a smile and simply nodded at the comment.

"Do you know about batu?" Jenaro asked. "It's the most popular game here in the Andolins."

"No," she answered with a brief shake of her head.

Jenaro puffed out his cheeks and exhaled. Defeated, he wanted nothing more than to shrink into his chair, slide down under the table, and crawl away from it all.

The remainder of the evening was a blur of congratulations

and well wishes. As Jenaro sat in his room in the small hours of the morning, he could scarcely remember if he ate.

After a restless night, Jenaro rose before the sun and roamed the halls of the manse. He grabbed a near empty bottle of wine from the Great Hall and wound his way outside the manse walls to the hill where his bibi was buried. In the tradition of her people, her grave overlooked the ocean, marked by a simple stone with a bronze cup meant to hold offerings to the deceased.

"I wish you were here, bibi," Jenaro whispered as he poured the wine into the bronze cup. "Baba says this for the good of our people. Yaya said his blessing was for the good of his people. What about what's good for me? Why do I never get to choose what is good for me. I am only sixteen. What do I know about marriage? Why can't I be like Sharae, loving whomever she desires, whenever she wishes." Jenaro sighed. "You always told me I was destined to do great things. Why must I sacrifice my life of adventure for marriage and a throne? Why must I give up on my dream?"

"Because you're the son of the Cacique," he heard a voice say.

Jenaro turned to see To'guey strolling toward him.

"It is too early for Anki's lessons, so what brings you here, behique?" Jenaro asked.

To'guey took a seat on the grass next to Jenaro. She casually shrugged. "My mind was drawn to you during my sunrise meditation. I took that as a sign from the cemi that I should check on my former student."

Jenaro jeered. "So now you listen to the cemi?"

"I have always listened to the cemi, Jenaro. Just because I do not agree with their words or actions does not mean I fail to hear them or see how they move in others."

Jenaro turned his head away in shame. "I don't know what

to do, To'guey. No part of me is okay with this betrothal. My mind is not just fearful and anxious, it is reluctant. My heart is saddened and angry. You always said it was my destiny to use my blessing to save the people of Ke' from the influence of the cemi. How am I to do that if I'm forced to sit on the throne for the rest of my life?"

To'guey *hmphed*. "Do you remember our lessons, Jenaro?"

"Some of them."

"Some?"

"There were so many!" Jenaro threw his hands in the air. "Six days a week, for hours a day. Sometimes seven when Atabey eighth day rolled around. How could I possibly remember ever single thing you ever said?"

To'guey turned to Jenaro, pulled her retch rod out of thin air, and slapped him on the hand. Jenaro pulled away and winced. "Still no self-control, I see. Always quick to answer, but slow to listen."

"Some things never change," Jenaro said with a grin.

"Our lessons on Andoli government," To'guey continued, "do you remember those?"

"They were dreadful, but yes, I do. I was a good student, To'guey, if a bit rambunctious."

To'guey ignored Jenaro's attempt at justifying himself. "I will say this, and then I will speak no more on the subject. As with other things in life, like love, consent is of utmost importance, even as the Andoli government is concerned. Caciques have never simply handed over their dujo to their heirs."

"Ah. If I'm honest, I don't remember that lesson," Jenaro admitted.

To'guey sneered. "Sometimes, the right to rule went to a sister or cousin. Sometimes it went to a completely different family. Sometimes it skipped a generation entirely." The behique rose to her feet. "Perhaps you should revisit your knowledge of our government, Jenaro." With that, she dusted the grass and dirt from her robe and walked away.

Jenaro remained by his bibi for a while longer, contemplating To'guey's words. She always seemed to speak in riddles, never saying outright what she meant. It was her way of teaching. She wanted Jenaro to use his brain, to think deductively and creatively; to solve problems on his own rather than having someone show him how to do it.

The smells of breakfast wafted to his nose before Jenaro left his bibi and hurried to the archives in the temple of the behique. He only had one more day to figure out To'guey's cryptic message, one day to decide if he would give up on his dream of adventure, say goodbye to the love of Sharae, or marry Hildy and begin his ascension to the dujo. Time was not on his side.

The archives were young compared to the books and scrolls they housed. During the waxing months of the war with the Ultan-Meres, a group of industrious behique (with the help of some local masons) built a series of underground bunkers dedicated to the safekeeping of Andoli literature. The behique managed to stow away countless books and scrolls. The Ultan army searched for these bunkers but thankfully discovered a meager two. While many books were unfortunately lost because of this, a good portion of Andoli literature survived.

Upon learning of these secret bunkers when she arrived, To'guey ordered every one of them opened and every single book brought to the temple. In less than a year, the archive stacks were built, and the collected wealth of knowledge ready to be shared with the people.

The archives were open to the public. Any Andoli could register and spend the day lost in the stacks. No fire of any sort, be it candle or lamp, was allowed through the doors, which meant one could quite literally only spend the day perusing the collection. A series of mirrors directed sunlight and occasionally, only with To'guey's strict supervision, torch light, throughout the entire facility. Jenaro had spent many hours reading and researching as a part of his education. To'guey usually directed him to a certain book or ancient tome, but every so often she would simply give Jenaro a clue and make him go find it. It meant the boy spent hours in search of a title. Fortunately, his adventurous side made it a game he reveled in.

He checked into the front desk, received his pass, and immediately headed to the historical tomes. Jenaro vividly remembered the scroll from which he originally read about the foundations of Andoli government, and it was exactly where he remembered it would be. He remembered the tarnished brass handles and the feel of the parchment. He remembered how the age-old scroll smelled and how heavy it felt in his scrawny young arms. It felt much less heavy now.

Jenaro carefully carried it to a nearby table and began to unroll the scroll. The scroll, of course, was only a translation, written down from the oral tradition passed from behique to behique, established long before the Andolin Islands were discovered by the barbarian Ultan-Meres and subjugated for centuries. However, translation or not, it was invaluable.

Jenaro smiled as he blew the dust and dirt from the delicate parchment. The Andoli runes were ancient, faded, and in a dialect dissimilar enough to make Jenaro cringe. He hated on the spot translations, especially without a lexicon. Jenaro barely made passing marks during those lessons.

It was deep into the afternoon and the mirrors were shifted to make the most of the now descending sun's waning light. Jenaro spent the rest of the day reading the scroll, forgetting about his hunger and thirst, reading despite an aching stomach and dry mouth. His head had just begun to pound when he reached the exact section he was searching for: succession.

The words flew off the parchment. His eyes consumed each rune. His mind translated the defunct dialect with ease. An idea began to form, to take shape in his mind. This was the key.

Jenaro read aloud mumbling the translations to himself. "The title of Cacique should only be bestowed on those deemed worthy to lead the people. They must be a–I don't know that word–virtuous and just, one who–okay, okay–it shall not be an heirloom, inherited by ones kin, rather a position to be filled by one respected by the caciques menores." His eyes went wide. This was exactly what he needed. This parchment would solve all his problems and allow him to, for the first time in his young life, wrest control of his destiny.

A plan quickly formed in his mind. He would present the scroll and let everyone know he would not accept the title of Cacique. That if the people truly wanted Marohu's line to rule, then Anki would be the next best choice. He hated to throw his sister to the wolves like that, but she was a bright little girl. She could handle it. Then he and Agostin would meet Sharae and the three of them would leave. Where to, he did not know. "I can figure that out later."

Jenaro looked at the dying light in the archives and nearly lost his breath. It was close to sunset. The feat of families would start soon. He stood from the table and rolled the scroll shut, looking around, quickly and quietly, trying to spot any behique roaming the stacks. Once he was satisfied, he was not being watched, Jenaro tucked the scroll inside his tunic–a deed that was sure to result in a whipping from To'guey if he was lucky–and hurried down to the first floor. He slowed his pace and relaxed his shoulders. There was no need to draw attention to himself. He only needed to exit the archives and make his way back to his room before the feast of families that evening. When he reached the outside, he breathed a sigh of relief and jogged back to the manse. A sly smile crept across his face as he ran. It would be a memorable feast of families.

Before making his way to his room, Jenaro snuck into the Great Hall. It was empty except for the servants who were busy preparing it for the feast. Jenaro walked as inconspicuously as he could to the dujo. He moved the cushion forward just enough to conceal the scroll then replaced it and hurried out of the hall.

Repercussions

The feast of families was an Andoli tradition that took place on an evening before a wedding ceremony. The two families would spend the night eating and drinking and celebrating the union of the soon to be married couple. It was a private and casual affair, unlike the betrothal announcement, with only family and close friends in attendance. Jenaro knew it would be his first and only chance. The wedding was tomorrow and by then, his dream would be gone as would Sharae. The most important people who needed to hear his words would be there and he could be sure to make his point without embarrassing or dishonoring either party.

Jenaro, dressed in his nicest yet most comfortable tunic and trousers, stood at the doors to the Great Hall. Hildy stood next to him, as tradition demanded, and the two of them welcomed the evening's guests to the feast. She said little and kept her head down, staring at the floor, even when addressed by name. Jenaro felt sorry for her. She deserved better.

Octavio and Ines were present and already at their table as were Marohu and little Helena. To'guey entered through the side to avoid the crowds. Jenaro nearly passed out when he noticed Alonso and Yahima Campos next in line. In a moment of panic, he searched the crowd for Sharae. Thankfully she was nowhere to be found.

"Mister Alonso, I had no idea you'd be joining us tonight, or else I would have informed my betrothed of your greatness."

Alonso chuckled appreciatively. "Thank you, my young lord."

"We were quite surprised when your father invited us to your feast of families," Yahima said with a bow.

Jenaro bowed in return. "Hildy, Alonso is one of the greatest batu players in all of the Andolins and Yahima actually made this tunic."

Hildy smiled and blushed, nodding at each in turn. "I'm afraid I don't know much of your batu, but the tunic is lovely," she said in a heavily accented voice.

"Congratulations," Yahima said to Jenaro and Hildy and joined the rest in the Great Hall.

Agostin arrived just as the last in line entered the hall. He seemed flustered and preoccupied.

"Hildy, I don't know if you've met yet, but this is Agostin, my carib and best friend." Jenaro nodded at Ago.

Hildy bowed but averted looking directly at Agostin. "What is a carib?"

"It's a position of great honor, sort of like a bodyguard and closest advisor combined. Right Ago?"

Agostin nodded quickly. "Yes, that's right."

"Are you okay?" Jenaro asked.

Agostin gave Jenaro a consolatory grin and quickly said, "Yeah, yes, I am," then hurried into the Great Hall.

"He seems…odd," Hildy said.

"Yeah, I was thinking the same thing," Jenaro replied then felt a tug at his arm. It was Helena. "My little Anki, have you met Hildy yet?"

"Of course," she said rolling her eyes, then looked to the pair of little girls standing next to her, Marisol and the Oleloan he had seen earlier. "See what I mean, he's so dumb."

Jenaro chuckled. "Who is your new friend?"

"I'm Heidi," the little girl said. "Hildy is my sister."

"It is an honor to meet you, Heidi," Jenaro said, giving her the palm of peace.

Heidi grinned and met the eyes of Helena. "So dumb." The trio giggled.

"Heidi is my new best friend," Helena declared.

"Best friend?" Jenaro asked. "You two have known each other for what, a day?"

"When you know, you know," Marisol chimed in.

"Marisol is our best friend too," Heidi added, pulling her to her side. The three stood, arms on their shoulders, giggling.

"You look like a trio of troublemakers to me," Jenaro said. The three girls laughed and turned to walk away, but Heidi look back.

"You had better not hurt my sister, or the three of us will hurt you," she stated.

"Yeah!" Helena and Marisol agreed.

Jenaro raised his hands and said, "I wouldn't dream of it." He turned his attention back to Hildy and said, "I am genuinely afraid of what those three will accomplish." He saw the hint of smile curl the corner of her lips.

"You seem good with her, your sister that is," Hildy said, somewhat surprised.

"It wasn't always that way, but yeah. And your Heidi seems like fierce ally."

Hildy nodded. "She is. I wish I had her fire."

The feast started without fuss. Toasts were given and food brought forth from the kitchens. Jenaro had learned of Hildy's love of seafood and made sure the menu for the evening was prepared thusly. There was grilled and fried and baked fish all resting on roasted potatoes. Camarones were skewered then fried or grilled to perfection and arrived on beds of rice. Platters were brought forth with mounds of clams and oysters and crab legs.

The aroma of butter and lime and peppers accented the air. Rum and wine were served to every guest, except for the children present, who enjoyed coconut water.

In between dinner and dessert, Jenaro stood from the table and made his customary rounds to the dinner guests. He noticed that Agostin was not at the table, but instead on the balcony arguing with himself. Jenaro briefly excused himself from his duty and walked swiftly toward his carib. He had not seen Agostin since the day before and very much wanted to talk to him about what he learned from the scroll.

Jenaro stepped out onto the balcony. Agostin went silent and straightened up. He turned away from Jenaro and leaned on the balustrade, preferring to stare at the city lights then meet the eyes of his friend.

"What's the matter, Ago?" Jenaro asked. "You're acting strange."

Agostin's shoulder drooped. "I–I tried to find some way to fix this, to make it so you didn't have to give up, but I failed. No matter where I looked or who I talked to I couldn't come up with a single idea that would change the fate before you. I couldn't bare face you knowing I had failed you so."

Jenaro immediately threw an arm over Agostin's shoulders and pulled him close. "Ago, my friend, my brother. You are the truest companion anyone can ask for. I'm sorry to have troubled you with so much, but I want you to know, that from the bottom of my heart, I love you and appreciate all you do for me."

"Even if I can't protect you from this?"

"Of course."

Agostin nodded and took a deep breath. "I feel bad, Jenaro, like I brought this upon you. Me and my damn witch eyes."

Jenaro chuckled. "You don't have that sort of power, Ago. You and your keen sight did not cause this."

"It's not just that," Agostin continued. "The more I thought about it, about you getting married and eventually becoming Cacique, the greater my dread. I fear our adventures together will end before they even started. Our babas spent their youth warring and sailing to new lands. Our days will be spent indoors, settling disputes between caciques menores and angry merchants."

"That is an understandable fear and one I share with you. It also has some bearing on my news. I met with To'guey this morning and she may have given me a way to stop this betrothal."

Agostin said nothing, merely looked at Jenaro.

"What is it, Ago? Do you not think I should stop this betrothal? You just said…"

"I know what I said, Jenaro, but fear aside, is that the wisest move?"

Jenaro sighed. "I don't know, if I'm honest. But I do know it is what my heart wants. Say you will have my back. Say you will support whatever decision I make."

"Of course I support you. That will never be in question."

Jenaro and Agostin grasped forearms and shoulders. Agostin leaned forward and placed his forehead on Jenaro's. The two separated with a nod and walked back into the Great Hall together. Jenaro stopped by the dujo to grab the scroll, stuffing it under his tunic once more. He took a deep breath.

Once back at the feast, Jenaro finished his rounds then joined Hildy at the head of the table. He remained standing. It was customary for the groom-to-be to give a speech. Hildy tried to smile but doing so only drew more attention to the crippling fear he saw in her eyes.

To'guey reclined in her chair next to his baba, smoking on her pipe and staring almost through him. She gave him the most subtle of nods. He scanned every face at the feast while they quieted, readying for his words. That was when he saw her.

Sharae was in attendance. She wore a simple sleeveless dress of the most vibrant yellow, which complemented her skin tone perfectly. She sat at the last table, the farthest she could get from Jenaro. Her face was downtrodden. Her eyes, avoiding his, were full of deep sorrow. Jenaro swallowed hard. It was time.

Jenaro raised his hands to draw the attention of all present. "My friends and family, I want to thank each and every one of you for joining us today for this feast of families." He paused for a small round of applause. "It is customary for the bridegroom to give a speech, to wax philosophical about his upcoming union, or to sing the praises of his betrothed."

A hum of approval ran over the feast. Jenaro met eyes with a few onlookers before he returned his gaze to Sharae. Sharae…he had always found her cocoa-colored skin and half-braided hair to his liking. He thought her ebony-colored eyes and husky voice were beyond comparison. He even liked how she was a hair taller than him. But for Jenaro, it was her stubborn nature, fearlessness, and confidence that drew him to her. She never shied away from conflict with him, even if he was the son of the Cacique. She always spoke her mind. She enjoyed all the things he enjoyed. Best of all, she made him laugh and smile. He wanted her more than anything.

She finally raised her eyes to meet his gaze. And it was then Jenaro realized how much he loved her.

Jenaro took a deep breath and pulled the scroll from underneath his tunic. He glanced at To'guey. Her mouth tightened around the tip of her pipe, a tic Jenaro recognized as shock. He could have sworn she nodded ever so slightly. "According to the original documents framing the government of our people, the line of succession is a fluid thing. The dujo of our islands was never meant to strictly be passed down from father to son, but from worthy ruler to worthy ruler, regardless of their placement within the family or position in our society!"

Jenaro looked at Marohu. His baba's face was cold and stern, his eyes wide and cutting. Jenaro had come too far to stop the tide now.

"I have come to realize that I am not worthy of the great dujo of the Andolins. It is my decision and my right, as laid down by our forefathers in ages past, to abdicate my place in the line of succession to my sister, Helena Meleloa del Rios, or whomever the gathering of caciques menores deems worthy." The rumbling in the Great Hall grew to a roar. Most of the Andoli present rose from the seats and began shaking fists or pounding the table. The party from Hal'e shifted uneasily, including the guards who gripped their spears. Little Anki stared at Jenaro, eyes wide, little hands covering her mouth. Jenaro cleared his throat and yelled above the clamor, "Thus this betrothal is null and void!"

An eerie silence struck the feast. A paralyzing cloud gripped every single person present. The Suma Behique exhaled an elaborate trail of smoke rings. Her eyes twinkled in approval.

Jenaro then turned to Sharae, whose trembling hands were covering her mouth. The moment Jenaro's eyes met Sharae's, she stood from the table and ran from the Great Hall. Her flight freed everyone from their stupor. Cries of anger and sadness rose up. Marohu stood with outstretched arms and called for peace. People rose to leave. Hildy's face turned bright red. Tears streamed down her face as Heidi and their matron ran to embrace her. The guards from Hal'e quickly surrounded the two and began to usher them from the Great Hall. Jenaro didn't care. He had to catch Sharae.

Jenaro sped after Sharae with quickness. He caught up to her just as she exited the manse and he reached out, grabbing her wrist. The two came to a halt on the front steps. Tears streamed down her face, her lips trembling.

"Why did you do that, Jenaro?" she asked angrily.

"What do you mean?" Jenaro asked back. "I did that for you. I did that for us, so we could be together."

Sharae shook her head. "We can be together, but not like that! It was never like that, you fool! You never truly understood our relationship, Jenaro. I don't believe in marriage and will not be your consort or paramour. I don't belong to anybody and there is no 'us'."

Jenaro stood flabbergasted by her words. He wanted to speak, to find the words to say what was in his heart, but none came. He realized as he released his grasp of Sharae and watched her run off into the night that his own selfishness guided his decision. He selfishly ignored Sharae's desires. He selfishly threw away his betrothal and single-handedly destroyed relations with the Andolins longest and most steadfast ally.

The autumn evening air turned cold, shaking Jenaro to his bones. He dropped to his knees on the steps to the manse and stared into the heavens. The stars above looked dim and shrouded. Marohu's words rang in his ears. "You always have a choice. The truth of the matter is whether you are man enough to live with the consequences of your choices."

HILDY

Unexpected Results

The last words dripped slowly from my mouth, the slower than expected speed adding a gravitas I did not intend. I paused for a moment and scanned the room. The same five faces that I examined before I began stared back at me. Their faces were not hard or angry. Not even confusion beamed from their blank eyes. Even Isadore seemed less than impressed. I don't know what else I expected from my meager crowd of sleeping drunks. They simply looked on, as if my speech was given to the statuary not twenty yards away.

I gave the tent another once over and spotted Luisa. My heart stopped. My throat tightened. She had stayed after all. Why did she stay?

A wave of insecurity swept over me as I bowed my head and made my way from the stage. Each footstep seemed to take an eternity to land, failing to take me away as quickly as I wanted. I parted the curtains and threw all manner of pretense and propriety to the dirt, breaking into a run to my small, curtained enclosure at the back of the tent. I burst through the curtains and began ripping the atrocious ceremonial vestments from my now slick, sweat covered body. It was like peeling the skin from a pig. The harder I pulled, the more the thin, revealing fabric clung to my flesh.

I wanted to scream. I wanted to cry out, not just because I hated the damned ceremonial garb or because the ermine paint was running down my face and into my eyes, but because of what had just transpired.

"How did I ever think that was a good idea?" I interrogated myself. "Likening the story of creation to Jenaro…"

I trailed off. I finally managed to disrobe just as Isadore parted the curtain. She stopped and stared at me.

"What?" I asked in anger. I didn't care to dress, to even cover myself in front of her. It wasn't as if she had never seen me this way; naked and distraught.

"Hildy," Isadore said, slowly, quietly.

I shook my head and sat at my table. I put my arms on the table, burying my head in my arms. I wanted to sob, to let my tears flow, but nothing came.

In moments, Isadore was by my side on the bench, arm on my shoulder, pulling me close. "Hildy, that was incredible," she said. "I would have never thought to relate the story of the first cave, the story of creation, to the actual creation of Jenaro! Brilliant!"

I raised my head. "You don't have to say that Izzy," I replied.

"When have I ever sugarcoated the truth to you?" she asked, offended. "Never in all our years together have I ever refrained in telling you exactly how it is. Why would I start now?"

I dropped my head to the table once more.

"It was incredible," Isadore repeated. "You should have seen those people once you left. They were all smiles, every one of them. They immediately ran to the Suma Behique to tell her how much they enjoyed the first night of the Telling. I even heard one say she was bringing her entire family to tomorrow's Telling."

I peeked my head from under my arm and sniffled. "They weren't angry or upset?"

Isadore shook her head. "Why would they be? The Telling

is boring dogma. What you presented was a real-life, real-world example."

"And the Suma? Luisa?" I asked.

Isadore shrugged. "The Suma Behique is hard to read. Luisa, on the other hand…" Isadore trailed off, muttering a curse under her breath.

I looked up and noticed that Isadore's words had mysteriously summoned my sister, the Cacique, to my room.

"I would ask to speak to my sister alone, Isadore," Luisa commanded from the entrance to my quarters.

I rested my chin on my arm. I watched as Isadore bowed low and removed herself from the room. Luisa's face was tight and grim; her teeth clenched and jaw tight. The vein on her forehead was bulging, a sure sign of her rage.

"Hildy, you are my sister and I love you, but please stand up and put some clothes on."

I refused to move.

Luisa rolled her eyes. "Who gave you permission to change the Telling? There is a reason it is told the same way every year. This is the most religious education our people get. If they wanted fairy tales, they could sit by their grandparents' feet. You can't go about altering the story just because you feel it is inadequate for your fantasies!"

"Alter it to my fantasies?!" I asked, slamming my hands on the table, and rising to my feet. "Luisa, you are my sister and the Cacique, but let me educate you."

Her face changed from anger to shock.

"My decision was approved by the Suma Behique so if you have an issue with my Telling, you are more than welcome to take it up with her. And if this is such an important event, there'd be more than five drunken Jibaros in attendance! Furthermore, do not ever lecture me about my fantasies. I don't criticize your lusts for power or how you dreamed of sitting on the dujo for as long as I remember."

Luisa's shock transformed to disgust. Her disgust morphed back to rage.

My sister's rage was a quiet tempest. Her venom was slow and painful as it attacked your psyche. She would smile and whisper curses that forever scarred even the hardiest of guazabara. I had never been one to trifle with my sister, even as children, and as my anger faded, fear crept in.

Luisa took a quick and deliberate step forward. Her eyes blazed; her jaw clenched tight. Her fists were balled. She leaned close to me, almost touching her mouth to my ear.

"Tomorrow, you will give the traditional Telling," she whispered into my ear. It wasn't a request. It wasn't a demand. It was the word made flesh. It was an assured vision of the future.

She stepped back and smiled at me. Her teeth were daggers, dripping venom and ready to strike. Her tongue was forked and foul.

"You are the moon of my life," she said sweetly.

"And the stars of my forever," I replied equally as sweet.

Luisa left in a flourish and Isadore was immediately by my side.

"Have I told you how much I absolutely adore when you stand up to her?" Isadore squeaked excitedly.

My shoulders dropped. I turned back to the table and slipped into my small clothes and robe. "She told me to p–perform the traditional Telling tomorrow," I uttered. "And…so I will."

Isadore's face twisted. "What? Why?"

I shrugged. "B–because she is the Cacique, and I must obey her commands."

Isadore exhaled sharply and shook her head. "No," she

grunted. "No, Hildy. That's bullshit. This is your Telling," she said forcefully as she grabbed my hands. "This is your Telling."

I shook my head. "You don't understand, Isadore. It wasn't a request."

Isadore raised my hands to her mouth and kissed both. "This is your Telling," she repeated, only this time, sweetly. "Not to mention she cannot direct the business of the Temple."

I lowered my head and Isadore lowered our hands, keeping them clasped together.

"Look, you have an entire day to consider what she said. And if my words hold any weight in your decision, I don't think you should listen to her."

I nodded and pulled my hood over my head. "Are you hungry?"

"I could eat," Isadore responded casually.

I quickly dressed and tried to smile as we locked arms and exited my quarters. Yet, my heart was heavy. We didn't make it far, though, for the Suma Behique was standing right outside.

"Suma B–behique," I stammered.

She said nothing. She did not have to say anything. Her simple smile and nod were enough. She was pleased with my Telling. I nodded back and pushed Isadore around the Suma Behique, trying my hardest not to hurry away from her presence, holding my breath as if the simple act of breathing would disturb her. As soon as the curtains to the main assembly flapped closed, I exhaled with a whistle.

Isadore giggled. "Why am I more frightened of the Suma Behique than I am of your sister?"

"I was about to ask you the same thing," I responded. We shared a short giggle then hurried into the batéy.

The evening festivities were in full swing. Dancers were parading through the batéy accompanied by their respective drum corps and singers. Isadore showed me her sneaky, conniving smile; the same smile she wore every time we ended up in trouble.

"Let's join the parade!" Isadore shouted over the music, dancing in place, shaking her hips, and bobbing her shoulders up and down to the beat.

Isadore was an incredible dancer. She once told me it was her dream to dance professionally and lead a team during the festival of Areíto. I was not blessed with her gift of rhythm.

"You go ahead," I said.

"Come with!" she pleaded.

I shook my head as she pulled me into the pathway and began to gyrate.

"I can't, Izzy!" I shouted above the crowd. "What would the Suma B–behique think?"

Isadore scoffed and leaned close to my ear. "You're not a full behique yet, only a novice. Come on!"

I reluctantly gave in to her demands and we danced with the group for a while. Isadore pirouetted and twirled and rolled around, her body a slave to the driving beat and the soaring vocals. I did my best but was sure I looked foolish shaking next to all the dancers.

We danced in line until the procession made an about face and marched back toward the center of the batéy. Isadore and I jumped out of the convoy and hugged each other tightly. Isadore was drenched in sweat, a glistening, beautiful mess.

"That was so much fun!" Isadore cried aloud as she embraced me once more. "Now I am definitely famished."

I nodded and forced a smile. "Let's grab a p–plate from the nearest vendor and make our way to the manse."

Revelations and Confrontations

I woke before the sun the next morning. Isadore was sleeping gently next to me, her breathing a slow and steady prelude to the dawn. I carefully rolled out of bed and slipped into my robes. For some reason, I felt compelled to grab the little knife given to me by my baba. I strapped it to my forearm and hid it under the sleeves of my robe. As I began to tiptoe to the door, Izzy rolled over and mumbled.

"No…you take the fish, mister caguama…" her voice drifted sleepily to my ears.

I immediately put my hands to my mouth to keep from waking her with my laughter. Isadore talked in her sleep as long as I could remember. Half of her sleeping conversations occurred between herself and this mysterious mister caguama.

I moved to my bedroom door and quietly exited. The manse was nearly abandoned at such an hour, save the sentries stuck with the night watch and the cooks beginning their prep work for the day's meals. The royal manse at Puerto Zafiro was celebrating its quincentennial during this year's Areíto. During the daylight hours of the festival, guided tours of the building and grounds were offered to citizens of the Andolins. It was always surprising how many people took the chance to see the artwork, tapestries, sculptures, and architecture in the manse. It was an expansive and spacious building that was once home to all executive and legislative offices of our islands. The original edifice was erected like a cylinder and built entirely of seastone quarried from West Andolin and shipped across the straits to East Andolin. It stood three stories high with each story greater than fifteen feet from floor to ceiling. The building initially had no windows. The warm, tropical breezes were allowed to flow through the manse unhindered. Windows were added after several consecutive storm seasons attacked the islands. They were the first of many additions. Over the years the garden was expanded, the walls strengthened, a stable and livery added, and a small home was built for the carib of the Anacaona clan. A second edifice was constructed about a century before I was born which became the new living quarters for the royal family. After its completion, the original building was restored and decommissioned. It is now basically a museum.

I made my way to the kitchen, nodding politely at each patrolling guard. When I entered, the two cooks, Feliz and Marcos, were amid an argument. Their voices carried above the roaring fire, bubbling pots, and searing sounds coming from the stove.

"No, no, no," Marcos chided. "We've been over this a million times. You must boil it with water then add the milk."

Feliz shook his head sending tremors to his chubby full cheeks. "If you cook the rice in milk from the start, it becomes a thicker, creamier dish," he shot back, reaching for the milk jug nestled snugly under Marcos's arms.

The spritely Marcos danced out of Feliz's grasp. I couldn't help but laugh at the antics. My giggles alerted the cooks to my presence. They immediately stopped their bickering and bowed slightly.

"It is a bit early for breakfast, behique," Marcos said as he motioned for me to take a seat at the counter island in the middle of the kitchen. I know he meant no harm using my future title, but the distant formality hurt. After all, I had been a regular fixture in the kitchen for eleven years now, ever since Izzy and I could wander the manse alone.

"I know, Marcos," I responded. "I was only looking for some fruit, maybe a p–papaya or mango…" I trailed off, scanning the kitchen and inhaling deeply. The delicious aroma of bread in the oven and stock pots full of rice and farina filled my nose. A slab of bacon sat on the counter, waiting to be sliced. It was then my stomach informed me that maybe fruit would be insufficient at this juncture.

Feliz stepped forward and, in one seamless motion, palmed a mango from the hanging racks above the island, and tossed a beautifully ripe one at me. I caught it easily as he winked in my direction. Marcos, on the other hand, went white as a ghost.

"Falta respecto–throwing fruit at the Cacique's sister…"

I chuckled lightly as I pulled my knife from its sheath on my forearm.

"Can I ask you something, your grace?" Feliz posed to me, emphasizing my title. There was the formality again. It made my breath catch in my throat and heart hurt.

Marcos rolled his eyes and returned to the boiling pot on the stove.

"Surely, Feliz," I answered as I sliced the cheeks of the mango sending its sweet nectar rolling down my hands.

"When you think of arroz dulce, do you prefer it creamy or syrupy?"

"Aye," Marcos groaned and moved from the stove. "Leave her out of this!"

"I only ask to prove a point, my good friend Marcos," Feliz said, tongue in cheek.

"You ask to irritate me," Marcos fired back. "And we are not friends. I am the chef, and you are my assistant."

I smiled widely as I sliced the mango into my mouth. "I think I'll sit this one out."

Feliz's grin grew larger. He nodded his head. "A wise decision from a soon to be behique."

Feliz couldn't know how his words turned sour in my ears. My smile faded and I stuffed my mouth with the remaining slices of mango. I stared at the counter for a few silent moments that created a thick fog of awkwardness in the kitchen. Feliz quickly returned to his work, until I spoke up.

"Feliz? Marcos?" I asked just above the clattering chaos in the kitchen.

Both men turned to face me.

"Yes?" they asked in unison.

"Did you always know you wanted to be a chef?" I inquired. "I mean, was there ever any doubt?"

Feliz grunted in approval, but Marcos left the pot and motioned for Feliz to take over the stirring. Marcos pulled a chair to the counter island and sat with a gentle moan reserved only for the aged.

"I wasn't always a chef, young Hildy. Before I came to work in the service of your bibi and baba here at the manse, I played batu."

I gave him a skeptical stare. "You were a b–batu player?"

Marcos nodded.

"You…I knew I recognized your name!" Feliz cried joyously from the pot. "All these years working side-by-side and I never once brought it up, but I knew you were *the* Marcos Macuya."

"Hush, you," Marcos reprimanded.

Feliz chuckled and flashed a toothy, mirthful smile from the stove.

"When I was young, my only dream was to play batu. I donned the stone bracelets and belts from an early age, soon as I could wear them. My father played batu, you see, and he was my hero. There is even a statue to him in my hometown.

"I was good, good enough to play with the men's team by the time I was fourteen, even won several Areíto tournaments. When I was seventeen, I collided with my best friend during a match. My body went one way, my knee the other. I tried to get back into it, after it healed, but my knee was never the same. Unfortunately, with an injury like mine, I could never again move with enough speed.

"I retired from batu at nineteen, a full fifteen years before the age my father had retired. It destroyed me. I left home, lost, without direction, not knowing what I would do the next day let alone the rest of my life."

"How did you b–become a chef?" I asked.

Marcos bobbed his head left and right. "It took me five years to come to terms with my disability. When I finally did, I realized my love for batu was simply from a desire to please my father. I wanted to make him proud by becoming as great as he was at batu. I didn't play the game because I loved it, I played for approval. Once I realized that, I began to explore what I loved to do, the things that interested me. I remembered how I enjoyed cooking with my bibi and abuela. This led to that and before long I was a chef for the Cacique." Marcos sat silent for a moment, shoulders back, head raised high. When he stood up he look like a general ready to lead his troops into battle. "Do you understand?"

I nodded and rose from my stool. I nodded somberly. "Thank you for the mango, Feliz. And thank you for the lesson, Marcos."

Marcos hazarded a smile then pushed Feliz away from the pot.

"You're over-stirring it," he barked.

Feliz hopped away with a chuckle.

Rather than return to my room, I made my way through the

manse to my mother's private garden. The darkness of night was subsiding, and dark gray washed over the sky. The lamps were still lit, illuminating the path to a set of benches underneath my favorite tree. I walked along quietly taking a seat under the enormous twisting branches of the ancient ceiba. I placed my hand on the trunk and whispered, "Good morning ceiba, oldest and wisest of all the trees in the Andolins."

As soon as the words escaped my lips and reached the trunk of the ceiba, the branches shimmied and shook, chattering with the morning breeze. I smiled and closed my eyes, choosing to meditate on the words of the tree.

My mind was restless, though, and could not stop thinking about Marcos's story. He always seemed like an ornery, tightly wound perfectionist. Imagining him running around the batu court, diving at the ball, volleying it back and forth with the stone bracelets, entertaining the crowds with his skill seemed unbelievable. Yet, it was not his calling. He was never meant to walk in his father's footsteps. Maybe I am the same, I wondered. All this time I believed becoming a behique and dedicating my life to the cemi was my purpose. I am the middle child after all. I don't have the military ambition and strategic thinking that Arecibo has, or the drive to rule like Luisa. The priesthood sounded like the natural choice, but was it my only choice?

My bibi had always wanted a child to serve in the temple of the bchique. It was her legacy. Every woman from her line had a child in the Temple. Her youngest sister had chosen the priesthood and my oldest cousin by my tía as well. Luisa would never have gone for it. The priesthood offered little by way of her ambition. And Arecibo was the only man-child. There was no way our baba would have let him choose a life of celibacy over progeny. So, it was left to me.

In some ways, I envied my siblings. Luisa was born to be

Cacique. Years of bossing everyone around, from Arecibo and I to the staff at the manse, prepared her for it. After our baba passed and our bibi stepped down it only seemed natural she stepped into the role. Arecibo, meanwhile, was always an adventurer. There was rarely a week where he wasn't running away or asking to join the guaza. But what did I ever desire but peace and quiet with a fishing pole, my flute, and Isadore at my side dancing to my tunes. No daughter of the Cacique could be part of such a bohemian lifestyle.

When I opened my eyes again, it was dawn. The coqui ended their moonlight symphony, and the sun was climbing its ladder to the heavens. The loro were stirring and the morning breeze brought the warm, briny smell of the summer sea to my nose. I pulled my flute from my belt and began to play. I couldn't rid my mind of the melody from 'Baile de la Grulla.' I knew that song inside and out. It was one of the first tunes I ever mastered. My fingers deftly danced over the finger holes as the song glided perfectly from my flute. I smiled as I hit the final note. I knew the misstep from the previous day had to have been nerves. I turned my attention to the path from my mother's quarters in time to see her, my bibi, and Isadore's Tía Celia approaching. Celia walked slowly beside my mother, who was too stubborn to use the wheelchair. She instead preferred to amble awkwardly forever clutching to Celia's arm.

To say she looked fragile was a hilarious understatement. The woman stumbling toward me was a shadow of the strong and vibrant former Cacique of the Andolins she once was. That image had crumbled away to reveal a sick, feeble crone, with the only thing remaining of her past self her smile. It still illuminated her face and beamed warmth that only she and my baba could give.

"Hildy, my love," she wheezed as she approached. "You don't have to stop playing on my account."

I stood from my tree root and hurried to her side. It always startled me how conflicted my relationship with her was. My bibi, Tinima, was overbearing, meddling, and insensitive, yet I loved and respected her more than anything.

"You are the moon of my life," Tinima rasped as she kissed my cheek.

"And the stars of my forever," I completed the motto and helped her to the bench.

She slowly lowered herself to her seat, exhaling sharply once she landed.

"I heard of your Telling yesterday, Hildy," my bibi said.

I inhaled through my nose and exhaled slowly through my mouth. She never was one to beat around the bush.

"Luisa says your Telling was…nontraditional?" she asked, but I knew it wasn't a question.

I shook my head. "B–bibi, the telling as you very well know has always been just as much about the b–behique as the story of the cemi."

"Try your best not to stutter, my dear. How is anyone supposed to understand you," Tinima said and my heart fell to the pit of my stomach. Her eyes were cold and distant. Her smile had faded from her face. "Must you always make waves, Hildy?"

I stood from the bench and nearly shouted but cut my voice off before making that error. "Was this what you wanted to see me for, b–bibi?" I asked quietly, careful not to raise my voice and incur her wrath. "To ridicule me and judge my decisions?"

Tinima scoffed. "No, my child, I never ridicule you, nor do I judge you. You are my flesh and my blood, and I only ever want what is best for you. I merely wanted to spend a morning breaking our fast like we did when you were young."

I sighed. She had a way of stabbing at me and treating the wound in the same sentence. I sat back down and bowed my head. *Yaya, give me strength.*

My bibi nodded to Celia, who swiftly exited the courtyard. Moments later she returned with a small envoy carrying a table and bowls of assorted breakfast treats; mango and papaya, cheese and peppers, bacon, even the arroz dulce Feliz and Marcos were arguing over. We ate in relative silence. My bibi made small talk while she avoided most of her food. I ate sparingly, not wanting to hear lectures about my weight, but attempting to avoid concerns over my lack of appetite.

"Luisa tells me you shared some rather private information about our family during your telling," Tinima said between bites.

I froze.

"Is that the wisest thing to do with Luisa's important decision coming shortly?"

I chewed my food for a few more bites then swallowed hard. "It was nothing that the p–people wouldn't b–be able to learn on their own. The temple library is open to the p–public."

"I agree, I just wish you would understand that there are some things the people don't need to know." Tinima leaned back slowly and sighed, crossing her arms on her chest. "There are times I wish you would have inherited my prudence instead of your baba's indiscretion."

"Arecibo got your p–prudence. Luisa got the dujo. It would have b–been nice to inherit something, anything from you, b–bibi, other than your complete disdain for me." I said and immediately regretted. My eyes went wide. My breath caught in my throat. I could feel my cheeks begin to flush. I cautiously looked at her face and immediately turned away. *Why would you say such a thing?*

"Your foolhardiness is definitely a trait of the Campos

blood." Tinima's disapproval quickly shifted. "You are not to speak of Sharae again in your Telling." Her voice was cold and stern. "Hildy, it is imperative."

I breathed a silent sigh of relief. Luisa must have told her. The thought of revealing Jenaro's indiscretions had never crossed my mind. I had assumed that mentioning her name and the fact that they were always lovers didn't count as one of those indiscretions, but apparently I was mistaken. Instead of voicing that thought, I simply nodded at my bibi.

When we finished, the same envoy carried away the meal, leaving us alone in the garden once more.

"I think I will make the trip to the batéy this evening. I am interested in hearing you speak, daughter."

My heart skipped. My hands instantly became slick with sweat. I could feel my face grow cold as my blood rushed to my extremities. "You don't have to do that, b–b–bibi," I stuttered, wincing at my moment of weakness in front of her. "You shouldn't risk it in your current condition."

She smiled and reached for my hand. I had seen that smile countless times before. It was the same smile I got from Luisa; a piteous grin only a cacique and mother could give. "Don't worry about me, child. You already have enough to occupy your mind."

I swallowed hard and rose from the bench. I bowed low and kissed her hand, then both cheeks and her forehead.

"Goodbye, bibi. I will see you this evening," I said as gently and warmly as I could muster through my embarrassment. "You are the moon of my life."

"And the stars of my forever," Tinima responded, her voice flat and humorless.

I nodded and smiled at Celia, who smiled softly. Her face told me to keep my head up.

I took the long way back to my quarters. I figured the walk

would calm my nerves. I was almost surprised that my suspicions were correct. Seeing the city sprawling down the slopes of the mountain, the many-colored banners flying in the wind at the Batéy del Albizu, witnessing the sails in the harbor, smelling the sweet and savory aromas rising from the various Areíto feasts being cooked, tasting the briny sea air…all of it soothed my spirit and refocused my attention on the day ahead.

Isadore was nowhere to be found. This was an occasional occurrence; she had other responsibilities pertaining to a carib that sometimes required her to be away. Security meetings, intelligence briefings, even simple maintenance of mind, body, and blade were necessary for the carib. I never questioned it but did feel a tiny bit of abandonment each time. Isadore was, after all, my truest friend and confidant. I wanted to be always by her side.

I took the opportunity of solitude to enjoy a bath. I undressed, drew a tub full of hot water, and soaked until my fingers and toes began to prune, until every ounce of heat had disappeared from the water. I closed my eyes and concentrated on the evening's Telling, on the progression of Jenaro's story. I knew in my heart what I wanted to do. I knew what came next in my version of the telling. I knew of the three most heroic of Jenaro's deeds and how to relate them to the cave of life. Yet, the knowledge of having Luisa and our bibi in attendance made my body shiver and my skin crawl. And thanks to bibi's warning, I could not stop thinking of Sharae Campos.

I finished my soak and was toweling off when Isadore returned. She came barging into my quarters almost skipping toward me with a look of pure elation plastered on her face.

"Hildy, oh Hildy, you will never guess what the talk about Puerto Zafiro is!" she said with a sing-songy delivery.

I sat at the edge of the tub and wrapped my towel around

my head. I motioned to Isadore's side, calling for another towel to wrap around my still dripping frame.

"I'm kind of p–preoccupied at the moment," I responded as I wrapped the towel around my body..."

"Oh–right, sorry. Is it your bibi?" Isadore asked. "How was breakfast?"

I sighed. "P–perfectly normal in the truest sense of the word."

Isadore frowned. "Did she tell you you're fat? Or did Luisa tattle on you and tell her that poor old Hildy was mean to her?" She imitated Luisa's voice. Her mockery was spot on.

"She heard about the Telling," I replied. "She wasn't happy with my version."

Isadore rolled her eyes. "If she wasn't there, how could she judge what you said?"

I shook my head. "I love my b–bibi, but the cemi be damned if she doesn't take every opportunity to b–belittle me."

Isadore frowned again. "Try not to worry about it, Hildy. Family will always be your harshest critic."

"I thought it was yourself?" I chuckled.

"Huh?"

"I think the saying is 'You will always be your own harshest critic.'"

Isadore shrugged. "Whatever. My point is, and this kind of brings me back to my news...your Telling is on everybody's lips today!" She grabbed my hands and lifted me from the edge of the tub.

"What?" I gasped.

"It's early, but word in my security meeting is that there will be double the normal guard to handle the expected members of attendees. Everybody is talking about it. Nobody had ever heard a Telling like yours. Even the tourists visiting for Areíto are planning to attend."

My mouth hung open and I nearly lost my towel. I began to tremble. "What…why?"

Isadore put her hands on my shoulders and smiled. "Your Telling was not only a success–it's also already being talked about as one of the best our people have ever heard. Taking boring old doctrine and relating it to their hero, our hero, Jenaro, was a stroke of genius."

I swallowed hard. My jaw shuddered. "So, they're expecting a crowd?"

"A crowd? Hildy, they think it will be the largest crowd in the history of modern Areíto!"

I took a long blink and flexed my hands by my side. My mind was spinning with a thousand different scenarios simultaneously. I clutched my towel and hurried into my room, where I paced back and forth from my armoire to my bed, changing my vestment choice over and over. I snatched a pair of undergarments from my dresser, then another pair, and then I reached in and grabbed every pair I owned and threw them on the bed.

By this time, Isadore had followed me out of the bathroom and sat herself on the edge of the bed. I was so unaware that I managed to throw my underwear all over her.

"I thought you'd be excited," Isadore said, pulling a pair of panties from her face. "What's wrong?"

I sighed and plopped down on the bed next to her. "My b–bibi is p–planning on attending."

Isadore's eyes went wide. "That's…that's great. I mean, I had no idea she was well enough to leave the manse."

Her words were kind, but her tone was full of dread. The news was a shock to her as well.

"She isn't," I grumbled as I tussled my hair one last time with the towel on my head.

"But that's amazing news. She wants to hear your Telling."

I shook my head. "That's not why she's coming. She wants to make sure I stick to the traditional form of the Telling instead of my version."

"What?" Isadore's face fell. "I had no idea, honest. If I knew I wouldn't have bothered to tell you…I mean I don't want to be the cause of your…distress."

I forced a smile. "Never. You never have to apologize for sharing your excitement with me."

Isadore nodded. "And don't worry about your stutter."

I puffed my cheeks with an exhale. My stomach performed a few acrobatics.

Isadore hopped off the bed in a flash and grinned from ear to ear. "I have an idea. You and I are going to spend the day relaxing and keeping your mind off tonight, okay?"

I stared blankly at Isadore for a moment before nodding reluctantly. "Okay."

I finished dressing quickly, then Isadore and I hurried out of the manse. She led me through back passages and small stairways and servants' passages. I wondered her reason for the secret escape but kept quiet and followed her lead. We exited the manse and Isadore immediately grabbed my hand. We hurried down the mountainside and into the heart of Puerto Zafiro.

Desires of the Heart

Day two of Areíto was already in full swing. The streets were full of festival goers dressed in crimson and ermine. Cheers from the batu games being played in the batéy rolled through the streets, a steady chime floating above the laughter and conversation. I figured Isadore would want to spend the day eating and carousing with the other festival goers, but she instead brought me to a carriage company near the edge of the Batéy del Albizu.

"Where are you taking me?" I asked Isadore with a squint and a frown.

She smiled and replied, "Just wait and see."

The carriage ferried us out of the city and down the coastline. The populace dwindled, leaving behind towering buildings of wood and stone for smaller, one room shacks. The carriage stopped at a hut neighboring a well-worn, narrow footpath that led toward the coast. Isadore paid the driver as we disembarked then grabbed my hand and began down the trail.

"I thought you'd have figured it out by now," Isadore chuckled haughtily.

I gave her a curious look, but then as we eclipsed the last rise to the sea, it struck me.

"Baba's fishing spot…" I whispered in delight.

Isadore's smile was infectiously wide.

Comerio's Cove was my baba's favorite fishing hole. It was a public lagoon, surrounded by squat, verdant cliffs. The waters were a beautiful teal and broad enough to support both top swimmers and larger, deep-diving fish. Baba and I often spent our fishing trips in the family dinghy, alongside the people of the islands. Baba would say, "a cacique must know the people he governs," and on those trips, he said, he would grow to truly know his people. Those were my favorite days; days that disappeared with his death.

I realized I had stopped walking. Isadore looked at me, concern painting her face.

"Is it too much?" Isadore asked.

I looked at the lagoon. A precious few fishermen were scattered in its waters, and my father's old dingy was prepared by the shore. It was a fourteen-footer, painted half red and half white. The interior was clean and polished with the natural veneer of two-toned wood. The oars were also two toned and covered in Andoli runes of strength and speed. We approached and I noticed our fishing poles nestled carefully in the boat. I turned to Isadore as a tear rolled down my cheek.

"It's p–perfect," I said through a sniffle.

We spent the rest of the morning and early afternoon anchored in the middle of the cove, casting our lines and enjoying each other's company. Isadore stocked the dinghy with all manner of supplies for both fish and human: a bucket of bait, lures, a net, two flasks of mango wine, a loaf of freshly baked bread, and two sausage links. I frankly was surprised she only put one a piece in there. Isadore entertained me with elaborate rumors overheard in her briefings, gossip that she felt I just had to know. I reminisced about the times the two of us spent in the cove with my baba. When we could no longer stand the heat from the sun, the two of us stripped to our small clothes and jumped into the water, scaring off any fish that may have been tempted to bite. We didn't care. We laughed and splashed water at each other, free from responsibility and from prying eyes.

"Sometimes, I wish we could just b–be like this forever," I

stated, lounging in the prow, drying off in the sun as Isadore rebaited her hook.

"Be like what?" Isadore asked as she set her rod in its nook.

"You know, happy, content to simply spend our days on the water, fishing, singing," I trailed off.

"Living," Isadore finished my thought.

I nodded. "Living," I repeated.

"Hmm," Isadore grunted, whether in agreement or in thought, I did not know.

"Don't you agree?" I asked after a few moments passed.

Isadore shrugged. "Sure, living life day-to-day, focusing on the moment sounds grand, but what about family? Obligations? Where would we sleep? How could we afford to eat?"

I gave Isadore a sideways look. She had never spoken like that before. Izzy was the epitome of free-spirited. How could she talk of responsibility and obligation?

"I guess so…" I muttered and returned to my pole. That was when she started laughing.

"You look so hurt, Hildy!" Isadore laughed.

I frowned and turned my face from hers.

"Are you upset?"

"No, b–but I am serious."

Isadore wedged her rod in between the hull and center thwart and shuffled to sit next to me. "How serious?" Isadore asked.

I shrugged. "I don't know. I started thinking about becoming a b–behique and everything that has been happening lately and I can't help but think that maybe I'm doing all this b–because the influential people in my life wanted me to. Did I make this decision on my own?"

Isadore nodded with a slight frown on her face. "You've been talking to Marcos again, haven't you?"

My eyes went wide. I could feel my cheeks flushing.

"It's okay, Hildy," Isadore assured me. "I talk to him too. I told him of my dream of being a dancer. He told me the Anacaona oath only goes so far as the carib desires. I mean, I would never leave you, but…sometimes I wonder…"

I gasped, offended. "You wonder what life would be like without me?"

"No, not without you," Isadore answered. "Without the oath. Without the responsibility."

"See?" I asked her. "See what I mean? Why are we torturing ourselves with these questions, with the uncertainty, abandoning our desires, when we can just leave it all and live how we want?"

Isadore grinned and chortled. "I'm going to grab these oars and row us to freedom." I giggled. "But to be the voice of reason in the conversation, something you know I hate doing; you can't just leave the behique, nor can we just sail away from your name and title."

"Why not?" I shot back, knowing she was right. The feeling of defeat began to creep up on me.

"People would notice," Isadore replied. "Your bibi would send the guaza after us. Luisa would have us both imprisoned on some ridiculous charge, not that it would be hard to spot a del Rios lady and an Anacaona roaming the countryside together."

"We can disguise ourselves," I said weakly, realizing the ridiculousness of my desires.

Isadore put a hand on my lap just as her line began to spin uncontrollably. She jumped to her rod and began to reel in her catch.

Isadore caught a sizable bacalao and we returned to shore. I played a few melodies on my flute after lighting a fire. Isadore gutted the fish. After our lunch, the music continued. At

Isadore's request, I played her favorite song, "Did Not Fall to Fate." As the intro reached its climax, she began to sing:

> Clouds of red, bloody night
> Luysa pilots her ship through
> The waters rage, the wind did howl
> And soon the beast begins its doom
>
> Some say she's born on eagle's wings
> Some say she lives under the sea
> The only thing I say to you
> No greater captain be!
>
> The architus attacked her ship
> Six armed beast from hell below
> It swung and screamed and battered Mourn
> But only angered the captain so.
>
> Some say she's born on eagle's wings
> Some say she lives under the sea
> The only thing I say to you
> No greater captain be!
>
> Luysa flew like harpy to
> The beast that clung aboard the Mourn
> With club in hand she struck the fiend
> So mighty a blow she killed her foe.
>
> Some say she's born on eagle's wings
> Some say she lives under the sea
> The only thing I say to you
> No greater captain be!

Some say she's born on eagle's wings
Some say she lives under the sea
The only thing I say to you
No greater captain be!

Isadore danced along the shore as she sang. She beckoned me with each verse, until I finally joined her in the surf. We danced and sang in the sand, waves gently rolling over our feet up to our ankles, until the sun turned the sky a tawny shade and painted the turquoise waters of the lagoon a brilliant gold and chartreuse. I knew the fun would soon end, but for the moment, I simply danced. Afterwards, we plopped down, side-by-side, into the sand next to our little fire, and Isadore served the fish. We ate and giggled about everything and nothing.

"You dreamt of mister caguama again last night," I teased, tongue out, as I held a steaming piece of bacalao next to my lips.

Isadore laughed. "You would not believe what he's been up to these days."

"Well, go on, tell me!"

"He's taken to stealing fish from nets and crabs from traps," Isadore whispered.

I laughed and threw my piece of fish at her. "You b–brat, that's nothing new! Mister Caguama has b–been thieving fish and crabs for years now!"

Isadore ate the piece of fish and threw a piece of her own at me. "But I think he's doing it for the thrill of it now. I mean, before he would steal to eat, steal to live. Now he's obsessed with the rush."

I smiled and shook my head. As we stared at the horizon, eating our fish and laughing, I became overwhelmed with emotion. I pulled Isadore in close and embraced her tighter than I ever had. "I love you, Isadore."

Izzy giggled and replied. "I love you too, Hildy."

Packed House

The carriage ride back to the Batéy del Albizu was quiet yet satisfying. I sat with my head resting on Isadore's chest, listening to her heartbeat. Isadore hummed her favorite melody from the lagoon and ran her fingers through my hair, gently massaging my scalp.

"Do you think you could learn to play 'El Tiburon?'" Isadore asked. "I want to learn that dance from last night but need the music to go with it."

"Of course!" I said, elated. "You know I love watching you dance. I can't let you do it unaccompanied."

"And I can't dance without your music," Isadore said.

"I'm sure you'd dance just fine to someone else's music."

"No, I wouldn't," Isadore replied. "Your music just feels different. It fills me up, lights a fire in my soul. Your music is the only music I want to dance to."

I couldn't hold back my smile. I tilted my head to show her how happy I was and saw the brightest smile I had ever seen on her face. I wrapped my arms around her and squeezed as tight as I could.

The second evening of Areíto was in full swing when we set foot in the batéy. The batu tournament quarterfinals were just ending, setting the matchups for the semi-finals later that evening. The first of the evening's parades marched through the plaza. The dance troupes traipsed to the beat of the drums, spinning and jumping around to the beat.

We quickly snaked our way to the center of the batéy, back to the plaza of the cemi and the behique tent. I held Izzy's hand as she led the way, still beaming from our day together, making sure to occasionally give it a squeeze. The joy evaporated like the morning dew the moment we spotted the tent. Sure enough, just as Isadore had said, the numbers from the day before had multiplied; where once sat five inebriated, cautiously pious Andoli now easily numbered several hundred. The number of those that could not fit in the tent was twice as many. Andoli from all over the islands jostled for seats near the front. Jibaros stood at the back; their wide brimmed hats off and hanging on their backs. I spotted a small group of Meres smiling and pointing, not understanding the gravity of what they were about to witness. An Itiban couple stood reverently, dressed in fine silks and outlandish jewelry, heads bowed as if in prayer. There were even several Cibao Ara' all the way from Cike'o sitting quietly near the entrance. My hands grew sweatier the more people I counted.

Borinkens brought entire families to the Telling, from the youngest new-born babes yet to reach their name day, to the eldest members of their clan. They sat in their respective family groups behind the Nitaino, who, unsurprisingly, brought seat cushions and servants to wave fans and keep themselves and their siani cool. They monopolized the best seats in the house. In the middle of the wealthy Nitaino, sitting together in the royal litter and accompanied by a detachment of guazabara, were my bibi and Luisa. I turned to Isadore, eyes wide and lips trembling. Isadore grabbed my sweat-soaked palms, leaned in, and kissed me.

"You'll be amazing," she said sweetly. "I'll stand right here by the entrance. Just like last night, okay?"

I nodded slowly, lethargically, as if a doll under a spell. "Tell me everything will b–be okay," I mumbled.

"Everything will be okay," Isadore said.

"Tell me I can do this."

"Not only can you do this, but you're also going to do it so well that everyone will be talking about it for a generation."

"And if it goes wrong, you and I will escape together on my b–baba's b–boat."

"I will have it outfitted and ready to sail before you even finish," Isadore said with a smile. "Now go!"

I let out a ragged breath, trying to force the anxiety from my body. My jaw trembled as I nodded quickly. She squeezed my hand one more time then left me to prepare.

I hurried my way behind the curtains to my ready room. My fellow behique had laid out my ceremonial vestments as they had done the day before, except today, the Suma Behique accompanied all my various accouterments. She sat at my table surrounded by the thick smoke of cassava snuff, and slowly looked up at me as I approached. She reached for my hand and held it fast. The effects of the cassava made her limp wristed. I was surprised she had any grip at all.

"Hildy," the Suma Behique began in a low, mysterious voice, "it is strange that I am visited by the same vision from yesterday. Again, I saw you and again a strong tempest descended upon you, only now I could see myself. I stand in the crowd and stare at the storm. I too am swept away. The cemi share an important message with me yet I cannot comprehend. It must be the reason for the redundancy."

She rose in a strange, methodical fashion and bowed to me then as if suddenly overcome by a wave of unexpected clarity, she embraced me. "The cemi approve of your Telling. Remember that." Her eyes were clear and bright, her smile, warm. She smelled of snuff and coffee. "May Yaya bless your Telling," the Suma declared, then left me alone to prepare.

I sat down in the seat the Suma had occupied and placed my

hands on my vestments. My bibi and Luisa would be expecting a return to the Tellings of old. It was what they wanted--no, what they expected me to do. The people would be anticipating more of yesterday's Telling. It was the very reason they packed so tightly into the tent. If the cemi were truly behind my decision, then whatever I decided would be simply an extension of their will. I exhaled and trilled my lips.

"What's the worst that could happen?" I muttered to myself.

Ten minutes later I was dressed and standing just beyond the curtains, waiting for the Suma to finish her address. I was welcomed on to the dais with an uncomfortable air of reverence. It made me shudder, from my shoulders to my heels. My eyes met those of my bibi and Luisa. I could do nothing but force a smile and nod at them as I began the ceremony.

I raised the rod and pipe over my head and clapped them together.

Every person present clapped their hands above their head. It was a bewilderingly reverent sound.

I cried out to Yaya in the ancient tongue.

"Yaya send your blessings down upon your people," I said, finishing the salute. I couldn't believe I didn't stutter.

"May we live in your favor!" the crowd roared in response.

I brought the rod to my mouth and mimed swallowing it, then lowered it to my side.

I brought the pipe to my nostrils and inhaled; only there was no snuff inside.

I turned slowly and placed both pipe and rod on the table of relics behind me. I inhaled through my nose and exhaled sharply through my mouth. Still, I was not sure which version of the story I was going to tell. When I returned my attention to the worshippers, three hundred pairs of eyes stared back. Three hundred faces dripped with excitement for the Telling. Yet no eyes were sharper or harder than the four of my bibi and Luisa. I met their gazes and quickly looked away, scanning the crowd for Isadore. Sure enough, she had taken her place by the door, only tonight she was not alone. Standing at her side was my brother Arecibo. They both wore brilliantly wide smiles. Isadore waved.

At first, my heart stopped. Had Arecibo come home just to hear me speak? It couldn't be. He had to have already been home. He was the spitting image of our baba, in look and demeanor, and in that moment, I saw the two become one.

I tried to find a reason for his mysterious appearance. Regardless, I looked upon his smiling face and knew I couldn't disappoint him—my brother nor my baba. I decided then and there. The people deserved to hear of Jenaro. That was why they were here, after all.

I took a step forward and raised both my hands. "The second cave," I proclaimed, louder than I expected, "is life itself."

THE SECOND CAVE: LIFE

The Crimson Sails

A Sudden Change of Plans

The gentle touch of fingertips on his scalp woke Jenaro. The sun was beaming through the thin summer curtains that hung on his windows; its rays resting warmly on his face. A quiet breeze whispered its way through his room, bringing with it the briny aroma of the sea and stirring the acrid smell of stale wine and sweat that had settled in his sheets. A small babble from the city below crept to his ears. He could sleep through all that—but her touch stirred him. He smiled slyly as her fingers caressed his head, from his crown to his temples. It drew a giggle from his consort.

Sharae leaned her face close to his and gently touched her lips to Jenaro's ear.

Jenaro opened his eyes and flashed a smile at Sharae. He could feel the warmth of her skin as she pressed against his arm and chest.

He was grateful that things were back to how they once were. Repairing what he nearly destroyed was not without its difficulties. After the debacle of the betrothal dinner, Sharae refused to see him and disappeared from Puerto Zafiro. Only recently, two years later, did she resurface and begin to contact Jenaro once again. Jenaro was careful to be mindful of her feelings and soon, the two eighteen-year-olds were once again in each other's arms.

"Did Agostin stop by with breakfast?" Jenaro asked as he swung his legs off the bed, leaving Sharae pouting over his departure. "He said he would meet here in the morning, and we would head to the manse together."

"There was a knock some time ago, but you were asleep," Sharae said as she lay back down on Jenaro's bed, pulling the covers up to her chest to cover her body. Her glowing skin was the perfect contrast to the pale silken sheets. She playfully patted and tucked them under her body, leaving a sensual outline for Jenaro to drool over.

Jenaro stretched, first skyward, then touching his toes then rotating at his hips; left and right. His gaze never left Sharae's blanketed silhouette. "How long ago?" he asked Sharae.

She shrugged her shoulders. "Hours; it is nearly midday, Your Grace."

Jenaro laughed but was immediately hit with panic. Surely, she was lying. He could not have slept the morning away. Yes, he and Sharae had spent the small hours of the morning engaged in lustful enterprises. Yes, he was a heavy sleeper, especially after consuming the better part of a barrel of mango wine and carousing the night away. But to oversleep on a day like today was unthinkable! "Do not toy with me, Sharae," he warned as he bounced around his room, clumsily gathering his clothing.

"What reason would I have to lie?" Sharae asked, her tone more offended than not. "Your attendant came by nearly after sunrise. It is almost the zenith now. Just look out your window."

Jenaro cautioned a glance out the two windows that towered opposite his bed as he fell to a seated position, pulling his sandals over his feet. He couldn't tell from the tiny window. Regardless, panic rose in his chest. "Maboya take me," he cursed.

Sharae scurried to the side of the bed as Jenaro pulled his tunic over his head. "What troubles Your Grace?" she questioned, placing her hands around his chest and resting her chin on his shoulder.

"Sharae now is not the time for sweetness," Jenaro slithered from her grasp, rose from the bed, and stumbled toward the door. "My father required my presence at a meeting with the admirals today. The admirals! I was getting my own ship today!" he shouted as he burst from his single room hovel, leaving Sharae alone on his bed.

Ever since the disaster with the betrothal, Jenaro had resided in the tiny room above the luthier's shop, the same luthier who taught him to play. It wasn't free. Jenaro worked for room and board, stringing lutes, and providing lessons, refusing the help from his baba and even his little sister Anki.

Baba... Conversation between the two had been few and far between since the incident. So when the opportunity to mend fences arrived, Jenaro jumped at the chance. Baba suggested he learn to sail and maybe a life of discipline aboard a military vessel would be just what he needed. Jenaro nearly balked, imagining having to "yes sir–no sir" Admiral Gueybana, but couldn't bear to lose his baba again. So, he went to all the meetings, trained with all the sailors, in between lute lessons of course, and became a competent sea dog. Now, thanks to one lusty night with Sharae, he was about to piss it all away.

Jenaro made it to the manse in record time, skidding to a halt next to the stairs that lead inside. He took a moment to fix himself, smooth down his hair and adjust his embarrassingly wrinkly clothes, then continued his way to the Great Hall.

The halls of the Cacique's manse were wide and airy. Most were open on one side, granting those traversing with large sweeping views of the city below and the ocean beyond. Large arches ran their length with plants and herbs hanging between. Jenaro moved like a cyclone, rocking each potted plant as he passed.

Each hall was filled with attendants and guards donned in crimson and ermine, all of whom paused from whatever business was keeping their attention to extend the palm of peace to their prince. Some greeted him warmly, others simply saluted. Regardless, Jenaro returned each palm and word in kind, trying to refrain from exasperation in front of subjects who adored him so. He reached the Great Hall, surprised to find Agostin waiting for him outside the doors. Jenaro slid to a stop and placed his hands on his head to aid his breathing.

Agostin, Jenaro's best friend and carib, was reclining on a bench, slicing a papaya with his dagger and slipping each sliver of juicy fruit between his teeth. He continued to do so even after Jenaro arrived.

"Please, catch your breath, Your Grace," Agostin said without removing his eyes from his fruit.

"Tell me they're still in there," Jenaro managed through ragged breaths.

"Whom do you speak of?" Agostin responded. "The Cacique, your father? The admirals? The Guazabara?"

Jenaro moved to speak, then noticed Agostin's curious sideways glance and wicked smirk. Jenaro raised his fists. "You whore's son, you," he cursed at his friend before feinting a swing but kicking instead. Agostin nimbly slid off the bench, avoiding Jenaro's strike, and tossed the half-eaten papaya at Jenaro. Jenaro caught the fruit and snarled. "It is not even fore-noon, is it?"

Agostin hopped to his feet and sheathed his dagger. He patted Jenaro on the shoulder and said, "It should be eight bells any moment now."

"Sharae?" Jenaro asked.

Agostin smiled. He knew the question without Jenaro having to ask. "We planned it yesterday, after the ales, but before you opened the barrel of the mango wine. Truly it was her idea."

Jenaro took a slice of the papaya and tossed the fruit back to his friend. Together they stepped toward the door. "She has regained her old boldness."

Agostin laughed. "That she has, my friend. That she has. I didn't think you'd leave the house in your pajamas though. This is an important day."

"Do I look that bad?"

Agostin grimaced then waved it away. "It'll be fine."

The two pushed open the double doors that lead to the Great Hall and strode boldy into the room. A cursory glance around the blue-pearl granite and opalescent seastone surfaces revealed the ceremonially dressed guazabara, but not the admirals. The two men paused only briefly before noticing the Cacique was also not on his dujo, the throne which sat only two stairs higher than the floor. Instead, the meeting convened around a long table to the left of the dujo close to the veranda, shrouded by sheer linen curtains that danced in the gentle sea breeze.

As Jenaro approached, he could see Admiral Gueybana leaning in toward his father. The admiral's face was like stone, but the rate at which his lips moved and the intensity with which he whispered into Marohu's ear were the actions of malcontent. As Jenaro and Agostin reached the table, the Admirals rose and saluted the Cacique. They each in turn presented a raised palm and smile to Jenaro and exited the room. All except for Gueybana, who simply nodded as he brushed past him.

Jenaro shrugged with upturned palms and a twisted grin. "I thought we were to have a commission hearing today, baba."

Marohu rose from his seat, which prompted Agostin to bow,

back away from the table, and head to the door. The Cacique walked to his son, gliding his fingers along the glossy wood inlays of the granite tabletop as he moved. He placed his hands on his son's shoulders. Jenaro lowered his head in respect. Marohu kissed his forehead.

"Walk with me, my son," Marohu said, less as a command and more as a request.

Jenaro walked alongside his father. They could have passed for twins, from the thick dark hair and olive skin to unusual height and lean build. The only differences between the two men were the streaks of grey hair adorning Marohu's temples and the scraggly beard that Jenaro wore instead of the thin mustache most del Rios men chose. Even though they stood the same height, Jenaro always felt small next to his baba. It was more than just the thin silver crown that twisted like feathers upon his brow, or his rich silk tunic with silver brocade, or even the velvets that composed his breeches and slippers. Marohu's demeanor commanded respect. He walked and spoke with an air only the Cacique could muster.

Jenaro was not immune to the effects. He loved and respected his baba, but as they reached the veranda, it was fear that consumed him. Jenaro lowered his head and noticed the wine stains on his tunic and the small tear in his pants from where Sharae yanked them from his body. He didn't need his baba to tell him what had been decided. He already knew.

Marohu placed his hands on the seastone surface of the balustrade that bordered the balcony. Gardeners tended the large terrace below, pruning bush and shrub and tree; every plant flowering and bearing fruit. Jenaro leaned next to his baba and stared at the ocean that swallowed the horizon. The steady roll of the waves added a gentle rhythm to the toils of those below.

"Jenaro, my son," Marohu began, placing his hand on Jenaro's back.

"I was denied a commission," Jenaro said before his baba could. "I didn't get a ship."

Marohu joined his son in leaning on the railing. "Hmmm," he muttered with a nod.

"Gueybana?" Jenaro asked.

The Cacique remained silent for a moment then stood upright. "It does not matter the reason."

Jenaro slammed his palms on the balustrade and pushed himself from the railing. "He hates me, baba. He despises me for, well, for what happened…" he trailed off. Jenaro looked at his baba and noticed the flash of disappointment in his eyes that disappeared as quickly as it had come.

Marohu shook his head. "Regardless, it may be several seasons before you may again be considered." When Jenaro remained silent, he spoke once more. "It seems you are bound and determined to forsake all the good I do for you."

"What?"

"I try my hardest to give you a good life and a prosperous future and you spit in my face every chance you can get."

"Baba, I never wanted to be a ship captain," Jenaro tried to explain.

"It's not just this, my son," Marohu turned his attention away from Jenaro to the city below. "It is the business with Gueybana's daughter, the moving out of the manse to fix lutes, the fiasco with delegation from Hal'e, I could go on."

"Then by all means!" Jenaro said angrily.

"Your bibi once made me promise that I would protect you from harm. I never imagined that harm would come from yourself. Why is it so hard for you to simply act like the son of the Cacique?" Marohu's gaze met Jenaro's, full of sadness and rage.

"Because that's not what I am meant to do! Do you remember nothing of that journey to Cidra, the vision of the cemi, or To'guey's oath to me? I am blessed of Yaya. I am not meant to sit in Puerto Zafiro dealing with matter of state. There's a great chance I won't live to see the day! I am meant to journey throughout Ke', saving its people from the influence of the cemi. That's what I want to do. That's what I'm meant to do." Jenaro sighed. He frowned, lowered his face from his baba's gaze, and said, "If you will allow it, baba, I will take my leave."

Jenaro exited the Great Hall expecting to see Agostin waiting, but instead nearly collided with his sister, Helena. Next to her was her carib and Agostin's youngest sister, Marisol.

"Cemi be damned, Anki," Jenaro cursed under his breath. The term had, over the years, evolved from a hateful nickname to a term of endearment. "I thought you had lessons with To'guey this morning?"

"You know damn well today is Karaya, natiao. To'guey never teaches on Karaya." Anki sneered playfully at her brother. "You think she drinks cassava juice all day?"

Jenaro grinned. "I think she prefers the snuff, if I'm completely honest."

Anki giggled. "Was she this prickly and ornery when she taught you?"

"She's only gotten worse," Jenaro replied with a shake of his head. "Are you going to see baba?"

"We've been studying affairs of state ever since you renounced your claim to the dujo," Anki nodded, "which you would know if you spent any time at all in the manse."

Jenaro rolled his eyes. "Does she give you the same sort of guilt trip, Marisol?"

"They are ten times worse when directed at me," Marisol chuckled.

Anki turned her head to Marisol and frowned. "You're supposed to be on my side," she pouted.

"I am always on your side," Marisol said with a smile.

Jenaro chuckled and stepped aside. "Have fun today, Anki."

"I would return the well wishes, but I know having fun has never been an issue with you," she prodded back.

"Oh, Jenaro," Marisol called to him with a wicked grin. "Tell Ago to buy you a watch."

"You were in on it?" Jenaro called back.

She waved and entered the Great Hall.

It was a long, spirit-draining walk back to his hovel. The thought of finding Sharae still in his bed almost lightened his mood. Unfortunately, she was absent. *Gone to work in her mother's seamstress shop. Or out with one of her other lovers.* Only Agostin was present, leaning against his door, eating yet another papaya.

"Are congratulations in order, my friend?" Agostin asked through a mouthful of fruit.

Jenaro opened the door and kicked off his sandals. "He rejected the commission," he stated. "I am his own flesh and blood, and he denied me a ship." Jenaro began to pace around his room.

Agostin ducked inside, set the papaya down on the open windowsill, and asked, "The Cacique?"

Jenaro ran a hand through his hair, angrily mussing his locks. "Yes, obviously the Cacique, Ago."

"How can you be sure?" Agostin asked. "Would it not have been Guybana."

"Gueybana was just decoy. The Cacique can overrule the admirals. No, Agostin, my friend," Jenaro started, "my baba has been lying to me under the pretense of protection for years now.

It has been a regular decision of his since bibi died. It was his decision."

There was a long silence between them. Agostin leaned against the wall, lightly drumming his fingers on his stomach. Jenaro exhaled sharply and stepped toward the window. He could just make out the bay from his hovel. A multitude of white sails skimmed its brilliant blue waters. They were fishermen returning from their evening at sea, merchantmen entering the port with trade goods from Hal'e and Cike'o, and lightly armed military patrols keeping watch over every activity. He envied the freedom of the seas. He longed to share in that life, to spend his days at the mercy of the cemi instead of under the thumb of his baba. He wished to be counted among those who witness the coming of the caguama. The great sea turtle was, after all, always his favorite creature.

"We go to sea," Jenaro murmured from the window.

"Pardon?" Agostin asked.

Jenaro slapped the windowsill and repeated, "We go to sea, Agostin. Who says we need a commission?"

Agostin chuckled and seated himself in Jenaro's chair. "To sea. To do what?"

Jenaro folded his arms across his chest and spoke but continued to stare at the shimmering jewel of the bay. "We adventure and make a name for ourselves; carve out our own destiny. Imagine it, my friend: the freedom of the sea, to live as we wish. To'guey always said I was supposed to save the people of Ke' from the influence of the cemi."

"Hmmm," Agostin agreed with a nod. "The only problem is that neither of us has a ship. And those of the royal navy that, for all intents and purposes, belong to your father, do not count." Agostin reclined, locking his hands behind his head and resting his feet atop the adjacent footrest. "What do you propose we do about this?"

Jenaro turned from the window, his arms still folded across his chest, and a wicked smirk painted on his face. "If my baba and the admirals refuse to give me a ship, I think I will simply take one for myself."

"Ha!" Agostin laughed. "The penalty for commandeering a vessel of any sort, let alone a royal one, is more than chastisement."

Jenaro strolled past his friend and pushed Agostin's legs from the footrest. "Then we will need to be decidedly inconspicuous when we commandeer a personal vessel."

Agostin smiled a wide, toothy grin and nodded in agreement.

The two friends spent the remainder of the day planning their evening and drinking. Jenaro outlined their route to the docks. Agostin informed him of the guard locations and rotations. Agostin listened intently, or as intently as the rum would allow, and made sure the two never saw the bottom of their glasses. He also criticized several minor points of the plan, to which Jenaro passively ignored.

"Have you considered bringing Sharae?" Agostin asked.

Jenaro nodded. "I have. I don't think she would be willing to live in a small boat with just you and I for company. But once we establish ourselves, have a fortune of our own and a mansion in Sandria, I'll come back for her. I'll always come back for her."

At sundown, Agostin stumbled away from Jenaro's hovel to gather the necessary supplies; a nearly impossible task while at such a level of inebriation, for anybody but Agostin. Jenaro chuckled as he watched his friend trudge away. The alcohol seemed to make him stronger, more determined.

After Agostin was on his way, Jenaro, as equally as

inebriated as his carib, dressed in his darkest sailing breeches and tunic, laced his boots tight, and covered his head and face in a scarf. He grabbed his drawstring knapsack packed with his dagger, a small flask, and a length of rope, and slung it across his shoulder. Quickly, he wrote a note for Sharae, leaving it on her pillow for her to find on her next visit. It read, "Went to sea with Ago. I'll be back for you. Love, J." Satisfied, Jenaro then killed each lantern in his room and climbed out of the window. He felt the need to move incognito. The city guard didn't really care what the disgraced son of the Cacique did, but he decided he'd rather not let word get back to his baba.

Jenaro spent most of his childhood scaling the trees and walls and columns that populated the manse. It often drew the ire of his baba and bibi. Yet, the long hours of climbing developed in him a keen sense of the manse and its ground as well as a preternatural muscle memory of every ledge, branch, and toehold. This skill was invaluable to the inebriated Jenaro as he scaled the city walls, more than once losing his footing and nearly tumbling to his death. The balancing act he performed across the top of the wall was equally as impressive. He held his hands out and thumbs up and told himself to keep the wall between his thumbs. The thought of how ridiculous he undoubtedly looked only crossed his mind once.

"I should have just chanced it with the city gate guards," Jenaro cursed.

Jenaro stopped to whisper a brief prayer of thanks to Yaya once his feet touched the stones below. He then quickly navigated the city streets, walking briskly and keeping with the crowds of citizens that ambled from tavern to tavern, singing and imbibing. Neither person nor guard paid him any mind and soon Jenaro was strolling quietly down the royal naval pier.

As he reached the naval shipyard, Jenaro was surprised to

find that the guard house was absent of its sentry. He crouched low and crept to each post. Both guards lay slumped on the floor. That was when he heard a whistle. He rolled forward out of the guard house and noticed through the dim lamps that hung on each pillar a figure traversing the spine of the gate. It was Agostin. He was perched atop holding a line of rope. Jenaro could see his smile shining through the dark.

The two friends slunk through the shipyard, slipping past guards, and taking shelter behind crates when necessary. Jenaro took the lead with Agostin following silently behind. Jenaro was thankful for the cloud cover and the wind that had moved over the island. The steady breeze moved out of the harbor in a hurry, bringing with it a drone that, when combined with the lapping of the bay, entirely masked their footsteps.

They arrived at the designated vessel without incident. Agostin crouched next to his friend and shook his head. "This?" he whispered to Jenaro. "Of all the ships in this harbor, you choose a cutter-rig instead of a piragua'?"

Jenaro turned to Agostin. "We needed a vessel the two of us could handle on our own, not a warship. Ago we went over this earlier. Look!" Jenaro pointed to the stern of the boat. "Can you not see those runes?"

Agostin leaned forward. "Gueybana. You love to kick the hornet's nest, don't you?"

Jenaro shook his head. "I have already forgiven and forgotten the man. He just has the best personal craft in all of Puerto Zafiro." Agostin shook his head and grinned. "Quickly, let's not waste another moment."

They hurried down the plank and hopped aboard the Gueybana cutter. Without saying another word, Jenaro and Agostin readied the ship, raised the sails, and casted off. The outbound wind carried the cutter quickly and silently through the shipyard. They cleared the locks before any alarm was raised. Both men watched as the city lights of Puerto Zafiro flickered and diminished below the horizon.

Jenaro's anxiety slowly disappeared as the cutter sailed farther into the inky black abyss of the open sea. It almost seemed too easy, their escape from Puerto Zafiro. Yet he shook his head and decided that it was a sign. Yaya had blessed their voyage.

Jenaro disappeared below deck to pilfer through the cabin. Just as he suspected, the galley was stocked with all sorts of dried food and alcohol. He grabbed a bottle of the finest Andoli rum and returned topside. He presented the bottle to Agostin and said, "A gift, courtesy of Admiral Gueybana."

Agostin was his usual carefree self. He lit the lamps and was swaying back and forth, sipping from his flask, and humming a tune when he saw the bottle. "Is that Mayaguez Black?" he asked with a smile that lit up his entire face.

Jenaro tossed him the bottle and he caught it one-handed.

They spent the next hour finishing off the bottle of rum and reigniting their stupor. Agostin led them in a collection of songs, culminating in his favorite tune, "The Barmaid or the Sea." Jenaro laughed and sang along with each refrain and even joined in on the last verse. They both reached the final note, only Agostin failed to add his deep baritone to the chord. Jenaro tilted his head and held the note as long as he could. When he finished, he turned his eyes on Agostin. His friend was gripping the hull of the cutter, eyes fixed on the bow of the vessel.

"What is it my friend?" Jenaro inquired.

There was no response, at least not from Agostin. The answer came in the form of a rolling boom that shook the very deck beneath his seat. Jenaro swiveled his head. The sky beyond the bow exploded in a brilliant flash. The sea raged on the horizon.

"Yaya does not seem happy with our theft," Agostin moaned as he hurried to the rig.

There was another flash of light followed by an echoing boom of thunder. Jenaro swore he saw the shape of the iguanaboina swirling in the clouds.

"I thought you feared no cemi, Agostin!" Jenaro yelled over the rumble. He moved to the wheel and looked at Agostin. He no longer saw unbridled joy, but concern and fear.

The storm overtook the cutter. Wind and rain assaulted the small craft. They worked quickly to lower the sails only to have the boom swing wildy, snapping the lines. Agostin caught it as it rotated, nearly tumbling overboard from the force of the swing.

"Tie it down!" Jenaro yelled over the raging storm. "I'm going for the rudder!"

Agostin managed to keep the boom locked then immediately slipped and slid his way to the bilge pumps. Jenaro held the rudder straight to keep from being tossed about on the waves. Each swell grew greater and more terrible than the last.

A giant wave surged over the bow and sent Agostin flying toward the stern. Jenaro reached out and grabbed his friend's arm just before the water took him. Lightning crashed allowing both men to see their faces. They saw nothing but terror and despair.

"I don't think we're going to make out of this one!" Agostin yelled.

"Nonsense! It's just a little wind and rain!" Jenaro shouted back as another bolt of lightning boomed through the sky, this time striking the mast of the cutter rig with a sickening crack. Wood splintered, lines cracked and popped, then the mast careened into the sea. The next bolt lit up the sky. To their horror, the bow of the little boat pointed directly at a rising wall of water. The ship fell as the ocean swelled and finally, the fury of the sea razed the ship in one giant stroke. Agostin and Jenaro were thrown from the vessel and swallowed by the waves.

Jenaro struggled to stay afloat. He saw the silhouette of a giant caguama just below the surface, the turquoise and verdant shell shining with each flash of lightning. Jenaro flailed and sunk beneath the waves. The caguama swam over him and under him. His feet glided across the mirror-like shell. For a moment, he could swear the beast was speaking to him. *Fear not, blessed of Yaya. I have use for you.* The caguama proceeded in swallowing him whole. He felt warmth and pressure about his flesh, a clammy but strangely comforting embrace. He faded out of consciousness.

The Mysterious Island

Daylight. It hurt his eyes. He inhaled deeply through his nose. The smell of dead fish and rotting seaweed was in the air. He could taste iron and salt in his mouth. Jenaro groaned as he lifted his hands to shield his eyes. An incessant, painful hammering assaulted his skull, no doubt a result of the alcohol from the night before. His body ached. There were bruises on his stomach and chest that screamed when he tried to move.

He managed to flip to his side. He cautiously opened his eyes. Fish large and small lay scattered about him amidst a field of debris. Planks of azure and silver, like the hull of the cutter he commandeered, were embedded in the sand like so many spears. Seaweed decorated every mound of rotting scales–he could even feel several strips plastered to his forehead and legs. He labored his way to a seated position. His breeches and tunic were torn and tattered. He was missing a shoe. His knapsack was nowhere in sight.

Jenaro sat for a time and watched the tide roll onto the beach. Each babbling wave brought with it more debris, more shattered pieces of the Gueybana cutter. He was almost disappointed. It was a beautiful little rig.

After he gathered his strength, he found his thoughts shifting to Agostin. His friend either jumped or was thrown overboard and most certainly met the same fate as he. That or worse.

"His death is on my hands," Jenaro whispered to himself.

Soon the sun became unbearable and forced Jenaro to seek shelter. He got to his feet and was surprised to find that he was saved the pain of broken bones. Although, the sand and dried seawater in his lacerations burned like fire.

The beachhead stretched on for miles. Behind him rose a field of small dunes. He could make out the tops of trees just beyond their peaks. Jenaro dreaded subjecting his wounds to more sand but plodded toward the shade of the trees regardless. Thankfully, the dune field was small and the grove of palms dense with plenty of shade.

Next was the thirst. Only a minute had passed under the protection of the palms before it set in. His mouth felt dryer than a desert, his lips chapped and cracked. Soon, his head started to spin. He lost track of time, unsure how long he had sat in the shade of the palms.

"Wait, how did I get here? Which direction did I come from?" Jenaro muttered as the confusion set in. He found it hard to concentrate on anything. The part of him that remained lucid knew a grove of that size had to mean a source of fresh water was nearby. He gathered his remaining strength and set off once more.

Jenaro stumbled around aimlessly, walking in circles, forgetting where he was going. He made it back to the palm trees and thought he had discovered another grove only to realize his mistake moments later. It took him a dangerously long time before he found a pond not far from the tree line. He nearly collapsed with joy. The water was clearer than the fountains of the manse at Puerto Zafiro. He could see the bottom and every fish that swam in the pool. He dropped to his knees and thrust his head under water, gulping as much as he could take until he collapsed on the banks. Jenaro pulled off his tunic and ripped the torn sleeve from his shirt. With it, he fashioned a head cover to protect his scalp from the blazing sun.

The water restored Jenaro to health, so much so that his

stomach began to cry out in anguish. "How long has it been since I've eaten. The last thing I remember putting in me was all the alcohol. Mayaguez Black," he stated, nearly gagging at the thought. "Must find some food." Now rehydrated, he set off again as the sun was halfway through its descent. He was not sure where to go but decided to continue walking away from the seashore.

The island he washed ashore on was of modest size. It only took Jenaro an hour to reach the opposite shoreline, which was free of debris, but just as vacant as the other. He traipsed across the island once more, hoping to find any semblance of life before sundown, yet his search yielded no such reward.

He happened upon a network of cliffs and jetties just as the sun was eclipsing the horizon. The way down into the hole looked dangerous, with a face as slick as wet marble and dozens of jagged stones below. Jenaro smiled. It was a challenge he eagerly accepted.

It was an intense climb down, even for one as skilled as Jenaro. He slipped and lost his footing more than once, only to be saved by a quick hand or toe in a crevice. He reached the bottom as the sun said its last goodbye. Much to his surprise, there was a cave. Even more surprising was the existence of bioluminescent algae on every surface.

The turquoise glow subsided not far from the entrance, replaced by the warm orange glow of torches. The humid, briny air turned sweet. Jenaro could swear he smelled roasted pig and heard the chatter of voices. His stomach churned once more.

The torches lead deep within the cave, winding in such a manner that Jenaro knew he could never navigate it on memory alone. Soon the path opened to an enormous room. Stalactites and stalagmites rose and fell on every surface. There was a clearing with a modest wooden shack and an outdoor hearth.

Rotating over the fires was a boar and sitting next to that hearth was Agostin.

"Jenaro Albizu del Rios!" Agostin shouted as he jumped from his stone seat. "You, my friend, are truly blessed of Yaya!"

Jenaro ran and embraced his friend. The two shared a chorus of boisterous laughter along with sentiments of relief.

"I was sure you had died," Jenaro told him as he took a seat next to the hearth.

Agostin raised his arm, flexed, and placed his other fist against his chest. "No storm can best an Anacaona man. But you look a little worse for wear."

Jenaro looked at the cuts that lined his skin like stripes. Not a single stab, slash, or puncture was present on Agostin's ebony skin. "It is some kind of dark magic that protects your clan." He replied with a smirk.

Agostin cackled.

As soon as Agostin's laugh dwindled, Jenaro asked, "What is this place? Surely the shack has an owner. The fire did not start itself nor did the boar take its own life."

Agostin shrugged. "I found it much like you did, boar roasting on the spit, cabin door open, and table set as if expecting guests. I tried to look around for the resident but found none."

"That is because I was needed elsewhere," a deep voice answered from the direction of the shack. Jenaro and Agostin leapt with surprise. Jenaro fell backward off the stone he was seated on. Agostin was on his feet and ready to throw a punch.

"Had I known I was to feed more than myself and my crew," the voice continued, "I would have killed another."

Jenaro quickly got to his feet and stood next to Agostin. "Please accept our sincerest apologies. We are shipwrecked and were unaware the island was inhabited."

"Well, it is as you said," the voice responded. "The fire did not start itself nor did the boar take his own life."

Jenaro slightly bowed his head in apology but kept his eyes on his host. As he stepped into the torchlight, Jenaro could see he was a striking and sinewy man, dressed in a dark coat that fell to his knees and a hood that shrouded much his face. He held his hands behind his back but made sure Jenaro and Agostin could see the gold and jeweled hilts that peeked from beneath his coat. His boots were sturdy black leather that seemed to consume the light of the hearth.

"I am Jenaro Albizu del Rios, son of Cacique Marohu of the Andolins. This is Agostin Anacaona, my carib and closest confidant."

Agostin nodded slightly.

Jenaro continued. "I assure you we meant no offense."

The man laughed a short, clipped howl that startled Jenaro. "All is well and good. If you are shipwrecked, then you are in luck. I am a captain myself. My crew and I plan to set sail in the morning. You are welcome to accompany us to our next port of call where I am sure you can arrange passage back to your Andolins."

Jenaro and Agostin exchanged glances.

"That would be most kind of you Captain…" Jenaro trailed off.

"Captain will do for now," the man replied.

"Aye, Captain," Jenaro repeated. "Shall we accompany you to your vessel?"

The Captain nodded. "Yes, but first we must carve the boar and grab a cask of wine."

Jenaro and Agostin nodded and went about assisting the Captain in any way they could. Jenaro helped pack the sliced boar in covered platters while Agostin gathered the two barrels of wine under his arms. He lifted one to his shoulder, leaned back, and opened the tap directly into his mouth. He looked at Jenaro and smiled wide. Once ready, the Captain snapped his fingers, and the fires of the hearth were quenched. Immediately, the bioluminescent algae came alive all around them, lighting a path next to the shack. Jenaro's eyes bulged in shock. He looked back at Agostin, who had gone pale. It was a short walk to the Captain's ship. The man whistled the entire way. It wasn't a tune Jenaro recognized but found pleasant.

The ship was a clipper, large and lean and the definition of motion at rest. It was a blade that longed to slice through every nautical mile of the Summer Sea. The glossy, black hull resembled glass, shining, and reflecting the light of the algae like a mirror does sunlight. The three masts resembled wrought iron spikes reaching to the heavens. Jenaro's smile was the widest he had ever known. This was truly the ship he desired.

The Captain whistled and the ship's gangway slid down from the deck. Jenaro and Agostin both froze in place. They watched as the sails unfurled into deep crimson sheets dripping like blood. The lanterns aboard slowly lit, bow to stern, all on their own. They heard no crew or clamor from the top deck. The ship's bell rang like a dirge. Jenaro looked to where he last saw the Captain, but instead he was greeted by empty space.

"All aboard, gentlemen!" the Captain's deep voice boomed through the cavern.

Jenaro and Agostin stood still. Jenaro swallowed hard, his joy at the beauty of the ship quickly receding. Agostin's face was grim, his jaw clenched shut, and his grip around the barrels so tight his knuckles were white.

"You haven't changed your minds, have you?" he called from the deck of the ship.

Jenaro gulped. "You disappear and reappear in the blink of an eye?"

The Captain chuckled. "Only to places to which I am welcome or needed; my ship, for example."

"What do you call her?" Jenaro asked.

"You see the black hull. You know the crimson sails. Why this is *Moin Hupia*!"

Agostin turned to Jenaro and whispered. "That's impossible. *Moin Hupia* belongs to Maboya. It is a legend. A fiction told by the behique and our abuelos."

"I know," Jenaro stated. "Yet, there it is before us, moored in this cavern." Jenaro inhaled and took a step toward the ship. "If this is indeed *Moin Hupia* that would make you –"

"Maboya!" Agostin gasped.

The Captain shouted with a whoop. His laughter crashed around the walls of the cavern, making Jenaro flinch.

"Yes, Maboya! I am so very glad you know it! I was not in the mood to keep up the ruse." Maboya's hysteria continued for several uncomfortable moments before his laughter subsided. "I knew my identity would shock him, but you Jenaro? Why we are old friends! I've known you since you were a child. Have you already forgotten our first meeting? It was such a memorable one."

Jenaro glowered. "I have not forgotten, Maboya."

Agostin turned to Jenaro and said, "So it was true? The glade, the cemi, all of it?"

Jenaro nodded then Maboya continued. "Now that it is revealed, you have two choices. The first: come aboard willingly. Eat, drink, and sail with me. Then maybe I will take you to the land of your ancestors."

Agostin took a step forward and stood next to Jenaro. "And the second?" he asked harshly.

Maboya leapt and disappeared only to reappear, balancing perfectly on the *Moin Hupia*'s bow spirit. "Refuse and I make you permanent additions to my crew."

"What guarantees do we have that you will keep your word?"

Maboya laughed. "Guarantees? None. I give you none. You either join me or die alone on this island."

Jenaro shook his head and stepped to the gangway, but Agostin did not move. He set the casks down on the cave floor, crossed his arms and beckoned Jenaro to his side. Jenaro nodded and turned his attention back to Maboya.

"If you will, great captain Maboya, I would like a moment with my companion," Jenaro said.

Maboya waved dismissively. "Fine, fine, take a moment, but make it quick. I have duties to attend to."

Jenaro nodded, set the packs of meat on the casks, and walked away from the gangway out of earshot. Agostin was right behind him. When he was a sufficient distance from the ship, Jenaro turned and crossed his arms on his chest.

"What is it, Ago?" he asked.

Agostin shook his head. "I have concerns."

"Such as?"

Agostin sighed. "The Maboya from all the old wives' tales was a trickster, that much is true, but the Maboya we learned about from the behique…that Maboya only appeared to the dead and dying."

"You think we're dead," Jenaro said, rather than asked.

Agostin shrugged. "I don't know the cemi as you do. I simply remember hearing that during my lessons."

"It is a valid concern, Ago," Jenaro assured him. "I unfortunately can't respond to it, but it is valid. What is the other?"

"If we are truly alive and not trapped in some limbo between the caves…well, doesn't it all seem very convenient? How did we end up on this island Maboya just so happened to be at? And why would he offer to ferry us home? What does he stand to gain from being helpful?"

"It is suspicious, I agree," Jenaro nodded slowly. "However, as it stands, I believe we have no other option. We cannot put our trust in Maboya, so trust me instead. I will figure this out, my friend."

Agostin sighed and nodded. The two returned to the gangway. Jenaro nodded at Maboya, and the cemi waved them aboard the *Moin Hupia*. Agostin set the casks of wine on the deck and Jenaro tossed the packs of meat atop. Moments later, sails unfurled with a snap and without the assistance of a single crewman. Maboya standing at the wheel reached up and threw off his hood. It was the first time Jenaro saw his true form; the form of Maboya, not as maja, but as near to man as a cemi could be. His head appeared serpentine, gaunt, with leathery skin pulled tightly over the skull. His sockets were empty except for dancing flames where his eyes should have been. Strangely enough, he had many teeth and seemed to have a permanent smile affixed to his ghastly face. Jenaro shuddered and turned away. He and Agostin stood and watched as the clipper flew from the cavern and out to sea. The island was soon a memory, swallowed by the horizon.

Once out in open water, Maboya brought forth an enormous feast. There were platters of roasted boar, rabbit, and fish, all garnished with peppers and pineapple. Mountains of corn cakes and yucca mingled with cinnamon dusted plantains resting on beds of rice. There were even bowls of candied mango and papaya. The casks of wine were tapped. Bottles of rum were brought by unseen forces from below deck. It was indeed a banquet for a large crew; a crew surprisingly absent from the affair. Regardless, Jenaro nearly wept as the sweet, savory aromas of the fruit and meat blended beautifully with the brine of the sea air. He wanted to resist, to deny such a decadent spread. All of the old tales claimed the food of the cemi would change the Borekua in horrible ways, but his body shouted for sustenance. His mouth watered and his stomach audibly churned.

Jenaro caved first. Agostin watched in horror as he placed a chunk of plantain in his mouth, for he, too, knew of the warning against the cemi's food. Yet, as he chewed bite after bite, morsel after mosel, Agostin's resolve faded. The two ate for hours. They ate as if it was their final meal. They ate until the table was covered in crumbs and bones licked clean of every shred of slow roasted meat. Maboya chuckled when Jenaro slid back from his spot and moaned in delightful gluttony. It was not long before Jenaro drifted to sleep with a full stomach and a mind full of contentment, despite his predicament.

In his dreams, Jenaro saw the caguama. He stood on a beach while the beast slowly swam to him. Riding atop its giant shell was the shimmering shape of a human, in the same way Yaya revealed himself to Jenaro all those years ago. It called to Jenaro with a melodic voice, saying, "He has reneged on his oath and so I will take back what is mine. Help me, blessed, and I shall reward you."

Aboard *Moin Hupia*

Moin Hupia was at a standstill when Jenaro awoke. The movement of the ocean and the creaking of the hull were not unlike an anchored ship. Yet the Summer Sea was deep and wide, and no measure of rope or chain would allow an anchor to hit bottom. Jenaro's first inclination was that Maboya had piloted them into the doldrums. The phenomenon was not uncommon at the far reaches of the Summer Sea, but there was no way they had traversed so many miles in a day. Jenaro was so curious that he neglected to notice he was no longer on deck but lying in what looked to be the captain's quarters. He jumped to his feet, exited the room, and found his way to the top deck. Agostin was already awake, standing on the bow, one foot on the spirit, the other planted firmly on the deck.

"The ship seems abandoned," Jenaro said.

Agostin nodded as Jenaro approached. "Our host has once again disappeared."

Jenaro looked around the deck then asked, "Why are we no longer moving? The sea looks as if it is completely avoiding the *Hupia*."

"The wind has disappeared as well," Agostin added.

"Another trick of Maboya?" Jenaro questioned.

Agostin shrugged.

"Can't be," Jenaro announced as he turned from Agostin. "The air is the realm of Yúcahu, not Maboya. It must be a spell or some enchantment, or –"

"It is neither, Jenaro del Rios," Maboya proclaimed from the wheel.

Jenaro stopped and gave Agostin a sideways glance. Agostin gulped.

Maboya once again wore his hood, except now a tricorne rested atop. It was black as night with blood red trim. Standing next to him was another Andoli. He was an old man, with wispy white hair and a long white beard. His skin was covered in spots. His eyes were deep set and surrounded by dark bags. His clothes were rags that were barely held in place by his body. Clasped tightly around the man's neck was a shackle of black iron. A chain ran from the shackle to Maboya's hand.

The cemi, whether noticing the unease of the Andoli, or simply wanting to gloat, chuckled. "Oh him?" he motioned to the old man. "Merely performing the task so graciously assigned to me by the great Yaya–gathering souls."

"And delivering them to the third cave, correct?" Jenaro asked.

Maboya scoffed. "To answer your previous question, the other cemi and I have an agreement, of sorts. So long as I am on one of their errands, my ship remains where I disembark. It makes it easier to find in case I…" he mulled over for a bit, "get lost." His tone was disinterested, nearing disdain. He held up a hand and waved. Mysteriously, the chain moved from his hand and began to drag the old man below deck.

"Well then Maboya," Jenaro called to the cemi, "since you have returned, my friend and I would very much like for you to sail us to our island."

Maboya strolled down from the helm. For the first time since they met, Jenaro laid eyes on the cemi's hands. His right was nothing but bone, held together with several sinewy strands of flesh around each knuckle and joint. The left was just as bony, except for the charred, leathery skin like that of a dessicated snake. Gripped in his left was Jenaro's knife, making Jenaro's breath hitch. He feared it was lost as sea with the rest of his belongings.

"Why would you desire to leave such merry company? Can you not see I have brought you a gift?"

"The knife my mother gave me?" Jenaro's eyes narrowed. "You gift me what is already mine?"

Maboya smiled. Jenaro spied his teeth grinning from just beyond the shadows of his hood. The cemi took a step forward, flipped the knife, and handed it to Jenaro hilt first. Agostin took a step forward and inserted himself between Maboya and his friend. Jenaro placed a hand on Agostin's shoulder, calming him and signaling to him to stand down. He grabbed his knife. Maboya let go and retreated.

"A captain always rewards his first mate," Maboya told the Andoli.

Jenaro shook his head. "While I appreciate you returning my dagger, I cannot accept such a commission."

Maboya scoffed. "And why not? Is it not what you have wanted since you were a boy, adventure, a life at sea?"

Jenaro stood quiet.

"I was trying to save you, you know," Maboya snickered. "I know it's hard for you to believe, but I truly was trying, in my own way."

Jenaro scoffed. "You bit me. You injected poison into my heel."

"I am a snake, Andoli. What did you expect?"

"Please, enlighten me as to how killing me was saving me."

Maboya sneered. "We have already been over this, dustling, because death is better than being enslaved to Yaya!" Jenaro and Agostin both jumped at his ferocity. The cemi let the air settle before adding, "It's not my fault you followed me to the glade where Yaya was sitting. Your kind die from snakebites all the time."

Jenaro scoffed.

"Do you not see his treachery?" Maboya hissed as he quickly closed the gap between them. "He stripped you of your soul and for what? So, you can blindly obey him for half your usual lifespan? So, his insecurities and ego are stroked by your undying devotion?" He spit. "Death is better than that, Andoli. Death is better than blind servitude."

"And the man you just sent below? What of him? Seems he is destined to an eternity of servitude."

"A necessity," Maboya stated. "Someone must crew my ship. His sacrifice will be remembered."

There was a dead silence that hung between them. Nobody moved. Nobody breathed. Not even the lapping of the ocean or the rushing sea breeze encroached on their bubble.

After a few tense moments, Jenaro spoke. "You say Yaya enslaved you?" he asked.

"Is the Andoli who cares for dead and decaying bodies the most revered on your islands? Yes, I am a slave. And I bear the burden of it!" He spread his arms. "Do you think I willingly transformed myself into this hideous creature?"

"I see. And how would serving you help your cause?" Jenaro asked.

Maboya's smile returned. "The half of your soul still enslaved by Yaya is released upon your death. That means the part of you that lives on through eternity is damned to wander, never rest. If you stay aboard and assist me, you will at least have a chance at peace in this afterlife, that is, if we succeed. Until then, you are free to live as you please, so long as it's in my service."

"It seems to me that I would simply be trading on master for another."

Maboya scowled. "Don't you see? We would be equals! I would not lord over you because I cannot lord over Yaya's creation. You and I would be free to do as we please, to tell others of Yaya's treachery and save countless other souls from him."

Jenaro turned from Maboya and began to pace from port to starboard.

"You require our souls," Agostin stated plainly. "You want us to forfeit our souls and we're supposed to just believe we won't immediately become like one of your invisible crewmen?"

Maboya jeered. "I require his soul," he stated eerily then raised his desiccated hand, made a series of gestures, and pointed at Agostin. "You may awaken from this nightmare, Agostin Anacaona. I am not ready to transport your soul just yet."

Jenaro made a quick about-face and looked at Agostin. Agostin's face was full of terror. Slowly he began to fade away, as if he was star twinkling out of existence. After a series of heart-wrenching moments, Agostin had disappeared from the deck of *Moin Hupia*.

A burning, white hot rage rose in Jenaro's chest. His heart began to pound out of his chest. His arms shook with a terrible fervor. Tears of sadness and anger blurred his eyes. With a fierce howl, Jenaro unsheathed his dagger and sprinted at the cemi. "What have you done to Agostin?!"

"Be still, Andoli," Maboya answered. "Your friend is safe."

Maboya laughed and vanished only to reappear several steps away. Jenaro was unfazed by the blink. He somersaulted forward and slashed upward. Maboya laughed as he dodged Jenaro's attack and countered with a swift palm to Jenaro's face. Jenaro was thrown back, slamming his back against the mainmast. His dagger clattered harmlessly away from his reach.

"Where is he?"

"He is back on your island, or as near enough as counts," Maboya said, as if such a feat was commonplace among Jenaro's people. "His suspicions were correct, after all. I don't reveal myself to just anybody; only those with the blessing," he pointed to Jenaro.

Jenaro scowled and kept moving toward Maboya, but then Maboya snapped and Jenaro was immediately restrained by unseen forces, his arms held outstretched. He struggled against his invisible bonds, growling at the cemi.

Jenaro spit in his direction. "Unhand me, Maboya!"

Maboya turned his back on Jenaro and raised a finger. Jenaro felt a shove and was forcibly directed below deck. He wanted to struggle, but realized it was futile to waste his energy against an unseen foe. The specters transported Jenaro to the captain's quarters and tossed him to the floor. His knife followed, landing an arms-length away. Jenaro ran to the door, but it was bolted shut from the outside before he could reach it. He slammed his fists against the wood and shouted for Maboya to no avail.

Jenaro saw the sun set and rise three times from the window of his prison cell. The ship moved constantly throughout that time. He could feel the swaying and rocking of the hull as it sliced through waters of the Summer Sea. Things about *Moin Hupia* slowly shifted and transformed the longer he was aboard. He began to hear chatter from amidships, the sounds of voices chuckling and arguing. When his door opened for breakfast and his platter of food brought in, he could now see a foggy specter transporting it. The food itself seemed to turn rotten in his mouth.

Jenaro passed the time by pacing his makeshift brig and combing his mind for a way out. The door was the obvious first choice, but even when it opened and the now shimmering shapes of the crewmen brought his food, he felt too paralyzed to even attempt to bolt. The porticos were too narrow and sealed by some mysterious force. On the morning of the third day, Jenaro decided he needed some sport, something to take his mind off his predicament. He pulled his knife and scrawled a target on the door to the cabin then proceeded to toss the blade from the opposite end of the room. He continued in this manner until he heard a pounding at the cabin door. Two shapes that vaguely resembled men barged in, restrained him, and dragged him up to Maboya. He was released with a shove and nearly lost his balance.

Maboya was standing at the wheel, ghastly, lizard-like hands tightly gripping the obsidian wood. "What game are you playing down there, Andoli?" Maboya asked angrily. "Whatever it is, I demand you stop with the noise."

Jenaro scowled. "Listen here, Maboya," he demanded with a point. "You are the only one playing games on this ship." Jenaro stopped and looked at his blade. He stared at the cemi and remembered the tales of Maboya told by the behique, the same stories Agostin mentioned with his concerns. The cemi of the dead was shifty and he enjoyed using his wiles to swindle mortals. He never stood down from a challenge, especially when a soul was involved. Jenaro wasn't positive that the Maboya of the behique was the same cemi that stood before him, but given the circumstances, it was a chance he would have to take.

"Tell me, Maboya; is it true you enjoy challenging mortals for a chance at stealing their souls?"

Maboya stared for a moment before chortling. "Where did you hear such nonsense?"

Jenaro shrugged. "It doesn't matter. If it is true, though, why not gamble a little with me?"

Maboya tilted his head in curiosity. "What do you propose? Dice? Cards?"

Jenaro rotated his shoulders and adjusted his torn and ragged tunic. "There are three games. The best of three wins."

"And what are the stakes?" Maboya asked.

"The life of my friend," Jenaro said.

"He is alive I assure…" Maboya began but was interrupted by Jenaro.

"If he is alive as you say then I'll raise the stakes. We play for the *Moin Hupia*."

Maboya stopped, startled and confused. "My ship. You want my ship?"

Jenaro nodded. There was a flicker in Maboya's red glowing eyes, a glimmer of delight.

"And what do I get in return?"

Jenaro took a breath. "I will join you and become your first mate, as you offered."

Maboya smiled. His forked tongue flicked quickly in and out of his mouth. "I accept your terms, Andoli."

Jenaro smiled and laughed to himself. Out of all the stories the behique told, he was so glad they were right about the tales of Maboya. He nodded and said to Maboya, "We should find an island; somewhere you and I can compete without interruptions, somewhere neither you nor I will have the advantage."

Maboya's grin remained constant; toothy and wide, a permanent fixture on his face. "I know of a place."

Games

Maboya piloted the *Moin Hupia* westward, following the arc of the sun overhead. It was not long before the ship reached a small atoll. Maboya commanded the ship to anchor then motioned to a small dinghy. The boat was lowered to the sea below. Maboya appeared on the boat in a blink, and Jenaro quickly descended, joining him. He gave a command to row. Jenaro sat still, waiting for the dinghy to respond as *Moin Hupia* did to Maboya's commands. When nothing happened, Jenaro realized the command was for him. Jenaro frowned and grabbed the oars.

Once ashore, Jenaro took a brief inventory of the island. The water amidst the atoll was crystal clear and full of coral of every color and shape. It teemed with all manner of sea life. A meager stand of palms lined the ring on the opposite shore they landed on. Jenaro could see albatross and gull circling above. He looked down at the rags that still hung on his body. His dagger was the only thing of worth. It would be difficult to fool Maboya. He knew he would have to play to his own strengths.

"Andoli!" Maboya called to Jenaro. "Out with it already! The shadows will soon be long. What is your first challenge?"

Jenaro pointed toward the copse of palms. "We need to head to the trees. There will be our first challenge." It took the two of them mere minutes to traverse the circumference of the atoll and reach the palms. "We climb. First to the top to retrieve an egg from the nest of the albatross wins." Jenaro thought that Maboya's steady grin wavered slightly. "I will toss my blade skyward, and we begin to climb the moment it impacts the sands."

Maboya nodded.

"Maboya, remember, I said climb. You cannot simply blink to the top and back not shift into the form of a maja and slither your way up the trunk. You must climb."

Maboya snarled, "Yes, yes, Andoli, I know the meaning of the word."

With that, Jenaro flung his knife. He flew from his spot the moment the blade hit the sand. He leapt to the tree. His barefoot landed on the trunk and propelled him up the palm. It took a few short strides for Jenaro to reach the bottom of the fronds. The saw-like teeth snapped at his hands but failed to stop his ascent. Jenaro stretched out his hand, cautioning a glance at the tree across from his; Maboya's palm. The cemi was struggling to find enough traction to climb his palm tree. His bony hand slipped on the surface of the trunk. His leathery palm was no better. His boots failed to provide any help. Jenaro chuckled to himself as he grabbed an egg from the nest of the albatross. His descent was swift and as soon as his feet touched the sand, he claimed his first victory.

Maboya was livid. "This was not a fair challenge, Andoli. You are suited to climbing. It would be as tilted as if I challenged you to soul harvesting."

Jenaro smirked and nodded his head. He tossed the egg gently from hand to hand then crouched and placed it in the sand, retrieving his knife in the process. "It is amusing to hear you, Maboya who slinks and sneaks and steals in the night, talk of fairness. But I concede. Since I am a good sport and desire for a fair and balanced challenge, I will let you choose our next game."

Maboya strolled to the center of the atoll, to the shoreline encased within the island. There, next to a large stone, he knelt. He reached into his long coat and brandished a dirk with a wicked blade that oozed and dripped as if it were covered in blood.

"Pinfinger," Maboya stated plainly. "I assume an islander such as you are familiar with the game?"

Jenaro knelt opposite of Maboya and placed his hand upon the stone. "The Andoli learn knife play as soon as they can wield a blade. Of course, I know the game. What are your terms? First to draw blood? Although I assume you have none."

"You assume correctly," Maboya answered. "No, first to sever a digit."

Jenaro swallowed hard. "Those terms seem rather unfair coming from one who, not moments ago, complained about fairness."

Maboya scoffed. "You have ten fingers. What damage would it do if you lost one?"

"That's a fair assessment, Captain," Jenaro replied. He brandished his dagger with a flurry, spinning it with his fingers and slamming the blade down between the middle and ring finger of his left hand. "Shall we begin?"

Maboya's smile widened. They set an even pace as a warmup. Blades hopped between fingers, ringing against the stone. Maboya's dirk occasionally sent a shower of sparks flying with a successful miss. Jenaro's knife work was nimble and deliberate. He and Maboya fixed their eyes on one another; Jenaro's twinkling with determination, Maboya's flaming with psychotic glee.

Their speed increased. Clink-clink-clink sang their blades in unison. Faster they went. Jenaro began to grit his teeth. Although Maboya's assessment was true, he did not desire to lose a finger.

Faster. Maboya's blade sparked with nearly every strike. Jenaro knew it was an effort to break his concentration.

Maboya increased the speed again. This time, Jenaro could

not keep pace. He began to slow only to be startled out of his concentration by a particularly large shower of sparks from Maboya. Jenaro's blade came down on the ring finger of his left hand, just below the first knuckle from his nail. A surge of pain shot up his arm. He lifted his hand from the table in reflex but did not raise the blade. Unfortunately, the initial impact did not completely sever the finger. Jenaro's reflex finished the job. He let out a cry. Maboya burst forth in laughter.

"You are not as quick with a blade as you think, Andoli," Maboya chided after his outburst.

Jenaro sat in the sand, squeezing what was left of his finger to stop the bleeding.

Maboya shook his head and reached down for Jenaro's hand. Jenaro recoiled briefly then let him see the damage. Maboya chuckled and brought forth his blade. The dripping from before had intensified. It danced across the blade as if it were made of fire itself. The feeling that shot up Jenaro's arm when it touched the wound confirmed the blaze. The blade was unnaturally hot and cauterized the wound on Jenaro's finger. Jenaro winced and growled. He could feel tears welling in his eyes. He became dizzy. When Maboya released the blade, he said, "Go and wash it in the waters." Jenaro plunged his hand into the pool. The water boiled and steamed and soon the burning of his missing finger ceased. The flesh, though, continued to throb. Jenaro removed the tatters that covered his head, tore a small strip, and wrapped his finger.

"It would seem we are on an even plane, Andoli," Maboya proclaimed.

"It would indeed," Jenaro agreed. "The next game decides who will be victorious."

Maboya returned his blade to his pocket. "Do not for a moment think I will take pity on you because of your injury."

Jenaro nodded and looked back toward the trees. "We

should head back inland." They arrived at the stand and Jenaro immediately retrieved the egg he had previously placed in the sand. "This one will be easy," Jenaro told Maboya with a grin. He explained the rules of a simple game of catch. They would toss the egg back and forth. With each successful catch, they would take a step back, increasing the distance between themselves. Whoever broke the egg was the loser.

Maboya stared suspiciously at Jenaro. "I can simply toss the egg at your head and declare victory."

Jenaro shook his head. "The game depends on both a good throw and a successful catch. If you purposely make an errant throw, the broken egg will be because of you. Thus, ensuring your loss."

"Get on with it then," Maboya grunted.

Jenaro gently tossed the egg to Maboya, who cradled it with his leathery hand. He lifted his head and squinted angrily at Jenaro then tossed the egg back. It landed like a feather in Jenaro's hands. He would have smiled except for the bolt of pain from his missing finger. They continued to toss the egg back and forth, stepping backward with each catch until they were nearly fifteen fathoms apart. Jenaro noticed that Maboya caught each throw with his leathery hand, using his bony right hand to stabilize his catch. He also seemed reluctant to move in any direction that would jeopardize this. Jenaro cleverly tossed the egg as high as he could, aiming for Maboya's right side. Maboya was slow to react. He shuffled to his right, attempting to get his left hand under the egg. When Maboya realized he would not be able to catch it as he desired, he lowered his hands to cradle the egg with both. The egg, however, was moving too rapidly. It landed primarily in his right hand, bursting on the bone, and spilling its yolk over his palms.

Maboya slowly raised his head, his permanent smile an

ironic display of shock and disgust. Jenaro swore his eyeless sockets blazed with the rage of betrayal. "You are a cheat, Jenaro del Rios!" he shouted.

Jenaro held his hands up. "It was a clean throw, Maboya."

"You were seeking to make a fool of me, and you have," Maboya growled, angrily shaking his head. "Now if you do not have any other tilted diversions, we should return to the *Hupia*. You are, after all, my new first-mate."

Jenaro laughed. "You are mistaken Maboya. The *Hupia* is my ship now and you are no longer allowed on board."

Maboya snarled and tore his dagger from inside his coat. In the blink of an eye, he was behind Jenaro with the blazing hot steel pressed to the Andoli's throat. "The *Hupia* will forever be mine."

Jenaro cringed as Maboya spoke. He could feel the heat of his breath burning his cheek. He could smell it, a putrid mix of sulfur and decay. The knife began to sear the flesh of his neck. Maboya sent Jenaro toward the dinghy with a push. Jenaro reluctantly walked. He looked to where he had lost a finger and noticed his family dagger still resting on the stone. Maboya forced Jenaro to row. He sat, back toward the glimmering black hull of the *Moin Hupia*, and worked the oars. Maboya still clutched his dagger. He lounged rather uncomfortably and watched Jenaro, tossing his blade up and down, flipping it from hilt to blade in his bony right hand.

"It is a shame, really," Maboya mused. "You were so close to winning your way out of here and back to the land of the second cave."

Jenaro eyes briefly darted to Maboya's face then back to the oars.

"Yes, you see your friend was right. It wouldn't have mattered anyway. Even the blessed of Yaya cannot stay trapped between the caves for too long. Surely you must have noticed? You must have seen things change; the food is suddenly less edible; my crew grows more and more visible to your eyes."

Jenaro remained silent, concentrating on his rowing.

"Do not be angry, Andoli. Our partnership is just beginning. Let us begin on equal footing, eh?"

Multiple Blessings

Night had fallen and the stars were out by the time they returned to the ship. The lanterns were lit, but the ship appeared abandoned. No sound of Maboya's crew could be heard over the gentle lapping of the sea. The dinghy pulled up alongside the *Hupia*, but as they arrived Jenaro saw the rope ladder was no longer lowered. Maboya growled, stood up, and pounded on the hull. "Lower the rope you imbeciles! Did you not see us approaching?"

There were several awkward moments of silence before the ladder rolled its way down the side of the ship to the dingy. Maboya motioned for Jenaro to climb aboard. Jenaro scaled the ladder and reached the deck of the *Hupia*. When he turned to look down, he noticed Maboya blink out of sight, presumably to appear on the ship–but he didn't move from the dinghy. This happened several times before the cemi shouted in frustration.

"What have you done, Andoli?" Maboya cried from below.

Jenaro shrugged. "I cannot control your movements or the peculiarities of nature, Maboya."

Maboya readied his dagger, aimed at Jenaro, but hesitated. "You have made a deal with her, haven't you?"

"Her?" Jenaro asked.

"You know of whom I speak, Andoli," Maboya hissed. He sat down, toothy grin still painting his face, and began to laugh. "You made a fool of me and now I have lost the thing most dear to me."

Jenaro opened his mouth to reply, but instead heard a furious, angelic voice respond from his side.

"You have made a fool of yourself, Maboya."

Jenaro turned to see a shining form hovering next to him. It was a pillar of cloud, just as he had seen in the glade as a child. The brilliance slowly dissipated revealing the stunning form of a ruddy and radiantly skinned woman hovering inches above the deck. Her lengthy, black hair fell in curls and shimmered like opals in the sun, floating close to her body, covering her most intimate parts. She looked at Maboya with eyes like a dark, merciless sea, full of rage and power.

"You mean to renege on our deal, Atabey?" Maboya asked.

Jenaro was surprised. The once boisterous and undaunted captain was now subdued, brought low by a creature much like himself.

"You are mistaken, Maboya," Atabey shot back, waving a finger adorned with sparkling sapphires. Her other hand gently cradled her pregnant stomach. "It was you who reneged when you decided to use my vessel for your own personal gain. It was once a beautiful ship, verdant and alive. Now it is a mar upon my seas." She paused, as if mourning for the *Moin Hupia*. "My ship was meant to speed the passage of creatures like him to my bosom," she said and motioned to Jenaro with a wide sweep of her hand.

"I am more than just a chauffeur of souls, sea witch!" Maboya hissed.

Atabey fumed at the curse. "Indeed, you are, serpent! And until a time in which I deem your penance complete, you will perform your deeds of deceit aboard the meager vessel in which you now stand!"

At that, Atabey raised both her hands above her head, moved her arms in a great circle toward her chest, then pushed her hands forward toward the horizon. In response, a swell of great magnitude pushed the dinghy far away from the *Hupia*. Maboya shouted curses and pumped his fist at the ship until he faded into the distance and his voice melted into the low rumbling of the wind and waves.

Jenaro smiled and turned to Atabey. The rage that veiled her face had subsided. Her mood now mirrored the sea about them, calm and quiet.

"What is your name, son of dust?" Atabey asked.

"Jenaro Albizu del Rios," he replied with a low bow.

Atabey smiled. "Yes, I do recall hearing your name from Yaya. Tell me, Jenaro Albizu del Rios; is it typical of your kind to stand tall in the presence of my kind?"

Jenaro smiled. Her voice was soft, and she seemed genuinely interested in his answer. He chuckled lightly. "No, great cemi, it is not typical. Many of my kind would cower before you. But do not take my lack of fear as a lack of respect."

She nodded and gingerly set her soles on the deck. The iridescent shells that adorned her legs and feet rattled melodically as she moved. The music continued as Atabey made her way to the wheel. Jenaro followed alongside.

"The caguama that saved my life was you, was it not?" Jenaro asked.

Atabey placed her right hand on her chest and bowed ever so slightly. "I took a chance by revealing myself to you. Not lightly do cemi do so to your kind. Yet, my intuition served true and now I am indebted to you, Jenaro Albizu del Rios. Without your assistance, Maboya would have continued to run rampant across Ke' doing all he desired and neglected that which Yaya, in his wisdom, created him to do."

Jenaro was silent until they reached the wheel.

"My ship is now in need of a captain," Atabey said.

Jenaro trembled at her words. His desire to pilot the beautiful and powerful *Moin Hupia* was strong. But another gift from a cemi was the last thing he needed–he did not want to be twice indebted. Jenaro took a deep breath before bowing his head respectfully to Atabey. "It is indeed a mighty gesture, Atabey. Yet, I cannot accept such a gift. My spirit is not as hardy as that of Maboya. I cannot spend eternity transporting souls for you."

Atabey laughed. "Worry not, son of dust. Maboya will continue to do so from the modest vessel in which he now finds himself. No, Jenaro Albizu del Rios, the *Moin Hupia* is yours to do with as you wish, so long as it is in keeping with the laws of Yaya. Use it until that time in which Maboya once again returns to your shore to claim your soul."

Jenaro shook his head.

"Why do you spurn what is freely given?" Atabey asked politely.

Jenaro forced a smile. Even if he could, he knew there would be no arguing with the mother of all life. It seemed he could not reject her blessing just as he could not turn aside the blessing of Yaya. "It is a kingly gift, great cemi, and one which I will treasure until my dying breath."

Jenaro stared out over the bow of the ship. The stars that shone were strange and foreign, heavenly bodies he never once observed. Each constellation sketched unrecognizable symbols across the inky black abyss above. He lowered his head and thought of Agostin. Was he indeed alive and safe in Puerto Zafiro?

"Great cemi, am I standing between the caves, stuck in some realm not living but not yet dead?" Jenaro asked.

Atabey nodded. "Fear not, my ship will sail you back to the cave of the living. I assume you are more than eager to return. As it happens, the sea calls me back to my home."

Jenaro presented the palm of peace. Atabey bowed her head in return and raised her arms. The deep crimson sails of the *Hupia* unfurled in response. A great westerly wind arose, as if on cue, and with a gust, propelled the *Moin Hupia* forward. Atabey raised her head and smiled at Jenaro. In the blink of an eye, she dove overboard. Jenaro ran to the edge and noticed the silhouette of a great caguama swimming alongside the ship until the shadow of the giant turtle slowly faded into the deep.

Jenaro stood in awe at the sheer speed of *Moin Hupia*. It felt as if the clipper were racing the sun, daring it to rise before it reached the Andolins. Jenaro held fast to the wheel but knew the ship did not need his input. He wondered if Atabey herself was pulling the ship along.

Soon, the morning rays of the sun combined with the lighthouse of Zafiro Harbor in welcoming him home. Jenaro could see the shining seas of the bay, the sails of those fishermen returning from their evenings abroad, and the banners and standards of the royal navy. It was those banners that caused Jenaro to stop. Without any way to declare his allegiance, the navy would more than likely open fire on the *Hupia*. Jenaro looked to the masts. *Moin Hupia* had no standard, no banner to announce whether it was friend or foe. His heart jumped. He ran from the wheel to the nearest line and began to climb.

The crimson sails lowered, and the speed of the ship decreased as he climbed. The clipper slipped into the bay proper. The alarm sounded, the horns of war screaming from the shipyard. In no time at all, *Moin Hupia* was surrounded by three small frigates. Admiral Cucybana's man-o-war was fast approaching. Jenaro reached the pinnacle of the main mast, wrapped both his legs and his left arm around, and waved his right hand. He was spotted before any vessel opened fire.

Moin Hupia refused to move farther into the bay despite the navy's attempts to tow it. So, Jenaro boarded the frigate *Pride of Caguama* and made his way ashore. He was met at the docks by none other than his baba and his carib, Agostin, alive and well.

Jenaro greeted both with a strong embrace and kiss. The two friends eagerly shared their combined tales to the Cacique as they walked back to the manse.

"Gueybana would have you arrested for stealing his ship," Marohu stated. "He has already called for it more than once."

"It is the punishment for the crime I committed." Jenaro paused before asking, "What would you have me do?"

Marohu stopped and turned to look at Jenaro and Agostin. He placed his hands on Jenaro's shoulders and said, "You bested Maboya. You sailed with Atabey. You no longer need me to tell you what to do." Marohu's voice caught in his throat. That was when Jenaro noticed the faint twinkling of tears at the corners of his baba's eyes. "You are my son, but you are grown. You have my blessing, no matter what you decide."

For the first time in ages, Jenaro was overcome with the need to embrace his baba. He quickly threw his arms around Marohu. When they separated, Marohu placed his hands on his son's cheeks and kissed his boy's forehead. He then leaned in close and whispered to Jenaro, "I envy you that ship. It is a treasure I have never seen."

Jenaro smiled wider than he ever had.

Marohu patted Jenaro on the shoulder and continued his walk, followed closely by Octavio and a small detachment of guazabara. He left Jenaro and Agostin alone on the cobblestone path to the manse.

Agostin walked off the path and leaned against the nearest tree. "You would not believe what I went through after I disappeared. Although it pales in comparison to what you experienced."

Jenaro smirked. "I imagine you suffered through a few interrogations about my whereabouts."

"Well yes, but that's not the interesting part. Two words: Sandrian Traders."

"You lie," Jenaro said with a grimace.

Agostin laughed. "I swear on my life. After Maboya sent me away I appeared on the deck of their ship. They pulled me out of the water and saved my life. Thankfully they were already on their way to Puerto Zafiro. In a week I was back. But let me tell you, that was the single most fascinating week I have ever had."

"Well, my friend, consider me jealous," Jenaro said with a chuckle. "But a week? It feel like I've only been gone for three days."

Agostin shook his head. "It has been more than a few weeks since we were aboard *Moin Hupia* together. Apparently, time flows differently in the presence of Maboya."

"Apparently."

"So what's the plan?"

"Well, there's a certain seamstress's daughter I'd like to see, but only after I have a bath and a new set of clothes. And then we must put together a crew."

Agostin grinned and nodded. "A crew? For what"

Jenaro crossed his arms on his chest and said, "Adventure."

The Timbered Hound

A Captain's First Voyage

Two weeks after his return, after groveling for forgiveness from Sharae and sharing his plans with her, Jenaro and Agostin were finally ready to sail. It took longer than he expected to prepare for the journey, fully stocking the holds of the *Moin Hupia*, and even longer to put together a crew.

On the day he was set to depart, Jenaro found himself strangely reluctant to leave. He bathed twice, and meticulously cared for his wounds. He spent the better part of an hour deciding on what to wear for such an occasion as his first voyage as captain. The del Rios family regalia proved too formal for such an event. Yet, his more casual apparel appeared to lack the needed gravitas. After four wardrobe changes, Jenaro finally settled on a crimson and ermine striped toggle tunic with rough leather waistcoat, breeches dyed a brilliant azul that stopped just below his knees, and oiled leather shoes. He wrapped his head in a scarf decorated like the multicolored tail feathers of an inriri. Jenaro took a step back from his mirror and nodded. He slowly packed a rucksack with an additional tunic and a pair of socks, anything else he thought he might need for an extended voyage.

He moved to his desk and opened the chest that rested on top. Inside were his cemi pipe, several blades, as well as his personal coin purse with Andoli gold marks. He quickly added those to his rucksack. As he moved to shut the chest, he noticed a glimmer. Underneath his variety of personal effects was a small charm necklace.

His heart nearly stopped. Jenaro swallowed hard and removed the necklace from the chest. It was just as he remembered; a thick, woven gold chain with a tri-faceted stone, a feather, and the fang of a maja. It was a gift to his mother after his encounter with Yaya.

He pictured Helena, basking in her sunroom, smiling, and laughing at his father. He saw the six-year-old version of himself, sitting at his mother's side and giggling at his father's antics. He looked at his mother and saw the necklace. She looked at him and smiled.

Jenaro blinked back to reality. The three charms rested in the palm of his hand; the woven gold chain dangled into the chest. He nodded and placed the chain around his neck. Still feeling anxious, he moved to his desk and penned a long love letter to Sharae. He struggled with what to say, striking through sentences, balling up the paper and restarting the letter more than once. His heart hurt to leave her yet again, and he teared up writing the same promise as before, "I love you and I will be back for you.", With a sigh and a nod, he sealed it with wax and the del Rios family emblem.

Jenaro was finally about to leave his room when there was a knock at his bedroom door. He gathered up his things and opened the door, hoping that whoever had called would see him on his way out. Unfortunately, standing outside his hovel door was To'guey.

His former teacher and behique had not aged well. Since their last lesson, five years earlier, To'guey appeared to have progressed several decades. She now hobbled slowly, resting most of her weight on a polished ceiba cane. Her once wild and uncontrollable hair turned wispy and white. Her skin was sagging low and lethargic, and her eyes were beginning to look glossy. Despite all this, she still managed to fill out her robe.

"I hoped to catch you before you set out," the behique said with a bow of her head.

"It seems your timing is perfect, Suma Behique," Jenaro responded, holding open his door and allowing To'guey to pass inside.

To'guey moved to Jenaro's sitting room and took a seat, groaning as she did. "My bones cooperate less and less these days," she said with a sneer. "It is the price I pay for living so long."

Jenaro breathed a sigh of relief, grateful for the diversion. He did love and respect To'guey and now appreciated her even more for delaying his departure. "What brings you to my humble home, To'guey?" he asked as he sat next to his teacher.

To'guey lowered her head. "The ship in the harbor...not lightly does Maboya relinquish ownership of his property."

"Atabey herself bestowed it upon me. Believe me, To'guey, it was no simple task to gain such a prize," Jenaro sighed, showing his teacher his missing finger.

"The cemi tighten their grip upon you," To'guey uttered as she examined Jenaro's hand. "I fear for you, Jenaro. Soon, you will have no choice but to obey their will."

Jenaro reached down and grabbed his teacher's frail hands, squeezing them tightly in his. "I, too, am afraid. I was reluctant to accept Atabey's gift. Yet, if you taught me anything it was that I am strong enough to make my own way, to live how I want, according to my own will."

To'guey nodded. "I know this all too well, but please, if you will, let an old woman dote over her student." At that, To'guey reached into the pockets of her robe and pulled a small leather pouch from inside. She pressed the pouch into Jenaro's palm and rose from her seat.

"Safe travels, my intrepid Jenaro," To'guey said, smiling and placing her palm on top of Jenaro's head. "I hope to see you when you return."

"Behique, before you leave…" Jenaro trailed off.

To'guey turned and looked to him with interest.

"Will you deliver this letter?" Jenaro asked, removing it from his tunic.

To'guey smiled slyly. "I will personally deliver it to her," she said with a wink.

Without another word, To'guey ambled slowly from Jenaro's room. Jenaro sat for a moment, eyeing the small leather pouch in his palm. He carefully unfastened the leather strap and peered inside. The Suma Behique's finest consecrated snuff was carefully wrapped within. Jenaro smiled briefly then stuffed the pouch into his rucksack and made for the door. "I think I've dawdled long enough."

It was late afternoon when Jenaro met Agostin at the royal family's private pier. It had taken Jenaro nearly four hours after midday to prepare to sail. If Agostin was overcome with impatience, Jenaro could not tell. His best friend raised the palm of peace as he approached. Jenaro returned the gesture and smiled. Much to Jenaro's surprise, his sister Helena stepped out from behind Agostin's shadow.

"I was beginning to wonder if you'd show," Agostin said after embracing Jenaro.

Jenaro nodded. "Just nerves, is all. I mean how often do we get to do something as this."

"You're right, such a momentous event and you couldn't even be bothered to let me know?" Helena said, arms on her hips, face twisted in disappointment.

"Strange, I didn't notice Marisol when I arrived. Here to see me off, Anki?" Jenaro asked his sister.

Helena's frown deepened as she crossed her arms on her chest. "You arrive home after disappearing for nearly a month and just decide to disappear once more? And without saying goodbye to me, yet again?"

Jenaro chuckled lightly. "It was insensitive and inconsiderate of me. I apologize, Anki."

Helena glared playfully at Jenaro before lowering her arms. "I guess I accept that apology, but only if you tell me where you're running off to now."

"I'm not entirely sure," Jenaro shrugged.

Helena scoffed. "Typical Jenaro. You run headlong and eyes closed into a field of brambles without noticing the perfectly clear path around."

Agostin and Jenaro laughed as Jenaro pulled his sister in for a hug.

"I'll bring back a gift perfect for a little Anki," Jenaro said.

"It had better be gold plated," Helena added.

Jenaro nodded as he released his sister. Anki bowed and left, turning around to wave goodbye as she stepped off the pier and back onto dry land.

Jenaro turned his attention to Agostin. "How's the crew?"

"They are ready and waiting, *captain*," Agostin replied, emphasizing the word with a small bow.

Jenaro smiled wider than he had ever smiled in his life. He looked past Agostin to the radiant, sable clipper resting motionless in the harbor. "Captain," he repeated. "That has a nice ring to it."

Agostin rowed the dinghy to the furthest reaches of the harbor before the island shelf gave way to the deeper waters of the Summer Sea. As they boarded the *Moin Hupia*, they were met by a small group of twenty-nine sailors. The crew looked rough and capable, just the sort of people Jenaro wanted on ship. Yet, the number proved inadequate for the size of the *Moin Hupia*, even after Jenaro and Agostin offered them more than any other merchant, even more than they would make enlisting in the navy. I think it was the ship. Nobody wanted to sail aboard death's ship.

Jenaro was greeting the crew when he noticed a new face among them: a woman standing in the back of the group, head down, trying to stay inconspicuous. Unfortunately, she locked eyes with Jenaro and nearly made him gasp.

"Luysa Bayamon," Jenaro called to the sailor. "Are you Luysa Bayamon?"

The woman stepped out of the crowd bowed her head courteously. "My lord," she replied in a husky contralto voice. Luysa Bayamon was the shortest, yet by far, the most imposing Andoli woman Jenaro had ever encountered, her face stern and her eyes a cold gray.

"Is it true?" Jenaro asked, approaching her and trying to contain his excitement. "The story of the architus?"

Luysa pulled the sleeve of her left arm up past her elbow. The beads and shells that decorated her sleeves jingled. Her skin beneath her sleeve was blotchy and purple with strange markings snaking from her wrist past her elbow. "The beast left its mark," she said.

Jenaro whistled in awe at the sight of her arm.

"You are not only an accomplished sea captain, but also a world-renowned navigator, are you not?" Agostin asked. She nodded.

"You were the first person to circumnavigate the globe," Jenaro beamed. "And they say you did it without a compass or sextant."

"I don't use them," Luysa said plainly as she lowered her sleeve then rested her hand on the twisted club hanging on her belt. With the other hand she reached into her blouse and pulled a small pouch attached to a chain. Inside the pouch was a milky white stone. "This is all I need."

A wave of awe and admiration swept over Jenaro and Agostin.

"What is that?" one of the crew asked.

"It is a guidestone," Jenaro said. "It uses the light of the sun to tell your exact position on a map. It's majick."

"Old majick," Agostin muttered and shook his head then wrung his hands.

Luysa grimaced at Agostin's discomfort. "They say these stones are cursed, chico," she said to Agostin, voice dripping with disdain at the idea.

"And what do you say?" Jenaro asked.

Luysa replaced the stone back in its pouch and stuffed the pouch back down her shirt. "Why should I fear something that allowed me to accomplish such great feats?"

Jenaro smiled and nodded.

Agostin grumbled and continued the introductions.

Jenaro turned to Agostin and nodded at his friend. "Shall we?"

Agostin's face beamed. His smile encompassed his face.

"Ready the ship!" Agostin yelled.

The crew jumped at his command, quickly doling out tasks as if they had been sailing together for years. Jenaro and Agostin traded smiles and walked to the helm.

"Thirty sailors," Jenaro said. "I know you are no man of Yaya, yet even you should be in awe of the surprise act of piety."

Agostin groaned. "It is nothing but coincidence, your grace."

"I wouldn't be so sure, Agostin Anacaona," Jenaro continued to prod. "Thirty is a holy number."

Agostin scoffed.

Jenaro laughed and took the helm. With the aid of the warm sea breezes, he piloted the *Hupia* out of Puerto Zafiro. Once in open waters, he consulted with Luysa and set course westward, deep into the rarely traveled reaches of the Summer Sea.

Arrivals

Moin Hupia was a curious vessel, as Jenaro and Agostin soon found out. The ship did not seem overly fond of its new captain, and did not respond as easily to Jenaro as it once did Maboya. The sails and anchor seemed reluctant to raise and lower on command, as if most of the ghostly crew vanished along with their master and the few that remained only aided their new captain begrudgingly.

The ship no longer bent the sea to its will but, despite the minute niggles, *Moin Hupia* still radiated a majick Jenaro had never experienced. The ship sliced its way through the Summer Sea at speeds Jenaro did not think possible, as if the wind was not even required for the ship to sail.

Every evening, minutes before sunset, the ship's lanterns would light on their own. Bow to stern, poop deck to orlop deck; the ship became a beacon in the dark. It was a pleasant surprise during the crew's first night at sea that brought with it much revelry.

The sails themselves were another surprise. Even though they no longer unfurled at the snap of a finger, it seemed that the crimson sailcloth remained strong and supple. No amount of battering from wind or rain deteriorated their condition.

They sailed for several weeks, traversing the Summer Sea in search of riches and infamy. Unfortunately, they found neither. This made the crew restless and in need of some amusement. So, Jenaro and Agostin met with Luysa and, in a matter of moments, plotted a course to Cu' Ciba. They were surprised at how close they had sailed to Cike'o. Apparently the *Hupia* could cover nautical miles faster than any ship they knew. Before long, the cry went out from the watch.

"Land! Land-ho!"

Jenaro spotted it before the call came down from the crow's nest. It was the sky. It always took on a greenish tint when land was just beyond the horizon. He turned and nodded at Luysa, who nodded back in turn and placed her guidestone back in its pouch.

"Do you think it's Cike'o?" Agostin asked.

Jenaro nodded. "If Luysa's stone is to be believed–," he began but was interrupted by Luysa.

"The guidestone is always correct," Luysa interrupted as she descended from the helm to take her place at the mainmast.

Jenaro chuckled.

"Cike'o," Agostin echoed with a nod.

"Land of the Cibao Ara'," Jenaro said, turning and smiling at his carib.

"I wonder if all To'guey's tales are true," Agostin said.

"We'll find out soon enough," Jenaro replied.

Moin Hupia continued to slice effortlessly through the waves until the horizon gave way to the continent of Cike'o. The capital of Cu' Ciba was located on a peninsula, nearly two hundred miles wide, which jutted southwest into the Summer Sea and away from the main bulk of the continent. It was marked with towering white cliffs hiding thousands of jetties and berths. It was no wonder the United Principalities of Cike'o chose the peninsula as site for their capital.

Cu' Ciba, the city itself, was founded as a small village at the cliff's edge but expanded into a massive center for Cibaoan culture. The city first grew on the tip of the peninsula, expanding from cliff face to cliff face until nearly half the peninsula was part of the metropolitan area. Then the Cibao Ara' delved into the cliff, creating a network of halls that stretched for miles into the white stone of the peninsula. Lastly, and leaving no space unused or forgotten, the city of Cu' Ciba built floating sections. Giant Cibaoan-made islands dotted the sea proper and developed into a thriving port district, housing everything from trading companies to brothels. Every need a sailor had could be satisfied on the islands.

Just as with Puerto Zafiro, *Moin Hupia* slowed to a halt immediately outside the bay proper. No amount of wind or current moved her hull closer to port. Jenaro lowered anchor regardless of her immobility.

The crew assembled by the dinghies. Each member wore a face of hope and anticipation. They were antsy to disembark. Nearly two months at sea with a skeleton crew makes the best of sailors weary. It was a painfully palpable truth that Jenaro felt to his bones. He should not have allowed it to get this bad.

"The Cibao Ara' require payment to be allowed access to the city. I know we are all in need of some rest and relaxation, but until we know if we will even be allowed in, it'll have to wait a little longer." Jenaro felt some of their hopeful air leave their lungs. "I want you to remain here in case we have any overly curious residents. Luysa, you will accompany Agostin and myself ashore and return to retrieve the others once we receive clearance."

The crew nodded without complaint and lowered the dinghy. Agostin rowed while Luysa steered. Jenaro sat in the prow and looked forward. The sights and sounds of the Cike'on capital grew exponentially as they approached. The hustle and bustle of the docks rang out over the harbor like the chatter of dozens of gulls.

A horn blast nearly sent Jenaro overboard. He and Agostin turned and gaped as an enormous, steamer chugged past. Large, metal wheels paddled the vessel to port, creating a wake that would have capsized the dingy, if not for Agostin's quick steering. Large, billowy clouds expanded skyward from a towering stack amidships.

"How is that possible?" Agostin gasped.

"Steam," Luysa responded. "The Cibaoan are technologically superior to us in every way imaginable."

Agostin shook his head in disbelief. "Steam," he repeated quietly.

"Have you had dealings with the Cibao before?" Jenaro asked. "I don't remember a story of you ever visiting Cike'o."

Luysa shrugged. "Only once or twice. Nothing of note to speak of."

Jenaro grinned at Agostin. "Nothing of note to speak of."

The steam and smoke only increased as they rowed closer. Columns of each rose from every surface, from the docks to the caverns to the city on the cliffs. It filled the air with an unnatural fog and turned the sun's rays into a hazy, fuzzy glow. As they pulled to the first dock they encountered, a young Cibao ran to the side and directed them to another wharf.

"Smaller craft such as yours need to dock at Pier Seven, near the harbor master's office. You'll pay your dock fees and entry tax there."

Luysa maneuvered the dinghy to the appropriate berth. Meanwhile, Jenaro began to smile, filled with memories of home. Seeing the liveliness of the dock was one thing, but the further into the port town they rowed, the more the usual smells of the dock overcame the odor of the smoke and steam. The dampness of the wood, the mixture of freshly caught tuna, bream, and spices, the brine of the sea, the bitter smell of rust on metal; every odor, every aroma ignited Jenaro's emotions ablaze. He loved everything about this life; the sights and smells that only a sailor could love.

They docked at Pier Seven and disembarked. Jenaro, Agostin, and Luysa were directed, rather nonchalantly by a pair of short and stout dock workers, to the harbor master's office. Jenaro found their casual disregard extremely curious. The Cibao scarcely noticed the arrival of the *Hupia*. He was certain the black hulled, blood-soaked sails would spark fear or amazement in the eyes of all who saw it, but everyone at the docks just couldn't be bothered with the appearance of a ship that used such ancient technology.

"We seem to be of no consequence to them, Agostin," Jenaro said with a chuckle. He turned his attention to his surroundings. The pier itself was a triumph of craftsmanship. Stone was married to metal, metal interwoven through wood. The slats of the walkway allowed for the free flow of air and water without sacrificing traction.

The harbor master's office was a one room marble and gold building that served as entrance to the port city islands. Unregistered arrivals would pay a harbor fee and state their business, then be admitted to Cu' Ciba. The harbor master's mood often determined whether a visitor was allowed entrance to the city. Inside the office was one long desk with several agents at different stations working to ensure the flow of arrivals never stopped. Each station had a small queue, and each queue was at capacity. There were marble benches lining the wall opposite the desk full of men from every continent on Ke', short and stout Cibao Ara' returning to Cu' Ciba, and even statuesque and stately Itiba Ara' waiting their turn at the desks.

Jenaro gave the Itiba Ara' a once over. They were dressed modestly, likely simple travelers or lesser merchants. Regardless of their profession, Itiba tended to be solitary when away from their country of Itibanen. Few made trips from that desolate wasteland and those that did were often in search of majick.

Agostin shook his head. "What a waste; generation after generation devoting their life to such nonsense," he scorned. "Hunting majick."

Jenaro shrugged. "I'm sure some say the same about the Andoli and our cemi, Agostin. No one knows why they continue to hunt after their legendary defeat. And furthermore, it is not our place to belittle their culture. Did we learn nothing of our own recent history; the struggles between the Ultan-Meres and the Andolins?"

Agostin physically backpedaled. "Our oppression was different. Theirs is self-inflicted."

"We are alike in more ways than not, my friend," Jenaro answered. "Let's not worry about Itiba. We are standing at the doorstep to Cu' Ciba, gateway to Cike'o! Technological center of the world! Let's enjoy ourselves."

Luysa nodded. Agostin smirked. "It is just like you to be so diplomatic," then took a seat on the bench.

The queue moved rather quickly and before long Jenaro was at the front of the line. As luck would have it, Jenaro was served by the harbor master himself, a Cibao named Turek. He was wrinkly and exceptionally long in the tooth, with a lengthy braided white beard, and a bald, liver spotted head. Yet his eyes were lively and shone like emeralds. He wore an exquisite marble bangle decorated with sapphires on his left wrist. It appeared heavy but did not slow his movements.

"Name," he demanded of Jenaro in his native Cibaonan. His voice was a curiously nasal tenor.

"Jenaro Albizu del Rios," Jenaro responded in kind.

Turek looked up from his register and squinted. "Andoli?"

he asked in surprise. "We don't get many of your folk here. What brings you to Cu' Ciba?"

"Resupply for my crew and ship. We have coin and some trade goods…"

Turek shook a hand, waving off Jenaro and interrupting. "Son, I do not care to know the minutiae of your stay. You could be here to carouse which is fine and dandy. Please keep your answers short and simple. I only have space for succinctness in this register."

Jenaro smiled and fought back a chuckle. "Resupply," he repeated.

Turek nodded as he wrote. "Ship's name and berth?"

"*Moin Hupia*," Jenaro said, then paused, curious to see if the name conjured any emotion from the ornery old Cibao Ara'.

Turek sighed. "Berth," he repeated in exasperation.

"No berth. Our ship is anchored in deep waters. We were directed here by your agents."

"'None' is a fine response," Turek rolled his eyes and shook his head. "Five silver denarii. I assume you plan to pay with Andoli pieces?" Turek stopped and turned to his abacus. His fingers danced on the rings, sliding back and forth for several seconds. "Sixteen silver Andoli marks."

Jenaro reached into his satchel and pulled a thin, two-by-four inch gold mark from inside. He placed it on the register. Turek slid from his stool and stomped to the back of the office. He opened a safe twice his size and pulled a rectangular book from inside. He slammed the book on the desk once he returned and leafed to the next empty page. His hand furiously scribbled Cibaoan runes as he mumbled a number to himself. He shut the book, tossed it aside then reopened the register. He transferred the number to Jenaro's entry.

"According to current rates, your payment will allow you

access to Cu' Ciba and the lands of Cike'o beyond the capital a total of nine times. That number is subject to change with market fluctuation and can be revoked if you are imprisoned or killed. Your vessel will remain tied until your return." Turek paused his speech and handed Jenaro a bundle of strange metallic planks no bigger than the palm of his hand. "Keep those with you at all times. They are your entry keys. Enjoy your visit."

Before Jenaro could even respond Turek yelled, "Next!" and shooed Jenaro from the desk.

Jenaro waved to Agostin and Leke who both abandoned their spots on the bench and met him outside. On the opposite side of the door was Cu' Ciba. They could see the islands, each one connected by glistening marble and wood walkways and bridges. Small craft navigated the canals, puffing little tugboats carrying men and goods alike. Beyond that, the cavern and cliff districts rose from the horizon like the tip of a giant glowing dagger. The sun reflected off the stone like a mirror. Steam-powered lifts worked their way up and down the cliff face. At the pinnacle of the cliff was the union house, flying the standards of Cike'o, each white and gold flag waving majestically in the wind.

Jenaro turned to Agostin and Luysa with a roguish smile plastered on his face. "Luysa, take this," he said and handed a metal token to his navigator. "That will give you and the crew access to the city. Head back to the *Hupia* and spread the word. You have three days to enjoy the city. On the fourth, resupply and prepare to sail."

Luysa's perpetual frowned straightened out in what Jenaro guess was a smile. She bowed slightly and said, "And you, captain? What will you do?"

Jenaro nodded at Agostin. "Explore the city, of course!"

At that, Luysa jogged back to the dinghy leaving Jenaro and Agostin ogling at the city before them.

Land of the Cibao Ara'

It was more than either of them could take. As he walked, Jenaro found himself staring, mouth agape, at the sights of Cu' Ciba. That was until he collided with a female Cibao, knocking him and Agostin from their revelry.

She spun and landed flat on her backside with an *oof*. Her knapsack spilled a variety of woodworking tools clattering across the marble and wood walkway. She had a small hatchet that slipped loose and careened to the water's edge. Before Jenaro could help her up or utter an apology, she was on her knees scurrying after the hatchet. It teetered on the edge of the walkway, threatening to take the plunge, but was rescued moments before.

"Would you watch where you're standing you…you… tourists!" she shouted in Jenaro's tongue. "What kind of idiotic, simple-minded, buffoon moves like that on a walkway?"

Jenaro was amused by her anger but bowed by way of apology. "I apologize on behalf of my friend and myself. We are merely overwhelmed by your great city."

"My city?" she jeered and as she gathered up her belongings. "Not mine, and thank the makers for that!" She stood upright and brushed the dirt of the dock from her clothes.

Jenaro introduced himself and said, "My companion here is Agostin."

She scoffed, tossing braided auburn hair to rest in the small of her back. "Do all Andoli introduce themselves to strangers?"

"Only the polite ones," Agostin replied, voice dripping with sarcasm.

"You speak our language almost without an accent," Jenaro continued.

She squinted suspiciously and shifted her bag on her back. "You have to know every tongue if you're a Cibao Ara'. How do you think we mastered trade with every nation? Been part of our education for ages now. I assume your Cibaonan is atrocious."

"I wouldn't say atrocious," Jenaro replied in Cibaonan.

The Cibao took a step backward as if to flee then shook her head and groaned under her breath, "My father would collapse from shame if he saw how I'm treating visitors." She straightened up and, with a nod, said, "The name's Rahe of Stone Point, daughter of Hano and Brindha. I accept your apology. Now, if you'll excuse me."

Jenaro took a step forward. "If I can have just a moment of your time before you leave. I did have a couple of questions about the city."

"I am not a tour guide, can't you see?" Rahe questioned him.

Jenaro and Agostin shrugged. Jenaro looked the Cibao up and down, trying to find the reason for her statement. Her skin looked well accustomed to the sun, an obvious mark of an outdoor trade. She wore a maroon-colored shirt with sleeves to the elbows and dark brown canvas pants. Jenaro was puzzled. That was when Rahe shook her wrist, jingling a bangle.

The purest gold circled her wrist, more extravagant than anything he had seen in the Manse of Puerto Zafiro. The afternoon sun's rays danced majestically on its surface. Upon closer inspection, Jenaro noticed the band was etched with ancient Cibaonan runes of dazzling quicksilver. The runes appeared to glow and pulse with otherworldly light. He thought for a moment and recalled the bangle that decorated Turek's arm. The harbor master wore marble with sapphires.

"Your bangles denote your profession?" Jenaro inquired.

"Yes," Rahe answered with a roll of her eyes. "Dock workers wear seastone and marble. Tour guides wear polished ironwood with ruby inlays. Soldiers wear black iron."

"And gold with quicksilver runes?" Jenaro asked.

"It means I'm a Scholia recognized artisan."

Jenaro gasped with delight. "A true artisan registered with the Scholia Regium?"

"That's the school that used to teach majick, correct?" Agostin asked cautiously.

"Almost a thousand years ago," Rahe answered. "Look, I'd love to stay and chat with you, but I have business to attend to. Find yourselves someone wearing an ironwood bangle."

Jenaro raised his hands. "Please, before you go, allow us to buy you a meal or a drink by way of apology. You do need to eat, correct?"

"A strange offer for such minor offense," Rahe reflected. "What's your game, foreigner?"

"No game," Jenaro responded. "I feel compelled."

Rahe sighed. "There is no swaying you, is there, Jenaro of the Andolins?"

Jenaro shook his head and smiled. "I would be honored to eat with an officially recognized artisan."

"Well, I do have to eat," Rahe answered. "I have one more delivery to make, so you can accompany on my errands. Then we make our way to the north gates. My favorite place is by the walls anyhow."

Rahe led Jenaro and Agostin through the island district to the lifts located in the caverns. Despite her earlier complaints, Rahe acted as a guide to the dumstruck Andoli, explaining how the islands were developed and the technology keeping them afloat; a complicated machine using steam and air for buoyancy.

The lifts themselves were enclosed metal platforms that rose and fell through the entire cavern to the cliff district above. Powered by steam, the lifts operated rather autonomously. While each lift had an orange clad Cibao maintaining the pressure, ride speed, and lubrication, the riders themselves controlled the lifts. Jenaro found them awe inspiring. Agostin on the other hand was wary and needed extra motivation to board the "metal box," as he called it.

It took four minutes to ascend to the cliff district. Jenaro and Agostin were greeted by the sights and sounds of the capital. Marble towers rose to the heavens, the pinnacles of which were hidden by the clouds of steam and smoke that clogged the city. Cibao Ara' dressed in every conceivable color and fabric, some wearing bangles, others not, scurried along the gilded marble streets. Jenaro saw others, too, Ultan emissaries, a Sandrian envoy, a couple of Itiba dressed as clerics, and even an Andoli trader, who raised the palm of peace to Jenaro and Agostin as if he spotted old friends. Yet, even amid so many Cibao Ara', it wasn't until they passed the gates of the Scholia Reguim that Jenaro spotted another gold bangle. The wearers, two wizened, white bearded Cibao, one clutching a spectacularly elaborate battle axe that doubled as his cane, the other with an arm full of books, waved to Rahe. Jenaro smiled. The gold and quicksilver runed bangle seemed to bring with it an enormous measure of esteem and respect.

"I have to run inside for just a moment," Rahe stated. "Can you two wait here without running into anyone else?"

Jenaro grinned. "Of course."

"I know what you're thinking," Agostin said after Rahe disappeared beyond the gates of the Scholia.

"It's right there, Ago," Jenaro smiled and pointed at the towering edifice. "The Scholia! She's not too far away. We can follow her and see the only place on Ke' where majick is still taught."

"No, we told Rahe we would stay here, and here is where we'll stay."

Jenaro huffed. "Since when are you the level-headed one?"

Ago chuckled and pulled Jenaro to a spot along the wall where they two stood and observed the comings and goings of the Cibao Ara'. It didn't take long for the pair to be dumbstruck by yet another Cibaonan marvel. Chugging its way down the middle of the boulevard was a contraption the likes of which they had never seen. A steam powered carriage rolled along metal rails, whistling, and wheezing its way to a stop across the boulevard from their spot.

"What in the frigid seas of death is that?" Agostin cursed.

"You islanders are so easily amused," Rahe laughed as she reappeared by their side. "It's a rail car. It provides public transportation throughout the cliff district all the way to the villages at the north end of the peninsula. We'll be hitching a ride."

Agostin's eyes went wide. "I don't know if I can handle much more technology."

"Come now, my friend," Jenaro said as he strolled past his carib. "This is the adventure of a lifetime!"

The train rolled Rahe, Jenaro, and Agostin through the streets of Cu' Ciba's cliff district to the gates at the northwest side of the peninsula. They disembarked just outside the gates and directly in front of Peak's Pub. It was an old establishment, even by Cibaoan standards. It, like every other building in the area, was made entirely of ironwood. The charcoal-colored wood had a natural sheen that made each wall seem like metal. Peak's Pub had several windows, hand-made glass tempered by Scholia artisans, and a red and green stone and clay tile roof. Inside, the walls were decorated in traditional Cike'on fashion. Dulled axes and swords, attached to plaques, hung from almost every surface. There were stuffed elk heads, each with a magnificent and unbelievable number of antler points. The bar stools, tables, and chairs were all ironwood. There was a large hearth at one side of the bar with four large iron stock pots sending the aroma of stewed meat and vegetables throughout the tavern.

"My da and I used to eat here every time we came into the city," Rahe said as she guided Jenaro and Agostin to one of the only unoccupied booths. "It was…his favorite spot in Cu'Ciba."

Jenaro slid into the booth across from Rahe, and Agostin sat next to him. "Does he not come into the city any longer? Or, is it something worse?" Jenaro asked.

Rahe sighed. "He's no longer with us."

"I am so sorry," Jenaro apologized. "I know how hard it is to lose a parent. My bibi passed on when I was nine."

Before any more words could be said, a surly barmaid stopped by the table. "Hello, Rahe. Who are your friends?"

"Out of towners," Rahe said.

"Well, I can see that! The name's Garbe," she said with a quick wave. "Me and my partner own Peak's Pub."

"I am Jenaro and this here is Agostin," Jenaro said, raising the palm of peace.

"Rahe here's been eating at Peak's since she was a little girl, only," Garbe put a hand on her hip and looked the Andoli up and down, "she's never brought friends in. I wasn't even sure she had any."

Rahe cleared her throat. "Okay, that's fine, how about some stew, Grabe?"

Grabe smiled. "Three bowls of our famous stew."

"And I wouldn't mind some ale," Agostin added. "I hear the Cibao Ara' are famous for it."

"Three stews and three ales," Grabe said with a nod. Jenaro slid an Andoli mark across the table before Rahe could reach into her coin purse.

"On me," he said with a smile.

Grabe picked up the mark and scrutinized it before placing it in her mouth and biting down. Her face lit up. "Three stews and all the ale you can drink," she said with a smile.

There was a moment of awkward silence that lasted until the stew arrived. Grabe placed three steaming hot bowls and three steins of ale on the table, then scurried off to serve the newest arrivals to the tavern, a pair of Itiba Jenaro found curiously similar to those encountered earlier that day at the harbor master's office.

Jenaro elbowed Agostin and whispered while staring into his mug of ale. "Those Itiba are oddly familiar."

Agostin nodded without turning his attention to the elves. "I was suspecting the same thing. It cannot be mere coincidence, can it?"

Jenaro shrugged as he wafted the savory aroma to his nose and glanced over at Agostin. He had already begun to feast.

"Grabe's stew is legendary," Rahe grinned as he spooned it into his mouth. They all ate in relative peace and quiet, finishing their stew and the first round of ale. That was when Rahe sighed. "My da was found dead in his workshop," she began. "Authorities suspected foul play, yet no Cibao was found to have done the vile deed."

"That's terribe, Rahe, I'm so sorry," Jenaro said.

"Thank you," she replied. "I haven't been able to shake it, mostly because..." she trailed off.

"Because?" Agostin asked.

Rahe frowned. Her face grew dark, suspicious. She gave a quick look around the pub before she leaned as far as she could over the table. "They say it was a baelor, but I know better. I saw the creature. It was no baelor I've ever seen."

"Baelor?" Jenaro asked, a little too loud for Rahe's liking.

Shushing him, she said then shook her head. "I must be crazy for even considering this but, if you want to know, I can tell you, just not here. The people don't like when I talk about it, not even Grabe."

Jenaro and Agostin shared a curious glance. "Where then?" Jenaro asked.

"Let's finish up. If we're lucky we can catch the last train to Stone Point."

Cibaoan Hospitality

Rahe's cabin stood on the foothills outside of Cu' Ciba proper, in the small village of Stone Point. From her front porch, Jenaro could see the towers of Union Hall and the cliff district to his left and the southernmost reaches of the Taicaraya Mountains to the right. As the sun dipped below the horizon, the steam and smoke that filled the cityscape transformed to a blaze of ocher and violet and swatches of every color in between muted by the veil of Cibaoan made smog. The Taicarayas were the exact opposite. They were a towering wall of midnight from which no light could be seen. Jenaro felt a chill run up his spine. He shook it off and entered Rahe's home.

It was a quaint and cozy one room affair. There was a fireplace opposite the door with a kettle. A braid of garlic and rope of herbs hung from the mantle as well as a plucked bird Jenaro did not recognize. At the north end of the house was Rahe's worktable. Blocks of wood and tools littered every space. Saw dust filled the floor like a carpet. The south end of the house was her living space. An unmade bed and half open dresser, a wash basin with plumbing and an enclosed lavatory. The ceilings were low for Jenaro and Agostin, who both had to crouch to move around. Rahe deposited her bag on her workbench and directed Jenaro and Agostin to the rug by the fireplace. Placed in front of the hearth was the pelt of an enormous animal. The head was mounted above, but the claws remained on the rug.

"What manner of beast is this?" Agostin asked as he sat on the pelt.

Rahe appeared puzzled. "It's a baelor. You don't have baelor bears on your islands?"

Jenaro and Agostin shook their heads in unison.

"The professors at the Scholia call them ursus something or others. They're native to Cike'o but also found in Ultan-Mere. They run wild in the Taicarayas which is why they say, 'Never travel the woods without your axe.'"

"Sound advice," Agostin responded. He ran his hands through the brown and white fur. "How did you slay such a massive beast?"

Rahe laughed. "I didn't. It belonged to my da. He got it as part of payment for a job. He was like that, you see. If you didn't have money to pay, da would take a trade; barter."

At the mention of her father, Rahe trailed off. Her eyes began to gloss momentarily. Jenaro took that as a cue.

"I assume you are quite the woodworker to have earned a golden bangle," Jenaro said.

Rahe nodded almost absentmindedly. "I am. Not as skilled as my da but accomplished in my own right. Oh, how could I forget?" She scrambled to a small chest and pulled a glass bottle holding a copper-colored liquid from inside along with three tin cups. She flipped the lid shut then hurried to her guests. "It's customary among Cike'ons to toast to your guests with your finest alcohol."

At that, Agostin perked up from his place on the baelor. "Alcohol?" he chimed melodically.

Jenaro chuckled. "Agostin considers himself a connoisseur."

Rahe nodded as she poured three cups. "Well may I present to you humery, or slack as we commoners call it."

Rahe distributed the cups and raised hers to toast. "To bonds stronger than steel and friendships harder than stone."

Agostin wasted no time and downed his drink. Jenaro and Rahe imbibed with a little more reserve.

"Hoo…" Agostin exhaled. "Humery…a grain?"

Rahe swallowed her sip. "It is a distilled malt of barley and honey. The original recipe used crushed jakenstone as a filter and aged it in unrefined ironwood. Bottles like that, like this, are expensive and hard to come by. I got this bottle as payment for a fine bedroom set."

Agostin began to voice another alcohol related question when Jenaro interrupted.

"I don't mean to be rude or interrupt your bonding, but you mentioned a strange creature prowling around your father's shop," Jenaro said.

Rahe's face immediately turned grim. She swallowed hard and cleared her throat before placing her cup on the mantle. She spoke, face fixed on the fire. "It started a little over three months ago. I have never been keen on visiting my father's workshop, especially since his passing. Some say it's the memories associated with losing a family member." Rahe paused. Her stare intensified. "I know loss. I know how it feels. This was different. Always was, always will be. There was a darkness that hung on the air at his shop; heavy and cold. But it worsened once he died. Almost as if the essences themselves moved in, took over, choked all the joy of life from that cabin."

"Essences?" Jenaro asked. "Your father was a mage?"

Rahe shook her head. "Enchanter. He couldn't use essence to summon flame or freeze the air. He could only bind essence to things and in turn give items majick properties.

"It was subtle, at first. Things would be out of place or missing, tools lost their sharpness immediately after being sharpened, and items fell from shelves. Slowly, it grew worse until my last visit."

Rahe trailed off.

"That's when you saw the thing, this creature?" Agostin asked.

Rahe nodded, "Two to be exact. The first attacked me. I fell backwards, my body recoiling from unseen blows. Then my father's axe floated toward me, drawn to the spirit by some invisible malice. The axe rose to end me when the second spirit appeared. This one had form and shape. I thought it resembled a baelor, at first, but after replaying the event in my head, it was more of a dog."

"A rather common creature here and abroad," Agostin responded. "Are you sure it was a spirit?"

"Yes," Rahe answered, rather annoyed. "It was no ordinary hound. Its skin looked like wood as if it were covered in bark. It had shoots and leaves growing from its body. It had deep, hollow eyes that glowed green. There was a mysterious swarm of torch bugs floating around it and crawling over its bark. It even moved like a tree, or as a tree would move, I guess. It was like wind through trees, creaking and moaning with each scrape. It howled as it moved forward; a far-away cry, as if made through a hollowed-out log."

Jenaro smiled once more and looked to Agostin.

"Opiyelguabiran," they said in unison.

"Beg your pardon?" Rahe inquired.

"It is definitely not a bear you describe," Jenaro stated through a chuckle. "It is Opiyelguabiran."

Rahe's face changed from fear to puzzlement. "Opi–what?"

"Opiyelguabiran," Jenaro and Agostin replied in unison.

"It is a spirit," Jenaro began, "a cemi of old, a legendary creature. It guides the spirits to the third and final cave. It fits your description perfectly, only it is not a bear, but a dog."

"What would one of your gods be doing here in Cike'o?" Rahe asked.

Jenaro and Agostin shrugged and shook their heads.

"O-pee-yellow-brain?" Rahe attempted to pronounce it.

"Opiyelguabiran," Jenaro said, slower, emphasizing each syllable. "It is the patron cemi of my family and clan."

Rahe shook her head. "I'll just call it Opi."

Jenaro chuckled. "Opi would find that amusing."

Rahe squinted, unsure of what he meant.

Jenaro shook his head in amusement. "Please continue," he said.

"So, Opi howled," Rahe spoke. "The axe fell to the floor and the presence vanished. The hound then led me away from the cabin, pulling at my shirt sleeves with its strange, wooden mouth. I didn't even have time to gather my father's tools and plans, the very reason I was there.

"It was midday when I arrived, but the sky around the grove resembled the dead of night. There was no sun, no stars, and the moon was gone. Even the light from the lamps inside the shop were swallowed by the darkness. The only light came from the torch bugs swarming around Opi.

"It led me down the mountain and back to the light of day. In fact, the closer we got to daylight, the further Opi faded from my view. Its glow diminished until it disappeared altogether.

"I've tried returning, tried to get back to retrieve the tools, his gold and quicksilver bangle, and the volumes of plans my da had stowed there…they were his legacy, you know? Every time I near the grove, I am once more greeted by the dark. Opi's light appears in the distance, but no matter how I try to follow it, it only ever leads me out o' the grove and back down the mountain where I started, almost as if it's protecting the darkness."

Jenaro shook his head. "No, it's protecting you from the

darkness. That's Opi for sure, but what it's doing out in Cike'o is curious."

"Curious? Frightening is more like it," grunted Agostin. "Cemi," he shuddered.

"Do you two not share the same beliefs?" Rahe asked.

Agostin rolled his eyes and shook his head.

"Anacaona men are infamously impious," Jenaro stated. "Yet, what they lack in piety, they make up for with fierce loyalty."

"The fact that you two can get along so well is amazing," Rahe complimented.

They both smiled.

"Difference of opinion should never hinder the intimacy of your relationships," Jenaro preached.

"And has your opinion of me and my problem changed? Are you still willing to help even after hearing all of that?"

"Of course, we will help, Rahe," Jenaro reassured her.

Before they turned in for the evening, the three discussed the route to the shop in the mountains. Rahe reminded them of the danger of the baelors and asked if they had weapons. Agostin showed her his dagger and cutlass. Jenaro had only a dagger. Rahe offered her woodcutter's axe to Agostin, who accepted the gift with honor.

"Listen, Jenaro," Rahe said as she finished filling a lantern for him, "I can't go with you. I…I just don't think I'm ready…"

Jenaro raised a hand and shook his head. "Please Rahe, there is no need. I understand."

Rahe lowered her head. "Please don't take any unnecessary risks," she said in hushed tones. "If you make it to the shop, just grab my da's belongings and run."

Jenaro nodded. "I will return your father's things to you. I promise."

Journey to the Taicarayas

The last vestiges of night were dissipating as Jenaro and Agostin marched out of the tiny village of Stone Point. The sky teased at morning, the blue-black of evening slowly changing into a smattering of grey. Jenaro glanced back at Cu' Ciba. Even in the small hours before dawn the city in the distance was shrouded in smoke and steam, a hazy glow. For the briefest moment, Jenaro swore he saw two figures dart out of sight.

"I am quite sure we are being followed," Jenaro said quietly.

Agostin nodded. "I spotted them too. It's those Itiba Ara' from the harbor, the same couple from the tavern. What business could they possibly have with us?"

Jenaro grunted. "I think they might be Wanderers."

"We are no majick users," Agostin spat as he adjusted Rahe's pack.

"No, we are not, but maybe they overheard us at the tavern. Maybe they sensed something in us. Maybe what they call majick we refer to as the power of the cemi."

"It all seems a bit hypocritical," Agostin said with a frown. "Wanderers use majick themselves, yet they hunt and kill majick users."

Jenaro nodded. "They see their use of majick as harmless. They use the essences to understand foreign tongues, or as lamplight, or to create eternal fire. They hunt those who use it to greater degrees, in ways they deem dangerous."

Agostin shrugged, "I'll keep my eyes on them."

"As will I," Jenaro agreed.

Towering before them were the southernmost slopes of the

Taicarayas. The sun was slowly rising yet despite the morning rays, the mountains lay covered in shadow. The dark only increased as the path led them into the ironwood forest that choked up the slopes.

The ironwoods were towering trees of shimmering gray graphite bark with needles so dark and green they looked nearly black. The shimmering needles carpeted the ground like a brocade of jewels.

At the first junction, Jenaro and Agostin followed Rahe's directions and headed left. The overgrown thicket of a path was a steady incline that wound its way up to the peak. The only thing marking it as a path was the trees on either side that had yet to encroach on it.

"Rahe said the darkness begins not far after the fork," Jenaro whispered.

Agostin chuckled. "You don't have to whisper. We are not in the archives back home."

As soon as the words left Agostin's lips, darkness deeper than a starless night descended upon them. Jenaro nearly gasped as his vision was reduced to nothing. Even more alarming was the sudden and terrifying silence brought on by the dark. The hum of the insects stopped. The rustling of the branches ceased. No bird or creature dared make a sound. Jenaro held his breath for fear of disturbing whatever stalked the abyss before him.

"Agostin," Jenaro called barely above a whisper.

"Already on it," Agostin replied from the dark.

Jenaro heard his carib rustling around in his pack. The clank of metal and glass emerged, followed by a knife on stone. Soon, a small aura of ocher light surrounded them. Unfortunately, it did not cast farther than that.

"Is that as bright as it goes?" Jenaro asked.

"Unfortunately, so," Agostin answered.

"It'll have to do," Jenaro sighed. "I'm sure Opi will see it and introduce itself.

They continued slowly down the path. The light of the lamp revealed their surroundings with each step, but didn't show the ground any farther than an arm's length away. There was no way of knowing, before they got there, whether their next few steps forward would lead to more of the path or a sinkhole. Jenaro hazarded a look around. He even toyed with the idea of turning back, yet with a look behind he noticed the darkness swallowed their retreat. He wasn't even sure if what was behind still existed.

After several minutes of painfully slow progress, Jenaro heard a faint shambling in the deep before him. It was a distant sound but clear enough for him to recognize: wood scraping against wood, rubbing along the thicket of grass that made the path. Jenaro came to a halt and dropped to one knee. Agostin joined him by his side.

"Do you hear it?" Jenaro asked sotto voce.

Agostin nodded. "Like wind through the trees."

"Just like the stories."

"I don't see it though. Rahe claimed it was surrounded by torch bugs."

Jenaro nodded. "We should continue toward the sound."

They moved forward at a snail's pace, cautiously placing one foot in front of the other until the gentle green glow of a swarm of torch bugs appeared in the distance. This light was a beacon in the dark. It did not banish the darkness but stood out, nonetheless.

"There," Jenaro pointed.

Their pace quickened toward the slowly blinking green signals. Yet the torch bugs never seemed to move any closer. Before they realized it, Jenaro and Agostin were out of the forest, on the trail leading back to Stone Point. The torch bugs were gone, yet they were not alone. Standing before them on the road were the robed figures and top-knotted heads of the same two Itiba Ara' they had assumed were following them.

There was a moment of surprised hesitation by their appearance that was quickly followed by the ringing of steel from scabbards. Agostin dropped the lamp and immediately jumped in front of Jenaro, Rahe's axe in one hand, dagger in the other. The Itiba Ara' tossed their robes aside and assumed a side-by-side stance, each wielding large, single edged swords with curved blades. Beautifully intricate, gilded light mail–made for the deserts where they resided–protected their copper skin.

"Who are you? Why are you following us?" Agostin shouted, readying Rahe's axe.

"What business is it of yours where we decide to tread," the taller of the two Itiba shouted back in a thunderously deep voice.

"It becomes my business when we are threatened by Itiban Wanderers!" Agostin fired back.

"Gentlemen, please!" Jenaro cried, stepping from behind Agostin and sheathing his dagger. "There is no need for bloodshed this day." He put his hand on Agostin's shoulder and bowed his head before the Itiba. "I am Jenaro Albizu del Rios, son of the Cacique Marohu of the Andolins. This is my carib and friend, Agostin Anacaona. We search these woods for a wayward spirit."

The Itiba exchanged wary glances then reluctantly sheathed their blades.

"Then it seems our quarry is the same," the tall Itiba replied. He took a step forward and bowed slightly. "I am Aaru al'Yarra and this is my apprentice."

"Heba lo'Tane," his apprentice said with a bow, her voice as bright as her eyes.

"We heard rumblings of strange happenings in Cike'o.

Spriggans and sprites haunt the forests of the Taicarayas from the Summer Sea north, to the far reaches of the continent. The essences once sprang like water from the earth in these parts. The return of these creatures can only mean the majicks have returned."

"And you've come to harness the essences for your own foul deeds, haven't you?" Agostin accused, axe still at the ready.

Aaru's face grew grim. "Your master offers to treat with us. We sheath our weapons and still you hold your axe at the ready?" He turned his attention to Jenaro. "It may behoove you to muzzle your dog."

Agostin growled and took a step forward, placing himself between Jenaro and Aaru. He stood eye-to-eye with the Itiba, who was as lithe as a jungle cat, the polar opposite of the mountain that was Agostin. Heba stepped forward in response. Her hands were off her weapon, but her body tightly coiled like a viper ready to strike. Jenaro held his breath for a moment, afraid that any noise might cause bloodshed. Jenaro opened his mouth to speak, to send a swift rebuke at Agostin, but was surprised when his words were drowned out by a furious roar Jenaro had never heard before, echoing through the trees. The force of the blast made each of the four jump and turn, putting their backs toward one another.

"Yaya's mercy, what was that sound?" Jenaro asked.

"It is a baelor," Aaru responded, "an enormous sow, by the sound of it."

"We have never seen such creatures," Agostin spoke. "The Andolins do not have bears."

Heba's face grew grim. She nodded to the tree line behind them saying, "It seems introductions are inevitable."

Jenaro and Agostin quickly made an about face in time to see the beast lumbering out of the forest. Never had they seen such a monstrosity; larger and heavier than a yamuy by a large margin but with a face that could have belonged to a dog. It stood on all fours but easily dwarfed the Itiba. Its thick, black and brown fur rolled back and forth with each thunderous step. It grunted and rose to its hind legs, preferring to look down at them with its bloodthirsty glare. It raised its enormous paws, complete with terrifyingly long claws, and let loose a savage, slobbering howl that raised the hair on the back of Jenaro's neck.

"That, Andoli, is a baelor," Aaru said, sheathing his blade. "Run!"

They ran without hesitation from the crossroads up the path that led deeper into the ironwoods. The roar of the baelor continued to intensify as they ran, as if the bear was nipping at their heels. Only when greeted by the consuming blackness did the creature's howls cease to ring. A wave of silence washed over them. Only their breathing echoed in their ears.

"Damn that bear," Agostin grumbled in the dark. "I left the lamp at the crossroads."

"Fear not," Aaru said. Soon the four reluctant companions were bathed in a soft blue light. Unfortunately, as with the lamplight, the glow only extended around their persons.

Jenaro nodded at Aaru, whose lamp was nothing more than a luminous cerulean rod about the size of Rahe's axe handle. The Itiba held the rod in one hand and pointed it forward.

"How do you create light with no fire?" Jenaro asked.

Aaru's face remained stern as he ignored Jenaro's question. "We tried to track the beast but ended up back at the crossroads."

"The beast with the torch bugs swarming around it?" Jenaro questioned.

Aaru nodded and began to slowly trudge forward. "It's a spriggan, a magical creature of the forest. It's protecting something deeper inside."

"A spriggan? No, it's a cemi," Agostin corrected.

"A what?"

"A cemi," Jenaro repeated. "It's no magical creature. It's a spirit; a cemi of our people, the Andoli."

"Hmm," Aaru grunted. "Whatever it is, we must destroy it so we can find what it is hiding."

Without warning, Aaru began to jog down the path with Heba by his side, leaving Jenaro and Agostin in the dark. Both Andoli began to jog after the Itiba but stumbled over each other. Before they could rise and dust themselves off, they were out of the dark and back at the crossroads. The roars of the baelor had grown distant.

"The baelor crushed Rahe's lantern," Agostin lamented, raising the shattered remains of twisted metal and glass from the ground.

Moments later, Aaru and Heba appeared, both at a full sprint, and collided with the fallen Andoli, crashing to the ground in a heap of moans and groans.

"Impossible!" Aaru shouted as he climbed to his feet.

Heba rose to one knee, shaking her head at their predicament.

"Impossible," Aaru repeated, with marginally less fervor. "This power is beyond that any spriggan should possess."

"It's no spriggan," Agostin interjected through ragged breaths. "We told you–it's a cemi and if we plan on catching it, we're going about it entirely wrong."

Jenaro was doubled over, heaving, and coughing, trying to catch his breath from a Itiban boot to his stomach.

Agostin placed his hands on his head and began to pace.

Heba rose to her feet and helped Jenaro stand. Jenaro found the closest tree to lean against.

"You're right, my friend," Jenaro said. "Chasing

Opiyelguabiran has turned us into nothing more those failed hunters from the legend."

"This Opiyelguabiran, is a creature of the forest?" Heba asked.

"Heba, do not give credence to the religion of savages," Aaru grumbled.

Heba became angry. "Master, we cannot continue to run blindly into the forest only to return here. Maybe the beliefs of the Andoli hold a clue that will help us to our quarry."

"Your apprentice is right, Aaru," Jenaro said, rising from the tree. "If you continue to chase it, Opi will only lead you back where you started. It doesn't matter how ardently you try."

Heba turned back to Jenaro. She raised both his hands by way of apology and bowed her head slightly. "Please, tell us of this cemi of yours."

Jenaro spoke as he slowly started up the path. "Opiyelguabiran, or Opi as our new friend Rahe called it, is in essence simply a guide. It is the first spirit one sees upon death. Opi guides the dead to the *Moin Hupia* which takes souls to their final resting place, the third cave.

"Our behique tell stories of Opi, how many men tried to capture the beast for he resembled a great hound but could stalk through the jungles without disturbing other beasts. Yet, no matter how long they hunted, they always returned empty handed. It is said one hunter was lucky enough to snare him. Opi even followed the man out of the jungle then simply slipped his bonds and bounded back beyond the trees."

Heba nodded knowingly. "So, if what Agostin said is true, we have been going about it the wrong way."

"Yes, we have," Jenaro responded, nodding at Agostin.

Agostin nodded back.

"Tell us, Andoli, how do you plan to capture this Opi?" Aaru said, breaking his silence.

"I don't," Jenaro replied plainly.

"I beg your pardon?" Aaru uttered.

"We are not here to hunt the cemi," Jenaro informed the Itiba. "We want to find our friend's workshop and retrieve her father's possessions."

Jenaro noticed Aaru's agitation at the news, a flash of emotion he hid quite well.

"If we want Opi to lead us to the cabin," Jenaro continued, "to Rahe's father's workshop, we can't chase him. He won't cooperate. No bonds fashioned by mortals can tie it down."

"Then what is your plan?" Heba asked.

Jenaro stroked his beard and glanced skyward. "I have an idea. It's simple but might work to our advantage."

Confrontations

Jenaro led the party back into the darkness. Even after two journeys within, the transition remained startling. The sudden and complete darkness made Jenaro's heart skip a beat.

"No light," Jenaro commanded his followers.

"What do you mean, 'no light'?" Aaru snarled back.

"No light!" Jenaro snapped. "Opi is drawn to the light. Only the living carry lamps."

"Only the living fear the darkness and what creeps in the deep," Agostin added.

"We continue in the dark. If Rahe's directions were accurate, the path from the fork to her father's cabin is a straight-line up hill."

They fumbled onward, clutching at each other's shoulders and straps. More than once did they collide with each other. Aaru was completely unamused and cursed in Itiban with every fault and falter. Yet, they continued in this manner until the shambling echoes and glowing swarm marking the arrival of Opi appeared. Only this time, the dim effervescence provided a small measure of illumination to the world around them. Jenaro could make out a strange shape around which the swarm buzzed. He looked down and could see the silhouettes of his hands and the undergrowth that made up their path.

"We continue on this heading," Jenaro advised. "Ignore the cemi," he warned sternly.

The group pressed onward in silence, ignoring the light of Opi dancing to their left. The shambles followed them, as if the cemi could not handle being ignored. The swarm of torch bugs continued to highlight their passage. Faint, hollow howls reverberated from the wooden skin of the cemi until Opi itself was walking side-by-side with Jenaro. Jenaro looked down upon the face of his patron cemi; the face of a god. Its twisted visage was vaguely canine. It appeared to also resemble an Andoli, front legs and paws were human arms and hands. It had brambles wrapped around its neck with shoots of leaves jutting from every joint and crease in its wooden skin. Its eyes were hollow with glowing green orbs just as Rahe described.

The cemi seemed agitated. It was used to being followed and thus did not like following Jenaro and his band. Jenaro smiled and placed his hand on Opi's head between the tufts of bramble and leaf that Jenaro assumed were its ears. A muted whine echoed through the cemi's body.

Before long, Hano's workshop arose from the abyss. The pervading darkness hung heavy around the ironwood workshop, but a warm soft light emitted gently from its windows. Someone, or something, was home and had lit a fire.

Aaru was flabbergasted. "How did you know?" he asked.

Jenaro shrugged. "Opi is a hound. Hounds hate being ignored." He placed his hand on Opi's head and gave it a rub. Opi let forth another whine. Its eyes pleaded with him to turn back.

"It looks as if whatever spirit attacked Rahe is still inside," Agostin declared.

"A violent spirit resides within?" Heba asked, drawing her sword. "If that is the case, perhaps you should allow us to handle this, Jenaro."

Jenaro shook his head and ran his fingers through his hair. "I would exercise caution. Parley may be easier than open battle with a spirit we know nothing about."

"And we don't know if whatever is in there will be hostile toward us," Agostin added.

Opi whined again and began to back away.

"Your cemi seems to know," Aaru pointed out as he unsheathed his blade. "Stand aside, Andoli, I will dispose of whatever is in there."

Jenaro spun around and stared hard at Aaru. "No," he said. His voice was low and assertive. "Agostin and I will go in first. If things get violent, I will allow you to perform your Wanderer art."

At that Jenaro turned and walked to the workshop door without giving either Itiba a chance for retort.

The steps to the front porch creaked with Jenaro's weight. He cringed at the loss of the element of surprise more than the sudden noise. The wood of the porch moaned and groaned as he stepped to the door. Jenaro raised his fist to knock, but the door opened on its own. There came another creak behind him. Jenaro turned his head and saw Agostin frozen on the steps. His teeth were clenched and his shoulders tight as if readying for a blow that never came. Jenaro beckoned him to his side with a swift tilt of his head.

Inside the workshop resembled a beachhead after a hurricane. Nothing was in its right place. The table and chairs were upended. There was a smelting kiln next to the fireplace, both were absent of flame but emitting a mysterious glow regardless. Various tools were buried in the walls and ceiling between the kiln and the work bench where a simple woodcutter's axe was embedded in the top.

Sitting crossed legged by the hearth was a shadowy figure, about the height of a Cibao, but dark and translucent, distorting the world around it. Indeed, it seemed as if his flesh feasted upon the light, including that which unnaturally exuded from the hearth. Laying on the floor, resting on either side of the shade were Hano's things; a mallet and a set of tools on one side, a trade book and the gold and quicksilver bangle on the other. The figure delicately ran its fingers along the tools as if caressing the skin of a lover.

Jenaro looked at Agostin then motioned toward the figure.

Agostin shrugged and whispered, "What is it? I don't see anything."

"A spirit," Jenaro whispered back. Unsure how to make his presence known, Jenaro simply cleared his throat.

The shade turned its head but failed to rouse from its seat.

"Why do you sit alone, shade?" Jenaro asked politely.

At Jenaro's words, the shade lifted itself from the floor, bringing the mallet with it.

"You can see me?" it questioned, its voice cold and sad and sounding as if a multitude of voices were speaking in unison. It brought a chill to Jenaro's skin. Jenaro turned his head to Agostin, who shook his head to say he could not hear the voice.

"Yes, I can," Jenaro answered. "What are you?"

The shade was taken aback. It wavered slightly then took a step backward, dropping the mallet with a thud.

"I do not know, for I cannot sense or see what I inhabit," the shade explained. "I have never dwelt within such a thing; deep within the earth, yes, nestled with wood or stone, but never this."

Jenaro nodded. "Do you have a name then? Maybe with a name I can inform you of what you are."

The shade seemed to ponder the question. It fidgeted and twisted, contorting its body in peculiar fashion. After a while, it returned to its seat on the floor, staring into the vacant fireplace.

"Curious that such a question would evoke so many conflicting emotions in me," the shade finally replied. "I suspect I had a name once, as I suspect I have one now. But I have lost it. Indeed…this fact may be the reason for my anguish."

Jenaro took a cautious step forward and crouched, resting his hands on his knees. "Does this place feel familiar? Perhaps your identity is tied to this workshop?"

The shade fidgeted once more. "It fills me with nostalgia, this cabin does. The wood, the tools, even the air that fills this room are memories long forgotten. Yet, I also feel dread, a pang of fear as if tortured by the dark fantasy of violent happenings."

Jenaro smiled, suppressing a chuckle. "Well, I would say you are at least something instead of nothing, for only a something would be able to feel such things. A nothing would feel, well, nothing."

The shade shifted. "Perhaps, but to be something means an existence I cannot confirm, for I know not if I have existed before or will exist after this moment."

"I don't understand, shade. How can you exist and not exist, feel and not feel, be but not be? A being cannot be such a series of contradictions and manage to thrive as you have in this place. Your very existence before me swallows the light of my world. Your influence has expanded beyond this cabin to the surrounding wood. Soon, it will overtake the trees and flow down the slopes to the towns below. Surely only something can do that. If you were nothing, or nobody, such a feat would be impossible."

The shade found Jenaro musings to his liking. The darkness of the figure seemed to pulse and change shape, only to return to the silhouette of the Cibao. It chuckled.

"May I share my thoughts?" Jenaro asked.

The shade nodded.

"I believe you are, or once were, Hano of Stone Point, father of Rahe. This is his workshop, after all, and your silhouette resembles that of a Cibao, which he was."

"It was Hano of Stone Point, but no longer," Aaru declared from the doorway.

The words made Jenaro, Agostin, and the shade all shift their gazes to the entrance. Jenaro rose from his crouch and the shade stood in response.

"It is now simply an abomination," Aaru sneered with malice.

Agostin stepped back and placed himself between Aaru and Jenaro. He lifted Rahe's axe to the ready. "What does that mean, Aaru?" he asked.

"Yes, Aaru, what do you mean?" came a question from Heba who appeared behind her master.

Aaru grunted. "Hano of Stone Point wasn't an ordinary enchanter. His enchantments went beyond those which are sanctioned by the Scholia Regium, those deemed safe. It is why he relocated here, to the Ironwoods."

"And as Wanderers you hunt and murder such people," Jenaro accused the Itiba.

"No, we don't kill," Heba offered. "Right, Master Aaru?" Her voice wavered. Her resolve was shaken, her tone skeptical. "Hano of Stone Point had become unstable. He began to imbue items with dark enchantments, curses, majicks used to kill and maim. Isn't that right, Master Aaru?" Aaru remained silent. "Master Aaru?"

Aaru inhaled deeply. "Not entirely, Heba."

"What?" she gasped.

"I kill when necessary. And the misuse of the majicks is necessary. It is what brought the wrath of the gods upon our people so many ages past. I will not stand idly by while the fires of heaven rain upon this world."

"You killed him," Jenaro said quietly, ominously. "You killed Hano of Stone Point."

"I killed him to protect us! All of us!" he shouted. "Enchanting tools that never blunt or blades that do not require sharpening is one thing. Hano's enchantments created fire! So yes, I killed him. Then, as the body lay there, something happened that I did not anticipate. Hano was enchanting when I came upon him. He was connected to the one essence, body and soul. When he died upon my blade, his soul bonded with the essence. The essence drank of Hano's soul and vomited out the abomination you see before you, only, I could not slay it, for his daughter approached. I had to escape and plan my return."

"You!" a voice boomed from the shade, deep and full of anger. It was one voice, one mind, shouting in defiance.

Jenaro and Agostin turned to witness the shade transform. The figure of the Cibao stretched and bloated and soon tore itself into a cloud of dust and darkness. It filled the cabin with the screams of a thousand voices, banshees crying out for vengeance.

"Tell me you can see and hear that, Ago," Jenaro said.

"Oh I can definitely see and hear that." Wasting no time, Agostin grabbed Jenaro and dove aside from the raging shade. Aaru began to circle his quarry while Heba hesitated. She unsheathed her blade but did not engage the shade. She kept her distance, eyeing both her master and the abyssal creature.

With another blast of energy, the shade shifted into another form. It was an enormous, flaming beast, fire dancing and leaping from its frame. It was tall and horned; even with legs bent it towered over Aaru. It held a claymore made entirely of flame. The fiery shade let forth a mighty roar that sounded like a raging fire.

Agostin and Jenaro began to crawl toward the door but were impeded by a wall of flame created by a sweep of the fiery shade's claymore. The shade leapt and slashed at Aaru mercilessly, burning air and wood and metal with each sweep. Agostin pulled Jenaro to his feet. Both Andoli dove over the flame and landed in front of Heba.

"Get behind me!" Heba yelled as he took a step forward, sword at the ready.

Jenaro didn't hesitate. He pushed Agostin out of the workshop. He then placed a hand on Heba's shoulder and nodded at him. Heba nodded back then turned to battle.

The shade swung wildly at Aaru, who parried every strike. Undeterred by his agility, the shade reared back and charged. Aaru nimbly sidestepped and slashed downward. His blade sliced through the shade like cutting through air. The miss threw Aaru off balance. He stutter-stepped and stumbled forward trying to regain his footing. Aaru's eyes went wide, and, in his moment of hesitation, he was struck by the fiery shade's sweeping right arm. The flame hit his armor in an explosion of sparks and embers and sent Aaru flying toward Heba. The two Itiba careened off the porch and into yard. Heba rebounded first and, as he rose, pushed Aaru back at the shade. Her master glanced back at her, face full of anger and confusion.

Jenaro watched from the porch, wincing at each strike. The fires that blasted forth from the shade burned hard, quickly consuming, and spreading throughout the workshop and surrounding yard. He grabbed Agostin by the sleeve and the two rushed from the porch, putting distance between the raging fire, the shade, and themselves.

Aaru raised his sword. He sneered and taunted the shade, saying, "I will not back down, abomination! I will destroy you and the essence you merged with!" He furiously rushed forward, yet before Aaru could move to strike, the tip of an Itiban blade burst through his chest piece. His eyes went wide. His mouth filled with blood. Heba removed her blade from the body with a cry of anguish.

"Heba," Aaru said as he spat blood from his mouth. "Why?"

He began to collapse and Heba threw herself on the ground next to him, cradling his fall.

"You murdered him," Heba said through sobs. "We're supposed to help those who wield the majicks not kill them. Ours is not to pass judgement."

Aaru coughed. "And yet…" he trailed off, slowly raising his hand to the wound on his chest, "you so easily judge me." They were his last words. Aaru was no more.

Heba cried out in grief and torment, placing her forehead on that of her master. She sobbed freely, disregarding the burning workshop or the angry shade.

Realizing his quarry had been defeated, the shade extinguished the fires that surrounded it, including the blaze that ate away at the workshop. It slowly diminished in size until it was once again the size of a Cibao.

Heba gently set Aaru's head on the ground and slowly rose to face the creature. "Hano of Stone Point!" she cried out. "With the blood of my master, Aaru al'Yarra, your vengeance has been achieved. Be at peace." Heba sheathed her blade then spoke in Itiban, raising his index and middle finger to her lips.

The shade took a step forward and spoke. Its voice had changed and was now one steady tone, warm and baritone. "Do not be too harsh on her. She only did what needed to be done."

Jenaro raised his hands and said, "We do not pass judgment on the ways of the Itiba Ara'," he hesitated then continued, "Hano of Stone Point."

The shade's shoulders lifted at the name. It flickered in excitement. "I was once Hano of Stone Point, enchanter, registered and recognized artisan of the Scholia Regium, but no longer."

"My friend and I came here on errand for your daughter," Jenaro responded. "Do you remember Rahe?"

The shade's head dropped. "My daughter…" it trailed off.

"Hano?" Agostin called to the shade.

"I didn't mean to attack her," the shade said. "I couldn't…I–I–there was nothing I could do. I had no control."

"It was the essences, Hano," Heba said. She tried to place a reassuring hand on the shade, but only succeeded in grabbing air.

"But now you are free?" Agostin asked.

The shade remained silent, pensive. It moved to the fireplace, before turning back to the others. He bowed to Jenaro and Agostin. "You, Andoli brethren, and you," it nodded at Heba, "Itiba Ara' have risked your lives to avenge my death. Yet there is only one way I can be at peace."

Jenaro exchanged curious glances with Agostin and Heba.

"How can we help you be at peace?" Jenaro asked.

The shade answered: "The essences that inhabit my spirit must be destroyed…and I along with them."

A silence swept over the group. Gazes were averted. Breaths were held.

"The majicks are not an unlimited resource," Heba informed the group. "They can be extinguished, like a flame."

"How does one extinguish such a resource?" Jenaro asked.

Heba exhaled and grimaced. "Usage," she said plainly.

They watched from the path as the workshop went up in the raging flames of the reignited shade. Heba, holding her master's sword and satchel, had placed the body of Aaru in the workshop to be burned in the ways of her people. Agostin held Hano's belongings, and Jenaro placed a hand on the head of Opiyelguabiran who sat at his heels. The blaze burned hotter and brighter than anything Jenaro had ever experienced. Amid the roaring fire, Jenaro could just make out the voice of Hano. The fire blazed until every scrap of ironwood had turned to ash. With nothing left to consume, the fire slowly dwindled until even the embers faded to wisps of smoke.

Opi led the party out of the forest. The darkness that once pervaded every corner of the slopes now slowly dissipated as they walked. Trees began to take shape. Insects and birds started their discordant symphony. Jenaro inhaled deeply, taking in the cool mountain air saturated with the smell of oxidized metal.

"Just another reason they call them ironwoods," Jenaro mused.

Heba nodded. "The smell? I never thought of it before."

They reached the crossroads and Jenaro noticed Opi was no longer at his side. He turned back toward the path that led to the cabin. The timbered hound sat in the distance, just in front of the tree line. Jenaro could make out the glimmer of the torch bugs. Standing next to the hound was Maboya, but not as Jenaro had ever seen. The cemi looked Andoli, but with sallow skin. He wore an enormous, feathered headdress and traditional hides. *His true form?* Jenaro thought.

Maboya placed a hand on Opiyelguabiran's head and the hound's tail began to wag. Jenaro's face grew cold as he watched the cemi interacting. He knew they were connected; he knew they both dealt with souls after they left the second cave, but Jenaro hated that his patron cemi seemed so at ease next to Maboya. He stood for a long moment, gazing at the two until Opi let loose a sorrowful howl from its hollow innards then slowly disappeared into the underbrush. Maboya followed.

Rahe listened intently as Jenaro recalled their journey to Hano's workshop. He confirmed her descriptions of both the cemi and the spirit. When he revealed that the shade was really her father,

Rahe's face blanched. Heba knelt by the Cibao, held her hand, and told her of her own part in the tale, of Aaru's betrayal and avenging her father's death.

Agostin presented Rahe with her father's belongings. All the tears she had been holding back poured forth like a waterfall. Jenaro joined Heba by her side and embraced Rahe. While Rahe sobbed, Agostin grabbed four cups of humery and poured them each a glass.

"To Hano of Stone Point," Agostin toasted.

"To Hano of Stone Point," they echoed in response.

The next morning, Jenaro, Agostin, and Heba said their goodbyes to Rahe. Agostin embraced her and the two fought back tears. Rahe then handed her father's axe to Agostin.

"My father imbued this axe with some sort of majick," she said. "It's never needed sharpening as long as I've lived. Keep it, with my thanks."

Agostin smiled and nodded. "It is indeed a righteous gift, Rahe." His face lit up.

Heba nodded and bowed gracefully, leaving Jenaro to say his goodbyes.

"It was a good thing you did here, Jenaro," Rahe commended. "A right good thing."

Jenaro smiled and embraced Rahe one last time.

"You should thank Agostin and the rest of my crew," Jenaro commented. "Without them I might never have made it to your shores."

Rahe smiled back. "My da once told me, 'You can tell the measure of a man by the company he keeps.' You, Jenaro Albizu del Rios, in the company of Itiba Ara', and Cibao Ara', and Andoli, are a measure I cannot even fathom."

"But you, Rahe of Stone Point, are just like me. Here you

stand, able to call Itiba Ara' and Andoli your friends," Jenaro replied, then embraced her once more before waving goodbye.

Agostin and Heba waited for Jenaro in silence, standing side-by-side just beyond Rahe's front porch. The sun beamed bright. The smog of Cu' Ciba filled the morning sky. A horn blast in the distance marked the arrival of the steam train heading from Stone Point to Cu' Ciba.

"It is our third day in Cu' Ciba and we have yet to enjoy ourselves, eh Agostin," Jenaro said to his carib with a slap on his shoulder. "I wonder how the crew is faring."

Agostin shrugged, "We'll find out soon enough, I suppose."

"And you, Heba?" Jenaro asked. "What are your plans? We have room for one more aboard my ship."

Heba bowed slightly. "Alas, I cannot accept your offer, Jenaro, at least, not now. The death of my master requires me to return to Itibanen. His deceit must be made known to my order."

"What becomes of you?" Agostin asked.

Heba sighed. "Reprimand and discipline, I presume, although, I cannot speak to the severity of either."

Jenaro placed his hand on Heba's shoulder. "If you are ever in need, I will gladly stand on your behalf."

Heba nodded and smiled. "I will tell my people of your deeds here, Jenaro del Rios," she said. "If ever you or your kin sail to my shores, you will be welcome in the halls of Bo' Choreto, capital of Itibanen."

Heba stepped back and bowed her head in reverence. Jenaro smiled and pulled her close for an embrace. Heba was caught off guard but quickly welcomed the sign of affection. Heba then turned to leave but bowed reverently at Agostin.

Agostin extended the palm of peace and nodded in return.

They waited and watched as Heba walked south out of town, toward the cliffs on the eastern side of the peninsula.

"Where to now?" Agostin asked.

"Luysa and the crew are most likely wondering where we are at," Jenaro said. "I think we should make our way back to the docks."

"In that case, do you think we could find a cask of that humery?" Agostin asked as they started toward the train station. "We cannot leave Cike'o without purchasing a cask of humery."

Scales That Adorn the Serpent

…three years after leaving Puerto Zafiro

The Storm

A massive clap of thunder exploded on the horizon. It split the evening sky and sent a shockwave across countless miles of the Summer Sea. The blast hit *Moin Hupia* just as Jenaro, Agostin, and their crew finished their evening meal. Everyone jumped in place. Hearts raced. Eyes bulged. Jenaro and Agostin quickly turned their heads to the horizon. The sky was a swirling abyss, complete with flashes of lightning leaping from cloud to cloud. They billowed skyward in the shape of an anvil. The warm sea breeze quickly transformed into a cyclone. The sea became unruly.

Jenaro looked at his crew. This was the third storm in as many days and was shaping up to be the most intense they had experienced since leaving Puerto Zafiro three years earlier. They stared at Jenaro; eyes red and surrounded by dark circles, faces full of dread. Jenaro gritted his teeth and nodded. Their faces quickly transformed to sudden determination as Agostin shouted orders.

"Reduce sails!" Agostin barked.

Jenaro and Luysa ran to the wheel. His hands wrapped around the jet-black wood as the first swell hit the *Moin Hupia*. The wave slammed against the hull and dropped the ship like a boulder off a cliff. Jenaro nearly lost hold of the wheel until Luysa ran up beside him and added her strength. The drumming rain immediately worsened to a violent crashing of hail.

The crew climbed the masts like squirrels, chaotic and quick. Yet, for all their speed, Agostin was the definition of swift. He worked with the quickness of a barracuda, slicing through the waves to nab its prey. The main sail was down and Agostin halfway back to the deck before the rest finished. Agostin slipped a step from the bottom and landed awkwardly on his right leg just as a swell hit the ship sending a rushing wave laterally across the deck. One minute Ago struggled to his feet, the next minute he and a handful of sailors were gone. Jenaro cried out in horror.

Jenaro let go of the wheel, desperate to search for Ago, but Luysa's firm grip on his arm stopped him. "I cannot steer without your help!"

Jenaro growled, knowing she was right and returned to the wheel. A moment later, Jenaro saw Agostin, in the midst of the gale, hauling himself and one other man back aboard, right hand wrapped up tightly in a line from the center mast. Their eyes immediately met, both men nodding with palpable relief.

The storm churned hard, fiercely raging harder and harder as each moment passed. He turned to Luysa. She was still standing by his side, knees bent, one hand white knuckling the nearest line, the other on the wheel. There came an unending flash of lightning and thunder so terrible Jenaro felt it shaking his bones. The hail gave way to stinging, sharp rain that assaulted their face and hands.

Agostin appeared by his side. He was yelling, but Jenaro could not make out his words over the roar of the wind and crashing assault of the waves. Agostin had tied the line he carried around his waist which connected to the nearest railing. He reached around Jenaro's waist and did the same, then moved to Luysa before fighting his way back to the edge.

Together, they battled with each swell and depression. Jenaro gritted his teeth though every crash of water that quaked through the hull of the *Hupia*. The ship let out a sickly groan after each hit. Every time Jenaro needed a reprieve, Agostin would step in. Agostin would rotate out and hand the helm to Luysa and then back again. It felt like hours. It felt like days. Then, as quickly as it appeared, the storm lost its fury.

The last droplets of rain diminished to nothing. The throaty bellow of the storm slowly dissipated. The lightning was no more, and the thunder diminished until all they heard was the gentle lapping of the Summer Sea against the hull of the *Hupia*. Jenaro heaved and placed his forehead on the wheel, thankful for the respite.

After a moment of silence, he scanned the deck of the *Hupia*. There was still a layer of icy stones about the deck. Each line and sail remained perfectly intact thanks to whatever unholy force protected the ship. Agostin sat with his back against the gunwale holding the frayed remains of the rope that had once held them. Luysa's hat was gone, and the sleeves of her shirt had ripped to shreds revealing the dark purple marks of the architus.

Jenaro nodded at Luisa. "Surely that was worse than the architus."

Luysa only shook her head.

Jenaro took a breath and said, "I need a head count and a damage report. I fear we may have lost a few of our crew."

Agostin rubbed his aching leg but said, "Aye aye, captain," and hobbled down the stairs.

"Luysa, can you head below and assess the damage?"

"Aye, captain," Luysa said and took a step forward. She crossed her arms on her chest and said, "I think you're right. I saw the two get thrown overboard."

Jenaro hung his head. "There's was nothing we could do, right? The sea, there was no way to go after them."

Luysa shook her head. "It's not for you argue over what Guabancex and Guatauba take from those who sail on their ocean."

An hour later, Jenaro reconvened with Agostin and Luysa in his cabin. The captain's quarters were as much of a mess as they could have expected. The tossing of the ship scattered Jenaro's belongings from hull to hull. There was broken glass and spilled rum everywhere. Agostin leaned against the bulkhead, Luysa against the door.

"Damage report?" Jenaro asked.

Agostin spoke first. "Three staysails and a mizzen sail, the four we had the most trouble with, were torn to shreds. A jib is completely missing, probably torn off by the winds. The foremast took some damage from the hail as did just about every deck on the ship." Agostin took a breath before saying. "Including the two you saw, we lost eleven sailors."

Jenaro hung his head and grief before asking, "Luysa, how did everything look below deck?"

Luysa frowned. "Hail damage. Water damage. Bulkheads missing planks. And we're taking on a lot of water."

"I thought this ship was the ship of Maboya, some sort of majickal vessel," Agostin stated angrily. "How does a storm damage it?"

"Maybe it was no normal storm," Jenaro said.

"Are you saying this is another cemi thing?" Agostin asked.

"It could be. I'm not ruling it out," Jenaro stated. "What could damage a vessel from a cemi other than another cemi? Think about it?"

Agostin scoffed.

"What's the plan, captain?" Luysa asked. "The crew is

banged up. All our rations are soaked with sea water. We're missing sails. We can't limp around like this for long, especially taking on water.

"When last you checked, what was the closest port?" Jenaro asked Luysa.

Luysa shrugged, "Kauhale, I think. We were due west of there, or at least of the Hal'e archipelago. As fast as this ship sails it wouldn't take long to get there."

Jenaro groaned. "Is there another option?"

Luysa stood up straight and shook her head. "No, Hal'e was the closest by far. We could try for Sandria, one of the ports in the west, but they are more than a couple days away. And with our damage, we may not make it."

"She's right, Jenaro, it has to be Hal'e," Agostin agreed. "Let's not forget about all these storms we've been encountering. Three in as many days…if that trend holds, we'll hit another big gale this exact time tomorrow. If we decide to sail to Sandria, that puts us in the path of another storm. If we sail to Hal'e, we can get to port before having to ride out yet another one."

"I doubt we can ride out another storm," Luysa chimed in.

"If it has to be Hal'e then it has to be Hal'e," Jenaro said reluctantly.

The three gathered the crew and informed them of their plans. The sore and banaged group of ten sailors got to work readying the sails. Luysa returned to the helm. With the help of her guidestone, she navigated the *Moin Hupia* due west to the coast of the Hal'e archipelago. Shortly before noon the following day, Agostin spotted the verdant haze of land. Jenaro examined the skies and noticed that not a single cloud stood over the now visible islands. Mysteriously, the cover was thick and dark several miles from shore, surrounding the archipelago in a strange bubble of blue skies and cool breezes.

As if on cue, *Moin Hupia* reached the shallower waters of the Summer Sea closer to shore and stopped moving. The harbor was in sight, an easy row away, yet the *Hupia* refused to move. They dropped anchor and met in Jenaro's cabin.

Malu the Shipwright

The ship's condition had worsened by the time it stopped in the harbor outside of Kauhale. The damage to the mast formed a crack that ran from the deck halfway up its length and threatened to sever it entirely. The remaining sails showed more wear than initially thought. The bilge pumps struggled to keep the water out of the lower decks even after Jenaro assigned two sailors at a time in rotating shifts to keep them going. Jenaro felt an overwhelming fear that he would lose his prized possession, the ship gifted to him by Atabey, the vessel he won from Maboya. He called Agostin and Luysa to his quarters once more.

"There are some matters that complicate our arrival in Kauhale," Jenaro began. "I wager the island will not be the most welcoming place to me."

"Why is that?" Luysa asked.

Jenaro nodded and lifted a hand as if to say he'd explain later. "To make things even worse, I don't even know if there is a shipwright in the whole of Ke' that could repair a ship not of this world. Maybe once, in the age of majick, before the Itiba Ara's war, but not now."

"What should we do?" Agostin said.

"That's exactly why I've called you here," Jenaro replied. "We can try to find materials to save the *Moin Hupia*, or we can scuttle the ship and hope we can find another one."

"That'll be like trading gold for slop," Agostin groaned. Luysa hmphed.

Jenaro turned his attention to his navigator. "Do you have

any other ideas, Luysa? You've been at sea longer than I have. Maybe there's something I don't know about."

Luysa grunted softly. "I know a man in Kauhale. He goes by Malu or used to." They remained silent, waiting to hear more. Luysa sighed and removed her guidestone from its pouch. "The voyage where I encountered the architus was rife with misery, chief among these being the damage to my stone. It cracked, split in two, no longer showed me the way. The waters led me here, to Kauhale where I met Malu. He's skilled. He can fix things, things that can't be fixed. He fixed my stone. He…attempted to fix my arm. Maybe he can fix the *Moin Hupia*."

Agostin rose and said, "Then what are we waiting for? Take us to this Malu!"

Jenaro looked upon the capital of Hal'e as Agostin and Luysa rowed. In many ways, Hal'e was reminiscent of The Andolins. The blue-green water of the bay shimmered like a jewel. Hundreds of sails dotted the harbor creating a billowy white cloud upon the surface of the waves. He could see the entire city from the boat, spread out from the shoreline, up the mountain slopes. They passed several smaller vessels and were surprised to receive warm welcomes from each, waves, shouts of greeting, even a horn blast.

"If I am completely honest, Jenaro, I am not excited to be returning to Hal'e," Luysa said.

"Why is that?" Agostin asked.

"I've never arrived in Hal'e thanks to good circumstances," Luysa said. "It's always because of death or destruction. This place just feels wrong. Always has."

Jenaro nodded. "If I am completely honest Luysa, I am also

not excited. I would be uncomfortable under the best of circumstances."

Luysa asked, "Why is that?"

"Do you not know?" Agostin asked. "Our dear captain here was once betrothed to a princess of Hal'e."

Luysa's hard set face softened. What might have been a smile twisted the corners of her mouth. "Then the rumors were true. I remember hearing this. I had just hung up my captain's hat."

"Don't look so smug, either of you," Jenaro groaned.

They moored the dingy at the first pier they found. The beaches that ran up and down the main island of the Hal'e archipelago were as white as a pearl. The capital city of Kauhale lined the beaches with towering buildings. In the distance, shrouded in mist, was Pele, the volcano that spawned the archipelago. It would be an ideal place for rest and relaxation, had circumstances been different.

They entered the city proper. Luysa led the way. Kauhale's streets were livelier than Jenaro imagined for a normal afternoon. Men and women wearing hats of incredible sizes and shapes pushed carts full of fresh fish and clams or brightly woven fabrics. Street performers playing steel drums and flutes entertained for pocket change.

The brick pathways were laid out in a near perfect grid. The buildings were mostly wood, but plenty of fired clay bricks could be seen in every foundation. Many were open on all sides, save for a few sets of load-bearing walls, to allow the free movement of the warm ocean breeze throughout the edifice. Restaurants, taverns, inns, even merchant shops were breezy, open-air buildings.

The residents of Kauhale were as colorful as the buildings, dressed in fabrics of pink, white, and turquoise with flowers and feathers in oranges and blues hanging everywhere. Women wore long, floral printed skirts, and those who weren't topless wore thin airy tops. The men wore shorter skirts that wrapped around their torso and across one shoulder. All wore necklaces of flowers or shells as well as studs or hoops in their ears, noses, and brows. Each was also covered with geometric tattoos, some forming whales or dragons, others hibiscus blooms.

Luysa turned down a narrow, less populated street. The shop all had signs with green symbols painted on them and interesting, flora and fauna related names like The Honest Herb, Uluwehi's Garden, and Iekika's Potions and Tinctures. At the end of the block was a small, nondescript building that appeared weathered to the point of instability. The door was propped open, there was no sign out front, and there appeared to be nobody inside.

"Here we are," Luysa declared in a less than enthusiastic voice. "Right where I left it."

Jenaro stepped forward and entered. The building was sparsely lit. Most of the light came from open windows and one candelabrum with only two of its three candles lit, resting on a counter. Despite its exterior, the inside was surprisingly clean and tidy, bookshelves with neatly stacked volumes stood behind the counter and on either side of a door. Various nautical equipment hung from the walls as well as aged and rusty tools of the trade. A glass case held a variety of tools, each labeled with a card holding a description and a price. Four wicker chairs sat in seemingly random spots about the floor.

"Hello? Is anybody here? I am looking for Malu," Jenaro announced from the counter.

There immediately came a crash from beyond the door followed by a long string of curses. The door flew open and a husky young Hal'e rushed to the counter. He wore a sleeveless shirt and a blue and pink striped skirt. His warm, golden eyes sparkled, and a permanent smile was transfixed on his pudgy face. He was sweating profusely which plastered his thick black hair against his forehead.

"Hello, hello! Welcome to…" the youth's proclamation was cut short. "I see you've returned," he said, looking past Jenaro. Jenaro glanced over his shoulder and noticed Luysa standing just behind him. "Are you still unhappy with your arm?" the chubby youth said from the counter.

Luysa glared and held out her scarred, purple arm. "You said no mark. You said the procedure would leave no mark!" She stomped toward the counter, but Agostin outstretched his arm and caught her midstride. The boy nearly tripped on his own two feet as he backpedalled away from her.

"So, I was wrong," the boy behind the counter said. "At least I saved the arm. It could have been worse. And it was your idea anyway. You know I only work on inanimate objects!"

Jenaro was puzzled. "Wait a minute, are you Malu, the same Malu Luysa claimed can fix the unfixable?"

The boy bowed his head. "I am, and if you are an associate of Luysa's I should expect a majickal sword or enchanted sextant or some other absurd oddity that broke in a painfully ridiculous way. My talents are wasted on such."

"Oh, it's much bigger than a sword or a sextant," Agostin stated.

Jenaro shook his head in disbelief. "You can't be older than thirteen. How did you work on Luysa's arm and her guidestone. That happened before Ago and I were even born!"

"It's him alright," Luysa grumbled as she took a seat in one of the wicker chairs. "Go ahead, tell them maje."

"Maje?" Agostin and Jenaro said in unison.

Malu smiled at Jenaro. "The last of my kind. I was trained in Cu' Ciba at the Scholia Regium."

"Impossible," Agostin said. "The Scholia hasn't trained majicians in centuries."

Malu sighed. "Close the door, will you Luysa?" He waited until Luysa returned to her seat, then said, "I was one of the last groups of majes to graduate. Now, they only train lesser users, enchanters or illusionists. After the cleansing, my kind went into hiding. It was easy for us, our majick gave us latent abilities, things the Wanderer's couldn't sense with their diviner rods. I thought of hiding, going to the Andolins or Sandria, but ended up back here, back home."

"But that would make you hundreds of years old," Jenaro said. "I mean, To'guey once told me to wield the essences required considerable sacrifice, but I had no idea."

"It's the curse of the maje, Jenaro," Luysa said. "He isn't as young as he looks. The majick…it does things to his body. He is young in body, but his mind and spirit have lived for decades longer than I, centuries. He will likely look like that when he dies. If he dies. Malu may live forever, but he'll never see the third cave."

"It's true," Malu said. "Here I stand before you, body not a hair over thirteen, mind just under a thousand."

"I believe it," Agostin interrupted. "Jenaro, we've seen strange things together, but Malu would not be the only majick user we've encountered." Agostin released his axe and showed it to the boy. "Hano of Stone Point made and enchanted this axe. We met him in Cike'o."

"Hano…" Malu's voice faded. "I remember him. He did good work. How is he?"

"He died," Jenaro said softly. "Killed by Wanderers."

Malu sighed and shook his head. "I suppose it was only a matter of time. Death comes for us all, am I right? But enough about me. Who are you and what do you have for me? It's been ages since I've plied my trade on something other than a fork."

"My apologies, I am Jenaro, this is Agostin," Jenaro said, giving the palm of peace and gesturing to his friend.

Malu nodded. "Well, Jenaro, I am the best in Hal'e, maybe even the best in Ke'. Just don't hold my mess with Luysa's arm against me. So, what is it? The axe?"

Jenaro chuckled. "No, Agostin was not lying. It is a bit bigger than a sword or sextant."

Malu stood on the dock next to their dinghy and stared at the shadowy black ship moored in the deep waters of the harbor. The *Moin Hupia* looked weathered and ancient, even to Jenaro, a far cry from what it once was. "A ship. You have an majickal ship? The power it must have taken to create that thing! A whole ship! And of that size? How are the Wanderers not on your trail."

"It's more otherworldy than majickal," Jenaro said.

"So, the Wanderers don't really care about it," Agostin added.

"The enormity!" Malu gasped.

"It is large and has taken a lot of damage," Jenaro said. "It may not even be salvageable."

"I can't even begin to fathom what it's been through what with the storms we've been having. But a ship?" Malu shook his head. "That's impossible!"

Jenaro sighed. "Then I guess we have only one course action. Luysa, inform the crew to abandon ship."

"Now hold on just a second," Malu said turning to face Jenaro. He looked stern, angry almost. "Just because I said it's impossible doesn't mean I won't take the job."

"What?" Jenaro asked in confusion.

"This is just the challenge I've been looking for. No more knives and forks. No more swords and sextants. An entire ship!" Malu laughed maniacally. "Malu the shipwright is at your service, Jenaro."

Jenaro chuckled. "Well, okay then. What exactly do you need to get started?"

"Just my tool kit," Malu said with a grin, rubbing his hands together. "Just my tool kit."

"Luysa, do you think you could accompany Malu back to his shop to get his tools?" Jenaro asked the navigator.

"If it's what you require, captain," Luysa replied flatly. "And you?"

"If tools are all Malu need, then we have plenty of coin for a feast. Agostin and I will head to the markets to replace and resupply all our ruined rations. The crew deserves to eat and drink well tonight."

"I wouldn't say no to some Oleloan cuisine," Agostin said.

"And no need to wait for us, Luysa," Jenaro continued. "Once you return with the tools, go ahead and head back to the *Moin Hupia*. We'll signal when we're ready or just hire one of these locals to take us out there."

Luysa nodded and grabbed Malu by the arm. "Come on, little boy. Let's go home."

"Little boy?!" Malu pulled his arm from her grip. "You're lucky I like you, Luysa."

An Evening of Surprises

Agostin and Jenaro spent the day at the market trading Andoli marks for much needed supplies. After a day of bartering, the pair found themselves with several wagon loads of goods and in need of a fresh meal. Agostin asked around and was directed to a local eatery farther inland, closer to the palace, called "The Offering." Jenaro expressed his concern but relented after Agostin described the Oleloan cuisine.

The restaurant was small but visibly well-trafficked. Clear pathways to the counter and around every table showed in the worn wood floor. The décor appeared genuinely aged and stately, not purchased that way for aesthetic purposes. The droopy, fan blades turned by a thin adolescent pedalling a series of mechanical gears provided a welcome breeze and wafted the smell of roasted beef, pork, and chicken. Jenaro found a table and Agostin hurried to the counter to pay for a meal.

Jenaro sat near the enormous bay doors that opened to the street, soaking in the sights and sounds of Kauhale. An elderly couple sat at the table just outside the window from him. Jenaro couldn't help but overhear their conversation as he people watched.

Agostin returned with a plate of skewered beef and vegetables sitting atop a mound of fragrant seasoned rice and two large mugs of a white, milky beverage. "They call it Kalapa. It's like alcoholic coconut milk."

"Sounds amazing," Jenaro said as he took a sip. "Tastes amazing, too."

"I guess our detour to Kauhale wasn't as painful as you

though it would be," Agostin said as he lifted a skewer from the plate.

"Not at all," Jenaro replied. "But it has been interesting."

"Malu, right?" Agostin asked.

Jenaro nodded as the couple outside stood up and left their table. "Yes, for the most part. But listen to this. I overheard that couple talking about rumors of human sacrifices."

Agostin shook his head, swallowed a mouthful of rice, and said, "Do the Hal'e still practice that?"

"I don't know, but they seemed like it was old news. As if everyone knew the royal family offered human sacrifices to a god at the peak of Mount Pele."

"You royals and your weird relationships to the gods," Agostin chuckled.

"It makes me curious though," Jenaro said. "I don't believe in coincidence. I don't believe we just happened to land in Kauhale. What if there is a cemi up there, Guabancex or Guataba, controlling the weather? What if they sacrifice to appease the cemi?"

"Please, Jenaro, I'm begging you, let's not make this about the cemi," Agostin said, taking a swig of his kalapa. "Can we just enjoy a nice meal together?"

Jenaro laughed then noticed Agostin was not. He sat motionless with a skewer halfway to his mouth. Jenaro turned slowly. Immediately behind him was a young woman. She was of above-average height for a Hal'e, muscular but lithe. Her skin was a ruddy mahogany, her hair dark, shaved on one side and short on the other, just past her slightly pointed ears. She wore an airy, cream-colored linen tunic with a black, leather bodice peeking from her open collar. She had a green canvas skirt with black shorts underneath. Straps covered her legs down to her laced-up sandals. Her face was plain, but not homely, and her gray eyes burned like a strange, ethereal fire. She held a long, thin dirk to Jenaro's neck.

"An Andoli should not worry about the practices of the Hal'e," the woman said in their own tongue.

"Your Coquien is nearly accent free," Agostin said. "You must have studied with an Andoli."

The woman snorted as she brandished another dirk and pointed at the carib. "I've been following you since the moment you set foot in Kauhale. Your face is famous, you know. I would have never guess you'd speak slanderous rumors about the queen, rumors punishable by death."

Jenaro raised his hands and slowly turned his body in his chair. He looked directly into her cold eyes. There was indeed a familiarity about them, but one he could not place. "I don't know what you mean. This is our first time in Kauhale. We're merchants and would never speak ill of your queen."

"It's too late for that, Andoli," the woman sneered. "You see these blades? These are the blades of the *Kamahao*, the secret police. I fear your journey is at its end."

"What would the Kamahao want with us?" Jenaro asked.

"You'll find out soon enough. You two are coming with me, in irons if I must."

"What's to stop us from fleeing or overpowering you?" Agostin questioned.

As quick as a flash the kamahao placed the edge of dirk along Jenaro's throat. Jenaro winced as he felt the sharpness slice into his skin. "One, if you value your friend's life you will cooperate," she said, "or else I will not hesitate to exact judgement here and now. Two, neither of you Andoli have any measure of speed. I would gut you before you could raise a fist."

Agostin leered at the kamahao.

"We believe you and will come along quietly under one condition," Jenaro said.

She laughed derisively. "That you believe you are in a position to negotiate is amusing, but I'll entertain you."

"You will take us to the queen. I wish to plead my case directly before her grace," Jenaro said.

The kamahao glowered at Jenaro then just as quickly returned each blade to its hiding place. "That is exactly where I plan to go, as luck would have it." She pulled a length of chain with manacles from a small pack on her back. "Time to put these on."

The Palace at Kauhale

They marched single file out of The Offering and back toward the main road. Agostin led the way, followed by Jenaro with the kamahao, bringing up the rear. At each intersection, she would call out a direction and the party would continue to march. She led them through seedy back alleys and narrow streets, up stone steps and under bridges populated with foot and cart traffic, until the queen's palace fortress could be seen.

Unlike the Manse at Puerto Zafiro, it appeared that the entire city of Kauhale sprung up around the Queen's abode. It stood in a busy plaza with edifices on all four sides. It was walled in with a large iron gate and guardsmen in full combat gear, yet each guard nodded and waved at citizens as they passed.

"There is one thing that has been on my mind since you barged in on us," Jenaro stated.

"And what would that be?" the kamahao asked.

"You seem to know me and my carib first mate."

"There's a reason for that," she responded with an eye roll and a sharp yank at their chains.

"Well…I am at a loss to your identity. I only mention it because I feel that if we are to be hauled in front of the Queen of Hal'e as prisoners when I am a Prince of the Andolins and he my sworn carib, I would very much like to know the name of my captor," Jenaro paused and turned his head to look back at the kamahao, "to make sure she is justly rewarded for such a catch."

The kamahao chuckled. "Keep walking, prince," she spat the last word. "All will be revealed shortly.

They arrived at the gate just as the lamplighters finished

illuminating the grounds. Jenaro was surprised when the normal candor of the guards quickly transformed to a more respectful bow. He had never seen an officer of the law so well respected, let alone one who worked in the shadows as the kamahao obviously did. She bowed in front of the most senior guard. Jenaro thought she called him Kono. Kono then embraced her.

The kamahao led them up the steps. The palace itself was rather small in comparison to Jenaro's home. It was of rectangular shape, only two stories, and composed of white and gray bricks. Floor to ceiling windows surrounded the building. The roof was decorated with a frieze that Jenaro could only barely make out. Above that, he noticed more guards, with javelins and bows. He could see the tops of trees peeking above the marble fence and a flock of multicolored birds hopping and flitting from treetop to treetop. Inside the palace they were greeted by the queen's steward. The steward pulled the kamahao aside. They spoke in whispers. Jenaro tried his best to hear their words but could only make out "An'oli." The steward smiled and nodded to Jenaro and Agostin then raised one finger and wagged it toward the trio.

"I am Kino," the steward said with a polite bow of his head, "the queen's steward. It has been suggested to me that I take this fat Andoli to the *hale pa'ahao*; the cells in the basement."

Agostin growled rushed forward, protecting Jenaro with his massive frame but was just as quickly overpowered by three Hal'e guards about his same size. One of the guards unshackled Agostin from the kamahao's chains and quickly placed a chained collar around his neck.

"We are not criminals!" Agostin shouted. "Get your hands off of me!"

Jenaro stepped forward and confronted both the steward and the kamahao. "You are making a huge mistake. Free my friend now!" he ordered.

Kino smiled. The kamahao followed suit.

Jenaro flared his teeth and cried out after Agostin, "I will make this right, Ago! Don't worry I will make this right!"

Jenaro resisted the urge to grab them both by the collars when he returned his attention to the steward and the kamahao. "Take me to the queen, now."

The steward nodded, reached down, and unlocked Jenaro's manacles. "The Queen is expecting you, Prince Jenaro Albizu del Rios," he said. "She is expecting you as well, Lady Hildy."

Jenaro's eyes went wide. "Hildy?" He felt his heart pound nearly out of his chest. His stomach churned and twisted into three different knots. When he finally focused back on the kamahao, he instantly saw it... The chubbiness was gone, replaced with lean, toned muscle. Her hair grew wild, her skin rough,her eyes gray that danced silver in the light and flashed an otherworldly fire.

"There's no denying it. And I'm a fool for not seeing it," Jenaro managed, voice nearly cracking with disbelief.

Hildy held her head high and motioned for Jenaro to follow the steward. "After you, prince, or do you prefer Captain now?"

Jenaro struggled to contain himself. He could feel his arms trembling. Facing the Queen had been his idea, a plan depending largely on his silver tongue. Yet now, with Hildy behind him, scowling and hating his very existence, he felt all confidence leave his body. His tongue felt swollen, a burdensome mess inside his mouth.

They entered the state hall. It was a modest size chamber with two guards at the door and another two standing on the steps leading to the throne. The entire room was white, from the polished floors and walls to the ceiling to the drapery and standards of the queen. Even the throne itself was carved from the wood of the beautiful white koa tree. Queen Hannah was seated on her throne, dressed in an elegant white gown. She was crowned with the white gold diadem of the Hal'e and held the scepter of divine right, smithed from white gold, and adorned with diamonds.

Jenaro tried to swallow to moisten his throat, but nearly gagged. Even as he stood before the Queen, his eyes darted back and forth in a desperate attempt to remember why he was even in Kauhale.

Hannah spoke in perfect Coquien, yet her words fell upon deaf ears. Jenaro stared at her momentarily before he felt Hildy slap the back of his head.

"I-I-I'm sorry your majesty, could you repeat yourself?" Jenaro mumbled.

A smug grin came across her face.

"I said that I am pleased a member of the Andoli royal family has finally decided to appear before their oldest and most trusted ally." The sarcasm poured from her voice.

Jenaro bowed his head. "It is true, your majesty, that my baba has neglected such true and honorable friends as the Hal'e."

"It isn't the first time we've had to bear such an affront. It makes me wonder if our partnership is even worth the effort."

"I assure you; my baba values your partnership more than anything. If not for your support, he would not have defeated the Ultan-Meres. Without your support, a free Andolins may have never existed."

Hannah waved off Jenaro's entreaty. "Yes, yes, this we know."

"Well, maybe you can tell me how you knew I had arrived in Kauhale?" Jenaro asked abruptly.

She smirked. "You are not the most inconspicuous captain on the high seas. As soon as those blood red sails were spotted in our waters, my kamahao deployed around my islands.

Queen Hannah rose from her throne and slowly descended the stairs. "Hildy recognized you immediately and as you stand before me, I can honestly say I would have as well. You are the spitting image of Marohu."

Jenaro straightened up and stood tall as Hannah stopped before him. She slowly circled him like a tiburón toying with its prey.

"I am indeed my baba's son," Jenaro stated proudly.

Hannah finished her rounds and stopped in front of Jenaro. She placed her cold hand on his cheek. There was no warmth in the gesture. Jenaro wanted to pull away but was afraid of what Hildy would do.

"Did you know your father was once betrothed to me?" Hannah turned her back on him and climbed the stairs back to her throne.

Jenaro remained silent.

"Oh, I assure you, it is true," she continued. "Marohu and I had an arrangement. It is, after all, a tradition between our people. Yet, when he arrived in Kauhale all those years ago to take my hand in marriage, he was bewitched by…" her face twisted in disgust, "Helena. She was a simple handmaiden; a nobody, without a drop of royal blood."

"Watch your tone when you speak about my mother, your grace," Jenaro warned.

Hannah stopped for a moment. She looked away in a brief flash of pain before returning to her hard, stoic face. "My father was not upset. He was a romantic. He too had married outside of the alliance."

Jenaro took a step forward but Hildy's blades sang forth from her sleeves and quickly rested against his stomach and neck.

Jenaro cleared his throat. "Queen Hannah, I am sorry my baba broke your heart and reneged on his promise. I also profusely apologize to you and your daughters for my actions, but reconciling every sin of my family is not the reason I stand before you today."

The Queen nodded at Hildy. She returned her blades to her sleeves and joined her mother's side.

"And what reason would that be, Jenaro, Prince of the Andolins?" Hannah asked flippantly.

"I came to Kauhale only to find parts and supplies for my ship, nothing else. It is your daughter here who accuses me of wrongdoing. I wonder why the kamahao would detain a prince for simply discussing a rumor about your grace."

The queen grimaced. "Let me guess, you want to investigate this claim?"

Jenaro stood silent for a moment. He wanted nothing more than to board the *Moin Hupia* and sail away from Hal'e. But the idea of a cemi wreaking havoc on the people of Ke' stirred in his heart the words of To'guey. He was meant to help the people of Ke' rid themselves of the influence of the cemi. Jenaro raised his head high, puffed out his chest, and nodded, saying, "That would require access to Mount Pele."

Hannah's face shifted to surprise for a moment. She looked to Hildy then to Kino. "Perhaps we should continue this discussion in my private chambers," Hannah declared as she rose from her throne. She turned and quickly left the throne room followed by her guard.

Jenaro stood still and looked to Hildy.

Hildy motioned for Jenaro to follow. "What are you waiting for?"

The Queen's sitting room was the opposite of the state hall. Whereas the hall had an opulent, almost sterile feel to it, the sitting room was familiar and comfortable. The chairs were plush; there were plants and flowers, and an entire wall of floor to ceiling windows that overlooked a grove of white koa trees. The queen's two hounds were asleep on beds of exotic fabrics. There was a small round table with two crystal glasses and a glass pitcher full of fruit infused water. The queen was already in her chair next to the table and beckoned Jenaro to take the seat next to her. Hildy stood on her mother's right side.

Jenaro slowly took a seat, sitting on the edge, and poured himself a glass of water. "May I pour you a glass, your highness?"

Queen Hannah scoffed. "Enough with the pretense, Jenaro. Let's get down to business."

Jenaro smiled. "My father always said you were not one to mince words or stand on ceremony. I was wondering when I would meet that, Queen Hannah."

Hannah scowled and leaned forward in her chair. "I have a problem with a dragon. It is holding my daughter Heidi for ransom. I want you to kill the creature and end its reign of terror."

Jenaro's breath hitched. *Heidi…held captive by a dragon.*

"Mother!" Hildy gasped from her side. "You cannot seriously be considering –"

"I am, Hildy. For too long have we let this beast have its way." Queen Hannah slapped her hands on the arms of her chair. "No longer!"

Jenaro kept his mouth shut. *So that's it. She is sacrificing people to appease a dragon, no, a cemi.* He studied Hannah, her stoic resolve, her unwavering glare. He turned his eyes to Hildy. She wore a sudden air of insecurity.

"What exactly can you tell me about this creature?" Jenaro asked.

"It controls the wind and the rain. It keeps the summer storms from our islands in exchange for blood."

Jenaro inhaled deeply. "I do believe you are not dealing with an ordinary dragon. What you describe is the physical embodiment of Juracán, a cemi. It is his earthly form, iguanaboina."

Hannah chuckled. "Don't you try and push your religion on me, Andoli. It is a dragon, nothing more."

"A dragon that can control the wind and the waves? A dragon that requires a sacrifice as some sort of worship? No, your grace; that is no mere dragon. Only a cemi can be so sick."

"I don't care what you think it is. I want you to kill it. Kill it, save my daughter, and I'll spare the lives of you and your carib."

Jenaro took another long drink of his water. He looked at Hildy. Their eyes met. Her strength seemed to fail her. For the briefest moment, Jenaro thought he could sense her hesitation, her fear for her mother and sister. She looked away.

Jenaro placed his glass on the table and rose from his seat. He bowed his head to the queen and said, "I require my man."

"You can have your Andoli but my daughter will accompany you. Consider it insurance."

"I will fulfill my duty," Jenaro said with a bow.

Hannah nodded. "You have my blessing and my leave." She raised her hand and snapped. One of her guards hurriedly left the room. The other marched to Jenaro's side and raised a hand toward the door.

"I assume I don't have to tell you to use discretion, Jenaro Albizu del Rios," Hannah called from her seat.

Jenaro briefly stopped in his tracks, tightening his jaw before leaving the room.

Plans

Jenaro was escorted from the sitting room and led through the palace. It was a short walk to a rather nondescript stairway that led to the second floor. The queen's guard led Jenaro to a room at the end of the hall and opened the door, leaving Jenaro with a salute.

Jenaro looked around the guest room. The entryway was decorated with white marble counters and blown glass vases with white blossoms. There was a decanter filled with a golden wine, and two overstuffed chairs made of bleached fish leather and white koa wood. Jenaro peered around the corner into the bedroom. The four-post bed was draped in cream colored linen. A white gold candelabra cast a warm glow around the room. Jenaro nodded his approval of the elaborately decorated entryway when he heard Agostin's booming voice arguing from the hallway. In seconds, he burst through the door and offered a quick and furious bow to Jenaro. Jenaro forced a smile for his friend. Agostin returned the smile but was unamused.

"Agostin Anacaona, it is good to see you." Jenaro said. He closed the gap between him and his friend with a few long strides and slapped his hands to Agostin's shoulders. "I would say we are guests now, but guests do not usually pay such a price for hospitality."

"Guests are also not normally remanded to quarters by armed guards," Agostin waved a hand at the door. "And why was I freed?"

"That's what I want to discuss with you," Jenaro stood from

the chair and grabbed the decanter, taking a sip. "It's wine, I think."

Agostin nodded in approval. Jenaro poured two glasses, handed one to Agostin, and returned to his seat.

"Queen Hannah all but admitted that the rumors are true. She offered our freedom under one condition. She requires us to kill a beast that has been causing headaches…a dragon; the one creature that can speak the truth in all of this."

Agostin rolled his eyes and took a long sip of the wine. "I assume you accepted her offer; else I would not be here." Jenaro nodded. "Tell me about this errand we've been sent on."

Jenaro rose from his chair again, exhaled sharply, and ran a hand through his hair.

"Why are you so restless?" Agostin asked. "Speak, my friend."

"It appears that Heidi, is the recipient of a rather ill omen involving the dragon, which I believe to be a cemi."

"Heidi…the sister of your former betrothed?"

Jenaro nodded.

Agostin huffed and shook his head. "You realize your life seems to be at odds with the cemi at every turn?"

"It would seem so," Jenaro agreed. "There's more. The kamahao that detained us was Hildy."

Agostin shook his head and reached for the decanter. He poured himself another glass of the sweet golden wine. "I thought she looked familiar."

It was then they were interrupted by a knock on the door. The pair immediately grew silent. Agostin's eyes shot to the door, telling Jenaro to answer the summons. Jenaro held his breath, tiptoed to the door, and opened it slightly. He was surprised to see Hildy standing before him. Jenaro smiled and bowed his head to her.

"Lady Hildy Hal'e, to what do I owe the pleasure?" Jenaro asked.

Hildy rolled her eyes. "Let me in so we can speak in private."

"Of course, milady," Jenaro said with another bow of his head. He held the door open allowing her inside.

They entered the common room. Agostin met their gazes and froze mid-drink.

"Oh please, don't get up," Hildy said sarcastically.

Agostin finished his second glass of wine before replying, "I wasn't planning on it."

"Princess, please excuse my carib's manners..." Jenaro began.

Hildy cut him off saying, "Enough of the 'princess' and false cordiality. I'm here because we need to go over some important information about this dragon. I'd like to give ourselves the best chance of defeating it and your pompousness and begrudging will not help us."

Jenaro was shocked and yet thankful for her bluntness. He looked to Agostin and quickly flashed a grin. "Alright, Hildy, tell us what we need to know about this dragon."

They sat in common room of Jenaro's quarters for several hours. Hildy instructed Jenaro and Agostin on dragon anatomy including the toughness of its scales, its more vulnerable spots, and the speed in which it moved. She also told them of its more latent abilities. Jenaro was surprised to learn that the beast could hypnotize with only a look or a series of words. It could manipulate water, including that which occurs naturally in human bodies. She also spoke briefly about the lizard-men that ran wild throughout the islands; foes they may encounter on their trip to the spring.

"This dragon does not sound easily defeated," Agostin

grunted. "We could do it, but we'd need more people–soldiers, warriors, mercenaries. Or Luysa."

"Luysa?" Hildy asked.

"Our navigator," Jenaro said. "She's had experience battling enormous creatures. But no, Agostin, you are correct. We would need many soldiers, which we do not have. Maybe a head-on assault is not the way."

"What would you suggest?" Hildy asked.

Jenaro stroked his beard. "Parley with the beast, entreat with it, convince it that killing Heidi is not in its best interest and have it bow to our will without resorting to violence."

Hildy did not seem impressed with Jenaro's plan. "The more you speak to it, the easier it is to use its voice to control you."

"That does not mean we shouldn't try." Jenaro shook his head. "And I have qualms about slaying a cemi."

Hildy sighed, audibly frustrated. "Fine, we can try non-violence, but if things are not resolved quickly, you both need to be ready to strike those soft spots."

"Agreed," Jenaro nodded.

Agostin groaned, rolled his eyes, and begrudgingly agreed. "Why can't we just have a normal adventure? We're on an island full of beautiful women, strapping young men, and lots of alcohol, one where we sing and dance and satisfy our baser urges for a few days–but can we? No, it must be demons and cemi and dragons."

Jenaro chuckled.

"Get some rest," Hildy said, rising from her seat. "It is a long way to the peak."

The Ascent of Mount Pele

They left Kauhale as the sun rose the next morning, but not before Jenaro sent word to Luysa. Hopefully their absence would give Malu enough time to revive the majick of the *Moin Hupia*. The golden light splashed the gray sky with hues of yellow and painted the bottoms of the outlying clouds with streaks of amber and crimson. The city was asleep, save the night watch, the drunkards stumbling home, and the chatter from the fish market near the coast. Hildy led the way, guiding Jenaro and Agostin through the capital and onto the west road. They followed the road until they came to the first of many guard booths. This one was positioned strategically at a wide fork. Hildy nodded to the guards and proceeded down the wide, well beaten dirt path that forked north from the booth. The path snaked its way through the jungle and toward the mountains.

For the first time since they landed in Kauhale, Jenaro could smell the jungle, the damp earth, the fresh dew, and the flowering trees. The symphony of insects carried on the cool breeze, punctuated by the chirps of tropical birds. For a moment, Jenaro imagined he was back in the Andolins, marching through the jungle to his baba's ancestral home.

Agostin whistled of the Andoli drinking song, "Tilly's Heart." It was a crude ballad about a jilted lover stalking the woman who was once her beloved. Jenaro rolled his eyes and jogged past Agostin to walk by Hildy's side.

"This mountain is an active volcano, is it not?" he asked.

"No longer," Hildy answered curtly. "Once, centuries ago."

"You afraid it might erupt again?"

"No."

Jenaro sighed. "Listen, Hildy, I want to apologize for what happened between us."

Hildy stopped abruptly and glowered at Jenaro. "Oh, do you now?"

"Yes," Jenaro responded. "I was young and stupid. I was more concerned with…others than marriage and ruling the Andolins. But that doesn't excuse what I did."

"You're right, it doesn't." Hildy growled and shook her head.

"You're right," Jenaro said, bowing apologetically.

"Heidi was the only one there to comfort me after what you did," Hildy added. "You embarrassed me, no all of Hal'e, in front of the entire Andoli court, and it was her shoulder I cried on, all the way back to Kauhale. Eventually you just became a worthless memory to me, someone we laughed about when we toasted to your demise, but it wasn't without her strength and love I couldn't have done it without her." She scowled and stormed up the path to put distance between them.

Agostin was only several paces behind when he joined Jenaro, once again whistling the intro to "Tilly's Heart."

"Do you think you could whistle a different tune?" Jenaro asked in aggravation.

Agostin stopped his whistling and shrugged. "I found it a fitting melody for hiking through the jungle." He smiled ear to ear.

"Fitting as it might be a reprisal of that song may also come with a swift punch in the jaw."

Agostin chuckled. "Did you expect that to go differently?"

Jenaro sighed. "Honestly, yes I did. I was sixteen, Ago. As I recall, you were not the most convincing carib when it came to my royal duties."

Agostin shrugged. "I only promised to stand by you no matter what."

Jenaro shook his head. "Maybe I'll try another approach."

Agostin laughed. "You always were a glutton for punishment."

Silence prevailed once again until Agostin took up another tune. This time his humming was undeniably "The Pride of the Princess." Jenaro cringed and nearly tripped over his own feet when Agostin decided to sing the chorus at the top of his lungs.

"And she squawked, and she flapped for it was all she knew
'Cause the princess, the princess would not be moved.
The bars fell around her, the lock snapped, closed tight.
Yet no man could ever cage her unbridled heart!"

Agostin's tune made Hildy look back. Her jaw was clenched. Her lips were pursed. Her eyes burned through Agostin so fiercely that he immediately stopped his music. Jenaro caught up with Hildy but kept silent until she finally spoke.

"Is he always that annoying?" Hildy asked.

"You wouldn't believe it if I told you," Jenaro said, just above a whisper. "He would say it was charming, not annoying. Surprisingly enough, nearly everyone would agree."

"Maybe charming to a herd of cattle," Hildy said with a grimace.

"I heard that," Agostin called from the rear.

"I wasn't trying to whisper," Hildy fired back. "Is there really a song in Coquien about a bird too prideful to notice her imprisonment?" she asked suspiciously.

Jenaro nodded with a chuckle. "Our minstrels are not known for their subtlety."

Hildy scoffed back. "Obviously not."

"You mean to tell me that the songsmiths in Kauhale don't sing such moving tunes?"

"Most of our songs are about the beauty of our islands."

"Your songsmiths must have more respect for their art. Andoli bards are merely concerned with entertainment."

"Hal'e songsmiths are very artistic. We as a people don't believe that art at the expense of others can be classified as art."

Jenaro nodded and met Hildy's eyes. She smiled back, but quickly turned away.

They stopped for lunch and a trail break, eating the rations brought along by Hildy: coconut water and fish wrapped in flatbread. Agostin took a few sips of his flask when he thought nobody was watching.

"Is there anything else I should know about this dragon, or your sister, or even the ceremony that may help our cause?" Jenaro asked Hildy.

Hildy frowned. "Not much, if I'm being honest. I told you all the knowledge I have about the dragon, none of it practical. It came from old scrolls."

"So, you know nothing of the ceremony?"

"I didn't say that."

"Well then?"

Hildy rolled her eyes. "The serpent has entreated with our family for several generations now. It would visit the volcano and, in exchange for an offering, it blessed our islands with beautiful weather and bountiful crops."

"And take its furious wind and rain to other islands, like ours," Agostin muttered.

Hildy glared, "Correct."

"You said offering. Does it kill this offering?" Jenaro asked.

"No," Hildy said with a shake of her head. She inhaled slowly and exhaled through her mouth. "The dragon wouldn't leave. It started demanding human sacrifices, threatening to destroy all Hal'e. My cousin was the first. She ascended the mountain last year, and every season after that a new person was sent up Pele to the spring. That was when Hildy…she offered to stay to treat with the sea serpent until a solution was found."

"And the dragon approved of this arrangement?" Jenaro asked.

"We believe so."

"You don't know?"

"No, we won't know until…the next person heads to the spring."

"Seems like Jenaro was correct in his assumptions," Agostin said.

"So you were willing to sacrifice someone else?" Jenaro fired back.

Hildy rose from the ground. "No, we weren't going to send someone else to their death. I mean I don't think so."

"But it is a possibility. And there's no way to know if your mother was thinking the same thing."

Hildy shook her head. "Mother is not evil. I choose to believe she would not have such malice in her heart."

Jenaro shrugged. "Love and loyalty can make a person do things seemingly out of the ordinary, especially if it means protecting that which they love."

Hildy shook her head once more but did not speak.

"She was quick to request our help with the problem," Agostin advocated. "It could be her plan was to slay the dragon. It could also mean she found us to be acceptable sacrifices. Maybe she expects the dragon to take me and Jenaro, and for it to release Hildy to go with you. And then –"

"Can we please stop accusing my mother of such an act?" Hildy shouted.

Jenaro held his hands up for peace. "Agostin is only trying to make sure we're not walking into a trap."

Hildy crossed her arms on her chest. "Fine, that's fair."

"Right now, we don't know either party's intentions," Jenaro stated. "So I suggest we continue to make our way to the summit with the intention of parlaying with the beast."

They returned to the road and continued to climb. The path turned rough and steep as it began to ascend the mountain. Thankfully, the Queen maintained some level of safety and security for the climb. Quarried stone steps were placed where the path was too great an incline. When neither path nor step would suffice, long tunnels were mined through the mountains. Each tunnel was lit by a mysterious blue flame.

"An eternal fire," Hildy offered without question.

"I'm sorry?" Jenaro asked.

"It is an eternal fire. Most people ask about the flame. Ages ago these tunnels were built by Itiban miners. They believed a fount of essence existed at the top of the volcano. They brought mages with them to help speed along the process. The fire was placed by the majes. We've no idea how or even if it can be extinguished."

"It is not the first time we've encountered such a flame," Jenaro admitted.

Hildy shot a concerned glance at Jenaro. "You've spent time with majes?"

"Wanderers," Agostin chimed in with a measure of disdain.

Jenaro said, "They had these rods that were filled with blue flame. It appeared to be some sort of fire in liquid form."

"Where were you when you ran into Itiba Ara' Seekers?"

"Cike'o," Jenaro replied.

"In the Taicarayas," Agostin added.

"Sounds like quite an adventure," Hildy said. Her words conveyed amusement, but her tone was anything but.

"It was unexpectedly dramatic, that is for sure," Jenaro stated.

"Maybe you can tell me more before we stop for the night," Hildy said as they emerged from the tunnel.

"For the night?" Agostin asked, exasperated.

"Yes. It is a two-day journey to the peak, to the Spring of the Creators," Hildy answered.

Agostin sighed.

"Where will we stop?" Jenaro asked.

"There's a wayshrine at the foot of the last climb. We'll camp there for the evening."

Attack of the *Mea Palola*

They traveled for another few hours. Jenaro, desiring to build a level of trust between the three of them, told Hildy about their run-in with the Itiba and about Rahe and the shade. Agostin took over at certain parts, adding his dramatic flair to the encounter with the baelor bear. Hildy remained pensive, for the most part, listening to Jenaro's stories, but failing to respond.

As the sun began to set, Hildy called their attention to a small cube of a building with a pinnacled, thatched roof that rose nearly twice its height. It sat on the rise of the next hill.

"That is our wayshrine," Hildy explained. "It will protect us from any weather and allow us to cook indoors for the evening. Mother always has it stocked with dry goods and non-perishables for the pilgrims."

"I thought this was private land owned by your mother?" Jenaro questioned.

"It is, but the path and the temple outside the spring are public," Hildy replied. "Pilgrims often journey to the temple to meditate on the carvings. By keeping the roads safe and offering free supplies, my mother maintains a relationship with the temple and its patrons."

"And these lizard-men you spoke of…what's to stop them from raiding it?"

"Black iron," Hildy said matter-of-factly.

"Black iron?"

"They find it unnatural and even painful to the touch. The wayshrines are enclosed in black iron fencing. The doorways are wood framed in black iron. Even the windowsills are black iron."

"Can we pick up the pace?" Agostin asked, interrupting Hildy's lecture. "All this uphill climbing and talk of lizard-men is making me wish for a safe place to sit and rest my burning calves."

They hurried over the last hill and reached the fence of the wayshrine just as dusk fell. Rather than hurry onto the grounds and inside the shrine, Hildy stopped short and dropped to a crouch. Jenaro and Agostin exchanged glances and immediately joined her by the fence.

"What's wrong?" Jenaro whispered.

Hildy shook her head. "Something doesn't feel right. That far section of the fence looks damaged, and there's a campfire on the far side. See the glow?"

"What are you thinking? Bandits?"

Hildy shrugged. "I'm not sure, but we should be cautious just in case."

They slowly crept to the front gate, keeping low and using the fence itself as cover. The gate looked as if it had been smashed open by a large object. The iron was bent and broken with pieces half buried in the earth. Before anyone could say it, Agostin pointed at several sets of tracks dashing around the yard.

"Those look exactly like gecko tracks from back home, only…larger." Agostin's neck and shoulders flexed.

Jenaro and Hildy turned to look at the mammoth footprints dotting the dirt.

"The *mea palola*," Hildy grumbled.

"Lizard-men?" Jenaro and Agostin asked in unison.

She nodded as she dropped her pack and brandished both her dirks. Jenaro tossed his satchel to the ground and grabbed his dagger while Agostin pulled Hano's axe from its place on his back.

"Follow me and stay low," Hildy warned. "Try not to make a sound."

Hildy dashed from the gate to the closest wall of the wayshrine. Jenaro and Agostin followed. They could hear a strange clicking and cackling coming from inside. Hildy motioned to one of the windows and then to both Jenaro and Agostin. Jenaro nodded and waved Agostin to his side. Agostin raised a knee and Jenaro boosted himself to the window. He slowly peeked inside and saw three long shadows cast on the far wall before dropping to the ground. He then snuck back to Hildy's side.

"I think there are three of them," he whispered.

Hildy grimaced. "Three usually means a warmonger and two smaller ones, possibly sprinters."

"How can you be sure?" Jenaro asked.

"Years of tracking," Hildy replied. "They travel in strangely predictable numbers."

"You called one a warmonger?" Agostin asked from over Jenaro's shoulder. "That doesn't sound good."

"It's not," she confirmed. "They're big and mean. I mean really big, though sprinters are no easy prey. They're fast and can attack quicker than you can move."

"What if we just avoid the wayshrine?" Jenaro offered. "We can bypass it and head straight to the spring."

Hildy shook her head. "People use the shrine. If we leave, unarmed pilgrims will stumble into this trap. No, we must confront them."

"Plan of attack?" Jenaro asked.

"I'll draw them out of the shrine and into the open. Then we spring them from behind. That will give us time to at least get a few hits in before they know what is happening. Agostin, you're with me."

Agostin nodded.

"We're going to tackle the warmonger together." Hildy

turned her attention to Jenaro. "You think you can take the sprinters?"

Jenaro shrugged. "I have no idea. I don't even know what they look like, let alone how they handle themselves in battle."

"Think adolescents, but with razor-like teeth and two stone daggers," Hildy informed him.

Jenaro nodded reluctantly. "I'm going to need another blade."

Agostin unsheathed his cutlass and handed it to Jenaro. "You remember how to use this?"

Jenaro grinned. "Vaguely."

"Alright, follow me," Hildy told Agostin then pointed at Jenaro. "You, wait for my signal."

Hildy and Agostin stayed low and made their way around the shrine. Jenaro remained to the left of the entrance. In a few moments, he spotted both Agostin and Hildy as they turned the corner. Agostin held Hano's axe at the ready. Hildy gripped a sizable iron beam in both her hands. With a shove and a grunt, she tossed the bar to the stone steps. It hit with a crash and rang out over the wayshrine.

Before the ringing stopped, the lizard-men rushed from the shrine to the iron bar. Jenaro's heart stopped at the sight. The sprinters were indeed the size of skinny, teenage Andoli. They were both covered in green and yellow scales that shimmered in the firelight. They wore rough, tanned hide shirts and wielded cumbersome stone and bone knives.

The warmonger was entirely their opposite. Whereas they ran with bestial speed and agility, it lumbered on two legs, burdened by its enormous frame. It was a teal-colored beast with flaming red eyes and hands bigger than Agostin's torso. It wore skins and bone as its armor, including a helmet that was a larger *mea palola* skull, and gripped a club that resembled a small tree.

All three lizard-men stopped in front of the bar. They spoke to each other in clicks and grunts, pointing at it strangely.

Before they could turn around and return to the shrine, Agostin dropped to one knee behind the warmonger. Hildy sprinted to him and using him as a step, propelled herself skyward. She brought down both her dirks into the warmonger's shoulders. The beast shrieked in anguish and flailed its enormous arms, connecting with a retreating Agostin, sending him flying to the ground.

Jenaro jumped to his feet and dashed toward the sprinters who moved away from the warmonger to avoid its swings. Jenaro caught the first sprinter by surprise. He spun in a circle, slashing the sprinter across the neck with the cutlass then bringing his dagger into the middle of its back. The sprinter gurgled then fell forward dead.

The second sprinter, now aware of its predicament, spun around and struck Jenaro in the face with the broad side of his tail. Jenaro felt his nose burst from the impact. His vision went blurry as he flew from the body of the dead sprinter. No sooner had he landed with a grunt did the second sprinter grab Jenaro by the neck with his tail and lift him to his feet. Jenaro's head was spinning from the first strike. Panic began to rise in his chest as the tail tightened around his throat. He scratched and clawed trying to get free, but the sprinter only snarled, sending slobber at Jenaro's face. With a wild swing and grunt, it tossed Jenaro toward the warmonger.

Jenaro hit the ground hard and momentarily lost his breath. He looked up while heaving and saw Agostin hacking wildly at the warmonger. Hildy still clung to a dirk buried in the beast's shoulder. She raised her freehand to stab it once more yet before she could strike, the warmonger threw itself forward, curling into a ball. The action flung Hildy from its shoulders. She landed softly, quickly turning to greet the warmonger's defensive posture. Agostin swung once more but missed as the warmonger began to spin, sweeping Agostin and Hildy off their feet with its tail.

Jenaro stumbled back to his feet and turned to look at the sprinter. It raised its head and let loose a battle cry then charged at him. Its daggers flashed. Its teeth bared. Jenaro gritted his teeth and with a shout, met it head on. He parried the first swipe but was hit from behind by the sprinter's tail. Jenaro quickly flipped to his feet only to feel the tail once again send him to the ground. Growling in anger, he rose a third time, determined to land a strike. The sprinter continued to spin. This time, Jenaro dropped to one knee and braced himself.

He caught the tail mid-spin and managed to stop the beast. Before it could break free, Jenaro hacked as hard as he could with the cutlass and severed the sprinter's tail from its body. The sprinter screamed in horror as it hopped around, looking back in horror at the stump where once was its tail.

Jenaro ran forward then slid beneath the jumping sprinter, locking his legs around those of the beast. The sprinter felt forward to the dirt. Jenaro quickly rolled off the lizard-man and swung the cutlass straight into the sprinter's mouth, embedding it in the dirt below, severing half the lizard's head from its body.

Jenaro screamed in triumph, but only for a moment. As he pulled the blade from the earth, his eyes were immediately on the warmonger.

Agostin and Hildy were struggling to bring it down. Jenaro ran to their aid. The beast was back on its feet and swinging its massive club. Agostin repeatedly jumped back, narrowly missing each swing. Jenaro ran to his side. The two shared a smirk and nod, then grasped each other by the forearm. Agostin spun and tossed Jenaro at the lizard-man. Jenaro slammed the cutlass into the creature's arm with such force, he swore he saw a shockwave. Even so, the blade barely scratched the warmonger's scales. Regardless, it stunned the beast long enough for Agostin, still spinning, to plant the axe into the soft flesh of the warmonger's stomach.

Hildy saw the creature double over from the strike and flew into action. She once again mounted the beast attempting to remove its helmet, stabbing repeatedly at the soft skin of the its neck trying desperately to use her blade as a wedge and peel the helmet from its head. Her last strike bounced off the bone itself and caused the dirk to fly from her hand and careen to the ground.

By this time, Agostin had pulled the axe from the lizard. Jenaro sprinted forward, rolled, and scooped the blade off the ground. "Hildy!" he shouted as he tossed the dirk back.

The warmonger roared and stood up straight, pivoting toward Jenaro. The creature swung the club vertically at Jenaro's head. Jenaro recoiled as quickly as he could and leaned back but the club moved faster than he anticipated. The jagged tip of the weapon slashed down his face, slicing a trail of blood from his forehead down to his jaw, taking a sliver of Jenaro's right eye as it traveled.

Jenaro wailed in pain. He dropped his blades and clutched his face as he fell backward to the ground. The warmonger's club impacted the earth with a spray of dirt and debris that pelted Jenaro as he fell.

"Jenaro!" Agostin cried out, as did Hildy, but their screams were muffled by the searing pain that shot through Jenaro's body. Blood shrouded his vision, but fear and pain were quickly replaced by rage and adrenaline.

Jenaro stumbled to his feet, dazed and still reeling from the searing, pulsing pain on his face, and let loose a bloodthirsty growl. He lifted his dagger as he stood and pointed it at the warmonger. Jenaro flew at the lizard-man with the feral shriek of a desperate animal protecting its herd.

The warmonger gasped and quickly back pedaled, dragging the club with it. Jenaro swung wildly, but with only one eye, missed every single strike. He moved clumsily, unbalanced by his own flailing. Fortunately, the warmonger was struck with fear at Jenaro's ferocity. Before it could raise its weapon, the Andoli captain-prince was upon him. Jenaro took three steps then miraculously planted his foot on the beast's club, leaping skyward. With a vicious thrust, Jenaro stabbed the warmonger through the eye slits of the of its skull mask, completely burying the blade to the cross-guard. The lizard-man coughed and clicked then stiffened before careening to the ground like a felled tree. Hildy jumped from its shoulders as it fell. Jenaro held fast to his blade and landed atop the beast's dead body, standing on his conquered foe like a statue to his great deed.

He took a deep breath and pulled his dagger clean from the warmonger's head, wiping the blade on the leg of his pants before collapsing.

"Jenaro!" Agostin shouted as he ran to Jenaro's side, cupping his face as he knelt before him.

"My eye," Jenaro trailed off. "I can't see…"

Agostin gently moved Jenaro's face to the dim light of the fire in the wayshrine. Hildy was soon at their sides and helped Agostin examine the wound.

"Try to open your eye," Hildy said as Agostin held Jenaro's head steady.

Jenaro forced his eye open but witnessed no change. The grimace on both Agostin and Hildy's faces was all the confirmation he needed.

"We should go to the wayshrine so I can treat this," Hildy said.

They helped Jenaro to the way-shrine and took a seat around the blazing campfire. The walls and floor of the shrine were covered in soot and blood spatter. Burnt and gnawed remnants of a handful of pilgrims were piled in the far corner. Agostin immediately began kicking and tossing everything out of the way to clear a space.

Hildy moved close to Jenaro and gently cradled his face. Without saying a word, she pulled a handkerchief and her canteen from her satchel, soaked the cloth, and began to dab away the blood.

"You'll never regain sight in this eye," Hildy said plainly. "The only course of action is to clean it of damaged tissue and cauterize the wound to keep it from bleeding."

Jenaro swallowed hard and nodded at Hildy. "Do it."

Hildy nodded back and pulled her dirk from her sleeve. She placed it in the fire, resting the hilt on a piece of stone. Agostin knelt by holding a flask.

"For the pain," Agostin said. He tossed the flask at Jenaro, who tried to catch it in midair but failed. It hit the pavement and slid away from him.

Jenaro shook his head in frustration. Hildy handed it to Jenaro who consumed a healthy amount of the liquor before tossing the remaining amount on his wounded eye. He clenched his teeth and winced at the sting.

"Are you ready?" Hildy asked as Jenaro tossed the flask back to Agostin.

Jenaro nodded.

"Okay, Agostin, I'm going to need your help. I need you to hold Jenaro and keep him from pulling his head away from the blade. Can you do that?" Hildy asked.

Agostin hurried to Jenaro's side. He sat behind him and braced his chest and head with his arms. Jenaro raised his blade to his mouth and bit down as hard as he could on the cold steel. Hildy reached and pulled her dirk from the fire. The tip of the blade was glowing orange. Jenaro clenched his teeth and shut his good eye.

"Don't count down or hesitate," Jenaro stated. "Just do it."

Hildy pressed the blade to Jenaro's ruined eye as soon as he finished speaking. The searing pain shot through his body. His muscles tensed. His teeth clenched. He growled then screamed. He tried to pull his face away, but Agostin held tight. Hildy pressed the blade against his eye in short bursts for a couple of minutes, but for Jenaro it felt like hours. When Hildy finally finished the procedure, Jenaro had passed out from the pain.

Discoveries

It was shortly after sunrise when Jenaro woke. His face was hot and sore. His head pounded. His entire body ached. He slowly sat up and looked around the wayshrine. Hildy was nowhere to be found. Agostin was crouched by the still burning campfire, roasting something on a piece of iron rod from the fence surrounding the shrine.

"How are you feeling?" Agostin asked without turning from his spit.

Jenaro groaned.

"That good, eh?"

"That good."

"You should be happy to know your nose was not broken," Agostin stated, turning to Jenaro and smiling. "Breakfast will be ready shortly."

Jenaro nodded. "And Hildy?"

"She went to scout ahead to make sure there are no more lizard-men prowling the trail."

Jenaro spotted Hildy's kerchief from the night before. He grabbed it and wrapped it around his head, covering the scarred eye and joined Agostin by the fire.

"Must be burning something pretty powerful to have lasted all night."

"Hildy said the *mea palola* have a greasy substance that burns long and hard and…" Agostin trailed off when his eyes met Jenaro's face.

"What is it, Ago?"

Agostin looked pleased. "You look like a pirate captain."

Jenaro chuckled. "What's for breakfast?" he asked as he slowly joined Agostin by the fire.

"Lizard tail," Agostin smirked.

Jenaro stopped mid-sit and looked at his carib. "You jest."

"No, I do not. Hildy told me the tail was actually good eating and gave me some pointers on how to prepare and cook it."

"It doesn't seem," Jenaro paused, "morbid to you? I mean, we are eating the flesh of the beasts that nearly killed us. Intelligent beasts."

Agostin shrugged. "It feels like fate, if you ask me. They would have done the same to us." Agostin motioned with his head to the pile of human bones.

"He's right," Hildy called from the entrance.

Agostin and Jenaro turned their attention to her.

"Back from scouting? How does the rest of the trail look?" Agostin asked.

Hildy nodded, but frowned as she joined them by the fire. "There are tracks all the way to the spring, fresh ones, too. I didn't want to enter the cave for fear of ambush, so I doubled-back. No more dead pilgrims, though."

"That's some good news," Agostin replied.

She nodded then looked at Jenaro. "How's the eye?"

"Sufficiently toasted to a crisp," he joked.

Hildy tsked.

Jenaro put his hand on her knee. "Sore and hot, but on the mend. I think I'll make it."

Hildy put a hand on his and gave Jenaro an awkward, yet warm smile.

"Well, let's hurry and eat so we can make it to the spring," she announced, sweeping his hand from her leg.

Jenaro and Agostin were pleasantly surprised by the meal. It was tender and slightly fatty which gave it a saltier taste and almost buttery texture. The fatty exterior charred nicely giving a gentle crunch. They washed the tail down with some ale Hildy discovered among the wreckage of the shrine.

Before leaving, the three of them gathered up all the bodies and set them to burn. They cleaned out as much of the wayshrine as they could–some of the mess would require a deeper scrub then they were able to do–and piled it outside. Finally, Hildy lowered the flag to half-staff to warn any pilgrims of the possibility of danger.

Jenaro struggled for the first hour. The loss of his eye resulted in a lack of depth perception. He stumbled over his own two feet. He continually bumped into Hildy or Agostin. It made his head pound and the world spin in small circles. After the path leveled out, he found it easier to walk without swaying and managed to avoid help from Hildy and Agostin.

They reached the spring just before noon. The dirt path turned to ancient white marble. A knee-high marble wall and crumbling marble pillars shouldered the path up to a stairway that led to the cave entrance of the spring. A sage green moss clung to and hung on every surface.

"It looks abandoned," Jenaro pointed out.

Hildy nodded. "Mother is afraid that removing the moss will result in further damage to the marble. And if I'm honest, I enjoy the look. It makes the spring look ancient and mysterious."

"I have to agree with her," Agostin chimed in.

Jenaro shook his head.

Hildy smirked and continued climbing the steps.

"What is that building?" Jenaro asked as he followed. "Looks like another wayshrine."

"It's the temple of the spring, the final destination on the pilgrimage," Hildy informed him.

"Do you think we should check it out?"

Hildy shook her head. "I scouted it earlier. It's the same as the first shrine, desecrated inside and out."

"How was their presence not reported? Aren't there guards on the trail and at the spring?"

Hildy stopped and faced Jenaro. "It was reported."

Jenaro and Agostin appeared confused.

"The *mea palola* are always spotted on the trail. We get ten or twenty reports a month from pilgrims and guards alike. The last report was just discarded as a usual occurrence. Nothing to investigate."

"Are there guards at the spring?" Jenaro asked.

Hildy remained silent.

Jenaro's brow furrowed, and his eye turned to a narrow slit. It all began to make sense to him. The *mea palola*, the surprise at their sudden aggression, the storms; it was all so obvious. He clenched his jaw and inhaled slowly before speaking. "The spring guards are *mea palola*, and your family is well aware of that."

Hildy avoided Jenaro's gaze and took a step toward the cave. "It's not that simple."

"So why exactly are we here? If I didn't know your sister, I'd wonder if you even had one held captive by the cemi. All of this is making Agostin's idea of a trap seem more and more plausible."

Hildy was flustered. "No! The *mea palola* have always kept to the jungles. They've never bothered pilgrims."

"Then what would cause them to be brave enough to travel the roads unchecked?" Agostin asked.

Jenaro clenched his jaw and inhaled slowly before speaking. "I think I'm beginning to understand. The dragon isn't upset because the sacrifices aren't enough. You said it yourself, Hildy. It hasn't left the spring in ages. You don't give it sacrifices because it asks for them. People are sacrificed to appease it, to keep it from lashing out in anger at its imprisonment!"

"That's ridiculous," Hildy scoffed as she continued to climb.

"And the *mea palola* aren't random brainless monsters. I think they're working for the cemi. Why else would the instigate aggression?"

Hildy shook her head. "No…it's…it entered the spring willingly. We didn't…I mean…"

"Regardless of your intentions, the beast has obviously had enough of its imprisonment. What better soldiers than lizard-men. They are reptilian cousins."

"And the storms," Agostin stated.

"The storms?" Hildy asked.

Agostin nodded. "We encountered storms on our way to Hal'e. They were tempests only Juracán could summon. The storm was the physical manifestation of its rage."

Hildy remained silent.

Jenaro became angry. "If this is indeed the truth then you fools brought this all upon yourselves."

Hildy slowly lifted her head. She shot cold, sharp needles from her eyes. Jenaro stared back, unmoved by her rage. Hildy began to snarl and moved toward Jenaro, but Agostin stepped in between.

"I think we're about to find all the answers we need, my friend," Agostin said, pointing toward the cave entrance.

Jenaro and Hildy pulled their eyes away from each other and turned their stares to the cave. Standing guard at the entrance were two large, turquoise skinned *mea palola*. Each one wore a feathered headdress; one of stunning greens and pink, the other a more subdued white and blue. Draped upon their chests were bone and stone mail. Hanging from their hips were battle-clubs of charred wood and stone. Their stances were not aggressive. In fact, the lizards seemed to be beckoning them forward, as if their arrival was expected.

"Let's find out exactly what's going on here," Agostin stated, turning a sideways glance to Jenaro.

Jenaro returned the glance with a nod.

"They are the *kafe*, the chieftains. I've never seen them out in the open like this," Hildy gulped. "They keep to the caves and aren't usually violent."

"Regardless, keep your guard up, everyone," Jenaro warned.

They finished climbing the steps and stopped in front of the lizard-men. The standoff only lasted a moment before the lizard-men bowed and moved from the entrance. They held their arms out, inviting them all to enter. The three exchanged looks before Jenaro took the lead and entered the cave, followed closely by Hildy and Agostin. The two kafe brought up the rear, cutting off any sort of quick retreat.

The trail to the spring was dimly lit by streams of strange blue light that ran along the cave ceiling. The walls and floor of the cave were smooth and polished, making each footfall echo. Soon, the cave tunnel led to an enormous room peppered with stalactites and stalagmites. Sunlight streamed in through a series of vents in the roof and lit even the darkest corner with warm, white light. The polished path ended abruptly at a sandy beach surrounding a turquoise watered lagoon, stretching as far as Jenaro could see. In the middle of the lagoon, Jenaro noticed the bubbling, rising geyser of the spring. Its babbling calmly washed over the entire cave. They came to halt well before the shoreline. The two kafe circled the three intruders then turned their backs to the spring and pointed at Jenaro.

Jenaro moved his hand to his chest and patted as if to signal and ensure they were pointing at him. The kafe nodded in unison and pointed to the lagoon.

"I guess they want me to take a swim," Jenaro stated.

"Maybe they want you to speak to the serpent," Agostin said.

"Just me?"

Hildy shrugged. "If you and Agostin have had dealings with your gods and survived this one's storm, as you say, maybe it knew you were coming."

"I'm not comfortable with this," Agostin admitted. "Last time you were alone with a cemi, you lost a finger."

Agostin took a step forward, which prompted the kafe to raise their clubs.

"Whoa, whoa," Agostin responded, raising his hands in defense.

The kafe with the green and pink headdress placed the ball of his club on Agostin's chest and pushed him back.

Jenaro pulled Agostin behind him and calmly said, "Ago, I think we may have no choice if we wish to avoid more bloodshed." Jenaro took a step forward and the kafe separated to allow him to pass. He stepped to the sand, turned to Hildy and Agostin and said, "Wish me luck."

Conversations with a Dragon

Before another word could be spoken, the waters of the spring began to swirl. The roar of rushing water echoed throughout the cave as a whirlpool appeared. Rising slowly from the center was the lifeless body of a woman, encased in a floating orb of lagoon water. It was Heidi, only older. She had lengthy, dark hair that floated about the bubble, and wore a pale cornflower blue gown that gently danced about as if on waves. Hildy gasped at the sight and tried to push past the kafe but was knocked on her backside by their clubs.

The bubble balanced perfectly on the caudal fin of the silvery-blue sea serpent. The dragon rose from the water with a terrible shriek, sending waves of brackish wind at Jenaro and his crew. It dove under only to emerge once again, this time closer to shore. The entirety of its shimmering body snaked in and out of the water. As it got closer, Jenaro could make out individual turquoise and teal scales as well as silvery-blue dorsal and ventral fins lining its body from neck to tail.

The beast slid onto the shore and let loose an ear-splitting cry. Jenaro flinched and found himself instinctively reaching for his dagger. Rather than unsheathe his weapon and spark an unnecessary brawl, Jenaro walked to the water, dropped to one knee, and bowed his head in reverence to the beast.

"Great serpent! I am Jenaro Albizu del Rios, envoy of Hannah, Queen of Hal'e. I have been sent to retrieve Heidi Hal'e and return her to her ancestral home."

The dragon returned its gaze to Jenaro and continued to snarl. Its eyes flashed then a voice echoed in Jenaro's ear.

"What proof do you have of this?" the dragon asked. Its voice was slow and deliberate, drawing out each word with precise pronunciation.

Jenaro turned and looked at Agostin and Hildy. He smiled and whispered, "It's responding telepathically."

He bowed his head and replied. "Is my word not good enough for you, O great serpent?"

"No," it answered plainly.

Jenaro thought for a moment. The dragon showed its massive fangs.

"I am blessed of Yaya, oh great Juracán. I witnessed his glory in the glade of the heavens. Surely you can sense his power flowing within me. Why else would you let your *mea palola* kafe admit me to your spring?"

The great sea serpent shut its jaws. Its body seemed to relax, albeit with reluctance. "I am the iguanaboina, the physical embodiment of Juracán," it said with a growl.

Jenaro turned to his friends. Hildy's dirks were in her hands. Agostin's hand was on Hano's axe. The kafe held them back with the clubs. Both their faces were painted with fear.

"My friends," Jenaro called to them. "Go with the kafe. Everything is fine." Jenaro said calmly.

"What?" Agostin and Hildy asked simultaneously.

Jenaro raised a hand to the serpent and quickly walked to his friends. "It is giving me an audience to speak. The dragon won't harm me I can assure you."

Agostin shook his head. "I am not leaving you alone."

"Agostin, please," Jenaro pleaded. "Trust in me as you have always trusted in me. I can reason with it. I can free Heidi. And I can do it without unnecessary bloodshed." Jenaro stood tall with the confidence and determination only a del Rios could muster.

"We won't be far," Agostin nodded, removing his hand from the axe. "If we don't see you by nightfall…"

Jenaro flashed a quick smile and winked. "You'll see me well before."

Agostin smiled at Jenaro's boldness and turned to leave the cave.

"Come, Hildy. Leave this fool to his games."

Hildy gasped. Her face twisted with concern. "I hope that tongue of yours is as quick as you claim."

Jenaro smiled and winked at her.

Hildy's look quickly turned red, and her eyes filled with anger. "If you don't return by nightfall, I will personally sail your damned ship of the dead to whatever afterlife you are sent to and kill you once more."

Jenaro grinned. "I'll hold you to that."

Hildy shook her head and followed the kafe up the passage and out of the spring.

When Jenaro turned back to the iguanaboina, the sea serpent had slithered its way back beneath the waters of the cave. He could just make out its opalescent tail fins as it swam into the deep. Jenaro *hmphed* and took a seat near the edge of the water. He crossed his legs and looked out over the spring. Hildy remained catatonic in her bubble prison.

"I wonder if old To'guey knew I would face off against the iguanaboina," Jenaro muttered to himself. "What would she have done?" *To'guey…* he thought, then smiled at the vision of his teacher, always cross-legged, always smoking.

Jenaro pulled his shoulder bag to his lap and removed his family cemi pipe from within along with his small pouch of snuff. He methodically loaded and lit the pipe. He brought the pipe to his nostrils and inhaled deeply. The smoke swirled about his lungs. He felt his body go numb. His hearing heightened. He closed his eyes as he exhaled the thick, pungent smoke and began to meditate on the music within the cave. The gentle lapping of the water, the trickling of moisture down the smooth stone walls, the hollow whistle of the breeze from the surface as it rushed down the passage. He sat and let himself be drowned in the symphony of sounds.

The shadows of the cave were longer when the iguanaboina interrupted Jenaro's meditation with a splash. Jenaro opened his eyes to find the sea serpent had once again slithered its way onto the shore and curled its body around him. Water from the lagoon dripped off its scales and showered Jenaro.

"Is she alive?" Jenaro asked, nodding to the bubble.

"Yes, but only just," the dragon responded. "The hour approaches when I will be forced to decide. If I am not freed, I will consume her like the cattle these imbeciles feed to me."

Jenaro rose to his feet. A thin sliver of dread poked at his consciousness as he recognized the enormity of the dragon. He could not even see over its body and would have had to jump to even attempt to free himself from its coils. Its mouth was large enough to swallow one of the *Moin Hupia*'s dinghies whole. Consuming his frail, mortal frame would be no difficult task. "Queen Hannah would have me murder you to free her daughter."

The dragon scoffed. "She is a fool. She wants success without sacrifice. She wants bounty without work. For centuries her people lived and worked and thrived with the land that was given to them, yet for her it was not enough, so she imprisoned me here thinking that with my influence on her islands, her empire will grow to rival that of the Itiba Ara'. She is a fool."

"She would have me believe you only require another sacrifice; a soul to consume instead of the one whose life hangs in the balance."

"Then you are more foolish than her. I simply want my freedom."

Jenaro thought on the dragon's words. "If it is so simple, why not free yourself? Surely you can summon a storm to level this mountain."

The dragon sighed and lowered its head to his body. "In my current state, no, I could not. I am but a shadow of my past glory. Too long have I been away from the waters of the seas, the power of the waves that strengthens me. I tried, many times long ago, to escape this prison, but no matter my strength I could not seem to break these walls. It is as if they are cursed."

"Why not return the way you came?" Jenaro asked. "I would assume this lagoon has an outlet."

"Yes, deep underwater, many miles below the surface," the dragon said. "This lagoon was made by the Itiba Ara', ages ago, during their failed war against the cemi. Pele had long been dormant when they arrived and discovered its deep connection to the essences. They planned to continually harvest the power stored here. They used their knowledge of the majicks to reinforce the stone. They are the same stones the Hal'e used to collapse the passage back to sea."

"We did encounter eternal fire on the way here," Jenaro added.

The dragon growled in annoyance. "Yes, that fire, that wretched creation of theirs, formed out of pure malice. It was the only thing the Itiba Ara' found that could harm a cemi. The same force of evil that created the blue flame binds the stones here.

"The Itiba Ara' fortunately were never able to accomplish their task. Atabey and I flooded the chamber through the vents deep in the earth. Soon after, the war ended and the Itiba Ara' were stripped of their ability to manipulate the essences."

"But they continue to deal in the blue flame," Jenaro stated.

"If they can no longer manipulate majick, why do they still hold power over it?"

Juracán shifted uneasily. "That is one question I cannot answer. Rest assured though, their now meager control of the flame pales in comparison of what they could once do with it. Regardless, when the Itiba Ara' retreated to their now desolate home and left the Hal'e in charge, the Hal'e found the cave and the entire chamber full of sea water. It was a miracle to them; a mountain full of ocean water."

"It does indeed have the makings of the miraculous. So, tell me, Juracán, you knew of this lagoon?" Jenaro asked.

"Yes. I would, time and again, visit and commune with the people of these islands. Several generations ago, when my imprisonment began, I attempted to flee, but found my only means of ingress and egress had collapsed. The stones still bore the majick seal of the Itiba Ara' on them. No matter how much I assaulted them, they refused to budge."

Jenaro thought on this for a while before speaking again. "Free the girl, iguanaboina. Free the girl and I will free you."

The dragon snorted. "Do you think I did not try that tactic? I am not without sympathy. I offered this Queen Hannah the opportunity to save the girl. She is not concerned with the life of her daughter, only her legacy."

"Give me the girl. I will keep her until the queen agrees to free you."

The dragon snarled and coiled tighter around Jenaro. Jenaro's heart began to race. The serpent was slowly constricting his movement. Soon he would have no place to go.

"You would have me trust you, the betrayer? Yes, Jenaro Albizu del Rios, all cemi know of you and your treachery. The betrayer is your name. You would take the gift of Yaya meant to glorify your creator and instead use it to lead people astray. You combat the teachings of Yaya and teach his followers to rely on their own understanding, their own voices, and their own power! You are in no position to offer your services."

Jenaro inhaled sharply and held his breath before slowly exhaling. His ears felt hot. His heart continued to pound.

"No, Jenaro. As we speak the *mea palola* are beneath the waters, delving through the cursed stone that blocks my path. It is fortunate that their kind are not harmed by the malice in those stone." The dragon lowered its head and brought its enormous, hideous face as close to Jenaro's as it could.

Jenaro's jaw tightened. The dragon's bizarrely cold breath blew icy crystals against his skin. Its ferocious breathing rattled in his ears. He reached down to his dagger, pulled it free, then stared at the beast's eye, remembering the warmonger and how difficult it was to land a blow. It would be impossible to do so against the iguanaboina.

"Their assault of the city of Kauhale commenced early this morning; a ploy to keep the Hal'e occupied while the rest work to free me, unhindered by prying eyes. Soon, my vengeance will rain down upon the Hal'e."

The faces of the Hal'e in danger flashed before Jenaro's eyes, Hannah, Hildy, Malu. He saw Luysa and the crew aboard the *Moin Hupia*. Death and destruction would come to pass if Jenaro did not act. He shook his head, freeing himself from the macabre, and turned a fierce eye to the dragon. "It would seem I only have one course of action," Jenaro said as he raised his dagger.

The serpent was quick. It coiled tighter and snapped its jaws as Jenaro stabbed. His dagger hit nothing but air. Realizing his space was now severely limited, Jenaro chose the only available course of action and scampered up the body of the sea serpent. His reduced eyesight made it difficult, but he knew climbing was about more than just sight.

The iguanaboina began to uncoil itself and thrash about. It swung its tail and smashed the walls of the cave. Jenaro leapt from its body, hit the sand, and rolled to his right, running for cover. He narrowly avoiding a falling boulder in the process. He jumped and dove behind a stone, covering his ears as the dragon roared in anger. Jenaro shut his eyes while the howls shook the cave. Jenaro sat and covered his ears, then noticed a figure sitting next to him.

The figure next to him slowly began to take shape. He recognized the form, the feathery headdress and the sallow skin.

Jenaro snarled. "Not again."

"Unlike you, Jenaro Albizu del Rios, I still have a job to perform," Maboya said as the shadows dissipated revealing the cemi of the dead. "It is, admittedly and frustratingly, more difficult without my beloved ship."

Maboya gasped at the Andoli. He chuckled and ran a finger over his own eye. "It seems you have lost more than just a finger."

"Why are you here, Maboya?" Jenaro demanded; ignoring the slight as he peaked over the stone to locate the dragon.

"Why else would I be here?" Maboya asked in return. There was an evil twinkle in his eye. The cemi smiled. No matter what form he took, he was always had the same enormous, toothy grin.

Jenaro shook his head. "This beast will not be the end of me, Maboya."

"Oh, I know. Except, you are not the only person here."

Realizations struck Jenaro like a blow to his gut. He was breathless, frozen with fear. "Heidi," he managed.

Maboya laughed. It started deep in his gut and quaked through his rib cage before expelling like an explosion from his mouth.

"No! I will not allow it!" Jenaro shouted.

"It is not up to you, Andoli. Yaya decrees the number of your days. I simply retrieve and transfer souls to the third cave." Maboya gave Jenaro one last look. He spoke softly, with no ounce of malice. "It would not be this way if you would but join me."

Jenaro screamed and ran to the spring as Maboya blinked from behind the stone and appeared over the raging waters of the lagoon. He knelt and reached his hand below the waves, raising Heidi from her confinement. She opened her eyes. She was no longer unconscious, no longer imprisoned in her bubble, but she was also changed. This was the vision of a living Heidi.

Heidi's face was twisted and confused. She looked at Jenaro, cocking her head to the side before the shock of remembrance came over her. Then turned to gaze at Maboya. Maboya wrapped his right arm around her shoulder and with his left, waved goodbye to Jenaro. Both cemi and Heidi slowly faded to smoke and disappeared from the cave.

The wail of sorrow that escaped from Jenaro's mouth rang throughout the cave, louder than the Juracán's bellowing. He fell to his knees, fists balled, screaming until his cries turned to sobs. His body shook with anger and sadness as the cave quaked with the dragon's fury. Tears poured from eyes.

Meanwhile, Juracán thrashed and dove beneath the waves of the lagoon. The waters of the spring crashed against the shore and threw Jenaro back to the stairs. There was a great calamity as the dragon exploded forth from the lagoon and slammed its body against the farthest walls of the spring. Several deafening thuds rang out from beneath the waves. Jenaro lifted his head and watched as the water quaked and splashed then suddenly detonated from the surface of the lagoon. He remained flat on his back as the waves crashed around him, throwing him like a rag doll and pulling him toward the center. Jenaro fought against the current until his body impacted a boulder near the now submerged shoreline. He grasped it with all his strength.

The dragon roared once more then disappeared beneath the waves. Jenaro clung to his stone and watched as the water slowly returned to normal and he was able to set his feet upon the sand once more. His ears rang. His eyes burned. He could feel the tears welling. He dropped to the earth, raised his hands, and covered his face.

"I failed her," Jenaro sobbed into his palms.

Racing the Storm

The dragon never resurfaced. Jenaro figured the *mea palola* succeeded in opening the path back to sea. So, he exited the cave and was greeted by the fresh, open air and bright sunlight. It looked as if the path leading up to the cave of the spring was not spared the iguanaboina's fury. The earthquake split the marble stairs in two and crumbled several of the large moss-covered pillars.

Jenaro trudged through the wreckage, eyeing the crevasse that split the stairs in front of the cave entrance to the gateway of the spring. He turned his attention to the temple on the grounds and saw Agostin and Hildy standing outside. The *kafe* were nowhere in sight. Agostin noticed Jenaro first and waved, which prompted Hildy to turn and run next to him.

Hildy spoke with a speed that revealed her anxiety. "What was that quake? It drove the *mea palola* screaming to the jungle. And…you're alone. Why are you alone?"

Jenaro sighed and took a seat on the steps by the gate to the temple. "I couldn't save her. I couldn't save Heidi."

Hildy's shoulders dropped. Her face grew pale, and her eyes began to shimmer from the welling of tears. Her lips quivered as she turned her head from Jenaro. Without another word, she ran from him and into the temple, shouldering Agostin out of her way. Agostin quickly looked at Jenaro then back to Hildy and hurried after her. He reached the temple doors right as Hildy slammed them shut. Agostin dropped his head then slowly made his way and took a seat next to Jenaro.

"It escaped?" Agostin asked.

"It was all a diversion. The *mea palola* freed the dragon while assaulting Kauhale. They plan to aid in Juracán's vengeance in hopes of wresting control of the islands from Hannah."

"And Heidi? Is it true?"

Jenaro nodded. It was all he could do to keep from breaking down once more.

Agostin exhaled heavily. "Then we are doomed."

Jenaro clenched his teeth and jumped to his feet. "Don't you think I know that?" he shouted at Agostin. "I failed. I failed Hildy, I failed Heidi, and I failed you."

Agostin rose to his feet and grabbed Jenaro by the arms. "There's no need for that, Jenaro."

Jenaro pushed Agostin's hands away and started down the stone steps but stopped and turned back to his carib. "She was right there, Ago, right there. All I could do was watch… In one day, I signed two death warrants—Heidi's and our own—because I didn't have the power to save her."

Agostin climbed up the steps and embraced Jenaro tightly. "I have no words of wisdom or great soliloquy to give you, my lord and captain. Be angry, yes. Be upset. But don't let failure stop you from being who you are or accomplishing what you were meant to accomplish."

Jenaro stood silently for a moment before walking back up the stairs. He placed a hand on Agostin's shoulder and held it there briefly before continuing to the temple.

The inside of the temple resembled the wayshrine. The stink of death and burnt flesh hung on the air. Every surface was desecrated by the *mea palola*. The remains of unfortunate pilgrims lay scattered across the grimy marble. Anything that could burn lay in a charred and ashen heap in the center of the temple. Hildy was standing by an open window, chewing the nails of her left hand, and rotating the point of a dirk on the soiled, black iron sill. Jenaro approached and cleared his throat so as not to startle her. Hildy turned her head to face him. Tear stains ran from her red, swollen eyes, down her cheeks.

Hildy sniffled and slid her dirk back inside her sleeve before using her shirt to wipe her nose. "I always knew this was a possibility; that I would never see my sister again." She faced Jenaro and moved closer. She remained silent before shoving him. "Why did you go alone? Why didn't you let Agostin and I stay with you? We could have done something together. We could have saved Heidi. We could have overpowered those damned kafe and slain that dragon."

Hildy shoved Jenaro a second time, but he was ready for it and braced himself. It angered her and she began to pound his chest.

Her tears began to flow as she swung at Jenaro. Each strike landed with less and less force until she no longer swung but embraced him. She buried her face in his shoulder and sobbed.

"She's dead," she cried, "and I did nothing to stop it."

Jenaro wrapped his arms around her, and she cried. They stood that way for a long while, until Hildy no longer had any tears left. As soon as they ceased, she pulled herself from Jenaro's cmbrace, adjusted her tunic, and wiped her tear-stained face.

"The dragon is free. It used Heidi as a distraction while the *mea palola* gathered a force to attack the city. The remaining *mea palola* removed the stones blocking the dragon's escape. It made it seem as if this was all done last night, while we assaulted the wayshrine."

Hildy held her breath, then exhaled slowly and shook her head. "I need to get back to the city then."

They walked to the entrance when Agostin ran up the steps and through the doors.

"I think you two should see this."

Jenaro and Hildy followed Agostin out of the shrine. The temperature had dropped drastically. Black clouds circled on the horizon. A strong wind began to rush through the trees. The sky opened with cracks of thunder and brilliant flashes of lightning.

"It looks as if the circle of protection no longer stands around the islands," Jenaro stated.

"I don't think we can beat this storm back to Kauhale," Agostin uttered.

Jenaro nodded in agreement. "Yet we cannot stay here. None of these buildings look sturdy enough to withstand a gale of that magnitude."

"Why would you return to the city?" Hildy asked. "My mother will not take too kindly to your returning without Heidi."

Jenaro shook his head slightly. "We may have failed here, but maybe we can still help you and your people."

"There's a shortcut," Hildy sighed and stepped forward. "It's dangerous, and probably more so if we get caught in the storm, but it will cut our travel time in half. We can get back to the capitol before nightfall."

Jenaro turned to Hildy and asked, "Why didn't we take this short cut on our way here?"

Hildy quickly shook her head. "It's too steep to ascend and…" her sentence was cut off by a clap of thunder and the steadily increasing chatter of rain on stone. "Follow me and stay close. It can be treacherous, especially in the rain."

Death on the Air

Once off the mountain, and suffering only a few scrapes and bruises, Jenaro and Agostin followed Hildy through the trees until the brush gave way to the capital road. The storm was worsening, and the road was empty. Jenaro could barely see ten feet ahead of himself because of the heaviness of the rain.

Hildy began to jog and Jenaro and Agostin followed suit. The stone and clay road quickly turned slick with rushing water and washed-out mud. The wind threw debris over their path, leaves and twigs, pebbles and small stones.

Jenaro lost his footing multiple times as the deluge continued. Each fall brought new cuts and scrapes and a serious scowl upon his face. Agostin never failed to lend a hand and help his friend to his feet, even if it meant taking a spill himself. Hildy, on the other hand, remained nimble, almost dancing around each drop, and gliding across the water.

The sky grew even darker as the sun set behind their veil. "We should hurry. The rain is going to slow our pace, but we need to get back as soon as possible if we hope to help." Hildy shook her head then said, "Hopefully the casualties from the attack were minimal."

They made their way through the capital and toward the palace. Broken glass and splintered wood along with steaming, charred roofs of buildings around the plaza greeted them. Jenaro hung his head in shame at the state of things, blaming himself as he wondered if the damage was from Juracán or the *mea palola*.

Jenaro's horror continued as they approached the gates. The walls crumbled. Blood splattered on the gate and ran with the rainfall toward the sea. Inside the walls, physicians tended to guards and citizens alike. Two guards rushed to stop Hildy but recognized her and instead waved them through the line and to the steps of the palace. The guards stationed at the door quickly ushered the three inside.

It was chaos in the palace. Men with torches ran up and down the halls, splashing through rivers of standing water. Several palace servants worked to seal a fresh broken window while another swept up the shards of glass. Two women yelled about a collapsed ceiling while they limped arm in arm toward the physicians. Jenaro ran to their side. "Was anyone hurt?" he asked.

"Yes, us and many more," one woman answered. "They are all still back there."

Jenaro shook his head in disappointment. "Can you walk?"

"I can, but she cannot without help."

Jenaro wasted no time lifting the woman in his arms and hurrying her to the physicians. Without a second of hesitation, he ran down the hall toward the collapsed ceiling, Agostin hot on his heels. A palace guard was directing the effort to remove the rubble. "What do you need?" Jenaro asked.

"There are more trapped inside," the guard said. "Help us remove this rubble."

He and Agostin used their combined strength to lift and roll enormous piles of rubble out of the way. Agostin released his axe and chopped larger beams of wood down to more manageable sizes that Jenaro could lift and toss from the doorway. All the while, rain poured in from the hole in the roof. Once a big enough opening was made, Jenaro crawled through and helped those trapped inside make their way to the Agostin's strong arms, who pulled them from the hole with ease. The rubble began to groan and shift as the last person was removed.

"Jenaro! There's no time left. The rest of the roof is about to collapse," Agostin called.

"There are still bodies down here," Jenaro called back.

"It's too late!" Agostin cried as the roof moaned and began to give way. "Jenaro, now!"

Jenaro grabbed his friend's hand and was pulled from the hole just as the roof gave way, breathing a sigh of relief as they avoided being crushed. They then carried the wounded back to the physicians at the palace entrance. Hildy had taken charge of the recovery effort. She divided those well enough to help into teams and handed out orders. Jenaro and Agostin reached her side at the same time as Kino, the steward.

Kino shouted, "Hildy! Thank the gods you're safe!" He stopped in front of her and placed both his hands on her shoulders. The steward noticed Jenaro and gasped. "By the gods, what did that beast do to your face?"

Jenaro reached up and pulled his scarf lower over his eye.

"It was not the dragon, but *mea palola* who scarred my lord," Agostin answered for Jenaro.

The steward clenched his teeth and took a step back. "I see…" he muttered, his face adopting a far-away stare.

"Where's mother?" Hildy asked.

"She's upstairs. Those damned *mea palola* struck hard and fast. Then the storm crept up out of nowhere. The citizens are calling it dark majick." Kino stopped to take a breath, obviously exasperated from a day of chaos. "I'll let her know you've returned…and I'll fetch towels and dry clothes for you and your companions."

"Tell her we'll be in her sitting room," Hildy called after Kino.

Hildy led them into the queen's sitting room where they found two stacks of linens, towels and several elaborate robes.

Once they were covered in robes and towels, the three convened by the windows. The outside world was drowning in Juracán's fury. Lightning flashed across the sky. Thunder shook the windows. The rain battered the palace in a cacophony of drummed roof tiles and dribbling ceilings. The streets below were a raging river. Torrents of water took debris of all kinds and ferried it downhill, toward the coast. Several fires were burning despite the heavy rain. Jenaro could barely make out the city guard directing the few souls braving the storm to find shelter, corralling as many as possible into the gates of the palace. Yet, beyond the square was shrouded in a gray sheet of rain and gale force winds.

Jenaro grimaced as he thought of Luysa, Malu, and the crew of the *Moin Hupia*. Hopefully the ship was holding up. It survived many storms over the three years he captained her without so much as a scratch. Yet the last few tempests wore the shiny veneer thin. If it was indeed a majickal vessel, perhaps the essence was waning. Jenaro was so deep in thought, he failed to notice Agostin carry a stool to his side and sit himself down.

"They would have taken precautions, my lord," Agostin told Jenaro. "Luysa captained longer than we've been alive."

Jenaro shook his head and sighed. "I know. They are probably in safer waters than we are now. What are we even going to say to the queen?"

"For starters, you can tell me how exactly you failed," Queen Hannah said as she stormed through the doors. Her voice echoed through the sitting room, above the racket from just beyond the windows. "I tasked you to kill the beast and bring back my daughter and yet here we are, enduring a storm no doubt summoned by that demon."

"Mother," Hildy began, but stopped short when Jenaro held up his hand and stepped toward the queen.

"Tell me, Queen Hannah, what made you think you could outsmart a cemi?" Jenaro asked venomously.

The queen was visibly taken aback by Jenaro's newly scarred face, if only for the briefest of moments. She quickly rebounded and matched his tone. "I am queen of the Hal'e Empire, and that dragon is a dying relic of a long dead age. The gods left our world and took their majicks with them, yet that dragon thinks it can still claim dominion over us after centuries of absence? I think not." Hannah took a step toward Jenaro and jabbed a finger at his chest. "The age of deities has long been over. It is past time this beast joined the rest of its brood."

Jenaro clenched his teeth. "You put my life, the lives of my crew, and your daughter at risk because of your arrogance."

"Speaking of my daughter," Hannah said as she made a show of glancing around her sitting room. "Hildy? Where is your sister?"

Hildy's head dropped. "Heidi is…" she trailed off.

"Heidi is yet another victim of your arrogance, queen," Jenaro snarled.

The queen turned to Jenaro. Her eyes were wide, an unbridled fury within. "You, Andoli, have killed my daughter?"

Jenaro shook his head. "I did no such thing."

"Then the beast that rages against my city?"

"It is innocent as well. The blood of your daughter lies on your hands. Had you not imprisoned him in the first place none of this would have happened. There would have been no need for sacrifices or the deaths or your own family had you just been content to rule Hal'e without ambitions of empire!"

Queen Hannah's face twisted in rage. She stepped to strike Jenaro but was greeted instead by Hildy who caught her loose hand. She struggled for a moment with Hildy, and then dropped her hand. Hildy then pulled her into an embrace. "Heidi is dead, mother. There is nothing we can do about it. It was no fault of Jenaro."

Hannah's face was stone.

"Stop this ridiculous feud, mother," Hildy pleaded, but her speech was cut short by a crash of glass from the throne room. There shortly followed the sound of yelling and a howling wind whistling its way through the palace.

"There is no winning against a creature that can conjure such a storm," Hildy continued. "Let Jenaro and Agostin go free, pray for forgiveness, and maybe the beast will be satisfied."

Hildy released her grasp. Hannah's gaze had only grown harder. She raised her hand and slapped Hildy across the face so violently, it sent Hildy doubling over. Jenaro rushed in and saved Hildy from hitting the ground while Agostin stepped in front of the queen, shielding the two from the queen's wrath. The queen growled at Agostin and readied another strike, but upon seeing the fearless, unwavering fortitude of Agostin, instead turned, and stormed from the room. Jenaro helped Hildy to her feet in time to see a detachment of imperial guards enter the room. Jenaro was less than surprised to see Queen Hannah bring up the rear.

"Arrest them!" she shouted. "All of them! Put them in chains and throw them in a cell!"

Agostin raised his fists, but Jenaro stayed his hand.

"Even Hildy, your grace?" the guard captain, the one Hildy called Kono, asked.

"Mother!" Hildy shouted back. "What are you doing?"

"All of them!" the queen bellowed.

The guards closed in on the three.

Jenaro and Agostin went along peacefully. Hildy, on the other hand, did not take her incarceration with the same modicum of civility. The guards threw the three of them into the same cell, with the guard captain profusely apologizing to Hildy the entire time.

"How I managed to escape prison in the Andolins and yet face time behind bars twice in as many days here is both shocking and quite frankly an indictment on our justice system, Jenaro," Agostin said as he seated himself. "What's worse: this is the same cell I was in two days ago."

Hildy growled. "This is unbelievable! Captain! Let me out of here immediately! You have no authority to arrest a kamahao!"

Jenaro took a seat next to Agostin.

"Hildy!" Agostin shouted above her shrieks.

Hildy stopped and looked at the carib.

"Calm yourself and look at me," he said firmly. "Your shouting is not helping our situation."

For a moment, the only sounds in the cell were that of Hildy's heavy breathing.

"What are we supposed to do now?" Agostin asked.

Jenaro let out a sigh. "Await our execution."

The Necklace

No more words were said that evening. Jenaro sat with his head in his hands for much of the night. Agostin sat by the cell door, whispering what Jenaro could only imagine were the last rites of the Andoli. Jenaro nodded solemnly as he too recited in his head the Andoli sailor's prayer. Hildy paced for a while before curling up on the bench and falling to sleep. All the while, the rage of Juracán never ceased. The assault lasted well into the night. Water began to seep down the cell walls and stream its way down the steps and into the holding cells. A small layer of water covered the floor, which brought about groans of discomfort from the other inhabitants of the jail.

Agostin relocated to the bench and managed to curl his big frame into a ball and pass out. Jenaro, on the other hand, moved to the floor. He avoided sleep, simply staring at the empty cell across the way. Thoughts of grief over Hildy flooded his consciousness. He cried silently until he had no more tears, then his tears gave way to anger and resentment. He beat at his crossed legs until his fists hurt and his legs felt bruised.

Morning came and brought with it a lull in the storm. It also gave Jenaro a new resolve. He was not over grieving the loss of Heidi, but he knew rotting in a Hal'e cell was not his destiny.

Hildy stirred first, then Agostin. The water level in the cell had risen considerably. The other cellmates were also awake, grumbling their disapproval of their situation. Before long, a few guards appeared with a hand pump and a long, flexible tube and began to work the water from the jail. The guard captain also appeared. The dark circles around his eyes and a shadow of hair on his face were stark indicators of the harrowing night he had survived. After a few choice words with the mouthier prisoners, the captain stopped at Jenaro's cell.

"Get up, you three," the captain whispered in Coquien.

Jenaro raised his head. Speaking in his native tongue could only mean one thing. The captain was about to do or say something he did not want his troops to know.

"The queen was raving all night, talking about executing the three of you. The steward warned her of the repercussions of killing the son of a sovereign nation, especially an ally, but she did not listen. She had the steward taken by the kamahao."

Hildy gasped. "Oh no."

Jenaro sighed. "I don't need to ask what that means. Kino is dead."

Kono swallowed hard. "This is…" he paused and shook his head. "Kino told me to get you three out of the city."

Jenaro shook his head. "Why would he want that and why would either of you help us?"

Hildy answered, "Kono here and Kino, the steward, are brothers."

"Kino's loyalties were always to the people, not the crown," Kono said with a nod to Hildy. "It was one thing your companion here and my brother shared."

Jenaro and Agostin looked to Hildy. She avoided their stares.

"Enough talk. Quickly, we haven't the time to chatter. You must make it to your ship before the storm returns."

"But how?" Jenaro asked, motioning to the bars.

Kono smiled, "Hildy is more than capable."

The captain barked an order and one of the pumping guards opened the cell. The captain tossed each of them a bundle containing their dried clothes. He then rushed himself and the guards from the prison, leaving the cell wide open.

After they dressed, Jenaro yanked at the jail door. "It's no use; this thing is solid top to bottom." He was close to kicking it when he turned around at the sound of Hildy's voice.

"I can open it, Jenaro," she said as she pulled two twisted pieces of metal from inside her sleeve. "That's why Kono brought us our clothes."

"You can pick the lock?" Agostin asked.

Hildy smiled and moved to the door. In a manner of seconds, the lock snapped, and the door swung open. She quietly let them up the stairs and out of the prison. They crept through the palace, keeping to the shadows. Hildy moved swiftly and decisively, her knowledge of the hallways and passages invaluable.

She found a bare stone passage, barely big enough for one person. It was dark with no ounce of light to be found. Hildy held her hand up and crept into the darkness. Jenaro and Agostin kept their heads on swivels, prepared to jump into the dark if they were spotted. Soon, though, Hildy returned with a small lamp and beckoned them to follow.

The passageway sloped downward and turned many times. They walked for nearly half an hour until they came upon a heavy wooden door, reinforced with black iron. Hildy examined the door and the frame. She pressed her heel into a particular stone only, nothing happened. She stomped it over and over to no avail. There was no knob or handle and no lock. She pushed against it and frowned. "It's stuck," she groaned.

"Let me try," Agostin said. The three of them shuffled around in the passageway until Agostin stood next to the door. "This one?"

Hildy nodded.

Agostin raised his leg then stomped as hard as he could. The stone ground against its neighbors. Agostin slammed his foot down once more, which brought a heavy clunk a metallic whir from somewhere beyond the door. Then, with a gentle push, the door opened.

Agostin led them inside a sizable stone cistern. A footbridge spanned the cistern to a ladder. The ladder ran up several stories to a hatch. A drop from the bridge meant falling for about a story before landing in the murk Jenaro could only assume was water. The lantern light reflected brilliantly off its surface. There was also a chest by the ladder.

Agostin hurried over the bridge and opened the chest. It contained all their gear that was confiscated, blades, axes, and the like. He quickly and carefully removed their weapons and bags, and then paused before closing the lid. Jenaro was right behind him while Hildy ensured the door was once again sealed.

"What is it Ago?" Jenaro asked.

Agostin shook his head and wiped his face with his hand. He inhaled through his nose but did not speak. Jenaro knelt and investigated the chest. At the bottom, hidden underneath all their personal effects, was Jenaro's necklace–stone, feather, and fang shimmering in the low light.

Jenaro took the necklace in his right hand and smiled as he put it on. "The cemi it seems have a sense of humor."

Agostin climbed up the ladder first. Jenaro waved Hildy up behind the lumbering carib. She quickly concealed her dirks, strapped on her belt, and scurried up the black iron ladder. Jenaro brought up the rear and was the last one through the hatch at the top.

The room on the other side of the hatch was a rectory. It was clean and orderly, a sure sign of constant use. Bookshelves packed with volumes lined the walls of the round building. There was a desk with a small lamp and an open journal, an inkwell, and a used mug. Sitting above the desk hung a painting. Two men stood next to an aged woman. The men looked like Kino and Kono.

It was a sturdy building as the wind and rain of Juracán's fury had not damaged it. Agostin was waiting by the door when Jenaro finished his climb. He closed and latched the hatch and replaced the aged rug atop.

"I guess this is where we say goodbye," Jenaro said to Hildy.

Hildy turned and looked at him. Disgust painted her face. "What makes you think you can be rid of me that easily?"

Jenaro raised his hands in defense. "I just thought now that our task is complete, we would go our separate ways."

"So, you planned to abandon me?" Hildy shot back, arms akimbo, face stern. "I don't think so, Jenaro del Rios. You do not get to walk away yet again."

"We do not plan to stay here, Hildy," Jenaro replied, "and we will most likely never return."

Hildy took a step toward Jenaro and brought her face close to his. "My mother wanted to kill me alongside you. Kauhale is no longer the city I grew up in. This place is no longer my home…not without Heidi." She let her tears fall with a sniffle.

Jenaro took a deep breath and looked to Agostin.

Agostin nodded slightly before saying, "We could always use another crew member."

"You could do much worse than a kamahao," Hildy assured him, wiping her face.

"Can you get us to the coast unseen?" Jenaro asked Hildy.

Hildy squinted and turned toward the door. "What kind of dumb question is that?"

Agostin held open the door for Hildy and Jenaro. As Jenaro walked past, his eyes met those of his carib. Nothing needed to be said.

The rectory was located a short walk from the beachhead. Things were calm outside the rectory walls. The sky remained overcast. A steady drizzle continued to fall. The wind weakened to a breeze. The city of Kauhale, however, was not as peaceful. The streets were littered with debris: palm leaves, branches, trash, and glass. Several buildings they marched past were completely in shambles. The open-air construction which benefited from the mild, tropical weather, proved useless against Juracán's tormenting rain and wind. Cabanas and bungalows were flattened. Small numbers of people surveyed the wreckage along with city guards, each one visibly flabbergasted and overcome with emotion.

The beachhead was more of the same. Seaweed and debris were strewn about the sand, mingling with driftwood and the shredded remains of beachfront property. The harbor was loaded with flotsam; the remains of any unfortunate ship not lucky enough to be dry-docked. Hildy led them along the beach. All the while, Jenaro scanned the horizon for any sign of the *Moin Hupia*. He was beginning to lose hope of ever seeing the ship again when Agostin spotted the shimmering black hull. It was a speck on the horizon.

"There, Jenaro!" Agostin shouted and pointed. "It seems that Malu was successful. What else could glimmer so on such an overcast morning?"

Hildy stopped and looked in the same direction. "That's going to be an exhausting row. On a lighter note, you have quite the eyesight, Agostin!"

Agostin bowed his head. "Just another blessing bestowed upon all Anacaona."

"Please Hildy, he doesn't need his head to get any bigger," Jenaro said, rolling his eyes. "Where are you leading us?"

"There's a cove about a mile down the beach," Hildy replied, pointing over her shoulder with her thumb. "The kamahao keep several small craft in a cave. Hopefully they survived the storm."

They ran together to the cove. It was indeed home to three small craft, two skiffs and a dinghy. They stopped and examined each vessel for seaworthiness. The skiffs were damaged and taking on water. The dinghy was without a sail and oars.

"How often are these craft used?" Jenaro asked disappointedly.

"Not often enough," Hildy responded. Her mouth twisted and her brow furrowed. Then, as if struck by lightning, her countenance brightened. "Wait a second; we might have a way to your ship after all!"

Hildy ran across the dock toward an unimposing, nondescript boat house. The windows were shuttered, and the door was locked fast. Hildy fumbled with the lock and growled.

"Allow me," Agostin said, brandishing Hano's axe. In one swift blow, he severed the lock from the door then bowed to Hildy.

Hildy proceeded to throw open the doors. Inside was yet another boat hidden under a heavy canvas sheet.

"Help me remove this cover," Hildy said as she moved to one side.

Jenaro quickly moved to the other and raised the sheet. The vessel underneath the sheet made Jenaro smile and Agostin whistle.

"A Cibaoan steamer," Jenaro said as he ran his hands on the gilded steel frame. It was a modestly sized pleasure vessel with room for five or six passengers, a galley, and a single steam stack covered in Cibaoan friezes embellished directly into the metal.

Hildy nodded as she boarded the steamer. "My captain acquired this vessel after pirates had commandeered it and ran out of fuel north of our islands. They attempted to stuff the furnace with all sorts of flammable material, but the ship refused to move. The steamer used a particular fuel and would not move unless it had exactly that. Turns out the grease used by the *mea palola* worked, though not as efficiently as its regular supply. At any rate, the owners of the ship were found dead on board. The queen didn't see the need for such a craft, so it was left in the hands of the kamahao."

Jenaro threw open the bay doors before climbing aboard. He sat next to Hildy at the helm. Agostin took his seat near the prow.

Hildy pressed a few buttons and with a puff of black smoke, the ship rumbled to life. "Fuel levels look good. We should have no problem making it to your ship."

"Take us there," Jenaro said and reclined.

The steamer chugged its way out of the cave and sped out to sea. The waves were choppy, but the little steamer rode each one with ease. *Moin Hupia* sat motionless amidst the rough waters. Jenaro noticed Luysa and Malu standing at the helm. The little shipwright waved enthusiatically. He punched Agostin in the arm and shouted for joy then returned the wave. Relief washed over him. His crew and his ship were safe and sound.

Hildy pulled the steamer next to the *Moin Hupia* and Luysa lowered the ladder. Jenaro let Agostin and Hildy disembark from the steamer first. He needed a few more moments to compose himself. As soon as his feet touched the deck, Luysa ran and embraced him. The show of emotion caught Jenaro off guard.

"You have no idea how happy I am to see you two," Jenaro said.

"The feeling is mutual," Luysa concurred.

Jenaro properly introduced Hildy. The crew welcomed her warmly, save Luysa who shared the same cold, dissecting look she had given Jenaro when they first met. She asked several questions of Hildy's qualifications, yet Jenaro could not tell if her answers satisfied the former captain turned navigator.

"Malu, do you think you can pilot that steamer back to the island?" Jenaro asked the shipwright.

Malu grimaced and pensively wrung his hands. "Yes, Jenaro, but the truth is, I think I'd rather stay on with you. This ship may need more work. And you won't find a better shipwright."

Jenaro smiled. "You're more than welcome to stay. I guess we should keep the steamer then." The crew attached the vessel to the *Moin Hupia*'s cargo lift and brought the steamer aboard. Once they were finished, Agostin gave the order and the crew got to work raising the sails. After, Hildy accompanied Jenaro and Luysa to the helm.

Jenaro looked back at Kauhale and frowned. "The storm looks to be reforming to the east of the archipelago. Juracán is planning another assault."

"Juracán?" Luysa asked incredulously. "That how you lost your eye?"

Jenaro smirked and raised a hand to the scrap covering his wound. "We fought a trio of *mea palola*; lizard-men. I was overzealous during a lunge and did not leave myself room to maneuver. A shard of wood ran down my face and turned my eye into jelly."

Luysa nodded several times. "You're beginning to gather quite a collection of deformities," she said plainly. "It's the mark of a good captain," she said and motioned to her arm. "Where to, Captain?"

Jenaro mused momentarily before saying, "I've never visited Sandria. I hear it's a paradise. If we sail south, then west we can reach the continent in no time at all."

Luysa nodded. "A good plan. I'll plot a course," she said and left Hildy and Jenaro alone at the helm.

"Have you ever seen Sandria? Would you like to?" Jenaro asked.

Hildy smirked. "Since when does the captain ask his most junior crew her opinion?"

Jenaro smiled. "I'm not your normal captain."

Hildy nodded. "Sandria sounds lovely. So, what are your orders?"

"If you would see my first mate, Agostin; I believe he may have some duties for you."

Hildy grinned slyly then ran to the masts leaving Jenaro alone at the helm. Thunder boomed in the distance. A blanket of dark clouds rolled over the city of Kauhale. The rough waters of the eastern reaches of the Summer Sea battered the glimmering obsidian hull of the *Moin Hupia*. Jenaro could feel the ship beginning to rock back and forth with the waves. He couldn't help but wonder how long Juracán's fury would last. Would it drown Kauhale just to punish one woman? Would it tear the islands apart with its ferocious winds? Would it show mercy and return to the sea? His hand absentmindedly went to his necklace. He ran his fingers over the cold steel feather, tri-faceted stone, and fang on his mother's rope. He closed his eyes and envisioned her, laughing and smiling in the third cave.

HILDY

The Tide Rolls In

The silence was deafening. Every breath I took reverberated obnoxiously in my ears. Even the din from the batu semi-finals could be heard with perfect clarity. Each soul, every last Andoli in and around the tent of the behique waited on bated breath, as if frightened that the slightest noise would destroy what they had just experienced. For the briefest of moments, I forgot where I was and what I was doing. Why was I standing in front of this large and silent crowd? That was until I heard a *psst* from my right. I turned to see Isadore, off stage, beckoning me with both hands to join her. Behind her were the Suma and two other behique as well as Arecibo. I blinked back to reality and retrieved my pipe and rod from the table and quickly shuffled off stage.

Arecibo greeted me first, hugging me tightly and kissing both my cheeks. He hadn't changed a bit. He still dressed casually in loose-fitting, navy-blue trousers and an airy, linen tunic dyed an outlandish shade of orange. His boots were worn and scuffed. He wore his thick, dark hair the exact same way he had when we were children, miming the look of our baba. His eyes still gleamed mischievous, and his smile was still just a smirk, as if replaying a joke over and over in his head. I heard him speak, saw his mouth move, but couldn't make out any of the words. There was a dense fog about my senses. All I wanted to do was sit down.

I must have vocalized my desire because I was almost immediately swept from the main stage back to my ready room.

The behique waited outside, but the Suma, Isadore, and Arecibo ushered me in.

They gathered around me. I couldn't help but stare blankly at each of them. Their lips continued to move. Isadore waved her hand in front of my face. I don't know how long I stayed in that state of stupor. I only know it washed away the moment Luisa came barging in.

Her face was bright red. Her jaw was clenched shut. She took a breath and demanded with quiet rage. "I would like a word with my sister."

The Suma nodded and Isadore bowed, but I rose from my chair and put my hand out to stop them.

"No, they can stay. If there's anything you have to say to me, you can do it in front of the Suma B—behique, my carib, and our natiao."

The rage in Luisa's eyes began to smolder.

Isadore stopped cold. The Suma Behique turned to me, her face grave and dark.

"Hildy, she is Cacique," the Suma uttered.

"And as Suma Behique even she is subject to you in matters of faith and religion in the islands, is she not?" I asked. "At least until she decides to disband the Temple all together."

Nobody moved.

"I believe my dear sister is here to discuss a matter of faith and religion," I continued.

Luisa growled. "Impudence! I don't care if you are my itu d'itu; you defied a direct order given by your Cacique!"

Arecibo stepped forward putting himself in between myself and Luisa.

"What in Yaya's name is going on here?" Arecibo asked. "What is wrong with you two?"

My eyes remained locked on my sister's and never wavered.

"Luisa here is angry because after she tried to meddle in my Telling I disobeyed her."

"She spreads heresy!" Luisa shouted and pointed violently at me. "The Telling is not some family history! It is the tale of the gods, a word from the cemi themselves!"

"That is not entirely true," the Suma Behique stated.

We all turned to face her.

"I beg your pardon, Suma?" Luisa said, emphasizing the last word with a palpable measure of disgust.

"The Telling was never meant to be stagnant. It always was and always will be a living, oral history of our people. It was meant to teach Andoli about the ways of the cemi, not to bring about repentance or evoke feelings of piety. It was and always has been a teaching tool.

"What Hildy has done over the past two evenings is teach in her own voice and her own way."

Luisa was fuming. "In her case this means spreading heresies like the malevolent nature of Yaya or Jenaro adventuring to serve himself and not the cemi!"

The Suma nodded. "I have smoked the cassava and communed with our cemi. They do not object to her Telling which tells me one of two things. Either they do not care how we see them, the coqui beneath their heels, or her Telling is correct, and they have no way to defend against her accusations."

Luisa glared at me. "Be that as it may, I ordered you to perform the traditional Telling, especially with our bibi present and you disobeyed that order."

"You cannot order a behique to do things contrary to the will of the Suma or the cemi," I reiterated.

"Please, you two!" Arecibo cried. "Peace! Our bibi enjoyed the telling. I could see the look of pride on her face."

"I do not recall asking for your opinion, natiao," Luisa

growled. "Do you not have some royal errand you should be on? Or maybe you need a new assignment, perhaps to Itibanen or Ultan-Mere this time?"

Arecibo saw the threat, bowed his head and backed away.

I turned to Aré and reached for his hand. He gave me a curious stare then stood straight and stepped to my side.

"Oh, now you two defy me together?" Luisa mocked.

"The Telling is not yours to give, Luisa. It is mine. Stay out of it."

Luisa moved closer and raised her hand to strike. That is when Isadore leapt forward and shielded me from the blow. Luisa's hand landed hard against Isadore's face. Izzy recoiled, but stood tall, imposing. Luisa gasped and turned to leave the tent.

"I wasn't planning on doing this until after tomorrow's Telling, but I see no point in delaying it. The Telling is officially cancelled, and the Temple disbanded, effective immediately." She stopped and looked over her shoulder back at me. "That is one thing I can control."

She left as violently as she had appeared. The tent flaps to my room whipped and cracked as Luisa departed. I turned my attention to the Suma Behique. Her head was bowed, and her eyes closed tight.

"Can she actually do that?" Isadore asked. "I mean, disband the behique?"

The Suma breathed deeply before answering. "I will talk to Luisa in the morning. I think she needs some time to cool off."

"It'll take years for her to cool off," Arecibo scoffed.

The Suma turned to us with a smile. "Young ones, do not let this sour your Areíto. Go now and rejoice, celebrate, and keep all this from your minds." With that, the Suma nodded and took her leave.

Arecibo, Isadore, and I all breathed a collective sigh of relief.

"Maboya take me, I've never seen her so angry!" Isadore said as she began to pace. "It has me wound tight like a spring! I'm ready to fight someone now."

Arecibo laughed. "I forget you are usually excused from her rage."

I nodded. "That was pretty typical for Luisa."

"Well, I do not envy you two being her siblings," Isadore replied with a fervent shake of her head.

Arecibo and I exchanged knowing glances before I spoke. "Can you give us a moment, Aré? I want to change out of these vestments and into my normal robes."

Arecibo nodded and embraced me. "Of course, Hildy. I am on my way out of the city. I was only given leave for the day and must return to my post by sun-up. It was good to see you, and your Telling was illuminating. I don't care what Luisa says." He pointed at Isadore and smiled. "And you, carib," he paused.

Isadore stopped her pacing and stood at attention.

"With stone or steel," he said, reciting the opening lines of the motto of the carib.

Isadore forced down a smile and nodded instead. "With stone or steel," she repeated.

Arecibo left and Isadore let her smile beam through. "How does he know the creed of the carib?"

I shook my head. "If I'm honest, I'm not even sure what exactly Arecibo does for the military, save that he spends a lot of time in Itibanen."

Isadore seemed pleased with my answer. She took a seat at my table and asked, "What do you feel like doing tonight for Areíto? I was thinking we would go catch a game. There is still one semi-final tonight. It should be a killer of a match."

I shrugged and began to change out of my vestments. "I don't know, Isadore. I think I just want to go home. The Telling and the confrontation with Luisa have drained me of every ounce of energy."

Isadore smiled weakly. "Then let's go home."

I continued to change out of my vestments and into my normal robes in silence. Isadore helped fold my ceremonial vestments and pack away my pipe and rod in my chest. I was just starting to get my bearings back, and we finally were ready to leave. Unfortunately, the ill-gotten peace that filled my quarters was shattered just beyond the curtains.

Chaos

My fellow behique were running in every direction, little tempests of raging chaos and wildly flapping robes. They were shouting and pointing at things, grabbing everything they could in their arms or in the folds of their robes. Two women I did not recognize collided and fell to the dirt, dropping hammered metal bowls in the process. Another robed behique was pulling the Temple banners from their hooks and hurriedly bundling them together. I looked to Isadore. Her eyes were wide, her mouth a tight line. The color in her face had drained.

"What in the name of Yaya..." Isadore swore.

I swallowed hard. My teeth began to chatter, and I could feel my hands shaking. "This isn't...something is not right."

Isadore nodded. "And something tells me we won't be able to get out using the front entrance." She walked quickly to the outer wall of the tent and with one quick slash of her blades, made a makeshift door. She waved for me to follow her through.

The warm evening air felt strange on my skin. It was tinged with something foreign that gave me goosebumps. I was hoping for a refreshing contradiction to the temperature inside the tent but was sorely disappointed. That awkward feeling of discomfort grew stronger when I noticed the stirring at the front of the tent of the behique. A crowd had gathered and was roaring. Fists were raised and pumping. A few held lanterns on poles. There were people in the crowd from every area of the Andolins and representatives from all walks of life: Jibaros, Borinkens, and Nitainos. Men crossed their arms. Women waved their fists. All of them were angry, burning with a fire stoked by something I could not place.

"Do you think Luisa really disbanded the b–behique?" I asked as Isadore grabbed my hand and pulled me away.

"Hurry, Hildy," Isadore commanded me. "We need to hurry."

We ran out of the plaza of the cemi as fast as we could, through a sea of angry faces. People shouted at guards. Guazabara were corralling people toward the exits. A city guard and a guaza worked to stop an altercation. Everyone's faces were blurred by the dark. Isadore held fast to my hand as she shouted and shoved her way through the crowds. Several people moved to strike whomever it was that dared to push them. Yet when their eyes rested upon Isadore and me, they quickly moved aside, raising the palm of peace.

Soon we were out of the largest concentration of people and headed toward a small contingent of city guards directing people from the batéy. Their captain saw Isadore and nodded, calling to her.

"Isadore! Behique!" She shouted with a wave. "Over here! You need to leave the batéy immediately."

"What is going on, Captain?" I asked as we approached.

Her face grew grim. "You don't know?"

Isadore shook her head. "No, we left the plaza, and the crowds were already on the verge of rioting."

"It's the Cacique," the captain began. "She made a public announcement shortly after the Telling disbanding the temple of the behique and cancelling the Telling."

I shook my head. "This is all because of Luisa," I mumbled.

"Cacique Luisa said the behique were spreading blasphemies and could no longer be trusted. Nobody expected the crowd to react the way they did, but the behique have always been on the side of the people…"

Isadore leaned closer to me. I could see fear on her face. "We have to get to the manse."

"You should be safe. Nobody has harmed anybody, at least not seriously. There've been a few brawls, but order is almost restored." The captain paused before continuing in a lower voice. "Nobody would harm a behique. Nobody is that stupid."

As soon as her words left her mouth, a small crowd of people began to approach. Their voices were raised. Their heads held high, and their chests bowed out.

"Quickly, quickly!" the captain ordered. "Let the behique pass!"

"Get your hands off that behique!" I heard from the crowd.

"Don't you touch her!"

"I would have never figured the city guard side against the behique. Don't they guard the temple?"

"That is behique Hildy, the Teller!"

"We're coming to save you, behique!"

"Go!" The captain shouted again, pushing us through the gate.

Isadore and I wasted no time. We ran from the scene. My heart was pounding. My head hurt. My feet began to bleed as the sandals I wore rubbed the skin from my ankles and heels. Yet we ran, through ragged breath and aches and pains, driven by fear.

The streets of Puerto Zafiro were full of people, young and old. Most were shouting and moving toward the batéy. Some hung from their windows and peeked out of their doors. Nobody paid Izzy and me any mind. When we reached the gates of the manse, the guards quickly ushered us inside and barred and latched them behind us.

It took Isadore and me a moment to recover from all the

running. Izzy was doubled over. I ran my hands through my hair and kept them planted firmly on my scalp.

"Have Luisa and my bibi returned?" I asked the guard as I attempted to catch my breath.

The first one shook his head.

"If they have, they did not enter through our gate," the second guard answered.

"What in the world is happening?" I asked.

Isadore stood up straight and shook out her limbs. "Did Luisa expect a different response when she basically cancelled an entire religion?"

We walked into the manse, still heaving from all the running, and headed to my room. Even the servants were mumbling about what was happening right outside the walls. Their whispers echoed off the polished stone and marble like waves beating against the shore.

"This is all in response to your Telling," Isadore said as she closed the door behind us. "People heard your stories. They latched on to your message."

"No, it's just a Telling."

"It was something new and fresh, something they all wanted and needed but didn't know they needed. Luisa took it all away from them."

I shook my head. "We've had Tellings b–before."

"Hildy, the people hate Luisa. This was the last straw."

I shook my head again. "She may not be as loved as my b–bibi or respected as Arecibo, but I wouldn't say they hate her."

Isadore threw herself on my overstuffed chair, her usual spot. "You don't see it because you're her kin. The people love your bibi Tinima, this is true. They have always loved Arecibo and you; that fact is also true. But Luisa...she is shrewd, harsh, and ambitious, too ambitious for their liking. This is what they talk about when you're not around. These are the rumors I hear every day during my briefings."

"I don't think they'd riot just to provoke her."

Izzy kicked off her shoes. "As I said, this was the *last* straw," she said and began to rub her feet.

"Oh Izzy, your feet!" I cried. "They're covered in b–blood."

Isadore smirked. "It isn't the first time. I'll be fine, Hildy, I promise."

"You may be fine, but my chair will not be." I extended my hand out to her and snapped. "Come now; let's go take care of those."

Isadore sighed and took my hand. I marched her to the bathroom and began to draw water for a bath, but only filled it enough to wash our feet. I ordered her into the tub and joined her. We sat on the edge and submerged our feet.

"What are we going to do?" I asked.

"We're going to try and relax here in the manse," Isadore replied as she soaked her feet clean. "If Luisa is smart, she will let this all blow over. The people will be angry for a while, but if she decides to quench that anger, it's only going to get worse."

"What if she isn't smart?"

Isadore twisted her lips into a frown. "Then there may be violence."

I frowned as well. "I hope it doesn't come to that."

"I hope so too."

We finished in the tub. I changed into my night dress. Isadore stripped down to her small clothes, but not before running to the kitchen for some sustenance. When she returned, she had brought with her a platter with an array of goodies. Marcus and Feliz out did themselves–Isadore had pork stuffed fritters, rice, fried plantains, and a jug of mango wine dangling from her belt. We ate our fill by the window, consuming every bite in silence as we watched the city below.

Concentrated auras of lamp light danced up and down the streets. Some moved in great clumps, others scattered about like so many ants. Occasionally, clumps of light would meet and create a brilliant ocher corona. We sat there in silence, straining our ears to hear the commotion below, yet at this distance, the rumbling, shouts, and screams were but a faint buzz periodically punctuated by a pop or whistle. We both wondered what was happening. I was curious of the fate of the civilians and the captain who ferried us through her checkpoint. I found myself closing my eyes and praying to Yaya and Atabey, begging them to keep everyone safe, especially Arecibo, Luisa, and our bibi.

Soon thereafter, we went to bed. My stomach was full of food and wine and my head was spinning from the events of the evening. I'm sure the alcohol might have had a little to do with that as well. My nerves were a twisted bundle, a mess of anxiety and worry. If not for the wine, I might have stayed up all night. Yet thanks to the wine mixed with all my emotional and physical exhaustion, I soon gave way to the bliss of sleep, leaving behind my worry to the realm of the living and accepting the embrace of unconsciousness.

A Strange, Metamorphic Wind

It was still dark when the urgent pounding at my bedroom door startled me from my sleep. Isadore woke in much the same mood as me; sweating, swearing, and frazzled. Only she leapt from the bed with daggers in hand.

After a series of deep, stabilizing breaths, she said ominously, "I'll go see who it is."

I rolled over, lit my bedside lamp, and threw my feet to the floor. I heard Izzy arguing with someone, so I tip-toed to the edge of my bedroom to eavesdrop on the conversation. That's when I heard the distinct sound of my brother's voice. I exited my bedroom and just as I suspected, Arecibo stood in front of Isadore, pleading his case to my vigilant carib.

"You cannot stop me from seeing her, Isadore!" he whisper-shouted.

Izzy was rearing back, ready to fling an innumerable amount of insults at him until I spoke.

"Izzy, it's okay," I said gently as I placed my hand on her shoulder. She turned her head to me. The fire in her eyes diminished. Her face softened. She forced a smile and nodded then took a seat in her usual spot: my overstuffed armchair.

I examined my natiao in the low light of my sitting room. Dried sweat and grime stained his cheeks and forehead. Dirt and dust peppered his hair. A bright red shiner of a bruise showed on his jaw. His face remained stoic and still, yet his eyes revealed an unusual amount of panic.

"Hildy" Arecibo began as he bowed his head, "how soon can you be dressed and ready?"

"Ready for what, Arecibo?" I asked. "I thought you said you were heading back to your p–post?"

Arecibo waved away the question. "It is no longer safe in Puerto Zafiro. Things got…" he paused to find the right word, "out of control while you slept."

I gasped. "Bibi? Luisa?"

He shook his head. "It seems our worst fears have come to pass. Blood was spilled in these small hours of the morning. It's not safe for you, even here in the manse."

"Why wouldn't she be safe in the manse?" Isadore spoke up.

"A behique was killed in the riots," Arecibo explained. "Nobody knows how or why, or they're not telling how or why. The people grew angry and retaliated. That only led to a greater retaliation by the guaza. Word spread that the behique were inciting the riots. A regiment of royal marines has begun reinforcing the city guard as well as the manse guard. Guaza are being rounded up, but it is a difficult task. They are much more skilled than regular infantry, even the marines."

"Aré, why did you avoid my question about b–bibi and Luisa?" I tried to keep my voice as steady as possible.

Arecibo lowered his head enough to avert his eyes from my gaze. He took a deep breath and said, "I don't know where they are. My men think some of the guazabara got them to safety somewhere away from the batéy, maybe even out of the city."

"Has no one gone to look for them?" I asked with a squeak.

Arecibo nodded. "I had the captain of the marine contingent send a squad. They have yet to return."

"Can you trust your men?" Isadore spoke up. I couldn't tell if it was a question or an accusation.

Arecibo's confidence returned at Isadore's statement. He held his head high and shoulders back in a defiant defense of his position. "We protect the people of the Andolins. We didn't choose a side, but when guaza began killing people in the street, we couldn't stand by and do nothing."

"You didn't answer the question. Can you trust your men? Because it will only take one of them to do something stupid and turn this riot into a full-blown civil war," Isadore responded in a low, unamused tone.

"Enough, both of you!" I shouted. "Aré, if b–bibi and Luisa aren't found, I can't just leave. I have a duty to the people of the Andolins as much as you do."

"You don't understand, Hildy. The guazabara are saying this is all your doing. As numerous as the combined force of marines, city, and manse guards are, the guazabara still pose a very real threat to all our safety. A single guaza took down ten of the marines right in front of me. It took another ten to subdue her."

"B–but I don't understand…why me? Why not go after the Suma B–behique?"

"Because the guaza already slaughtered a number of behique in the city, including the Suma."

I felt my soul cry out as if it wanted to leave my body. My jaw began to tremble, my heart dropped to my stomach. I felt sick and frightened and angry all at once. My face grew cold, and a shiver began to overtake my body. The Suma's words began to echo in my ears: *A strange, metamorphic wind begins to blow. It sweeps around you and tosses all else aside.* I shook my head in disbelief. Isadore stood from her chair and walked to my side to steady me.

"Arecibo is right, Hildy," Isadore said. "We should go."

I wanted to cry. "I can't leave," I said. My voice cracked. I felt a lump in my throat. "Who will govern if they don't find b–bibi…or Luisa?"

Arecibo stepped forward. He cupped my hand in his. The

skin of his palms was rough and cold. I could feel callouses pressing against my skin.

"I can handle things here, but only if you're safe," Arecibo said.

I looked at Isadore. Her face was strained; concern lined the corners of her eyes and mouth. "Maybe this is our chance, Hildy," she said. "Remember Comerio's Cove?"

"I was only kidding," I stammered. "I couldn't leave. How would I survive?"

I looked into Isadore's eyes. For as long as I had known Izzy, those caramel-colored eyes looked on with a warmth and fearlessness I saw nowhere else. When we were children facing stern discipline, her eyes were hard as stone. When I was timid and afraid, her eyes gave me strength enough to do what needed to be done. I could always tell the measure of her person simply by her eyes. Now in the face of imminent danger, realizing that Arecibo's dire news would bring about uncertainty, her eyes twinkled with doubt. She was as scared as I.

"If I am to leave Puerto Zafiro, where do I go? What will I do?" I asked them both.

Arecibo nodded and took a deep breath. "There are some people who owe me a favor or two. I have already called on them to help. Where they go is entirely out of my hands, though. You'll have to pack light, travel as commoners, not Andoli royalty. You can be friends, lovers even, just nobody of consequence. Izzy, you're good with a blade which will fetch plenty of grunt work. Hildy, you know how to fish like a pro and can play that flute of yours and make snakes dance and birds sing. People are always looking for an entertainer."

I nodded, impressed by his plan. Aré was prepared. "If you don't know where we're going, how will you b–be able to find us or keep contact with us?"

Arecibo flashed a sly grin. "Don't you worry about that, Hildy. Now, quickly! Pack light! Oh, and here." He reached beneath his tunic and pulled out a shimmering gold rope. The necklace was long and thick. Three charms hung like pendants at the end: a polished three-faceted stone, a feather made of a strange bluish alloy, and a fang that looked like genuine bone from the mouth of a great serpent. It was the necklace, the family heirloom passed down through the generations from Jenaro Albizu del Rios himself. I was at a loss for words.

"Baba gave this to me before he passed on to the third cave. He said it had majickal powers meant to protect those of our family." He stopped and chuckled. "Looking back on everything I've done with the military… It's funny, I never believed him until this moment. Take it. It'll protect you now."

I nodded to Arecibo and immediately put the necklace around my neck, tucking it safely beneath my gown.

"Now hurry! Get packed and meet me at the slip outside the naval pier."

"The one with a weird gate?" Isadore asked.

Arecibo pointed and nodded. With that, he took his leave. Isadore and I were once again alone. I took a seat in my giant chair. Izzy squeezed in next to me. I looked down at my hands. They were shaking. Isadore reached over and clasped her hands in mine. Her lower lip was quivering.

"I'm scared, Hildy," she said to me.

I swallowed hard and replied, "Me too, Izzy. Me too." I touched the necklace beneath my gown and said, "B–but if the legends are true, this necklace should p–protect us."

We sat for only a moment before the urgency of our situation forced us to snap to and ready ourselves for exile. I ran to my room and snatched my pack from deep in my closet. The canvas rucksack was buried behind boxes and underneath old, worn shoes and shirts. I patted it clean, wafting away clouds of dust and disuse.

As I began to pack, I concentrated on the most important things first: my best boots and trousers and my warmest coat, because for some reason I imagined Isadore and I sailing somewhere cold. I tossed in a scarf for my hair and my favorite cloak.

That is when I looked up and saw myself in the mirror. A young Andoli girl with long, dark braids and tired, clean olive skin stared back at me with no sign of hard labor or stress on her countenance. The woman staring at me was a frightened princess of the Andolins, a novice in the temple of the behique, a storyteller, a girl who loved Marcos' famous mango treats, and playing daggers with Isadore and her Tía Celia. She was worried about her family and scared for her future.

I looked into my bag and turned it over, emptying all its contents on my bed. I quickly dug into my closet, grabbed my sturdiest boots, my least comfortable trousers, and my most plain cloak. I also grabbed a solid red scarf I had worn for a decade and a couple of simple, striped tunics. I pulled one last change of clothes from the closet, slammed it shut, and quickly changed into my hastily gathered outfit. I threw on a brick red tunic with long sleeves and tucked it into my old sailing trousers. I was momentarily surprised they still fit. I slipped on my shoes and threw a plain brown canvas cloak over my shoulders. I then ran to my chest and tossed my knife, my flute, and my coin pouch into my rucksack. After that, I grabbed my bag and ran to the bathroom, placing the rucksack in my washbasin.

I stopped to take one last look at myself before grabbing my braid and my knife. Without hesitating, I cut my hair and tossed the severed braid to the floor. I stared at the woman before me.

She was now frightened, but determined. Unsure, but courageous.

Isadore stood in my doorway, rucksack slung across her back, blades at her hips. She had quickly thrown on a long sleeved, olive colored knit sheath tucked into a pair of tight navy pants stuffed into tall black boots. A russet leather jacket completed her ensemble.

"Short hair looks good on you," Isadore said.

I gazed at the braid on the floor and ran my fingers through my short new locks. "It's just hair, right?"

Izzy nodded. "Come on, Hildy. We shouldn't make Arecibo and his contact wait."

Empty Streets

It had been years since I climbed out of my bedroom window and scurried down the walls of the manse. I felt confident in my ability, yet, standing on the edge brought a wave of fear and vertigo I had never experienced. I quickly turned my face, back to my window, closed my eyes, and tried desperately to regain control of myself. My breathing grew erratic, and my palms slick with nervous sweat.

"Hildy," Izzy called quietly from her spot down the wall. "Hildy, you can do it!"

I shook my head, more at my own fear than her unwavering belief in me. After a few deep breaths, and drying my hands on my sleeve, I started moving again. The ledge outside my window led to a corner with a series of jutting stones that were basically a makeshift ladder. We climbed down a single story before a sturdy branch from my mother's garden tree reached up along the side of the wall. Izzy and I were both able to reach the enormous branch with a bit of stretch. Izzy acrobatically leapt to the trunk while I gracelessly lost my balance and nearly fell to the garden if not for her quick instincts. Instead of climbing down the tree, we traipsed along the branches, climbing to a large limb that bent its way over the wall. It allowed us to step easily from the tree to the stone of the wall. I accomplished this transition with much less drama.

We followed the garden wall until it reached the thick outer wall surrounding the manse. Izzy called for a boost. I crouched near the wall and offered her my palms. She stepped up and I lifted as hard as I could. It was just enough. Isadore's hands reached the edge of the parapet. She pulled herself up, glanced left and right, and then quickly darted out of sight.

My eyes went wide. I inhaled abruptly then threw myself against the wall, trying to hide my frame in the shadows.

"Izzy!" I called softly, but there was no reply. That was when I heard the boots, several pairs, clattering along the seastone parapet. It was the watchmen of the manse guard performing their rounds.

I put my hand to my mouth in a desperate attempt to smother the noise of my breathing. Luckily, they did not loiter, but marched right past my spot. I peeked and saw the points of two lances bobbing away down the length of the wall. I cupped my hands by my mouth and once more cried for Isadore.

"Izzy! Maboya take me, where is she?"

I looked up and saw her face. She flashed me a smile before reaching down to me.

"Your bag first, then I'll pull you up."

I breathed a sigh of relief then tossed her my sack. She placed it behind her then reached down again.

"Jump!" Isadore instructed.

I leapt as high as I could but missed Izzy's hands by mere inches.

"Try using the wall as a step," she whispered down to me.

I nodded, took a few steps back then ran forward using the wall to help lift myself upwards. This time, my palm smacked just above her wrists. I held on tight, as did she, and used my feet to help kick my way up the wall as Izzy pulled me from her spot. Once on the parapet, I placed my pack on my back and followed Izzy. We ran single file down the parapet built to allow two men on horseback to ride abreast. Our lightly shod feet allowed us to run without any clicking of heels against the opalescent seastone.

We ran to the nearest guard tower. The door squeaked

loudly as we entered, causing us to pause in place, teeth clenched, hearts racing. Yet, the noise was not enough to stir the few guards playing a rather vocal game of cards a floor below us. Izzy held one finger to her mouth and motioned to the stairs. I slowly followed her up the stone steps leading to the roof. As I reached the landing, a chorus of shouts came from the card game. The sudden outburst made me squeak. I covered my mouth and looked at Izzy. She was baring her teeth at me in a look that screamed for silence.

We were statues, immobile, while the cheering continued. I held my breath the entire time, afraid to inhale and alert the guards to our presence. When we both realized my squeak had gone unnoticed, Isadore waved me on ahead. Up the ladder I went to the roof hatch and opened it to the roof. Isadore was hot on my heels.

She closed the hatch behind us and breathed an audible sigh of relief. "I don't know why, but I felt like we were about to get in trouble with your bibi just then."

"It's all the sneaking around," I said sorely.

"You're probably right." She responded as she removed a length of rope from her shoulder.

"Is that what you disappeared for?"

She nodded and began to unwind it. "That and I noticed the guards…didn't want our escape to end before it even began. It should be long enough to get us to the ground. We're only about three stories up at this side of the wall." Isadore tied the rope to the inside latch of the roof access and threw the rest over the edge of the tower. "You go first. I'll make sure you make it down safely. Leave your pack here though. It'll unbalance you."

Rope climbing was never my strong suit and to say I struggled was an understatement. I thought at first, I would lose my grip and fall. My hands screamed in pain from my white-knuckle grip. My arms burned and cried for relief. Even my legs were no more than a slip or gentle breeze away from simply giving up and letting me dangle. Yet, before I knew it, I reached the end. Unfortunately, I was still about four feet above the ground. I let go and landed awkwardly, feeling my ankle give. I resisted the urge to scream as pain ran up my leg and straight up to my watering eyes. I steadied myself and applied a little weight to it.

"It's not b–broken," I said to myself as I hobbled away from the rope. "I think it's just sprained."

I looked up and gave Isadore a wave. She waved back then dropped our bags, one at a time. I caught both and quickly set them aside. As soon as I turned back to the rope, Izzy was already halfway down. She descended like a mono descends a tree. She dropped at the end of the rope, standing up straight and smiling.

"You looked like a p–pro," I said in awe, "or the cacique of monos."

She stuck her tongue out at me. "Are you okay? You look like you're favoring that leg."

I grimaced. "I landed wrong. I'm fine; it's not b–broken, just sprained."

Isadore frowned and pulled a scarf from her pack. She folded it up then wrapped it tightly around my ankle. The pressure felt nice and relieved some of the pain. "We'll go slowly," she said as she stood and adjusted her pack.

A strange fog moved in to cover the city as we journeyed to the slip. It wasn't an uncommon sight in the small hours before dawn, but this mist felt dark, oppressive, and almost evil. It was a thick cloud, like syrup, and covered all the city lamps in a shroud giving them an appearance of a floating specter. The light emanating from various buildings appeared distant and foreign. To make matters worse, the low rumbling babble from the rioters quieted to a whisper and only came through in short waves, like a calm sea lapping against the hull of a ship. Screams rose and fell in swells.

Isadore slowed her pace. It was safer than accidentally running into a streetlamp or tripping over some upturned cobblestone, especially in my already injured state. We crept carefully down each street, keeping as close to the buildings as possible. The streets were nearly empty. It seemed the events of the evening were polarizing the populace, just as Arecibo said. Either they were enraged and rioting, as the ebb of shouts proved, or trying to hide inside in case they were needed for work in the morning.

The closer we got to the crossroads; the more debris littered the streets. Broken glass and shards of wood were strewn across the stones. Bruised and damaged fruit from a vendor's cart rolled past like tumbleweeds. A pack of stray dogs rushed by, barking and paying us no mind.

When we reached the crossroads, Isadore stopped and threw her hand up. "We should head south then double back up to the docks." Her voice was low, almost a whisper, and as unsure as I had ever heard.

"What's the matter?" I asked.

She nodded her head at the opposite street corner. I peered through the fog and gasped. Laying in a pile next to the streetlamp were several people–no. Bodies. Their throats were slashed, their faces twisted in ghastly horror. I quickly looked away and held my breath. It was all I could do to keep from vomiting. Isadore was not as lucky. She doubled over and retched into the street. When she stood upright once more, she had grown pale. I put my hand in hers.

"Lead us south, Izzy. We can do this."

She swallowed and wiped a mess of vomit from her chin on her jacket sleeve. "Do you think you can manage if we pick up the pace? I'd rather not come across any more sights like that, or worse, become part of the next one."

I nodded, but before we moved away, noticed something strange near the pile of the dead. A figure, vaguely the shape and size of a man, yet drenched in shadow, peered at me from behind the bodies. I felt my skin turn clammy and shiver run up my spine. I blinked and the figure vanished.

We moved quickly south and thankfully encountered less chaos. The streets were clear. As we neared our junction, a gang of city guards turned the corner. They were jogging toward the crossroads. We froze in place. There was no telling if that group of Andoli were dead by their hand or the groups of guazabara that Arecibo warned us about. Thankfully, they ran past just as the dogs had, failing to notice the two women on the opposite side of the street.

Pier Street was more of the same, except the bay itself seemed to glow from all the lamps of the naval ships. Arecibo had said they were on alert, but from the intensity of the glow, I gathered none of them had taken to open waters just yet.

"Where is this slip Arecibo spoke of?" I asked Isadore.

"This way," Arecibo's voice called from behind the curtain of fog.

I looked around in a desperate attempt to find his location but saw nothing.

"Aré!" I called back. "Where are you?" No sooner had the words left my mouth did my brother's silhouette appear in the fog. He emerged like a shadow.

Isadore was caught off guard by his appearance and brandished her blades, but quickly sheathed her steel when she saw his face. His tunic hung from his shoulders tattered and slashed to pieces. I noticed several lacerations on his skin: arms, hands, even face. His left cheek appeared scuffed and bruised. A lock of hair covered in blood plastered itself against his forehead. His right eye was completely swollen shut. He cradled his right arm with his left. A lantern dangled haphazardly from his free hand.

"Cemi be merciful, what happened to you!" I shouted and ran to him. Izzy did the same.

Arecibo shook his head and cracked a crooked smile attempting to deemphasize his injuries. "This? This is nothing. I just ran into a little trouble with a guaza."

"This is more than a little trouble, Arecibo," Isadore corrected gently.

He rolled his good eye. "It's fine. I'm fine. You two though must leave right now."

I gave Arecibo a concerned look then nodded. "Lead on."

He nodded back and beckoned us deeper into the fog. We walked along the pier toward Arecibo's hidden slip. The fog thickened and nearly swallowed everything, even the sound of our shoes against the street. The air grew heavy. I could feel it weighing on my lungs, forcing them to work harder for each breath.

I wanted to question him about his injuries but knew he wouldn't answer. Aré had always been stubborn and secretive. It was the typical machismo that plagued the males in my family. Even as a boy, when he broke his leg, he didn't make a sound–at least not in front of baba, Luisa, and I. Yet, that night, when he thought he was alone, I snuck in to check on him and was surprised to hear silent sobs.

I knew he was strong. Nevertheless, I worried for him. It had only been an hour since we last saw him and his condition had severely worsened. Whatever was happening in the city was clearly beyond what I could have ever imagined.

Arecibo led us straight to the strange gates Isadore

mentioned earlier in the manse. They did seem out of place in the Andoli capital, let alone at the naval pier. They were not forged of iron or steel, but rather peculiar pearly silver without a single speck of rust or sea spray stains adorning the surface. The traditional Andoli shapes were absent, favoring instead delicate spirals and sweeping leaves I recognized from my books on Itibanen architecture. They opened easily without sound or strain. Beyond that was a staircase that ran down and away from the harbor.

Arecibo descended slowly, and Isadore and I followed. At the bottom of the stair was an expansive hall that twisted out of sight. Arecibo placed his lantern on a small pedestal, grabbed a thin chip of wood, and lit it with his fire. He then tossed it at the wall. With a great whoosh, a thin line of electric blue flame shot across the walls of the hallway, speeding ahead of us and lighting our path.

"Where are we?" I asked in amazement.

"It's an old Itiban smuggler's tunnel, from before our independence when the Andolins were ruled by the Ultans." Arecibo explained.

"That would explain the excellent condition of the stone and the gate, in spite of the sea air," Isadore replied.

"And the eternal flame," I added, still flabbergasted. "It had no idea it could be quenched, let alone reignite like that!"

Arecibo shrugged. "I honestly do not know much about it, just that it fires up just a quick and is extinguished every single time I return."

"You and your men still use this tunnel?" I asked.

"In my position, you find yourself making allies in unlikely places," he said as we came to a stop. Arecibo placed a hand against the wall. I noticed he was growing pale.

"Aré, are you okay?" I asked, touching his shoulder.

He nodded. "I just needed to take a quick break."

"We can rest as long as you need," I said taking a deep breath. My muscles ached and my head slowly but steadily began to pound. I needed to lay down and sleep, but had no clue when I'd be able.

Arecibo cleared his throat and spat blood on the stones before standing up straight. Without missing so much as a beat, he continued walking and talking. "I saved an Itiba Ara' several years ago. Turned out he was second in command of an Itiban smuggling ring. The Itiba told me if I ever needed his services, he would readily oblige. So, I called in a favor. Turns out, he already knew of this hidden slip."

For a moment, I swore I saw movement deep within the darkness, a shuffling figure, trying to quickly move out of sight. I shook my head and continued following Aré.

"So, we're leaving the Andolins aboard a smuggling vessel," Isadore said. "You've entrusted our lives to pirates."

"I wouldn't call them pirates," Arecibo responded. "They're more of the ambitious entrepreneur types."

Isadore chuckled mirthlessly. "That's a cute way of saying criminal."

The tunnel made another sharp turn and opened next to a canal. They both ran on for as far as my eye could see. There were countless pathways that intersected with the canal tunnel. Some dead ended shortly after they crossed our path. Others disappeared into the blackness beyond the eternal flame.

Arecibo shook his head. "They are good at getting things in and out of places without much fuss, including Andoli like myself. It's either this or take your chances with the guaza."

"Do you think they would send someone after us?" I asked.

Arecibo bobbed his head in uncertainty. "Honestly, I have no idea. If Luisa gave them the order to kill the behique, then they're going to carry that order until every behique is dead, even if that means killing a member of the royal family. That absolute loyalty is how they are trained."

"Brainwashed, if you ask me," Isadore added.

Arecibo nodded. "Luisa and only Luisa can stop their rampage, and we don't know if Luisa is even alive or not."

I shook my head. "I can't b–believe our sister would even want me dead."

"You're a behique," Arecibo stated plainly. "She sees the behique as an obstacle to complete and supreme autocracy of the Andolins."

"But we're b–blood, siblings," I said, voice trailing as if trying to convince myself.

"I know. It is the only shred of hope I still cling to. Could Luisa commit such evil?" Arecibo shook his head. "All I know is that Luisa has only ever been concerned with one thing: control of the Andolins. With the behique out of the way, the last check to the throne is gone. She can now institute her will without the advice or input of such a meddlesome group."

A faint bubbling of water and the drip-drip of condensation falling from the ceiling filled the air. I was more than happy the air inside the tunnel smelled of briny ocean water instead of refuse or death. An occasional rat scurried past our feet, preferring the darkness over the eerie blue light.

"How much farther?" I asked. It came out angrier than I expected. I wasn't meaning to sound impatient. My ankle was beginning to hurt again, and I needed to sit and let it rest.

"Not long now," Arecibo responded kindly. He raised his arm with a wince and pointed to a stairway just coming into view.

The stairway led to an enormous underground cistern. The canal opened into a larger boat channel. Crates and barrels of increasingly impressive size and quantity lined the walls and sat on pallets. In the center of the warehouse, the boat channel flowed along to two massive bay doors that were shut and locked from the inside by a chain with links thicker than my arm. A footbridge crossed the canal near the opposite wall from the doors, connecting both sides of the warehouse. Resting at anchor was a sleek, Itiban khufu. It was a mono-hull vessel shaped like a dagger. There were a handful of smugglers aboard, shuffling about and passing boxes and crates to each other. A few were lowering a pallet below deck. One smuggler noticed Arecibo and whistled. Everyone stopped. All eyes rested upon the three Andoli now standing before the ship. With a passive wave, the smugglers returned to their tasks.

Arecibo held out his hand, calling for us to stop. He then continued to the ship and placed himself in front of the gangway as an Itiba emerged from below deck and ran to meet him. He wore only an open vest, of black satin with gold stitching, letting his chest and belly show. His belly swayed and jiggled with each word he spoke. His tree trunk legs were covered with purple silk trousers. He was barefoot. His ears, lips, and brows were pierced and decorated in gold and rubies.

Isadore and I stood and stared at the vessel. I had heard it said many times that Andoli shipwrights are second only to the Itiba but until now, I could not say I wholly believed it. It was a painfully beautiful ship composed of an ashen wood combined with the same silvery metal from the gate. Both wood and metal refracted light like beautiful gemstones. Each line aboard the craft looked as if it were spun gold. The sails were lowered, but I could tell the billowy sheets were the purest white imaginable. The multicolored standards that hung on the flag line were radiant with symbols and pictures I did not recognize.

After a few moments of hushed conversation, Arecibo called Izzy and me to his side. "This here is Eshaq al'Caiman, captain of the *Celes Fain*. Captain, this is my sister Hildy Rios and her carib Isadore Anacaona."

"Common names among the Andoli?" Eshaq asked. He was a towering behemoth, even by Itiban standards, with curly ebony hair and dark skin. A long-braided goatee fell from his chin adorned with stone runes and glittering gemstones. His burgundy eyes glimmered as he looked at us. Smuggling had been good to Eshaq, and it showed.

"Common enough," Arecibo replied.

"Hmm," Eshaq mused, twisting his thick mustache, curled at the tips. His fingers were garnished with gaudy rings on each finger. "We may need to consider aliases…" he said absent-mindedly. "But where are my manners. Greetings Hildy and Isadore, he said with a bow, "and welcome aboard my ship."

Isadore and I refrained from bowing. I feared attempting his Itiban flourish and failing would offend him and the custom. We, however, returned the gesture with the palm of peace. Eshaq appeared pleased and satisfied with our greeting.

"Your brother here has informed me of your troubles. We will give you safe passage to Itibanen as a favor between friends, but to avoid any questions from nosier dockhands, you'll need to become sailors and smugglers."

"My natiao made us aware of this, Captain Eshaq," I said with a slight bow of my head.

"Good, good," Eshaq said quickly. "Every sailor aboard works for their meals and their cut, whether that be maintaining cargo, maintenance, cooking, or watch. You'll be no different, I'm afraid, granted some measure of leniency will be given due to the sharp learning curve."

Isadore and I exchanged glances and nodded in agreement.

Eshaq grinned. "'Yes, Captain,' is the traditional and acceptable response."

"Yes, Captain," Isadore and I said in unison.

Eshaq then turned his attention to Arecibo. "I'll let you say your farewells. We sail as soon as you are aboard," he said to Isadore, and I then swayed up the plank.

I turned to Arecibo and tried to force a smile but only succeeded in tearing up and choking back a sob. "How will I know when I can return?" I asked.

"I'll get word to you, you don't have to worry about that," he said softly. "Things will turn out alright, Hildy, it just may take some time. I cannot tell you how long you may be away."

"And if they don't get b–better?"

Arecibo sighed and pulled me into an embrace. "Worst case scenario? You never return, but live a normal life with Isadore."

I held him tight and sniffed back a few more tears. "I'll hope to hear good news from you, Aré."

"You are the moon of my life," Arecibo said with a smile.

"And the stars of my forever," I replied and hugged him once more.

We separated and I noticed a few tears in his eyes. I wanted to comment but instead let him have his moment of sorrow. I watched as Isadore and Arecibo said their farewells. He was oddly more affectionate toward her than I expected, embracing her tightly and kissing her on both cheeks. It caught Izzy and me both off guard. He then waved goodbye and disappeared into the shadows.

The Sea Calls

As soon as we were aboard, Captain Eshaq gave the order, and the bay doors were opened. Soon, the ship started out of the harbor and toward the open sea. It was nothing like how I imagined leaving my home, especially for the first time. In my dreams the sun was shining, and the breeze was strong and swift. The sea shone like a jewel as Izzy and I watched our home fade into the horizon. Instead, the fog that hung thick over the city and the harbor shrouded my last view of home, even with the virgin rays of the morning beginning to peek over the horizon. Faint, smoky glows waved goodbye and disappeared, swallowed up by the dark nothingness of the sea. Isadore stood next to me the entire time. Our hands were interlocked, tighter than I had ever experienced. We were both afraid but having her with me was undeniably comforting. I couldn't ask for a better travel companion, even in exile.

Shortly after the Andolins disappeared from our sight and the *Celes Fain* shot its way to the open seas, Isadore and I made our way below deck to our shared quarters. The deck below was just as beautiful as the top deck. Carved ashen wood adorned every surface. The walls and decks were painted and polished and looked more like chiseled stone than wood. Our quarters were just as elaborate. It was a cramped little space with one trunk between the two of us and two hammocks as beds, one hanging above the other. The fabric of our new beds looked as expensive as they were comfortable.

The single trunk made unpacking a breeze. Shortly after, Eshaq's first mate, Lalia appeared to take us to our duty stations.

Lalia was a half Itiba Ara', beautiful if fair skinned, which I imagined she gained from an Ultan parent. Apparently, the captain had apprised everyone aboard of their new crewmates.

It was a long first day. Isadore was assigned to deck duty, and I was put in the mess hall to help with the ship's cook. I knew how to prepare meals from my time in the Temple kitchens, but that was for only a handful of behique. This, cooking for an entire ship, was hard work. I soon found myself with a greater appreciation for all Feliz and Marcos did. Dicing vegetables proved difficult when the floor you stood on rocked and rolled with the waves. I constantly dropped utensils for the sweat that coated my hands. I even fell once, dropping an entire bowl of salted pork. The cook treated me kindly, but I could tell my lack of speed frustrated him.

When we were relieved for the day, we both met back at our quarters, exhaustion dripping from our faces. I couldn't remember when I last slept. Before we knew it, we were both in our small clothes and laying in the hammocks, giving our new beds a try. I didn't think my sore muscles would cooperate so Isadore, thankfully, took the top bunk.

"I never imagined my first trip away from the Andolins would take me to Itibanen." I said.

"I never imagined I would ever leave the Andolins," Isadore replied. "Were you hoping the captain was headed to Hal'e or Sandria, you know somewhere tropical, like home? I've heard stories of the Sandrians. Those southerners sure know how to live!"

"No, I mean, I don't know," I said. "Just Itibanen never crossed my mind."

"Too bad it can't be a disappearing island or the Cibaoan capital of Cu' Ciba like in the Jenaro and Agostin stories."

I shrugged in my hammock. "I don't know. Jenaro and

Agostin never went to Itibanen or Ultan-Mere. Maybe you and I can have adventures they never even dreamed of."

"Maybe," Isadore responded.

She didn't say so, but I could hear the uncertainty in her voice. She couldn't promise me any adventure. She couldn't promise me the wise counsel and support that Agostin showed Jenaro.

I took a deep breath. "Things will be okay, Izzy. We'll be okay."

She sighed. "I don't want to think about it right now," she said dismissively.

"Okay," I said and left it alone.

"You know what I do want to talk about though, right?"

"How strange Arecibo's goodbye was?"

She giggled. "It was so odd. But no, I am a little upset that I won't get to hear the end of Jenaro's tale. I mean, I know how it ends, thanks to the history books, but I wanted to hear your version, your Telling."

"There's nothing stopping us from completing the Telling. If there is a speaker and someone to listen, the Telling can take place." I paused and sighed. The events of the day were finally beginning to take their toll on me. The third part of the Telling was meant to represent the third and final cave.

When I finally spoke once more, my words were soft and weak. "Well, the third part of the telling, the third cave, is meant to represent death. I'm starting to think we've had enough death and destruction for a while."

Isadore responded, but not with words. The slow and steady inhale and exhale of exhausted sleep rose from her hammock. I smiled and soon, I too succumbed to my own exhaustion, lulled to sleep by the gentle rolls of the ship.

I dreamt of home. I could see the sun shining off the

seastone walls of the manse. I could feel the warm, briny breeze tossing my hair and dancing on my skin as I studied in one of the outdoor plazas within the temple grounds. I could smell the savory and sweet aromas of Marcos's cooking and taste the freshest and sweetest mangoes Feliz always kept stocked just for me. But the joy was short lived, and the dreams quickly turned sour, replaced by flashes of fear and anger.

I saw fires ablaze all throughout the city. Rooftops burned trapping people and animals inside. The noxious smell of burning bodies made my dream self retch. Cries of horror assaulted my ear drums. Swarming crowds of blank-eyed Andoli overtook me. They grabbed at my arms, wrists, and ankles with cold, vicious hands that hurt me and left steaming marks on my skin. I cried out, but nobody heard my pleas until, when I thought all was lost, a strange figure shrouded in black parted the throngs of Andoli and scooped me up off the ground, saving me from harm. When I turned to look at my hero, its face caused me to scream in fright. The only thing I saw aside from the purest and deepest abyssal darkness flicked out from just beyond the nothingness, a forked tongue.

I awoke with a start. My heart raced nearly out of my chest. My sheet and small clothes, drenched in my cold sweat, clung fast to my skin. It took me several minutes to catch my breath. I sat in my hammock, listening to the soft whimpering sleep of Isadore. That was when I heard a voice calling my name, barely audible, quieter than a whisper. I thought it was in my head or simply residual from the dream. I would have even believed it had my eyes not spotted an eerie, spectral luminescence creep into my cabin, riding on the tails of a mysterious fog.

"Izzy?" I called out quietly, but my voice echoed as if in a vault. Once it subsided, I peeked over the side of the hammock and nearly fell to the floor. She was gone.

"She cannot hear you. You're alone with me," a voice spoke through the fog. It sounded hollow and hoarse with a raspiness only disuse could give.

I held my breath and let the words bounce around my skull. "Who is there?" I asked, but I knew who lay beyond the fog. I studied enough of the cemi to know their power and their ways.

"You know my voice," it replied. "It is the first time you have heard it, but you know it well. You've always known it."

"Maboya," I whispered.

"I've waited a long time for one like you to come along, another from that cursed del Rios line. I knew it would take something drastic for your spirit to finally awaken."

"Something drastic?" I repeated. "You started the chaos at home?"

"I only planted the seed of discontent. The malice that exists in all Yaya's creation made it flourish."

I looked around, desperately trying to pinpoint the origin of the voice. Would it be from the formless and void spirit, or the pirate captain, or the grim looking Andoli, or the maja, slithering on its stomach?

"What do you want?" I asked, hoping it could not hear the terror on my voice or sense the fear in my heart.

There was a long, pregnant pause. Only my breathing could be heard. Only the ethereal fog could be seen. I felt something draw near, a presence that made my skin crawl and my body shiver. I shut my eyes for a moment and opened them to see a figure, cloaked in shadow. Its vaguely human shape, about the height and build of an average Andoli, pulsed with eerie, ethereal wisps that resembled flames. The voided mass before me emitted no light, but instead seemed to be the source of the sickly green luminescence and fog that choked my cabin and distorted everything that passed its vicinity. Then it spoke.

"I come before you as I did to your ancestors, Jenaro and his kin. I come before you, Hildy Rios, to beg for your help."

To be continued…

GLOSSARY

Note to the reader:

The Andoli people, their culture, heritage, and language of Coquien, are based entirely on two actual, real-world cultures: the Puerto Ricans and their native ancestors, the Taíno. A handful of words and phrases that both real world Puerto Ricans and the fantasy Andoli use are in fact Taíno words and phrases. Unfortunately, due to the extreme lack of knowledge surrounding the Taíno people (for various reasons that will not be discussed), much of their language and culture was lost to history. Thus, the Andoli, and their tongue Coquien, are an amalgamation of the ancient Taíno and modern Puerto Ricans. The following is a list of words used throughout Stone Feather Fang *with Taíno or Spanish roots.*

abuela(o)–grandmother/father

aguila pescadora–osprey

Andolin Islands–a group of islands in the western reaches of the Summer Sea consisting of two main land masses, East and West Andolin, as well as a number of smaller islands totaling 33. It is the ancestral home of the Andoli people

Areíto–literally, festival of dances; a three-day festival in the Andolins occurring every three years, celebrating the cemi and all the heroic deeds of their ancestors, usually consisting of feasting, dancing, batu matches, etc.

Atabey–1. cemi of life and birth, mother goddess, wife to Yaya; through her womb, all races of Ke' were born. Often appears as a caguama. Her cemi is a pregnant woman astride a caguama.

2. Eighth day of the week, appearing once every four weeks

baba–father

bacalao–cod fish

batéy–historically, a rectangular plaza in the center of an Andoli village that served a multitude of functions (weddings, funerals, dances, batu matches, etc.). The batey grew in size with the growth of the city. The Batéy del Albizu became a renowned park with multiple batey within its walls.

batu–ball game of the Andoli, played on a stone or grass court between two teams of ten people. Each player wore stone bracelets on their wrists, elbows, knees, and ankles and would attempt to volley a coconut sized ball to their opponents. Each team had three attempts to volley the ball to their opponent's side. Points were scored each time the ball failed to make it across the center line in three hits or was dropped by the opposing team while attempting to return the volley.

behique–an Andoli priest or priestess in service of the cemi

bibi–mother

bisabuelo–great grandfather

Borekua–the race of man, youngest of all races of Ke'

Borinkens–derived from Borekua, group of clans of working class Andoli; most Andoli consider themselves Borinken

Cacique–literally chieftain, later used as king or queen

cacique menor–historically, minor chieftain, later used to

describe the number of men and women who governed the smaller provinces in the Andolins

caguama–giant sea turtle

camarones–shrimp or prawns

carib–literally strong man, term used to describe the personal bodyguards of the del Rios family. Most carib are members of the Anacaona clan

cassava–tree whose root had hallucinogenic properties. Roots were mashed into a pulp, dried and used as snuff along with tobacco; drained of their juice and distilled into alcohol

cemi–1. A god, or gods, of the Andoli, both singular and plural or
2. the statue or likeness of the god, worshipped by the Andoli

Cibao Ara'–literally, "The People of Stone," second oldest race in Ke'

coquí–small tree frog, sometimes considered the ancient symbol of the Andoli

flamboyán – ornamental tree with reddish-orange blooms, also known as the royal poinciana

grulla–a crane

Guatu'–fourth day of the week

guazabara–warriors, royal guard of the cacique of the Andolins

Guey–second day of the week

Hura–sixth day of the week

iguanaboina–sea serpent, or dragon; Juracán's most common form

inriri–woodpecker

Itiba Ara'–literally, "The Great People." The oldest race in Ke', original wielders of majick

itu d'itu–sister

Jibaros–name of a clan of agrarian Andoli from the west island.

Juracán–cemi of the raging wind and sea who appears in Ke' as the iguanaboina, or sea serpent; represented by a dragon holding an empty orb and a jug of water.

Karaya–last day of the week (7), except for the fourth week of the month when there are eight days making it the second to last day of the week

Ke'–the world created by Yaya

loro–parrot

Maboya–evil spirit and counter spirit of Yaya, appears as giant snake or as a dessicated corpse, represented by a cemi of a skeleton wrapped in the coils of a snake

maja–large snake, exhibiting characteristics of both a boa constrictor and a viper; often associated with Maboya

Moin Hupia–Maboya's ship, literally means *The Bloody Ghost*

mono–monkey

mucaro–screech owl; symbol of good luck to the Andoli

musaraña–island shrew; raised and hunted for their exceptionally fine coats

natiao–brother

Ni–third day of the week

niñera–nanny

Nitaino–group of clans of affluent Andoli, many of whom live on the east island.

Opiyelguabiran–(O pee yell wah bee ran) cemi who guided departed spirits to the third cave, often seen in conjunction with Maboya; represented by a timbered hound, half wood, half flesh

pernil–pork shoulder

Puerto Zafiro–capital city of the Andolin Islands, located on the northern coast of the eastern island

retch rod–long, thin rod of carved and polished cassava wood used to induce vomiting; thought by ancient Andoli to aid in communing with the cemi

siani–married woman

Suma Behique–formal title for the head priest or priestess, most senior leader of the temple

tostones–a dish of twice fried plantains, seasoned with salt and spices

tía–aunt

tío–uncle

Turey–fifth day of the week

yamuy–jungle cat, or jaguar

Yaya–1. Creator god of the Andoli, represented by a tri-faceted stone cemi, often seen in conjunction with his son, Yúcahu 2. first day of the week

Yúcahu–god of the air, often appeared as either a woodpecker or osprey, even in cemi form

ACKNOWLEDGMENTS

Back in 2015, before the pandemic, before the world of Ke' existed, I had an idea for a fantasy story. Like most tales in their infancy, it was chaotic at best. Nothing fit. It drew on too many things that already existed. The Andoli were a minor people with no real culture or history. I struggled to write anything that felt important to me let alone something I think anyone would want to read. So the idea fell by the wayside, gathering dust in my brain. And it would have stayed there if not for a couple of books and a handful of people who saw something I did not.

Fast forward to 2019. After finishing *The Silmarillion* by JRR Tolkien, I thought to myself, "Most fantasy novels are Eurocentric. What would a fantasy novel look like if it focused on Latino stories and Latino mythology?" After not writing for months, and at the behest of a good friend of mine, that idea from 2015 began to evolve and take shape. At the same time, I began to read about my own cultural history. *War Against All Puerto Ricans* by Nelson Denis sparked a reading frenzy. I experienced an awakening of sorts and through that, *Stone Feather Fang* was born.

Since then, my story went through countless rewrites and revisions. Characters changed. Themes disappeared. But throughout it all, the idea of a Puerto Rican and Taíno foundation for a fantasy novel remained. Thanks to all the arduous work, the countless proofreaders, beta readers, and editors that took a knife to it, *Stone Feather Fang* became what it is today. It may be cliché, but it really was a labor of love and I hope that love and pride, that orgullo Boricua, shines through it all.

None of this would have been possible without the help of a handful of people. Without them, *Stone Feather Fang* would still be just an idea, buried in deepest recesses of my mind. Joseph Easterly pushed me to write when I did not want to write. I may have given up on this dream of all together if not for him. Sandra Desjardins gave me my first break. Without her, "Jenaro and the Crimson Sails," would never have been published. From that short story, *Stone Feather Fang* gained real traction. Emilia Linley believed in this project when I was full of doubt. She saw potential when I wanted nothing more than to quit. She read, proofread, and edited every version of *Stone Feather Fang* and helped make it what it is today. Stephanie Hansen saw real potential in me and my story and decided to take a chance on me, and for that I am forever grateful. I also want to thank Craig, Christina, Cali, Ave, Francisco, and everyone else at Deep Hearts, YA, who read my little novel and decided they wanted to publish it and put it out into the world.

Lastly, I want to thank you, the reader. If the world I created brings you even a fraction of the joy it does me, then all of this will have been worth it.

Con paz y amor,
AG

ABOUT THE AUTHOR

AG Rodriguez is a Puerto Rican American, multi-genre author specializing in Latino/a/e/x stories and characters. He is the author of the debut novel *Stone Feather Fang* from Deep Hearts YA, a fantasy reimagining of Taíno mythology and Puerto Rican history. He holds a MFA in Creative Writing and has penned three published short stories along with four full-length manuscripts in the past ten years. They all have sequels planned, if he can just stop coming up with new projects to work on. He currently resides in the Land of Enchantment where the beautiful mountains and never-ending skies inspire all his work.

Also from Deep Hearts YA

The Aziza Chronicles:
Awakening
TreVaughn Malik Roach-Carter

Discovering her descent from mythological African warriors called the Aziza was just the beginning of Justice Montgomery's troubles. For not only has she been chosen to be their champion against supernatural evils—a demon is on the loose seeking to manipulate her into misusing her newfound powers.

Determined to do what's right and live up to her heritage, Justice trains and forms a band of allies, both human and supernatural. Yet the demon is determined to lead her astray, in the hope that her power might be used to enact an ancient prophecy.

Should she succeed, Justice might become one of the most legendary Aziza to ever live. But should she fail, she might resurrect a goddess of Hell, and doom the world.

Available now in ebook and paperback

Also from Deep Hearts YA

Of Gods and Boys
Harry F. Rey

Teenager Achilles is fresh out of juvie.

It wasn't even for something he did; he took the fall for a crime committed by his father, a member of the Greek mafia. As hard as prison was for Achilles, being outside is proving even harder. He struggles to reconnect with his former girlfriend Carla while getting his GED and navigating the bizarre parole condition of qualifying for a Greco-Roman wrestling competition. At least his mom, an ardent follower of traditional Greek religion, is there to help Achilles win the favor of the gods with animal sacrifices in the back garden.

When Principal McKenna sets Achilles up with a student tutor, out-and-proud Hispanic math genius Jesús, things start to turn mythical. After saving Jesús from a violent homophobic attack, the Gods want a word with Achilles. With the help of Underworld boatman Charon (in full drag), Achilles' heroic actions spark an epic adventure of mythological proportions that will force Achilles to confront, and defeat, all his many, many demons in order to win what his heart truly desires.

Available now in ebook and paperback

Also from Deep Hearts YA

The Reign of Ruth
Jazel L. Faith

In the Forest of Dahlia's depths, witches have long hidden from the clutches of malicious hunters. But as their numbers dwindle and hope fades, they turn to a sacrifice to create the most formidable witch to ever exist: Ruby, known only as the Red Demon.

Bound by fate, Ruby is thrust into a treacherous quest for freedom, her only ally being Lilith, a witch with the power to glimpse into the future. Together, they venture beyond their sanctuary, stepping into a world of hunters, life-changing discoveries, secrets, royalties, and magic to seek peace for their kind at last.

The girls will soon learn that no battle comes without sacrifice, and their choices hold the power to shape the destinies of all witches.

Available now in ebook and paperback